KNIGHT

KNIGHT

Matador
9 Priory Business Park,
Wistow Road, Kibworth Beauchamp,
Leicestershire. LE8 0RX
Tel: (+44) 116 279 2299
Fax: (+44) 116 279 2277
Email: books@troubador.co.uk
Web: www.troubador.co.uk/matador

ISBN 978 1780884 714 (Paperback)
978 1780884 721 (Hardback)

British Library Cataloguing in Publication Data.
A catalogue record for this book is available from the British Library.

Typeset by Troubador Publishing Ltd, Leicester, UK

Matador is an imprint of Troubador Publishing Ltd

Printed and bound in the UK by TJ International, Padstow, Cornwall

In loving memory of Marlyn;
the sunshine of my days, and the bright star of my nights.
– *from Wedding Vows, January 2003*

PART 1

CHAPTER ONE

And so it has come to this...

One last challenge, one last joust, one last chance to prove that the glory of all those campaigns, all those years in service to his king, all those wounds taken on the field of battle, all those nights spent carousing in the king's company were not just a dream, but a reality more compelling, more worthy, more sweet than any other choice of life he might have made.

And so he sits; thinking, waiting, reminiscing. The flanks of his horse beneath him quiver quickly, then stop. The sun shines brightly, and the smell of the grass rises sweetly from the turf below. He looks up, and notices how high the blue of the sky seems today; how immense the canopy of air, and sunlight, and soft white clouds appear above him.

His gaze moves slowly around the arena; moving across the crowds, who laugh and frolic and behave as peasants have always behaved; jolly and carefree and immensely happy, in these moments when they are not beating the searing, unwilling metal, nor slaving over raw, angry coals, nor tilling stubborn soil; the peasants, who on these carefree days, when the king declares a carnival or a tournament, seem to portray a profound, simple truth, concerning life lived in the moment, with no worries over property or possessions or power.

And now, with lance held upright in its rest, and visor awaiting closure, his gaze moves to the king's champion, seated on the charger at the opposite end of the course. The champion, whose bludgeoning martial strength has brought him to the front of the battle lines; the champion, whose lineage in the hands of a diplomat has forged an alliance and saved a kingdom in a time of uncertain conflict; the champion, whose smooth, easy charm and overly-good looks have impressed the lords and the ladies, and the inevitable sycophants who inhabit the courts of nobility. And now, here, on this turf, in this tournament, under the king's flag, the champion waits; the villain, the murderer, for whom there will never be any feeling other than hate; the champion, the personification of evil, and the constant reminder of all that was good and lovely and fair until she was cut down; early, violently, unforgivably.

His gaze moves further left, now; finding the nobles, the courtiers and the king himself; the royal entourage, for whom these days are planned and performed, and for whom the events are merely a pleasant diversion in their affairs, and not, as for him, a testing, a proving, a confirmation of his reason for existence, and once, a demonstration of his love.

And there, the empty box, where so many times she sat, and waved, and smiled, and poured out her love and her strength to him, across the yards between the spectators who watched, and the knights who battled; between those who loved, and those who proved their love; between those who watched and prayed and hoped and loved, and those who challenged and battled and sometimes rose to the occasion and sometimes fell in despair, but always loved in return.

And now he is focusing inwardly; closing his mind to the noise, the babble, the laughter of the crowd; focusing within a sphere growing ever smaller as he separates himself from the outside world and prepares for the challenge; his last tournament, his final appearance, the end of his active days as a knight.

His gaze drifts downwards over his armour. There are tiny spots of rust showing through now. The armour has served him well over the years; has taken many blows which would have felled him, has repelled many arrows which would have pierced him, has clashed and glinted mightily in the sunlight as he stormed across fields in sweating, glorious victory. But now, in the late summer sunlight, it appears as he knows he himself appears; slightly worn, slightly out of place, slightly unequal to the task ahead.

Lifting his head, he sighs briefly, then focuses, as he has been trained to do; focuses, as he has done on so many prior occasions, when the cause was just and the odds were appalling; focuses, and becomes absorbed in the familiar calm which descends upon him, feels the thrill of battle rising, and once more becomes the invincible warrior of his younger days.

Only this time, the limbs are older, the reactions are slower and the cause is a planned entertainment, not a righteous battle. Perhaps, this time, the incentives are not so compelling, the consequences of failure not so traumatic, and hence, the rush of blood will not be so strong. Perhaps, he will not achieve the sublime rhythm and grace, which came so naturally in years past, but, by God, he will put on a show, and if he finishes flat on his back, then what does it matter?

He is an old man now, already in his thirties, and no-one really expects he will be on his feet at the end. And besides, she is not there to watch; has not been there for two years now; is not there to cry out with heartfelt anguish as he is unseated, not there to cradle his head in her arms, and weep tears of disappointment for him at his loss, and relief for herself at his safety. No, it is just another tournament. He will give it his best shot, but in the scheme of things, it does not matter. Tomorrow will be a new day, the start of a new life, more comfortable, more restrained, more suited to an aging knight, whose glory days are past, and whose back aches in the mornings.

★

The heralds, the trumpets, the announcement of the joust, and now, the carefree gaiety of the peasants becomes muted; the babble recedes, the chatter subsides, and the world diminishes until it contains just him and his opponent.

A little tightness in the chest, a little perspiration on the palms, but the vision; oh, the vision is so clear, the focus is so precise. The beast beneath him senses the change in rhythm, in tempo, and her hooves begin to stutter on the firm grass of the track. Left hand up to pull down the visor, which falls into place with a metallic clunk. Breathing amplified now within the helm, deeper and more ragged as the blood begins to pump even though not yet needed. The world has reduced to a slit, yet in that slit, everything that needs to be seen is visible, can almost be touched.

A movement to his left and a hand is raised; a linen pennant rustles gently in the breeze. The mare is eager now; can scarcely be restrained as she paws at the earth, and snorts her breathing in a forceful echo of his own. Fighting now to hold her back, wheeling from side to side, nostrils flaring on both knight and charger, perspiration glistening on the body of the mare, and running down the arm of the knight, hearts pounding, two beings melding into one, two spirits responding in unison...

The pennant falls.

Spurs into the flanks, and body instantly leaning forward to combat the blow to the base of the spine from the high-backed saddle as the mare tears at the ground in acceleration. Lance coming out of its rest as they gain speed: Point of balance always forward, head of the lance coming down and the hilt rotating upward to nestle under the right armpit.

Tension on the reins reduced now as they reach full speed, and shield arm being cocked to take the blow from the champion's lance. Breathing hard now, blood pounding through bodies as the distance between opponents reduces at an alarming rate. Lance locked into place, balanced, unwavering, pointed at the heart of the champion; searching for an opening, the slightest chink in which the lance might find some purchase.

Massive, explosive impact as lances strike shields, splintering wildly and shields crash cruelly into the armoured ribs of the knights. Bodies are flung backward by the enormous impact, knees clinging desperately, and backs buffeted by the high-backed saddles keeping the knights upright, the combatants pull back on the reins, slowing the thundering horses. The first pass is over.

Visor open, he gulps in fresh air. The mare is still eager, and canters with a stutter as he wheels her around. They begin to trot back to the lines for a new lance. The champion passes within yards. Not the time to show weakness, not the time to admit any pain from the battering just received. He looks into the champion's smiling face and sees supercilious pity. His own face shows nothing; no expression, no feeling, nothing to give away the competing emotions of pain and hatred; nothing to tell the king's champion that an old knight will compete until there is no energy remaining, no part of his body left unbruised; nothing left in the vessel but raw pride. And even then, he will go on if the opportunity arises.

He has reached his lines; his squire looks up and asks the question. The knight nods, although he is aware that his right leg is quivering, then, taking the new lance from the squire, he lowers it carefully into the rest and looks up again.

The king is standing, drawn to his feet by the ferocity of the first clash. On other occasions he has bidden his knights desist when the first clash has been so brutal and in the spirit of carnival has awarded garlands to both, as shared victors. He hesitates, looks first to his champion, then to his favourite knight, hesitates again, then, recognising the end of an era, slowly sits again in muffled agitation, offering his faithful servant one last, futile chance at impossible glory.

No tightness in the chest this time, but in its place the steady throbbing of a spreading bruise. The mare, mature and strong, resumes the nervous staccato of her hooves. Her rider, regaining his breath, settles and once again begins to inhabit a world shrinking by degree until it is once again the tight, focussed sphere of battle. Breathing is deep, but steady this time, eyes are bright and vision is as clear as the first time. The lance feels a little heavier, but he knows this feeling, knows it is the after effects of the blood rush of the first charge, knows it will be replaced by another rush when the time comes, and so he remains calm, relaxed.

Although focussed, he allows his gaze to take in the empty box, as he always does; the box from which he drew his strength and his inspiration when tournaments produced formidable opponents. And, just for a moment, he sees her there; sees her long black hair, her smile, her almost imperceptible wave, and feels, once again, the warmth which such a love as hers was able to generate in his being.

The pennant is fluttering in the breeze as he returns his gaze to the champion, and pulls down the visor.

The pennant drops, and he is jolted forward by the eager mare as his spurs rake her sides. Body forward again, he lifts the lance from the rest and begins to rotate the head downward. Lance in place, couched under right

6

arm, grip on the reins relaxing as speed is reached, left arm coming up to position the shield to parry the blow from the champion's lance. Focussing desperately, searching for the chink, the opportunity, the one-in-a-million chance to make the hit stick. Closing too fast now, no time to think, no time to search, prepare to defend, prepare for the colossal impact about to occur.

A tiny pebble on the track, and the champion's horse skids an inch. Balance upset just a fraction; for just an instant in which the shield arm wavers; an instant in which the champion's defence is momentarily less than rock solid; an instant in which a lance crashes into the unsteady shield; an instant in which the champion's weight is not all directed toward the oncoming weapon; an instant in which the older knight's lance does not splinter immediately, but retains its structure for a fraction of a second before shattering; an instant in which the inertia of the lance defeats the inertia of the rider.

The champion's lance is nonetheless devastating as, in its wayward passage during the unsteady moment, it strikes a sickening blow at the base of the opposing knight's helm, before glancing off, spiralling skyward, then crashing, along with its champion, in a cloud of shredded grass and dust, into the turf.

★

Almost senseless from the battering to his armoured neck from the champion's lance, the older knight clings in desperation with knees and hands, roughly reining in his mount; ears ringing, eyes seeing nothing through a dark red mist, up and down indistinguishable from each other, time passing at an unknown rate. The beast beneath him is untroubled, remains eager, and is now a handful to control as he begins to emerge from the cacophony of sounds in his head, back into a world of distorted shapes, and the beginnings of some vague sense of order again.

Unable to remain upright on his mount, he clings drunkenly, then slides in ungainly fashion from the saddle. Leaning heavily on the mare, legs buckling under his armoured weight, he claws at the saddle, clinging upright, breathing in wretched gasps, desperately gulping air and willing his head to clear. Momentarily steadied, he reaches up, tugging at the helm, discarding it roughly, not caring where on the turf it falls, and, for the first time since the sickening impact, begins to find breathing easier again. The horizon steadies but the pounding in his ears remains.

He turns and sees the crumpled heap of the champion rising from the turf; sees the riderless horse at the other end of the course and realises the improbability of what has just occurred. From within his battered and bruised depths a chuckle emerges and a feeling of lightness begins to overtake him.

In this, his last appearance, he has unseated the king's champion. But the instant is momentary: once again the hatred he feels for the man overwhelms him and sanity sharply returns.

The champion is on his feet now. Helm discarded, he glowers at the older knight. Reason has no hold on him as he roars to his squire. Within an instant the champion's squire is lumbering forward, carrying sword and shield.

Now the situation is ugly, desperate, turning impossible again, but this time with malice; the threat of death now hanging in the air. His own squire has also responded and is charging forward urgently bearing sword and shield.

From the vicinity of the royal entourage, knights also run toward the combatants. The joust is over, further action is not necessary within the rules of chivalry and, as often happens, hot tempers must be restrained before knights who fight together on the field of battle, damage each other on the field of sport. Restraining hands, consoling voices, raucous back slapping, and cups of wine will be the order of the day as damaged pride and bruised egos are assuaged.

"Hold." The roar is commanding.

The runners hesitate, then stop. The king's champion, arm outstretched, armoured forefinger pointing accusingly at the advancing knights, snarls his command.

"Come no closer, my brothers; he is mine. His lucky joust may have unseated me, but I am the king's Champion; he who bests me, momentarily, does not walk away with glory; he must see it through to the bitter end, or be bested himself. This taste in my mouth, this taste of – what is it, defeat? – is bitter and unfamiliar. I will be avenged. *Je serai vengé.*"

The king, brought to his feet by the staggering clash of wood and steel and battered bodies, stands, feet apart, hands tightly gripping the wooden railing in front of him, and stares painfully toward the two knights and their squires, agonisingly holding the eyes of his favourite knight for a long moment, then straightens with steely resolve. The protocol is clear, the champion knows it and stands, feet apart, both arms outstretched, awaiting the king's signal to unleash him into combat. Still breathing hard, the older knight realises the impossibility of the situation facing his king and slowly turns, then, in one slow, graceful, fatal movement, draws his sword from the scabbard proffered by his squire. The die is cast.

The king turns away, unable to look, then, unwilling to avoid looking, sinks back into his seat, right elbow propped, chin buried in right hand, watching intently, fingers of the left hand drumming in agitation, assailed by memories of a strong right arm slashing through the air, foiling an axe within inches of his own head; an arm, which older now, but still glinting with unwavering steadiness in the afternoon sunlight, now holds a sword pointed at the heart of the king's champion.

The dance commences.

Averill and Bijou: The one, older and a little slower now, yet more experienced in battle, but still suffering from the lance to the neck; the other, younger, stronger and the king's champion, enraged and dangerous; the slightly out of tune vestiges of the once silky-smooth skills of a hundred ferocious battles versus the raw power and bludgeoning strength of the younger champion. And yet, within the mind of Averill, there is no fear. The earlier resignation of an aging knight in his last appearance is forgotten now. There is no world outside of this small circle inhabited by the combatants; no distractions, no thought of tomorrow. There is only here, only now.

A lunge, a strike and Averill's shield shudders as it parries the champion's ferocious opening blow. Such strength! Head still not clear, sharp pain in neck, throbbing pain in left ribs; need to be careful; need to fight intelligently or be overwhelmed by sheer brute strength. Bijou follows up immediately, in no mood to waste time, intent upon vengeance; pride bruised and hurting. Another crashing blow, parried again, Averill retreating; wary, watching, seeking desperately to clear the muddled brain.

Averill lunges. The movement is slow, seen early by the champion and disdainfully brushed aside. The champion immediately launches his own counter-attack, and Averill is again forced back a pace. Bijou's face alternates between the grimace of effort and anger as he strikes, and the cruel smile of supreme confidence in combat.

Both strike. Swords clash and bodies tremble, but the advantage is clearly with the champion. Averill stumbles, but regains his balance before the champion can capitalise. The king watches with foreboding, acutely aware of the prowess of his champion; aware of the humiliation to which his favourite knight is now consigned, yet unable to shake away the images tumbling through his mind; images of far-off fields of battle when two brothers-in-arms fought side-by-side through mud and rain and blood, through treacherous marshes and bristling undergrowth, and charged in screaming unison across wide fields of early morning mist and sunshine, hearts racing, blood pounding, wind whistling through visors and flowing locks, crashing with unshakable confidence into the oncoming hordes. He wishes, even though knowing the futility of the wish, that the relentless march of time did not have to be so uncompromising, and that today, for just one more time, just a little of the grace and skill of those former years might be granted to the old hero now struggling to make an impression below, and given the ugly mood of the champion, perhaps even battling for his life.

Another blow, and Averill staggers again.

The champion is smiling more now and grimacing less. The confidence, bruised by the ignominious and premature end to the joust, has returned. He is the king's champion and no-one deprives him of that. No-one takes more than a momentary advantage; and whoever dares do so pays seriously for such precociousness, such foolhardiness. The rage has subsided, replaced by supreme confidence and disdain, but the savagery of the attack remains undiluted.

The older knight's head is clearing now; horizon no longer lurching, legs no longer dismembered appendages beyond the reach of willpower. The ground is firm underfoot.

Another blow launched, but parried successfully, and this time, no stumble. Feet remain planted firmly, body sways at the hips, shield rises to meet the onrushing sword, but continues its motion, diverting the energy of the blow into a glancing slice, which, finding no resistance, causes the champion to lurch forward under his own momentum, at which point Averill's sword begins its own downward motion towards Bijou's exposed shoulder. But too slow, and the counter-blow misses... but not by much.

Bijou roars in anger. Averill watches, waits and feels the balance swinging. The champion's strength is his power, but therein also lies his weakness; for power must be countered by balance, lest it be exploited, and the returning rage is not conducive to restraint or to balance.

Another lunge, another slash, another miss, another stumble. The king is alert, upright, no fingers drumming now; both hands are gripping the arms of the royal seat; he is half-risen, for he too has sensed the swing; has fought beside Averill too often to not notice, to not share, to not understand what is happening.

Both men breathing heavily; the one carrying slightly more grimace than smile now, but arrogantly confident that victory is but a few slashes of the blade away; the other wary, steady-eyed, focussed.

Averill feints a thrust, Bijou parries upward to where the sword was expected, the delayed stroke now slashing cruelly across the exposed upper arm: sharp pain, but no damage; protective armour saving the champion's arm from more than a serious bruising. Averill nods minutely; the image of the raised arm with the exposed armpit now burned into his mind; the chink, the weakness, the target.

Another roar from the champion, but no delay this time as he launches a mighty strike against the older knight, who drifts sideways, avoiding much, but not all, of the blow; reeling drunkenly backwards from the sheer power of the attack. Bijou follows up with another mighty blow and again Averill parries much, but not all, of the blow, and once again stumbles backwards.

The champion senses victory now, and begins stalking the older knight: pace, slash, pace, slash. Each monumental blow crashes into Averill's shield, but the rhythm is familiar, and although being forced backward at each stroke, the older knight is no longer off balance.

Another pace, arm rising for another blow. Averill feints. Bijou counters with raised shield, then excruciating, agonising, searing pain. The champion's face contorts and the guttural roar of a wounded beast vomits from his mouth, as Averill's thrusting sword buries itself into the unprotected armpit of the champion, then rips free in one sublime, fluid motion, arcing up before slashing down upon the gloved right hand of the champion, severing metal, crushing fingers and shredding flesh. The finger plates of the shattered right glove drip blood, as does the left side of the champion's breast-plate, from armpit to waist.

The champion falls to his knees in agony as the point of Averill's sword reaches his throat. The shield drops. Bijou's sword lies where it was plundered from his shattered right hand.

"Yield."

CHAPTER TWO

A sudden draught of cool air as the wooden door opens, and Averill rises, with difficulty, from the warmth of the wooden bath in which he is soaking his wounds, and attempts a stilted bow.

"Majesty."

"I was sure I would find you here," smiles the king. "Be seated my old friend, be seated. May I?"

"Of course, Your Majesty, please sit wherever you wish."

Averill lowers himself gingerly back into the blessed warmth of the bathtub. Silence; the familiarity of old comrades.

"You look like shit."

"Yes, Your Majesty." A pause. "But so does he!"

The king erupts into laughter and the formality of the occasion is broken; banished from the intimate camaraderie which envelopes the two old warriors. Averill attempts to join in, but instead issues a groan of bruised agony and settles for a small chuckle and a very broad grin.

"You had us worried there, for a time, my friend."

"I had me worried there, for a time, my Lord. Much as I hate the man, he is still formidable."

"He's not your favourite person, is he?"

"Indeed, sire, he is not. Would that the rules of the tournament allowed me to take his life, then I would have slaughtered him on the spot and felt nothing of it, my Lord."

The king looks long and hard at Averill. "I know, my old friend, I know." Then quietly: "Do you think you will ever be able to forgive?"

"Ah, my Lord." A long pause as Averill thinks, and slowly shakes his head. Then looking up: "I believe I am an honest man, my Lord; and a fair man, and a man who holds few grudges. But there is a hatred burning in my gut that I cannot extinguish."

A pause, a shudder, an anguished look. "You knew her, my Lord. You loved her as everyone loved her. There is not a day goes by when I do not miss her; not a night when I do not weep for her; not a minute when her absence becomes tolerable."

The king holds Averill's gaze, then replies, softly. "I know, my brother; I know. Yours is not the life that any of us would have chosen, nor would we

12

have lived it as well as you have done. She was divine. She was everything a man could want, and more. She was the angel for whom you had waited so many years. I cannot even start to imagine how you live each day; and yet you do."

Abruptly the knight looks away, fighting to regain control of his emotions. "And I have a daughter, my Lord, who reminds me, constantly, of her. A beautiful daughter, now forced to go through life without her mother. Was it not enough that she spent her recent years in poverty, running from marauding brigands, living on the dregs of campfire waste? Is it right that now, just when she gained the family she had, for so long, been seeking, her suffering should return in this most sad and unexpected way?"

The king kneels down beside the bathtub, placing one arm around the shoulders of his greatest ally, and with gentle strength, draws the head of his old friend to his breast.

"She is young, Gregory; and strong. She will survive. And, she loves you dearly; almost worships the ground you walk upon, although you do not see it. She is the greatest reason you have for carrying on, my friend."

Looking up again, the knight smiles wanly, then tries earnestly to give voice to his feelings. "I know that a knight's vow requires forgiveness, my Lord, and I have tried, all these years, to behave as a true and worthy knight. I have run when you have said, 'run', I have fought when you have said, 'fight', I have sung victory songs with my brothers-in-arms, I have bedded women and enjoyed the lust of those fiery nights. But now, there is always emptiness; always the longing for what cannot be; for the life and the love I knew for so short a time. And, try as I might, my Lord, I find I cannot forgive. And I feel certain that the anger, the emptiness, the hopelessness that I feel, shall be my penance for the rest of my days."

Thus they remain, knight and king; the one nursing bruised and aching body, the other with head bowed, embracing his battered ally of a lifetime's battles. No words; no need; until the king slowly releases his comrade with a gentle, "Take some time, then come and join us in the Pleasaunce. We have a banquet to conduct, and I need a hero."

CHAPTER THREE

Such a meal, such a feast, so much laughter, so much raucous singing, so many very bad jokes.

But, as he had entered the banqueting hall, there had been a sudden hush, as no-one quite knew how to handle the situation. How does one greet the knight who has defeated the king's champion; especially given the ferocious manner in which today's contest had taken place?

The king, equal to the task, had, within seconds, recognised the potential for the celebration to turn ugly, and acted decisively.

"Sir Gregory, come sit with us, for we are celebrating the triumphant end to the days of my favourite knight."

Averill had bowed, rather stiffly and a little painfully.

"Your Majesty does me a great honour, and I humbly accept your invitation."

"Sir René Bijou is unable to attend this evening," continued the king. "The pains of combat, as we all know, can often be unexpectedly severe, even when the event is sporting. Nevertheless, his faithful brothers are here and we all welcome you to our table, for this day is yours. You have shown us all what it means to be a knight of this kingdom; what it means to carry one's pride to the end of one's days of active service, and not one of us would begrudge you the victory so richly deserved and so valiantly earned this day.

"My Lords, my brothers; join me in recognising the years of valiant service, the courage, the heart, and the steadfast refusal to acknowledge odds which were too high for average men to contemplate.

"To Sir Gregory."

The assembled company had enthusiastically joined in the celebration. Even Bijou's closest friends had acknowledged Averill's achievements this day and had commented that Bijou himself should be proud to have shared the arena with Averill in this piece of history.

But Averill's instincts had told him a different story; a story he knew was not yet finished.

★

14

Now that the feast is over, he has withdrawn to a quiet corner, resting on beautifully embroidered cushions, observing the merriment around him, but too tired, too bruised to take any further part.

"Goodnight Daddy."

He gingerly looks up and finds the beautiful, smiling, oriental face of his daughter. "Goodnight, my Odelia."

She leans down and tenderly kisses his lips. Almost a woman now; fourteen years old, and fourteen years young; at the stage where one never quite knows who is going to speak; the little girl or the young lady. She leaves, stops, turns, blows him a kiss, then continues on in animated conversation with her maid. He gazes after her, remembering that walk, those delightful, unpredictable surprises, that sparkle in the eyes.

He closes his eyes but the tears still escape.

He opens them again, looking around for some distraction; something to take his mind off the pain of his loss; something to focus upon; something to bring him back to the here and now, and leave him to visit his private world of grief another time, when he can close his eyes, and rest his head, and be absorbed into that sad, private world of memories which he inhabits from time to time, re-living the beauty, the happiness, and all that was good in the world for a time; for such a brief time.

His gaze wanders, slightly unfocussed, around the hall, where the revelry is becoming fractured as groups seek out their like-minded companions, to carry on the high spirits and bonhomie established earlier during the banquet; the boisterous group in the middle, engaged in serious arm wrestling; the quieter quartet above them, who Averill knows will be earnestly debating some quite philosophical elements of life; the various individual knights pursuing their romantic encounters with the many beautiful ladies who make up the softer aspect of the court; the larger group, mixed knights and ladies, who, as yet, have not established any pairings, but who, in the course of this night, might well do so; and the other large group, the recently-graduated squires who, wide-eyed and youthfully clumsy, are taking in their first court banquet as knights, some becoming exceedingly drunk, others bashfully clinging to the edges of the group, observing, and drinking in the intoxicating atmosphere of this night.

He notices her now, auburn hair, dark eyes. She is standing some few yards away, looking at him; looking at him as if not quite able to believe what she has seen this day; not quite able to accept that this slender man, whose hair is showing the first wisps of grey, whose face carries the lines and scars of battle, whose stride today no longer carried the spring which must surely have been present in youth, had walked from the field of the tournament victorious; had ultimately despatched the champion, even though he himself had been battered and bloodied in the process.

She looks away, and walks towards the king, nodding courteously as gentlemen of the entourage offer their compliments. And then slows, turns, and looks once again, directly at him; quizzically, uncertain, perhaps unable to push aside the prejudices which say he should not have been able to achieve this victory today; that it had most likely been a fluke, a once-off, an event not to be counted in the list of significant events, or of things upon which a life, or a love, could be based. She turns away again, and walks on.

He realises he is standing now, watching after her, his breath catching a little in his chest, his gaze following the sweep of her departing back, his heart slowing again after the initial lurch, his face slowly colouring as the feeling spreads; the feeling he had experienced, once, long ago, when an angel had looked up at him with terrified eyes when he stood, sword raised, feet planted firmly in the stirrups, and roared out his challenge to any who remained willing to fight.

A hand slaps him roughly on the back; the moment splinters into a thousand pieces, and the good humour of the night's revelry imposes itself upon him.

PART 2

CHAPTER ONE

A cold, grey morning, clouds scudding low across the hills; the thin morning light gradually revealing the shapes of men preparing for battle. The clink of metal, the thwack of leather as straps are threaded and buckles tightened, the light tapping of hammers on metal as last-minute adjustments to armour are made. Moist clouds of vapour, snorted from horses' nostrils, leave small, swirling clouds just above ground level; the squelch of hooves seeking firmer footing in the muddy turf provides a rhythmic background to grunted conversations.

Higher up the hill, more men, pacing slowly, occasionally sipping from tin goblets, engage in quiet conversation, fingers stabbing at lines drawn on parchment; battle plans; long deep blue cloaks with emblazoned yellow and white emblems, several richer maroon cloaks bearing black and white designs, and two in red and blue and gold; royalty.

A ray of sunshine breaks through, angling upward from the crest of a low hill. Conversations momentarily halt as eyes glance toward the east, and a perceptible sigh passes through the working throng; perhaps today will be favourable after all. The lift in spirits brought by the momentary sunshine is palpable.

And now, a closer huddle of the armoured and cloaked men as one of the red and blue and gold figures speaks. "Gentlemen, this day will mark the end of this campaign. Today, we will rout the enemy, or we ourselves will be destroyed. For, beyond those dunes, to the south, lies the sea; and if we are pushed back there, then that is where we shall die."

A muttered assent from the group.

The king continues, "Henry, my beloved son, shall lead the charge. And should he fall, then as always, his place will be taken by my champion, Sir Gregory Averill."

Once again, the muttered assent of men about their business.

"Our cause is honourable, and our forces are committed and well-trained. Yet, do not underestimate our foe this day. We have tasted his strength and his commitment in two skirmishes before this, and we can be confident that he will not tire, nor will he yield. He has strength, of that we are sure, for we have felt it; but we have also seen his weakness, for the very rigid thought that makes him formidable is also the constraint which limits his ability to react to changing circumstances. If we fight his fight, then we shall surely be defeated, for he has training the equal of ours, equipment the equal of ours, commitment the equal of ours and a larger force than we can muster.

"So, my Lords, as we have discussed, and as we have planned these last several days, it is tactics which will win the day. I do not need to labour the point; you all know your duties, and the pennants which will signal the phases of the battle; you all know the feints we will employ, and..." – here the king hesitates, aware of the precariously thin line which will separate comprehensive victory from shattering defeat – "... you must all act decisively when the final charge is signalled, for upon this our survival depends; upon this our nation's future is now gambled, and upon this, our own histories will be written, to be read with burning pride, or with abject dismay, by our children, and by our children's children.

"Go therefore, and prepare, for the sun rises, and we must be about our business."

Purposefully, the assembled lords depart, striding back towards their troops, to direct the unfolding of the day.

"Henry, Gregory, a word."

The two young men abruptly turn and sprint the few paces through the clinging mud back to the king, heads erect, eyes gleaming, hearts pounding, as foreboding fails in its competition with excitement, and deference fails in its battle with confidence.

Henry, tall, lean, with close-cropped dark hair and dark, intense eyes, looks with unsuppressed excitement to the king. "My Lord, Father, we can do this."

And Averill, an inch or so shorter than Henry, but slightly more athletic in appearance, and equally enthusiastic in his assessment, adds his endorsement. "Yes, my Lord, we can indeed do this, for I have never seen our men so ready as they are this day."

"Yes, gentlemen," replies the king, "we can do this. And be assured, I know your hearts, for I too have been young, and I too have felt the thrill of battle. But, I have also seen the faces of despair and of terror, and I do not wish to see them again this day. Therefore, I say to you, most earnestly, and upon this I will brook no dissention: You are my son and my champion; between you, you are the flower of this nation, and I demand – demand – your absolute commitment to the strategy we have devised. On this day, your bravery, your skills, your discipline and indeed your belief in your king will be put to the test, for, I tell you now, I will withhold the order for the final charge until the very last second, until our enemy is committed far beyond the point where we would normally attack, for I cannot – will not – accept the possibility of defeat; its consequences for our nation are too dire to contemplate. Therefore, if needs be, I will sacrifice more of our young men than I have ever dreamed necessary before, in order to draw our enemy into our snare, and ensure his inability to escape.

"Go therefore, and know this: upon you and you alone, the formation of this army depends; for if you break, if you accede to any impetuous impulse, the structure of our army will disintegrate, and our cause will be lost. This is my charge to you this day. Do not fail me, for my wrath will be terrible, but it will be nothing compared with the suffering you will have brought upon your country. Have I made myself clear?"

Young men mature in stages, and the transformations are usually only discernible in retrospect. But occasionally, very occasionally, a transformation occurs in one instant of time. Such an occasion occurs as Prince Henry and Sir Gregory Averill face their king.

"Kneel."

The prince and the knight, faces no longer alight with eagerness, but suddenly transformed into masks of determination, bodies quivering from the searing impact of the king's stark challenge to them, drop on left knees to the muddy turf. And the king, placing one hand on the head of each young man issues a soft blessing, in stark counterpoint to the ripping challenge just uttered, then turns and walks slowly up the hill toward the command post, the knowledge that one or both of his favourite young men may be dead by the end of the day, stalking the edges of his consciousness.

The day ticks one second onward towards its inexorable conclusion.

CHAPTER TWO

The bustle on the hill has increased tenfold as men, horses, feather, leather and steel, fluttering pennants and heavy-wheeled wagons move in a hundred different directions. And yet, as each minute passes, the unstructured gaggle of the earlier period gradually transforms into massed concentrations of forces and definite identification of the groupings of archers, foot soldiers, and armour-clad mounted. And, minute by minute, the mass of men and equipment appears to swell and then thin, as large groups assemble and then depart, disappearing into the heavily-wooded lower hillsides surrounding the large, open plain at the foot of the hills.

And, as discovered yesterday afternoon, the lower hills, when viewed from the plain, give the appearance of continuity. But here, when viewed from the line of pennants higher up the hills, the narrow valley between the two overlapping hills is clearly visible; narrow certainly, but not so narrow that a force, five horses abreast, could not charge through.

And, had the keen eyes of the king's falcon been trained on this scene, they would have discerned lithe, green-clad young men near the edges of the trees along the lower hills surrounding the plain; squires; watchers; charged this day with responsibilities which belie their immature years. Squires, knights-to-be, whose job this day is to watch and wait, without distraction, without loss of concentration; to watch and to wait, and then, at the unfurling of the designated flag, to charge back into the woods where the forces to which they are attached wait in concealment and readiness, and where their captains await the orders to attack.

And now, the earlier mist is evaporating and the sun is peering over the hill on the flank to the right of the king. He and his retinue are now partially lit, partially silhouetted by mild, early spring sunlight angling down across them, whilst further down the hill the now-positioned forces remain concealed in trees and morning gloom. As each second passes, the boundary between light and gloom creeps slowly across the grass and moss and scattered rocks which make up the lower reaches of the encircling hills, revealing details of the terrain, damp from the overnight light rain and early morning mist; terrain upon which so much blood will this day be spilt, and so many young lives will be forfeited.

Back within the valley between the folds in the two hills the bustle continues, as armoured knights assemble in clusters, and squires tug horses into rough position. On one side of the valley a little way up the hill, the prince; on the other side, Averill; each standing, hands on hips, observing, occasionally pointing and gesticulating as captains strung out along the line of the valley gradually bring order to the scene, and ranks of horses, five-abreast, become discernible.

★

From the king's vantage point, a distant scurrying appears on the far edge of the green plain. And, over the next ten minutes, the advancing mass acquires definition, becoming distinguishable as more than two thousand foot soldiers. Behind, now also discernible, come several hundred armoured mounted. Archers are nowhere in sight, but then neither are the king's own archers, so no store can be placed in their absence; at least, not yet. Time will tell.

The scouts, sent out over the last few days, had reported about seven hundred fighting men, but this, this is well beyond that figure. This was not expected. Dread and resignation compete within the king's mind; neither wins.

Assessment, calculation, re-assessment, re-calculation, revision of tactics, decision to not revise tactics, uncertainty, confidence, lack of confidence, mind shutting down under stress, need to walk, need to think quietly.

The king moves away and focuses; beginning to play-out the day in his mind. He sees the advance of the enemy with their rigid, structured ranks taking ground methodically, inexorably; sees his archers appear from the lower trees of the foothills, launching wave after wave of pain and death from the sky; sees the enemy ranks hesitate in momentary disarray, then sees them re-group, their number too great to be mortally impacted by the archery onslaught; thinned and visibly more cautious, but too doggedly persistent to be imperilled by the first wave of opposition.

Eyes now closed, he breathes deeply; dread now beginning to gain the upper hand. But a king is a king through achievement on the battlefield, and ability to out-think, out-manoeuvre, out-general an enemy, and so, though dread may curdle his stomach, it does not impact his will. He resumes the analysis of the unfolding day. And in his mind's eye, sees his own foot soldiers burst from the trees on either side to attack the flanks of the advancing horde; sees the enemy force momentarily ruffled again, sees it buckle just a little, then regain structure and begin the steady, methodical destruction of his brave young men; sees the enemy force dividing in two as they press their advantage to the flanks, thereby making a path for their mounted knights to charge through to attack the hill. And there, right there, the experience and the wisdom from a hundred campaigns yield their advantage, identify the weakness, and define the timing of the charge which his own knights will make; the charge, which will split the advancing enemy knights, forcing them into the milling skirmishes of the foot soldiers on either side, and from which there will be no recovery. But, as he had previously imagined, timing will be everything, and the charge will need to be late, very late, for the impact to be significant. And it will mean losses, heavy losses, as the enemy is allowed to hack its way into a position of vulnerability.

Grim, but satisfied at last, he turns back toward his entourage, noting the advance of the enemy during these last few minutes in which his mind has been elsewhere, scanning the trees for any sign of the concealed troops, and noting with satisfaction the occasional glimpse of green which, if you know is there, is just discernible.

He stares down at the valley between the two folded hills below him, where two rapidly maturing young men hold the reins to their horses, as forty ranks of five behind them do the same, and squires busily attend to the final details before the concealed force prepares to mount.

CHAPTER THREE

The terrain dictates that this battle will be done before the sun reaches its zenith; no more than half a morning will be required to see the destruction of an army; no more than the time it takes to prepare and bake a batch of bread, or to slaughter and dress a pig will have passed between the launch of the first arrow and the last plunge of the killing sword; and in that space of time, over a thousand young men will have died, and a kingdom will have been saved, or lost.

★

The noise is astounding; the continuous clash of steel upon steel, the guttural grunts of men hacking other men into maimed or lifeless parodies of humanity, the screams and whimpers of the wounded and the dying, and the background thunder of bodies and shields engaged in close combat; a scene of nightmare proportions.

The advancing enemy has withstood the initial archery onslaught; momentarily surprised and disarrayed by the sudden appearance of death from the skies, launched from the lower edges of the foothills on either side. But unsurprisingly, the reforming of the army has occurred within fifteen minutes and the archers have been forced back into the trees, their places taken by the mass of foot soldiers unleashed by the waving pennant near the summit of the central hill. Here a group of cloaked individuals stares intently at the unfolding scene below, conversing seriously from time to time, but mainly watching, observing, assessing and inwardly wondering if, this time, tactics may be inadequate against the size and the persistence of the enemy force.

An hour has passed since the advancing foot soldiers first clashed with those rushing from the trees, and the grass at the edges of the clearing is now slick with spilled blood. Further in, footing is unsteady as the muddy turf is churned by a thousand straining feet into a sticky cocktail of water and blood, shit and vomit. The field has divided into two separate battles, the enemy force split into two halves, each attacking a force which emerges from the trees, then retreats, only to appear again further along the foot of the hills.

The appearance of retreat toward the king's position on the hill is as convincing as it is real, for although the strategy was to draw the enemy further into the clearing and further toward the hidden valley, the pace at which it is occurring is frightening, and the losses in the king's force are more alarming than the captains had imagined or ever experienced. This will not be a protracted battle; the defending force is being steadily cut down, and the attacking force, originally numerically superior, is becoming progressively dominant. The day will be lost within another hour.

★

Two hundred knights pace backward and forward within metres of their horses, the sound of the battle echoing off the valley walls. But the battle itself is unseen from this position. The pennant on the hillside, which will signal their release, has not moved since it was placed in its scabbard before dawn. Other pennants have been unfurled, raised high, waved to and fro and then thrust forward, lance-like, to signal the commencement of a phase of the battle, but this one has not, and the frustration of the knights is mounting. Not being able to see the battle is a new, unsettling experience, and the wisdom of the decision to deploy the mounted knights in this fashion is, as yet, unproven.

Averill and the prince, armoured for battle, but with visors still up, pace backward and forward together, exchanging looks and words, kicking at the grass and generally reflecting the demeanour of hunting dogs on a leash. But, in both of their minds, the king's words, of not two hours ago, are still ringing, and their discipline, though battered by frustration and uncertainty and eagerness, remains intact.

The prince starts, a cry half-uttered, half-throttled in his throat; the pennant has been removed from its scabbard and raised high in the air, and two hundred knights are lumbering towards their horses. Frenetic activity has now replaced the frustration and poor temper of just ten seconds ago. A low pent-up growl of aggression begins to rise from the group as testosterone and adrenalin combine to fill the air with anticipation, aggression and fear. The outcome of the day is now being transferred to this fearsome band of combatants. But the scene into which they will ride remains totally unknown.

The pennant is being waved from side to side; only seconds now.

★

The enemy knights have entered the gap between their divided foot soldiers, and are steadily gaining pace as they move toward the near end of the plain. Their army on foot is clearly forcing the defenders back toward their king's position, and now, the capture of the king is uppermost in the minds of the advancing enemy knights.

The canter has now become a struggling gallop as the way ahead opens up. The din of furious close combat only metres away is partially drowned by the muffled thunder of hooves on soft turf. Oh, for the dryer ground of the foothills where the footholds would be better, even though the way would be upward; but, we are knights, armoured, protected, and there is no force now between us and the king. It will cost exertion, and sweat, but there is no death in sight; nothing now barring the way to the king on the hillside. Once taken, the battle on the plain will be over; there will be no stomach for more fight, and no reason either.

★

The pennant is still being waved to and fro.

"Why in God's name are we still waiting? We are mounted, we are ready, for God's sake release us; let us see the battlefield, the better to understand our opportunity; release us from this torture of ignorance and inactivity; let us at them; let us at them."

Knights struggle with powerfully eager horses, under orders issued with force and intensity and malice to those who would ignore them, to maintain the structure of the formation. Squires holding bridles are tossed aside as powerful war horses strain to be free. Three arms are broken; snapped by the hooves of horses intent upon rampage. A young squire lays dying; chest crushed by the falling hooves of another viciously rearing horse. The edges of pandemonium are visible; visible, but at bay; barely.

Averill and the prince react furiously to the delay; all about them trained men are swearing, fuming, held on check by the slender thread of discipline; a thread which is stretched almost to breaking point. And in the heads of the prince and Sir Gregory, the king's words echo ludicrously: "On this day, your bravery, your skills, your discipline and indeed your belief in your king will be put to the test."

Every sinew of their bodies is straining to be off, every nerve is at fever pitch, every instinct screams at them to fly.

They wait, cursing, which helps, wheeling violently as they fight their animals, which does not; but waiting.

★

The king's head is on fire from the pain of concentration, his eyes ache from the savage intensity of his gaze. He waits, a moment longer, then, "Now."

A second pennant is hauled from its scabbard, and waved to and fro for no more than three seconds, then thrust forward, lance-like. Immediately, two

27

streams of archers emerge from the trees on both sides of the king, running desperately to take up positions across the open ground of the hillside just below the king. Within seconds, the air is filled with feathered death, raining down upon the backs of the hapless enemy foot soldiers, now exposed by the passing of their knights. The slick brown sludge, which two hours earlier was soft green turf, begins to accommodate more dead and dying.

★

The prince and Averill scream protests of disbelief at the second pennant, already pointed forward, already having released its forces into battle.

"How long will this madness continue? When do I trust my instincts? When do I disobey my king; my king, whom I can clearly see, and who stares not in my direction, but over my head at a battle I cannot see; my king, to whom my loyalty is unquestioned; but should I question it; now, at this time, in these circumstances? What madness is this?"

★

The scene confronting the charging enemy knights rocks wildly as they urge forward horses beginning to break free of the soft, gluey sludge which has impeded their gallop to this point.

And a nagging oddity, struggling to come into focus; that's it, focus: maintaining focus upon the hill ahead is proving difficult. The world feels unsettled, for slightly left of centre and slightly right of centre the eyes are adjusting to something; something unseen, but felt; something not right; something disturbing; as if there were two hills, not one, as if, oh my God...

★

The prince and Averill are already moving as the final waving pennant on the hill is thrust forward. Behind them, forty ranks of armoured mounted, five abreast and swords drawn, structure intact, roar in unison as they charge forward through the folded hills and out onto the battlefield, less than fifty metres from the enemy knights still struggling to gather speed as they emerge from the mud.

Two sets of knights, five hundred in all, closing fast, react to each other less than five seconds away from impact. Panic and pent-up fury compete; panic loses.

The front five rows of enemy knights are still drawing swords from scabbards as their heads are severed from their bodies. Behind them, the momentum of horses being urged forward as they escape the mud draws the next wave of enemy onto the pointed tips of swords being propelled forward by sure-footed horses charging down the slight incline where the hidden valley opens onto the plain, and another swathe of death crashes onto the fresh, but now bloodstained, grass.

Now pandemonium, barely held in check in the hidden valley, is given freedom to reign. Enemy foot soldiers are dying from the king's foot in front and his archers in the rear. The enemy mounted are thrashing and flailing in the face of the manically-possessed king's mounted, who have stormed with terrifying power out of nowhere, turning the battlefield order on its ear.

The day is won, but doesn't know it yet; the methodical destruction of the early morning has become the insane hacking of terrified defeated.

Enemy mounted are fleeing the field, pursued by the king's knights, bent on releasing hell onto the plain and surrounding hills, and whatever lies beyond.

CHAPTER FOUR

The dappled morning sunshine, sparkling through the leaves of the canopy of trees overhead, provides soft, benevolent relief as knights and foot soldiers, weary from the battle of the previous day, move quietly along the wide, beaten pathway in the wood skirting the town of Marquise. Laughter finds no place in this scene as warriors contemplate their own survival as well as the loss of so many brave comrades. The clink of riding harnesses, the soft beat of horses' hooves and the background murmur of men in subdued conversation provide the only clues to the passage of an army.

The dead of both armies have been buried, the prisoners exchanged, and terms of surrender agreed between victors and vanquished. Thus has passed the afternoon and the evening of the day of the battle. The pursuing knights have wreaked their terror on the fleeing enemy, who is now a shattered and impotent force. Further aggression from this quarter is unlikely to come in the short term.

The column moves on, slowly, quietly, making its way toward Boulogne-sur-Mer, from whence they will begin the trip home. Already, messengers have been despatched to prepare for the embarkation.

At the head of the column, Prince Henry, sitting tall in the saddle, with the unmistakable dignity of nobility, and Sir Gregory Averill, more relaxed, moving smoothly in time with the gait of with his mount, lead the way with subdued but watchful purpose. The enemy army may have been defeated, but there are still small bands of rough, lawless men roaming the area; hardly capable of inflicting significant damage on the column, but a potential nuisance nonetheless, as well as a serious threat to the welfare of the peasant villagers who inhabit this region, and whose welfare has now become, to an extent, the responsibility of the victorious army.

Although alert to the current situation, both the prince's and Averill's thoughts remain fixed in the exhilaration and the terror of yesterday's battle.

"My Lord, you may not realise how close I came to breaking yesterday; I am still trembling at the thought of it. Another few seconds and I believe I would have failed in my obedience to our king."

"Dear Gregory, rest assured, I am aware, acutely aware, of just how much faith my father placed in us, and just how close we both came to failing him. In fact, I feel that I had already failed him, for I was already moving to charge as the signal came."

"As was I, my Lord; as was I."

A reflective pause, then Averill continues, "We have been victorious, and no doubt there will be accolades for our leadership, but, you and I know, full well, just how close we came to failing our king, at a time when his strategic vision was the difference between resounding victory and comprehensive defeat.

"I pray that I never again doubt the wisdom of our king, and I pray that, when the time comes, as it surely must, I will not fail you the way I almost failed your father on this occasion."

"Gregory, Gregory; do not punish yourself further. Recall my father's words: 'your bravery, your skills, your discipline and indeed your belief in your king will be put to the test'. He knew, long before we knew, that we would be tested, probably to our limits; that we would be pushed almost to despair, almost to breaking point, perhaps even beyond. But he also had confidence in us, confidence that we would hold our nerve. And even though we now doubt our recollections, he was right. His judgement was accurate. Even though we now break out in a cold sweat just thinking about it, we did not let him down, we did not falter when it counted.

"And this is what makes a wise king, and this is what I must one day emulate. Yes, he annoys me at times, and yes I know that I become petulant around him, because I think I can do better. But, this is my mountain to climb; to acquire the wisdom which has made him a great king, to learn how to analyse each situation as it unfolds and devise tactics which yield victory no matter how improbable the circumstances.

"And you, my friend, my brother-in-arms, will be my strongest ally. You will be my champion, just as you are my father's champion, and I know already that I will not regret these words, for we have shared our boyhood dreams, to become warriors together, and we have stood side-by-side before, and will do so again, many times.

"Understand that, whatever the circumstances, whatever the pressures, your judgement, your courage, your humility will always be needed by this kingdom, and will always be valued by this kingdom. And I shall always count you a friend as well as a valiant knight. This is my pledge to you, Gregory, my friend."

"My Lord, you do me honour where none has yet been earned. Therefore, I also make a pledge; that I will set my heart to never let you down, so that even through our darkest times, you will always be able to call upon me first, to stand with you, no matter how desperate the situation, no matter how misunderstood the cause, no matter how hopeless the odds. This is my pledge to you, my Prince."

Thus unburdened of their recollections, and buoyed by the freedom of confession, the two comrades ride on in silent reflection; the snorted breathing of their horses and the clinking of armour and bridles blending with the sounds of other mounts behind; the muffled chatter of fellow knights overlaying the steady background crump of the army's marching feet.

But the prince's exuberance cannot be contained. He turns in his saddle and fixes Averill with a manic stare. "But it was fucking incredible wasn't it? When we burst out from that valley, I couldn't believe my eyes. They were there, right there, right in front of us; you could almost touch them. And we were tearing out of that valley like hell's own demons. If I hadn't been so furious at being held back, I believe I might have frozen at the sight, just as they did. My God, I would not like to have been in their shoes. You saw them, just as I did; their eyes wide and filled with panic; poor bastards. They didn't stand a chance; like lambs to the..."

The words hang in the air as arrows strike both prince and mount. The animal screams as it crashes to the ground. The prince, falling heavily, left leg caught under the body of the dying horse, is pinned to the ground. The scene deteriorates into mayhem.

Horses following immediately behind rear violently, throwing more knights to the ground. Averill clings on desperately as his own mount shies violently away from the tangle of fallen bodies.

The forest to the side of the track suddenly spews forth mounted riders charging across the line of the column into the melee of skittering horses and unbalanced riders, swords scything through the air as they dismember indiscriminately then vanish into the trees on the other side of the track, as quickly as they had appeared.

Another wave follows, but the element of surprise has been lost now and the regrouping knights exact a small revenge as several of the attackers are felled; the rest causing little further damage before disappearing into the trees behind the first wave.

Averill, torn between pursuit and concern for the prince, wheels his mount viciously around to take in the scene of tangled and bleeding bodies. The prince, still pinned under his horse, but in no mood for sympathy, roars his command: "After them!"

Relieved on the burden of making a choice, Averill's thunderous "With me!" has one squadron of mounted knights charging into the trees behind him, whilst the others remain to deal with the recently-compiled carnage.

Without head protection, and with locks flowing in the breeze generated by their passage, the pursuing knights duck and weave through the trees, taking occasional painful batterings from creepers and spindly lower branches of the trees through which they charge at break-neck speed. The marauders have disappeared and the knights follow in the direction of their departure. But Averill's blood is up and the pursuit is on in deadly earnest.

Within minutes, the charging knights break out of the trees into a clearing; and are there confronted by a chaotic scene. Less than fifty metres away, a village is in flames. Peasants run screaming for cover as the marauders sweep through the village, slashing anything in sight, leaving a trail of maimed and dying. Then they abruptly rein in and turn. From the smoke and shadows behind them, a larger force emerges, also on horseback, and with menacing composure.

Averill's stomach lurches as he brings his partially-armoured squadron to a sudden, sliding, hair-raising halt. They have ridden headlong into the ambush and are only armoured for travel, not for battle. The lieutenants quickly range up alongside their captain, casting anxious glances around the clearing, looking for additional threats. Younger knights also look around, wild-eyed, breathing hard from both the sudden, mad dash through the forest and the rising fear from the scene confronting them. But the danger is concentrated in the force slowly emerging from the devastation of the village ahead of them; a force of mounted men; rough, armed, and dangerous; vicious men, lawless, and intent upon savagery.

Averill's face betrays his emotions. But where his lieutenants had anticipated worry and concern and, perhaps even fear, they see a chilling, fearsome and unnerving smile. Although seasoned campaigners of a score of battles under Averill's command, they remain in awe of him, unnerved by the transformation which occurs in the man whenever he smells battle; whenever he 'goes manic' as they say – but not to his face. The captain, the knight, the king's champion, is all of these things because of this, and the fear which had initially engulfed the knights, as they skidded to a halt before the brutal and sinister scene confronting them, is washed away by the flood of confidence and purpose inspired by their leader. Averill's muted laugh is chilling in its starkness. He speaks, almost to himself at first, then rising in volume, cold, precise and terrible: "This is what I want; a chance to pit ourselves against a dangerous foe, on his ground, on his terms. A chance to show that, under any circumstances, we are the best there is; not average, not good, but the best there is. Gentlemen, this will be a massacre. Let none of them escape."

And now in full-throated roar, "There will be no attacks upon my prince, no attacks upon my king, no attacks upon my knights which go un-challenged, un-met, un-punished."

Spines tingle and knights, worried and uncertain a moment before, now roar their support in unison; confidence unshakeable.

To his lieutenants Averill barks commands, "Gareth, Thomas, the left flank. Anthony, Bryan, the right. Robert, Charles, with me."

Fifty metres separate the forces.

Rough, angry, dangerous men, accustomed to launching guerrilla raids through this ragged, uncompromising territory, stare menacingly and intently at the squadron of partially-armoured knights, now identifiable as three distinct groups, fighting to control the war-horses which, sensing the impending clash, are barely restrainable.

Averill's mount also snorts and wheels in agitated anticipation of action, yet the knight controls the beast with apparent indifference, whilst he himself remains impassive, eyes narrowed, alert to the slightest change in circumstance. This time there is no waiting in a valley, no restraining external imperative. This time, the decision is his; the foe is visible, immediate, and unquestionably dangerous.

The signal from Averill is an almost imperceptible nod, and, at once, the two outer groups of knights spread to the flanks of the terrifyingly intimate battleground. The assembled marauders shuffle into a crescent to face the smaller but now widely-ranged force confronting them.

The ambush has succeeded in pitting the larger force on home ground against the smaller squadron of partially-prepared knights. But Averill's passion for combat coupled with his rapid, decisive deployment of forces has re-established the balance. Where, a matter of minutes ago, ruthless, menacing arrogance was pitted against disorganised professionalism, the theatre now arrays unrestrained relish for battle against unsettled bravado. And Averill is not in a patient mood.

Actions suddenly follow in rapid, bewildering succession. Averill's raised sword is echoed by those of the deftly-positioned knights, and his full-throated "Charge!" follows without pause. The enemy group spurs horses forward in response, but Averill's central group does not move. The marauders' response immediately becomes ragged and indecisive, while flanking knights, responding to their captain's command, launch their screaming, violent attack into the now-broken and unprotected sides of the enemy crescent. Riders turn to face the onrushing knights, whereupon Averill launches his central group into the now-distracted enemy. In the space of ten seconds, the shape of the battle has been established: the enemy has responded, abandoned the response, turned aside to face the new danger and been torn open by the original threat. Powerful warhorses, now unrestrained, propel knights into the conflict with fearsome intensity.

Within seconds, the battle separates into a series of individual clashes, as forty knights hack with disciplined ferocity, advancing mercilessly as each enemy rider is despatched. The battleground quickly engulfs the shattered, burning village. Peasants run screaming between the charging horses and flailing swords as, from the smoke, another small band of marauders roars into the battle. Villagers, caught between the brigands and the knights are trampled as riders rush headlong toward each other. Between them, a young peasant woman screams and cowers, terrified, unable to find a path to safety as the battle engulfs her.

The ferocious clash lasts less than fifteen seconds as powerful warhorses crash into the enemy's mounts, and knights' swords cut a terrible and bloody swathe through the onrushing horde.

A sudden stillness; the battle is over.

Averill, sword raised and covered in grime and sweat, swivels around, eyes straining wildly, looking for the next challenge, and, amazedly, finds none. Blood pounding, mind racing, he wheels his horse violently around in ever-tighter circles, then stands, sword still raised, feet planted firmly in the stirrups, and roars out his challenge to any who remain willing to fight.

Deathly silence.

Then, a whimpering almost beneath his hooves: the young peasant woman, caught up in the clash, lies sprawled on the dusty, bloodied ground, shaking violently with raw fear, and staring up at him through wide, terrified eyes.

Averill blinks, shaking himself out of the battle trance, and by degree, re-enters a world where death is not his immediate companion. Slowly, he dismounts, and stands, one hand lingering on the saddle, the other holding the bloody sword, still warm from the death it has dealt. Around him, knights survey the grotesque forms littering the battleground. At least three partially-armoured figures are among them.

The sword clatters to the ground as Averill takes a pace forward then drops quietly to one knee, slowly reaching out toward the bruised and bleeding shoulder of the terrified young woman, who appears more wild, frightened animal than hearty peasant stock.

A slight shuffle forward and Averill is able to place his arms under the young woman's back and thighs, gently cradling her as he lifts her from the dirt. He turns and begins to walk back toward the cool, soft, clean grass at the edge of the clearing, where the squadron of knights first entered the scene not five minutes previous.

Sharp fingernails suddenly rake Averill's face as the young woman shrieks and claws her way out of his grasp. The knight cries out in pain and surprise, the sudden ferocity of the attack causing him to drop the woman back onto the hard and dusty ground. A moment's hesitation as she lies, dazed, before she too recovers from the shock, and then starts to sprint across the ground, long black hair tossing in the breeze as she dashes, screaming unintelligibly, into a flaming, crumbling village hut.

Averill turns, stunned by the sudden turn of events, and watches as the woman hurls herself into the blazing hut. Raising his hand to his cheek he finds blood on his fingers. Anger rises, but fails to match the sudden weariness in the knight and he turns back toward the cool, beckoning grass at the edge of the clearing.

A few paces, he slows, then stops. A moment's pause, hands on hips he ponders, looking downward, a shake of the head and he resumes his trudging steps toward the grass. Three more paces and he suddenly whirls around and begins sprinting toward the hut, a growl rising in his throat as he reaches the crackling flames and shuddering timber beginning to fall around him. He launches himself into the blaze.

Thick, swirling smoke combine with flying cinders; the heat is intense and visibility is limited. Yet the hut is not large and the scrabbling form on the ground in the far corner is the only movement inside. Averill strides forward, brushing aside burning timber as it crashes around him, reaching the now huddled form in just five paces. Quickly reaching down he grasps the woman and lifts, crashing to the floor himself as the burden resists movement. The tangle of three bodies separates as the child cries out in terror and the mother whimpers in raw, abject fear.

Outside, the watching knights have sprinted to the hut, reaching it just as the burning doorway erupts into a cascade of sparks and flaming ash as Averill storms out, each arm wrapped around a body; one face down and feet dragging, the other, smaller, shivering in fear and clinging desperately to his neck.

Willing hands take the now limp form of the young woman from Averill's tiring grasp. The child cannot be prised away.

CHAPTER FIVE

Every field camp acquires its own unique character as a campaign unfolds, and every new pitching of tents adds a dimension to that character. But it is the nights after battles which have the greatest and most painful impacts, as personnel, be they knights or foot soldiers or archers, return to inhabit their spaces, and, for the first time, recognise the scale and the permanence of the sacrifice of those who have fallen on the field of battle that day.

And so it is following the battle of the plain, and again one night later after the skirmish in the village. Soldiers returning to tents exhausted and bloodied fall gratefully upon the sparse bedding lain on the ground and await the return of comrades. Some wait in vain, slowly realising that theirs will be the only breathing to disturb the forthcoming long night of tossing and turning, of dreams and nightmares.

And some tents harbour no breathing, no tossing, and no nightmares.

The night following the battle of the plain adds the largest chapter to the growing book of the campaign, as the impact of the king's bold, successful and ultimately devastating tactics, are finally felt in human terms. And the night of the clash in the village writes its own small, poignant addendum as three further tents echo the melancholy of diminished occupancy.

But once the army returns home, these painful adjustments gradually fade as the newly-completed tapestry of the campaign is rolled away and assigned its place in history, and knights and foot soldiers, archers and squires, nobles and armourers set about the business of relishing lives spared, and once again, piece-by-piece, become absorbed into the blessed bosom of home.

But for Sir Gregory Averill, this homecoming brings an unsettled peace. For, until now, Averill has been a loner; not in the way a hermit is a loner, but in the way in which he has not needed any external confirmation of his life's path. His prowess in battle has been undoubted and he has led his troops with skill, confidence and daring; his glamour in the eyes of the ladies of the court has been beyond question and he has enjoyed a number of passionate liaisons, any one of which could have ended in a stylish, courtly marriage; and, indeed, his own awareness of his course up through the ziggurat of chivalry has been undoubted and unquestioned and he has duly arrived at the top, where all who have known him, full well expected he would ultimately arrive.

Yet here, now, laying back on his bed, in the familiarity and comfort of his own chamber, reflecting upon the events of the recently-concluded campaign, he is aware that something has changed, something he did not even know was missing appears to have been found, and his heart beats a little faster and his stomach reacts to butterflies he has never known before, every time his mind sees those eyes which stared up at him in terror during the battle in the village; eyes, which, for him, now hold a secret which, for the first time in his life, he feels an undeniable imperative to unlock.

For the tiniest instant, Averill wonders.

But, of course this could not be love, for he hardly knows the girl; has no idea of her background or her station, could not possibly comment on her suitability as a companion for a knight, does not even know what language she speaks, and certainly has no concept of her personality and its likely compatibility - more likely, incompatibility - with his. And she has a child; presuming, of course, that the distraught little girl who clung to him in shivering terror those ten, or was it twenty, days ago, was her daughter. A daughter, and him a knight at the top of his profession? Now there's a complexity that just could not be accommodated. No, clearly, he is toying with a whim, a fantasy, and, in the morning, these thoughts and these images in his mind will appear for what they are; the idle musings of a slightly distracted knight drifting towards sleep.

★

But fate, however she is perceived, is a wily and cunning temptress and sometimes the morning after a good night's sleep does not bring the peace and resolution one anticipates. Paths cross, which might otherwise not have crossed, glances are exchanged where bowed heads might otherwise have passed unseeing, and small, trivial, almost inconsequential events leave lingering impressions, where, in other circumstances, they might have been brushed off with a quick smile and an amused shake of the head.

And so, as Averill strides down the castle corridor this morning, on his way to the stables, with thoughts of the mounts he is about to examine and assess, elsewhere the fates are conspiring to bring him undone. In a brief moment of battlefield sympathy, Averill had ordered the young woman of the village, along with her child, to be brought to the castle among the ragged assortment of the few fit and healthy survivors and potentially-useful chattels from the destroyed village, where she may find safety whilst being put to work somewhere in the vast organic mechanism which is the lifeblood of the castle.

But things have not gone well, for the young woman is a free-spirited and strong-willed being, more used to the harshness of the village where individual resourcefulness and fierce protectiveness are essential skills in the battle for survival. And here, in the depths of the castle, where subservience and obedience are paramount, her innate individualism has led to several scoldings, and at least one beating.

Another stupid rule, another argument, another slap across the cheek, another mixing bowl shattered on the cold stone floor, and the young woman once again runs sobbing from the kitchen. But defeat is not in her make-up and within a few seconds she has slowed to a brisk walk and proudly drawn herself up to her full height, head erect, long black hair flowing, right hand raised to wipe away the tears. And thus it is that this picture of injured beauty and fierce pride rounds the corner of the corridor and crashes into the hurrying Averill.

The eyes, the same eyes, the eyes of the village, the eyes of the dream, the eyes which have haunted him since they first stared up at him in terror, burn deeply into him again. But this time there is no terror, this time they do not belong to a victim, this time they flash a fiery pride, softened by the glistening of recent tears.

Averill's senses lurch as he grasps the young woman's arms, just saving her from crashing to the ground. Twin gasps echo in the silence which follows.

A second; neither speaks.

Another second; still no word.

The silence is shattered as the red-faced pursuing cook lumbers around the corner, comes to a startled and abrupt halt, then, recognising the knight, curtseys and withdraws as quickly as she had burst in upon the scene. The knight and the kitchen maid are alone again.

Still no words.

Averill's eyes are fixed upon the young woman's face, his breathing quickened from the successive shocks of impact and then recognition. Abruptly, he notices that the flaming eyes, which until this point have demanded his total attention, are framed by a strange and unique beauty. The eyes are almond-shaped, the face a soft oval, lips rich and full, skin smooth; a slightly olive complexion. On her right cheek, a smudge of flour where a hand has wiped at tears, adds a stunningly attractive adornment to the vision of beauty he beholds.

By contrast, the young woman's defiance against the recent injustice in the kitchen has not yet subsided. She remains silent and still, focussed upon the face of the knight who holds her arms, ready to defend herself once again, uncertain of the direction this sudden encounter will take.

Averill recovers. "I'm sorry, I was on my way to the stables, and..."

His voice trails off. There is nothing for a knight to say to a maid or a cook or a serving wench. He has never spoken to one before, has never actually been aware of their existence. His hands still hold her arms, but gently now.

Her guard lowered slightly, the young woman regains her decorum. Curtseying briefly she turns aside, gently breaking free of the hands which have been lightly holding her arms, steps around the bewildered knight and, with head now bowed, walks swiftly on. The rapid rise and fall of her breast and the sudden rising flush of blood to her cheeks are unseen by Averill, who stands mute, mind racing, as he tries to comprehend what has just occurred. He turns to look after her but there is nothing but an empty corridor and the scent of freshly-ground flour in the air.

★

Moments pass and Averill does not move. Confused images strain his senses: the terrified eyes staring up at him from the ground beneath his horse at the village had been framed in dirt and grime; the creature had attacked his face with claws and fled screaming, and he had only turned to her rescue in the fiery hut when rising human compassion forced its will upon him. There had been no desire in the act. And yet, ever since, he has been haunted by those eyes. For no known reason, he has been haunted; in sleep and whilst awake. But this time? This time the eyes were fierce, yes, but somehow soft too, and deep, and beautiful, and glistening and... there, just in front of him, inches from his face.

Instinctively, he raises his hand and reaches out. He could have raised his hand a moment ago and touched her face, should have touched her face, will forever regret not having touched her face.

Averill is undone; all thought confused, all resistance dissolved, all pride displaced, all purpose forgotten.

Oriental. He knows the word, has heard it applied to people from far-off lands, but has never previously encountered it. Oriental. So unique, so captivating, so unlike anything he has ever seen, or felt, or imagined before. Oriental. Averill will never be able to look at another woman, so affected is he by the impact of this chance, fated, impossible, wonderful, frightening, beautiful encounter.

Then, slowly, quietly, reality intrudes upon the smitten knight's senses and he becomes aware that he is standing, in a castle corridor, unsure of why he is here, but convinced there must have been a reason. But that is of no matter now. Now there is a more pressing matter. The questions tumble before him: Who is she? Where is she now? How will he find her again? Where did she come from? What was she doing in the village? If he speaks to her will she understand? Will he understand her? The torrent of questions causes his head to spin, leaving him unsteady, and, breathlessly, he reaches for the wall. Reassured by the texture of cold, rough, solid stone, his breathing steadies, glazed eyes regain focus. And then, vague and formless, the hopelessness of the situation descends upon him, and the strong, brave knight of a hundred ferocious battlefield encounters, drops his head in sudden despair, as the impossibility of the liaison engulfs him.

CHAPTER SIX

Three days have passed; three days in which Sir Gregory Averill, knight, commander and king's champion has called into question every concept, every tenet, every belief he has ever held true. Three days in which the brave, serious, self-sufficient knight of countless challenges, and dangers too numerous to recollect, has vacillated on almost every decision facing him, has lost focus on every task confronting him, and, more than once, has walked perplexed, head bowed and shaking in confusion, from the tilting course where he has been attempting unsuccessfully to concentrate upon the squires learning and practising their craft.

The very foundations upon which Averill's life has thus far been built have become illusory and inadequate, incapable of accommodating a new truth; a truth which is broader in scope than he had ever previously recognised, which encompasses a depth of feeling he has never previously experienced, which brings with it dreams of previously unimagined delight, yet which crushes him mercilessly with the certain knowledge that a formal liaison with the beautiful creature from the domestic bowels of the castle will never be possible. A shabby, hidden encounter of lust is easily achievable, but that will no longer satisfy the affected knight.

Since returning to the castle, he has been preoccupied with courtly duties, and has devoted scant time to thinking about the gaggle of survivors brought back from the village to the castle. But, day-by-day, as matters have been addressed and tasks completed, the image of the woman he rescued from the burning hut has begun to seep through the mental barriers, until, now, it consumes the knight completely.

Anger follows serenity, hope is engulfed by anguish, determination leads only to despair, and all compete for the upper hand in the maelstrom of the knight's mind. All impact his behaviour and his interaction with those around him, and all contribute to the growing view that something is amiss with the king's champion; something has occurred which has left the knight wounded.

Another morning, and Averill strides purposefully out into the bright sunshine of midsummer, determined to exorcise the demons which have possessed him these past few days; determined to conquer the malaise which has impeded him, and regain the verve and enthusiasm he has always known; determined to banish all fanciful thought of impossible romance from his mind, and become, once again, the determined, focussed, confident, self-sufficient knight upon whom a kingdom can depend.

Such intensity, such commitment; such folly.

A wooden pail of warm, still-steaming milk clutched in right hand, a drape of soft, dark-orange cloth over her left shoulder, a small milking stool held at arm's length for balance, she staggers back across the courtyard toward the heavy wooden door, still ajar from her earlier passage out to the milking shed. Momentarily, she puts down the pail and the stool, and raises her right hand to brush back the long clutch of dark hair which has fallen over her eyes. Taking another moment, she removes the scarf which has covered her hair, meaning to re-try it to manage the errant tresses. Head back, eyes closed, she swirls the scarf into position above her head, and is, for a moment, oblivious to everything around her.

And in that moment, as the scarf descends upon long black hair, shining richly in the early morning sunlight, and as two white geese look up, slightly affronted by the presence of a busy, gold-speckled hen pecking at the dusty ground at the maiden's feet, another being joins the tableau: a knight; determined, focussed, confident, self-sufficient, striding from the castle, slapping leather gauntlets against his thigh in purposeful reinforcement of his gait.

The footsteps falter, then stop.

The maiden's eyes open, startled. Recognition, and a sharp intake of breath.

No sound, no movement; nothing to challenge the growing power of the soft, silent spell which now shimmers over one small piece of courtyard where stand a knight and a maid, and three farmyard fowl.

The scarf, not yet tied, falls softly to the ground.

★

Hearts pound at imprisoning breasts, eyes engage, transfixed, unable to tear their gaze away from each other, bodies strain at the paralysis which immobilises them.

A wild, giddy, boyish, uncoordinated lurch and Averill breaks free, stepping forward to retrieve the fallen scarf. He rises, hesitantly, leather gauntlets in one hand, scarf in the other, and finds himself looking into deep, brown eyes set in almond-shaped lids, framed by the exquisite oriental features of a slightly upturned face, already flushing pink, only inches from his own.

Words; where are the words?

"Thank you, my Lord."

Composure; more than he has.

"My Lady." Madness, she is a maid.

"My Lord?"

"Forgive me, but I should not be talking to you. I should not even be standing here with you. It is not proper for you and me to... it is not the done thing here in the castle... well, outside the castle... that is, not actually outside the castle, just... outside this particular wall of the castle... in the courtyard... where we are now... if you see what I mean."

Foolish, boyish, uncontrolled babble.

"My Lord, if my presence offends you, I apologise. I will leave you now."

"No, wait. I mean... I was being foolish. Of course your presence does not offend me. It's just that..."

"What is it, my Lord?"

"It's just that... I don't know who you are. I don't know anything about you... I don't know... anything... apart from the fact that... your fingernails are incredibly sharp."

A gasp, a look of horror and the young woman instinctively reaches out to touch the recent scar on Averill's cheek. Immediately embarrassed, she withdraws her hand. But Averill's senses are already reeling, his command of speech further shattered.

Mute, he stands, mind racing, decisions being made and unmade, desires being acknowledged, banished, then reinstated, consequences recognised, rejected, then slowly, painfully, accepted.

Seconds pass. Slowly, inexorably, the die tumbles and comes to rest. Doubts subside, the gaze steadies, shoulders heave once, then relax, and, piece by minute piece, the babbling boy resumes the mantle of knighthood. Gently reaching forward, Sir Gregory Averill takes the soft, dusty hand and re-places it against the small, fading scar on his cheek. "For whatever comes of this moment, whatever happiness or distress it causes, whatever it ultimately costs, I accept all responsibility... my Lady."

A pause as Averill's words – all of the words – are considered.

Then slowly, distinctly, with every care to ensure that this is not a mistake, is not a beautiful declaration made in too much haste. "My Lord, I know not what you mean. I am a simple maid, working in the kitchen of this vast castle. I do not understand your words about 'distress' and 'cost'. And I know of no responsibility which you should bear on my behalf."

But the knight is too far gone now; too deeply drawn by the overwhelming feelings of tenderness, to know, or even care, if the soft reproach carries any truth. "Ah, my Lady. I think that, whilst you may be a maid here, in this castle, at this time, it has not always been so. I think... that you are as much a maid... as I am a cobbler."

Abashed, the young woman withdraws her hand from Averill's cheek and, head bowed, eyes averted, clasps both hands together under her chin.

The knight's voice is gently insistent. "I do not know how it happened, how you came to be in the village near Marquise, but you are clearly not a native of France. And whilst one may be forgiven for not knowing your status, no-one could mistake the fact that you are a foreigner, and I believe it is now time for us to unravel the mystery of who you are, and where you come from, and how you have finished up here, in a maid's costume, carrying a pail and a stool from a milking shed, in this particular castle, on this particular morning, just as I am on my way through this particular courtyard."

Half-expectantly, Averill waits. Breasts rise and fall; the young woman remains silent.

Softly, Averill continues. "Does it not seem to you that fate keeps thrusting us together? And who are we to ignore such signs? I, for one, would not be so foolish as to walk away from you now. Twice you have stumbled into my life, and twice you have disappeared again. And each time, you have left me bewildered and... alone. I could not go through all that again.

"Every time you appear, my heart leaps with excitement, I lose my balance and have to reach out to walls for support, I forget everything I was doing and stand, dumbstruck, thinking of everything and nothing. And every time you disappear again, I am left bewildered, not knowing where I am going, despairing that I will never see you again, knowing that it is hopeless to want you so badly, yet hoping against hope that there will be some way of making it all work.

"I try to put you out of my mind, but it is useless. At night, I dream about you, during the day I cannot think of anything else but you, my companions wonder why I am failing to achieve virtually everything I set out to do, even I am beginning to doubt that I can do the things which, up until now, have been as natural to me as breathing. There is something about you which, when you are not here, makes my life seem empty, and pointless, and... and I no longer wish to be without you."

Breathing heavily from the sudden outpouring of emotions, Averill stops, realising that he has said far more than he ought; far more than a knight would prudently say to a maid he casually comes across in a courtyard.

Then, cautiously, warily, delicately, he offers. "It is for all this, and all that may come of it, that I accept responsibility."

A soft breeze swirls the leaves at ground level, then dies. A pair of white geese waddle nonchalantly into a milking shed while a gold-speckled hen gives up the search for grain and wanders off. A tear rolls slowly down a young woman's pink flushed cheek and drops noiselessly to the ground in a courtyard of a castle. A knight reaches out across a gulf of silence and places his fingers beneath the young woman's chin, delicately turning her head towards his own. A further slight pressure and her face is raised until warm, brown eyes, framed in almond-shaped lids and swimming in tears, look up into those of a man falling in love. A small sniffle, a blink, more tears cascade down upturned cheeks, then the most wonderful, glorious, radiant smile flashes momentarily before disappearing again, as if startled by its own suddenness. Nervously, hesitantly, it re-appears, then, with gathering confidence, it spreads, encompassing eyes, cheeks, lips, outshining the morning sun, and lighting with it, every fibre of the knight whose hand still supports the trembling chin.

"Who are you?"

The smile is breathtaking.

"My name is Mariel. My father was from the other side of the world; from China. My Chinese name is Choy Dip. It means 'beautiful butterfly'."

CHAPTER SEVEN

Averill stands on the hillside, alone and brooding, staring towards the grey, scudding clouds of the rapidly advancing storm. Sudden flashes of lightning are accompanied by sharp, violent cracks of thunder, which resonate around the harsh, rocky terrain. The wind whips around the jagged outcrop where he stands, his heavy cloak snatching at legs clad in long, warm boots, which, as if of their own mind, have brought him here, to this place, where the elements are at their fiercest, and where a knight can clear his mind and concentrate on the problems of life.

A vivid flash of lightning and the almost immediate angry, sizzling crack of fractured air herald the arrival of the storm. Driving rain begins to lash the dark, grey rocks, flattening grass and creating small rivulets which snake and join and cascade down the hillside, but still, Averill does not feel impelled to move. If anything, the growing ferocity of the storm has drawn him into its spell, calling him to meld with the elemental forces of nature, and the knight, in response, has eagerly accepted the invitation, for his mind is no longer in turmoil, no longer uncertain, no longer subdued by the impossibility of the path ahead. Instead, his is a mind now fiercely committed to a course, and all of his thoughts are now focussed on the obstacles which confront him in the endeavour.

"Mariel."

The name sounds so sweet when he utters it.

"Mariel."

He can still hear her voice as she spoke her name; soft, melodious, gently-accented, imparting an exotic timbre to the name which made it attractive beyond belief. Or is it just his utter surrender to the thought of her which now focuses his mind and directs his footsteps? Whatever the truth, Averill knows, with absolute certainty, that he is in love; totally, completely, utterly, in love.

And this is where the difficulty lies; this is where all social convention, all accepted mores of behaviour, threaten to bring him undone. No longer is he unsure of his path. Instead, he has never been surer of a course of action. And yet, he knows it to be a path of unacceptability, a path of destruction, a path of ruin. For how could a knight – not just a knight, but the king's champion – engage in a liaison with a kitchen maid? How could the royal court tolerate such an association? How could the king retain his dignity and allow his

47

champion to walk openly, arm in arm, with a servant girl not even of the station of a lowly cook?

And yet, the anguish and the depression which had previously descended upon him when he considered this question, are no longer present, for he has met her, has inhaled her presence, has been overwhelmed by the warmth, the peace, the excitement, the tenderness, the passion she arouses in him, and has fallen utterly in love with her. He is in no doubt that he will go to her, and is just as certain that it will cost him everything he has achieved to-date; every honour, every friendship, every look of respect from his peers, and of awe from those who hold the knights in esteem. He knows, with absolute certainty, that nothing will stop him in this quest, and equally, he knows that the final, irrevocable consequence will be banishment from the king's court.

Lost in contemplation, oblivious to the buffeting wind and fierce driving rain, the knight has not heard the faint slosh of approaching footsteps.

An arm wraps itself, vice-like, around Averill's throat; the knight's heart lurches. His right hand sweeps aside the cloak, and in one fluid movement, grasps the hilt of the sword at his waist, withdrawing it as he simultaneously whirls to confront the intruder. The movement is immediately countered; the attacker's other hand, with strength and leverage, forcing Averill's sword arm downward; the sword remains half-drawn. Impasse.

Heart pounding, eyes wide, sinews taught and ready for combat, Averill waits. The attacker maintains his grip, pressing no further but neither relinquishing any advantage. Slowly, the arm wrapped around Averill's neck draws the knight's head backwards; a voice hisses in his right ear, "Why, Gregory, do you choose such godforsaken fucking places to confront your demons?"

"Bastard," Averill explodes.

Slowly, against cautiously diminishing resistance, Averill turns his head to look directly into the smiling eyes of Prince Henry, who, with one cloaked arm still maintaining pressure on Averill's neck, and the other still firmly gripping Averill's sword hand, has the champion in a grip as fierce as any likely to be encountered on the field of battle; for the prince knows the ferocity of Averill's reaction when startled and is well prepared for the response.

"Well, Sir Gregory?"

The knight's heart continues to pound, breath coming in fierce shudders through flared nostrils. A second passes, then the prince begins to relax his grip on Averill's sword hand. The knight slowly recovers from his state of readiness to kill.

Rain lashes down upon the warrior pair, who stand, indistinctly silhouetted against the rapidly-scudding dark grey clouds. The prince's left hand is now cupped behind Averill's neck, holding their faces no more than six inches apart, yet still Averill has to shout above the roar of the elements: "Because, my Prince, they are demons and a feather bed just doesn't cut it with them."

The prince chuckles, buoyed by both the response and his momentary surprise of his champion.

"Bastard," growls Averill, still struggling to regain his equilibrium. "My Lord," he adds as a precautionary afterthought.

Outright laughter now from the prince.

"Gregory, Gregory, it is not often that I get the chance to best you, but when such opportunities arise, be assured, I am not too proud to take them."

Averill simmers as he contemplates his prince, then, piece-by-piece, re-acquires his composure and his sense of humour.

"There is always training, my Prince, always training." A thinly-veiled reminder of the ferocity of some of the sparring sessions conducted between the knights.

A wry smile from the prince as he releases his hand from Averill's neck and turns slightly aside, looking out over the valley. "Ah yes, training." Then looking back, directly at Averill, he continues, "Funny, but the news which reaches me is that my champion has been singularly disappointing in recent training. In fact, I understand that my champion has walked away from several recent training sessions. Could it be that my champion is starting to feel his age a little?"

Averill is at once embarrassed and offended; embarrassed that word of his distracted condition has reached the prince, and offended that his staunch ally should even broach the subject of age at this stage of the knight's illustrious career. Indeed, so deeply is Averill involved in the subject that he has failed to recognise the by-play for what it is; one strong, confident young man taking the opportunity to take some fun at the expense of a dear friend, an ally, upon whom he knows he can depend, and yet who, for the moment, has lost his equilibrium to some unknown or at least, un-revealed, cause.

Averill grimaces. "It appears my Lord is well informed on these matters. And I must admit to having been somewhat..."

"Preoccupied?" prompts the smiling prince, gently probing.

Averill says nothing, looks directly at the prince and ponders how much to disclose, how much to reveal at this time; for this is a dangerous moment. Upon this moment now hangs the future composition of the king's army, not to mention the career of Sir Gregory Averill, companion, knight, and king's champion. For if he speaks, Averill will utter such words as place his prince in a position of choosing between convention and friendship, and Averill knows, with certainty, just how seriously the prince regards his royal duties, knows that whatever the consequences, the prince will act in the best interests of the kingdom, and knows, therefore, that the prince will have no option but to initiate the course of action which will lead to Averill's banishment.

But Averill is more a soldier and less a diplomat, more used to crashing through obstacles than to finding ways around them, more comfortable with direct speech than playing with words. And so, as Prince Henry waits, a gentle smile playing about his lips, Sir Gregory Averill inexorably moves toward the speech which will end his career, the speech which will expose his love for a servant girl and plunge a kingdom into embarrassed chaos for the time it takes to re-establish the chain of command within the king's army.

A sigh, a deep breath, a decision.

"My Lord, it is true that I have been less than effective in recent training sessions with my knights. And, indeed, I confess that there have been times when I have walked away, my mind in turmoil. And, as you bring me news that you have heard as much yourself, I must therefore accept that this is a viewpoint which is spread wide within the court.

"I do not seek to play down the situation, nor do I seek to avoid any of the consequences which may flow from my actions... or inactions. The fault is mine, and mine alone, and I will accept whatever... judgement... is determined appropriate."

There is stark contrast now between the demeanours of the two men: Averill, erect, serious, speaking with brave conviction, choosing words carefully, seeking a way to minimise the terrible fallout which is about to occur; the prince, gently watchful, wondering where this serious tone is leading, not yet alarmed by anything he has heard, but beginning to have the slightest doubts about the wisdom of raising the issue of his champion's malaise.

Averill continues, "My Lord, you know me well; you and I have played together as boys, we have been happy together, and we have been precocious together; we have stood back-to-back protecting each other from older boys who would cut us down to size, we have been pushed and cajoled and kicked into shape by the well-meaning knights of the kingdom, we have shovelled horse shit together and beaten metal with the smith, and we have grown into our destined roles together. I have been at your side and you at mine, forever, it seems.

"And you have listened to me when I have been drunk and infatuated; and we have bedded some of the loveliest ladies this court has to offer. And yet, I believe you know that my heart has never been given to anyone, my focus on my duty has never wavered and my commitment to my king has never faltered. But now..."

The prince waits, light-hearted calmness now giving way to a certain edginess, not certain where the conversation is going, not prepared to break the flow of Averill's words.

"My Lord..." Averill is hesitant, uncertain, desperately searching for a way to broach the subject which will destroy his career. "My Lord, I fear I am being drawn into a liaison which threatens..."

Prince Henry stiffens, now alert, now concerned as to what has embroiled his friend, and how it has occurred; worried that the friendship which has bound them together for so many years, may be about to be shattered; and immediately aware that the stability of the kingdom might also be about to be thrust into turmoil. And yet he waits, sensing the difficulty confronting Averill in his efforts to discuss the matter, and not wanting to deflect the focus of the confession, if that be what it is.

"... which threatens all that this kingdom holds to be right and proper."

A pause, then, "There is a woman..."

Prince Henry almost laughs in relief. It is not a defection, it is not a matter of honour, it is nothing more than a trifle. His lifelong comrade is involved with a lady of the court and has lost his heart to her. It is a trifle blown out of proportion by a lovesick knight.

Sensing the prince's relief, Averill's own concern deepens, for the prince has misunderstood. This is not an acceptable liaison with a lady of the court. This is something altogether different.

Committed to his path, Averill forces himself to continue; to complete the confession: "My Lord, I am not talking about a lady of the court; she is not of such noble stature; she is a..." and here the knight falters; here his departure from the norms of acceptability becomes accusingly undeniable.

But the prince is now forcing the issue.

"She is a what? Tell me, Gregory, what is she? Is she a peasant? Is she a cook? Is she a lady's hand-maiden?"

The prince's tone is goading, pushing Averill to spit out the words around which he is currently skirting.

"My Lord, I do not know her station in life. She is from a different world, but was caught up among a herd of stragglers brought to the castle some few weeks past; stragglers who were thought no better than work animals for the court."

The prince begins to understand about whom Sir Gregory is now talking, for the tale of Averill's rescue of the fierce young woman and her child have been told many times over since the army returned.

"Indeed, my friend, indeed?" spoken with gravity. "Then, perhaps, someone got it wrong. Perhaps there has been a mix-up. Perhaps whoever gathered together the survivors in the village was not sufficiently careful in identifying who they had in their little group. What do you think of that?"

But Averill, in the centre of the storm, is blind to the opportunity being laid before him. "Forgive me, my Lord, but I do not think there could have been any mix-up. There was only one small village, and only..."

With exasperated beneficence, the prince interrupts, "For God's sake, Gregory. Sometimes I wonder about you, I really do. Sometimes I cannot reconcile the mild, good-natured and if I might say, rather naïve, knight who inhabits our corridors, with the fearsome, terrifying being who commands our troops in battle. Sometimes I wonder if you will ever understand that I am royalty."

Silence. Averill hears but does not understand.

The prince continues, "I am royalty, Gregory. I make the rules. I am not bound by convention; I make it.

"She is yours, Gregory, she is yours. You saved her life in the village. You had her brought back to the castle. You didn't care enough to bother about what happened to her then; but now it seems you do."

Another pause as the words begin to sink in.

"So, what do you want her to be: a cook, a hand-maiden? Or, are you so affected by this creature that you want her to be a lady? All you have to do is say the word."

Averill's mind is reeling, his vision swimming. This is so far from the repercussions he was anticipating, so far from the ignominious end to his career that he had convinced himself was imminent.

But now the prince's gentle mocking tone, to which Averill has been oblivious, is replaced by a truly serious admonition to his champion. "But know this, my friend; know this and know it well: Neither you nor I have any knowledge of this creature; her culture, her upbringing, her manners. Once she becomes a lady – your lady – she will reflect upon you in everything she says and does. And as a result, she will have the power to embarrass you; forever."

Prince Henry waits, upright, hands on hips, watching the impact of his words upon his champion. Sir Gregory, hands also on hips, but head bowed, absent-mindedly kicks at several small loose rocks near his right boot, as he weighs the prince's words. A few seconds' silence, then the prince leans forward, gently placing his hands upon the shoulders of his troubled knight.

"Gregory, I am so sorry to have to tell you this," another pause, "but you must come to terms with the situation, and the consequences, of your decision. You must realise..."

Slowly, Averill looks up, directly into the unwavering eyes of Prince Henry. The knight's face shows no despair, no worry, no concern. He is smiling. "You are right, of course. I must consider the situation, and the consequences." A pause, and Averill appears momentarily lost in thought.

"But if you could see her my Lord, if you could but spend a minute in her presence, you would know, as I do, that she will not embarrass me, she will not bring me disgrace, but rather, she will bring to my life such grace, such elegance, such beauty that I may never again be able to wipe this smile from my face, my Lord.

"And I think, my Prince, that she has not always been as we see her now. I am beginning to suspect that, in truth, she was born a lady; somewhere far off, somewhere we have never seen or even imagined; for she carries such an air that I have, more than once, found myself speechless in her presence.

"My Lord, I will, with your consent, make her my lady; and together, I swear, we will make you proud."

Gloved right hands clasp, and in the pause which follows, two friends from boyhood regard each other with comradeship born of lives intertwined and adventures shared over so many years. Released from the intensity of the recent exchange, both notice that the storm has passed. The sun is dipping towards the horizon, light filtering through rapidly thinning clouds, though the dying wind is still gusting enough to buffet the grass and cause coats to flap.

The prince is also smiling. "Then go to her Gregory. Go, and make her yours, my friend. You have waited a long time for this; and I can see that this is no mere infatuation.

"Perhaps your angel has arrived at last."

CHAPTER EIGHT

"Oh shit."

The bright morning sun is intense. Bryan, on haunches, discoursing eloquently on the texture of a mole recently encountered on the inner thigh of a certain lovely lady of the court, stops mid-sentence. The five squatting knights look up, first at Anthony, whose expletive has utterly destroyed Bryan's story and whose eyes are now fixed on the approaching figure, then turn their heads in unison, and watch, with growing apprehension, as the tallish, willowy, unmistakable figure strides purposefully towards the group.

"Oh fuck."

Gareth, the gentle giant of the group, drops his head, fingers of his left hand massaging his temples. Concern. "I've seen him this way before."

"Uh huh. And we know what this means, don't we?" Anthony's question is rhetorical, but it helps to focus the thoughts, if focus were necessary, of the group gathered for the day's circuit work.

Gareth looks up again, breathes in through clenched teeth. "Well, I don't know what it was, but whatever it was, it's fucking over now."

A pause as they assess the situation, then Anthony, with resignation, "Yep. He might have been a bit off for the past few days, but he sure as hell isn't off now."

"Come on, ladies; better get your arses into gear."

The five knights slowly stand, smiles of greeting barely distinguishable from the grimaces of condemned men.

Averill, for so many days lethargic, indecisive, unfocussed, disinterested, stops three paces from the group, hands on hips, fierce, manic grin plastered to his face.

"Are we ready, gentlemen?"

"Oh, shit."

Gareth turns aside, places hands on hips, and stares toward the horizon, searching desperately for salvation, then, finding none, turns back to face his leader, who, head bowed, is busy adjusting the belt of the scabbard which carries the heavy broadsword at his waist.

The small three-sided courtyard is quiet, occupied only by the seven knights, gathered for a brisk training session. Crisp shadows angle down from the high eastern wall, stopping just short of the area where the knights have gathered.

A swift, fluid movement and Averill's sword is out of its sheath; the tip inches from Gareth's face. A flick of the wrist and the weapon twirls lightly in the knight's gloved hand. The manic grin has gone, replaced by steady, fearsome intensity.

"So, who's first?"

And now there is no doubt; the malaise which had affected their leader has been banished. And suddenly, the purpose, which has been missing for the best part of a week, ripples through the assembled group, and an unbidden, collective 'Yes' escapes their lips; the energy felt by every man present.

Training is back on the agenda; in earnest.

CHAPTER NINE

The clash of metal still rings in his ears and the dust from the day's activity, now a grimy, sweat-encrusted film, has found its way into every pore of the knight's body. Blood and bruises too, where the week's layoff was reflected in the ever-so-slight loss of tone, upon which Averill's eager knights have pounced, inflicting unaccustomed damage upon their leader. A rare day indeed, and hence more memorable for the achieving.

And yet the slightly battered knight is smiling as he lowers himself into the hot water of the large wooden tub. The energy rush from the day's clashes is still with him as he re-lives the encounters: Gareth's first thrust was a sudden, quality strike, parried late but effectively, but still requiring nimble footwork from Averill. The gentle giant had been affronted when Averill's sword had spun menacingly, not six inches from his nose. But Averill had sensed that his own slackness had spread to his knights, and had been determined to eradicate any lethargy without delay. Gareth had responded with predictable aggression; and Averill would have been seriously displeased had he not done so.

Charles and Robert had witnessed the ferocity with which Gareth had engaged in response to Averill's taunt, and had launched themselves into a clash of swords more willing than Averill had seen for a long time. Brotherly love had been put aside as they each tried to outdo the other, spurred on by the energy generated during the first session between Gareth and his captain. Even the watching knights had cringed on two occasions as first Robert and then Charles had landed blows which, without the thick leather arm bracelets each had been wearing, and the dulled edges of the swords used for practice, would have delivered serious injury to the sibling opponent.

And as the brothers had tired, Bryan and Thomas had taken up their weapons and eagerly launched into a display of sustained brilliance which had caused the onlooking knights to applaud when the dust had finally settled.

Word of the clashes had spread through the castle and soon the crowd of participants and onlookers had swelled to about fifty as knights, squires and stable boys had come from all corners of the courtyard to witness what was clearly not just a normal training session. Averill and his lieutenants were known for their intensity, but this was something else; this was a spectacle the like of which had not been seen in the castle courtyard for as long as any present could remember. Something had happened here, something which had its origins in Averill's transformation, and although no-one quite knew what had caused it, there was celebration enough that it had occurred. For there had been a growing concern that the king's champion was seriously out of sorts and with the ever-present uncertainties in Scotland and Wales, not to mention Ireland and France, an army led by a crippled champion was always going to be a liability.

The tempo had been lifted again when another tall figure had appeared at the edge of the watching crowd. No-one had noticed his quiet approach, nor could they later quite recall when he had appeared in the assembled crowd, which, in any case, had been totally engrossed by the action. In fact, his presence had been completely unsuspected until he had spoken.

"So, Sir Gregory, it seems you have found your direction again, and along with it, that of your knights."

The boisterous mood of the crowd, and its total involvement in the action of the sparring knights, had rendered many of the observers deaf to all speech. But Averill had instantly reacted to the voice and wheeled to face the speaker. Within a heartbeat the last excited shout and the last animated exclamation had been suppressed as all gathered had stopped their chattering and bowed before Prince Henry, whose right hand now brandished a sword, and whose eager grin marked a challenge not to be ignored.

But the prince had quickly assessed the situation and set his terms. "Not you, Sir Gregory, for I see that one of your lieutenants has already deprived me of the chance to make you sweat and bleed. However, yon Anthony looks remarkably refreshed for so late in the morning and methinks he would welcome the opportunity to put me on my backside."

And Anthony had responded; with circumspect words, but unrestrainedly aggressive swordsmanship. And both the prince and Anthony had, indeed, been put on their backsides at least once before they saluted each other and called an end to the encounter.

Yes, it had truly been a day to remark upon for some time to come.

★

But, little-by-little, as the warmth from the water infuses the exhausted and bruised body, the images of the day recede and the knight's individual recollections are replaced by a deeper, more profound awareness. Eyes closed, head back, resting upon the edge of the tub, Averill drifts from the here and now, losing contact with reality, surrendering himself to the pull of the dream. The sounds and the smells of the surroundings fade and Averill is transported to another world, another place, another time, where the soft outline of a beautiful oriental face hovers above him, and smiling almond-shaped eyes regard him with gentle, veiled amusement, and where, unbidden, the beautiful, foreign words return: Choy Dip... Choy Dip.

The knight lips move as he repeats the name, but nothing else disturbs the reverie.

CHAPTER TEN

Flying stones shower startled peasants and choking dust swirls violently in the air as the ragged and breathless rider charges through the gateway, under the raised portcullis, and on into the courtyard. Cruelly reining in his mount, the rider tumbles from the saddle as the distressed horse comes to a shuddering standstill, flanks heaving and breath whistling through wildly-flared nostrils.

Hitting the ground awkwardly, the man pitches helplessly forward as his left leg buckles from the impact. A muffled scream from the pain in the damaged ankle and the bleeding and dishevelled individual is on his feet again, struggling urgently towards the wide, grey stone steps leading into the castle. With no consideration for either rank or gender, he crashes, without apology, into several of the royal household making their way down the steps. A trail of sudden amazement, quickly turning to outrage, marks his passage.

Within seconds, a second figure is charging down from the top of the steps, also ignominiously scattering genteel courtiers and castle folk in his wake.

"My God, Anthony, what has happened to you?"

Averill, having spied the commotion from within the castle and recognised the battered rider, has rushed forth and bounded down the steps to his struggling lieutenant.

Gareth, a step behind his captain, already has the bloodied knight in his grasp, supporting him with gentle strength. Lowering himself to a sitting position, back against the balustrade of the steps, he cradles the injured knight in his arms as Anthony attempts to respond.

"Ambush, Gregory, ambush... in the woods near the village of Horsham... hard by the intersection of the rivers."

A pause, as Anthony grimaces in pain, from the now throbbing ankle, and the steadily mounting impacts of damage sustained during his wild ride to the castle.

Continuing through clenched teeth, "As you well know, I took a party to investigate the rumours we had received of unfriendly activity in the area. We found the village to be an easy five days' from here and spent a number of days scouting the region. We had begun to think the reports exaggerated, for although we saw evidence of small skirmishes, there was nothing to suggest that they were any more than the usual unrest of local factions."

Another pause, and Averill and Gareth exchange worried glances. Their companion is not looking good, and his pain and distress are obvious.

Anthony continues, "However, on Tuesday last, as we were making the climb to the top of the hills overlooking the village, we were set upon by a band of about fifteen riders. The six of us were absolutely no match for them so we fled. For a while we were in luck since our smaller number gave us the advantage of manoeuvrability in the forests. We left them behind and, knowing now that the reports were true, we forced a path generally in the direction of the castle."

The flow of words is interrupted as Anthony coughs, then stifles a gasp of agony caused by the sudden jolt within his chest. Averill's growing concern over the news is now overshadowed by his mounting alarm over the condition of his knight.

Gareth mops gently at the perspiration covering Anthony's face, and, as the sharp pain subsides, the latter continues, "Gregory, these are no local thieves and rascals, these are men accustomed to fighting, and once again they found us. I had posted a single guard each night, changing every four hours, but just before sunrise on Friday they descended upon us again. It was too dark to see well and the morning fog was thick, but I am sure it was the same group for I recognised their speech. They managed to kill four of our number, leaving only William the bowman and myself. We escaped only by the slimmest of chances, when we fell into a gully and tumbled to the bottom of the hill away from the main group. The horses had scattered, but, by chance, we came upon the beasts around midday the same day. Without that small piece of luck, we would still be somewhere in the woods between here and the village, and quite probably dead by this time."

Reaching out to grasp his captain's sleeve, the battered knight pulls himself up to within inches of Averill's face. Urgently, he implores, "Gregory, heed my counsel: these are men who know how to fight; they are not unfamiliar with battle, and they are persistent in their pursuit. I am deeply concerned that they are here. I have no idea of their objectives, nor do I know if they continue in this direction or not, but I urge caution and preparedness, for they are likely to be formidable if they are here in number."

Effort expended, Anthony slowly releases his hold on Averill's sleeve, and sinks back into Gareth's steady embrace.

It has been three weeks since the day Averill and his knights put on their exuberant and unplanned display of virtuosity in the courtyard; three weeks in which rumours of unrest in the surrounding countryside have filtered in to the castle; three weeks in which events have proceeded apace on a number of fronts; not all of them good. Averill's face reflects the agitation of his mind, for Anthony's news and his battered condition tell a worrying tale.

Softly, he asks, "What of William the bowman?"

Resting in Gareth's grasp, Anthony continues with unconcealed anguish. "Gregory, I know not what became of him. We had regained our horses and were riding for home with all haste, when we heard pursuit again. We urged our mounts on, but they were tiring. I turned in the saddle to see how much distance we had between us and our pursuers and I know nothing after that, until I awoke on the forest floor some distance from the path along which we were riding. I can only guess that I struck something, a branch perhaps, which pitched me from my horse and flung me into the undergrowth beside the path. It was dark when I awoke and there was no-one. After some time, I was able to stand and regained the path. I began walking in the direction we had been riding and came upon my horse an hour or so later."

Anthony hesitates, searching for words, but finding none, closes his eyes for a moment. Then, with a despairing shake of the head, he again looks to his captain. "There is little more to tell; I am here through luck and misadventure alone, and all my men are slain. I confess, I have seen enough to make me believe that we face troubled times ahead."

Anthony coughs again, and cries out in pain once more. Gareth feels the spasm in his friend's body, noticing also the sustained shiver which follows. Averill looks at his two knights, the gentle giant cradling his bloodied and bruised companion, and also observes the shiver which consumes Anthony's body.

Leaning closer and placing his hand behind Anthony's neck, he asks, "And you, my friend, how are you?"

Anthony smiles weakly. "I bear the cuts and bruises of the encounter as we have always done, Gregory. But, perhaps something inside is damaged, for breathing is difficult."

★

Henry's thinking is being disturbed by the pacing of the two young men before him in the small but well-appointed room overlooking the long shadows now stretching across the courtyard. With head bowed and fingers rubbing his temples, he has, for the last few minutes, been pondering the situation, ignoring the sounds of muffled footsteps and the visions of coloured jerkins passing backwards and forwards at the periphery of his vision. But now, it has become too much.

"Henry, Gregory, desist."

Abruptly the prince and Averill stop their pacing and turn towards the king.

"Sorry, Father."

"Apologies, Your Majesty."

The king waves his hand in dismissal. "No, no, I understand your concern; particularly with regard to Anthony. But we have larger issues to consider, and I cannot think clearly while you two are pacing backwards and forwards in agitation."

The room is silent as the king deliberates; only Averill's drumming fingers unconsciously betray the tension he feels; but these the king does not see.

"Now, Gregory, you say this all occurred within five days' ride of the castle?"

"Yes, Your Majesty." Averill is alert, awaiting the follow-up question, which must surely come.

"And Anthony is certain that the voices were French?"

"Yes, Your Majesty. Anthony is a capable linguist, and would have had no difficulty in understanding, sire."

For a moment, the king's thoughts drift back, to a time long past, when a much younger king experienced other foreign warriors threatening his life, his queen and his country; a time when fresh, raw men were tested to their limits, by aggression far more severe than any seen in the land these past twenty years, but which, in light of the recent news, might now be re-visited upon these young men standing before him today.

Regaining focus, he continues. "So, the question is: have we stumbled across the forward guard of an incursion, or are these men merely a small party, landed here to scout the surrounding areas and gather information?"

"Do you have a view, Gregory?" defers the prince, knowing that Averill has listened to Anthony's tale first-hand.

Averill is circumspect, but unhesitating. "I do, my Prince." And, turning to face his king. "Your Majesty, I suspect that these are scouts, landed on our soil and for the moment alone, but potentially a harbinger of a future invasion force. I believe we were fortuitous in encountering them, and that there is no larger force yet assembled here, for had there been, we would most certainly have come across more than one instance of them during these past few weeks."

The king has fixed Averill with an intense stare, as if trying to divine the reliability of the knight's assessment by observation alone. But then he nods, in muted agreement. "Yes, I concur."

A pause, a breath and the king arises and commences his own slow pacing. "Therefore, we must use our available time wisely." He stops, turns, and pointedly addresses the two. "Our army is not ready for battle. Most have returned to their homes, and we would need time to re-enlist and re-train before we would again be capable of defending our kingdom."

He resumes the slow pacing, the weight of decision plainly obvious in the slightly stooped stance. "So, we must watch, and wait, and prepare... and pray that our enemy, whoever he is, is not more impatient and more impetuous than our good endeavours can tolerate."

Once again he stops, and turns to face the listening pair. "And, we have much to learn about these scouting parties; how many they number, where they are from, the regions they are scouting, and ultimately, the size of the force they portend."

Another pause, and then the king is upright; the stoop, so visible just a moment before, gone, imperious strength in his voice, the address formal: "Sir Gregory, I leave this task to you."

Averill starts to respond, but the king has not finished. "Henry, you may wish to go with Gregory, but you will not. I have need of more strategic support. I need you to raise me an army."

And with that, the king sweeps out of the room, the door slams, and not for the first time, the two young men stand rooted to the spot, impaled by the abruptness and the intensity of the king's directives.

"How does he do that?

How does he lock you down with a stare and cause your limbs to tremble with the force of his command? How?" asks Averill.

Prince Henry's throat betrays the dryness in his mouth as he swallows before replying. "I don't know, Gregory, but every time I see it, or, as in this case, feel it, I wonder if I am really up to what it is going to take to be king."

A pause, then the prince continues.

"You know, there are times when I think he might be getting beyond it, times when I wonder if his grip on things might be slipping just a little; like when we came into the room and he listened to us, and put his head in his hands, and I thought, for a moment, it was all getting just a bit too hard for him. And sometimes, I say things which I shouldn't about his capabilities. And then, wham, just like that, he lifts his head and takes the situation by the scruff of the neck, and has the pair of us reeling and wondering what just happened. The power, the intensity; they just well up inside of him and all I can see is the father I have watched and loved from a little boy; the king I have always wanted to be.

"And, by God, when my time comes, I will do my utmost to..." Henry is breathing hard from the intensity of his outburst, and Averill, regaining his composure following the king's piercing command, smiles just a little. The prince stops.

"And what are you smirking at, may I ask?"

"Oh nothing," replies Averill, smiling even more broadly. "It's just that I'm standing here being overpowered by a king who roots us to the floor with his decision and passion and intensity, and a moment later I'm listening to a prince contrasting his own meagre abilities to those of his king, and, in the process, rooting me to the spot with his commitment and passion and intensity. And I can see no difference between them. The one I have followed for all the days I have been a knight, the other I will be proud to follow all the days left to me as a knight.

"You are, my Prince, as you once reminded me, royalty. And, even if you cannot see it, everyone around you can."

Henry smiles, a little self-consciously. "Sorry Gregory; got carried away a little there; but thank you."

Averill's response is brusque, avoiding any further sentimentality. "So then, shall we be off; you to raise your army, and I to investigate these incursions into our territory?

The prince smiles and nods his approval. Then Averill stops: "But first, my Lord, I have a knight to visit. Anthony is abed, but, if awake, may welcome an opportunity for conversation, now that he is back in safety."

The door swings softly closed, as the two young men stride from the room; one to visit an ailing comrade, the other to take another step towards donning his destined mantle of power. A low-angled shaft of sunlight reveals the swirling dust disturbed by their passage; the particles suddenly agitated, then slowing, and spiralling, in complex patterns, downward toward the well-worn wooden floor. The dust settles, the sound of boots recedes down the corridor, and only the phantom echoes of voices remain: the king was here today, as was the prince, and their champion also; an ordinary gathering, pondering an important problem, to be sure, but an ordinary gathering nonetheless.

How much, such ordinary gatherings will be missed, in the years to come.

CHAPTER ELEVEN

Rough-hewn walls, which by day appear off-white in the diffused and reflected sunlight, by night acquire a richer, more intriguing hue, compounded by subtle movement and mysterious shadow, as flames from the braziers lining the walls of the room spread their gently flickering light over the well-furnished room. In one generously appointed corner, fine curtains are loosely tied back, almost, but not quite, revealing thick, soft bedding, upon which the outlines of rich blankets and plush cushions can just be made out. The irregular play of reddish-gold light alternately reveals then conceals the finer details of the setting behind the curtain.

In front and slightly more centrally, additional rugs and cushions are strewn on the floor, amidst which a low table set with food, some consumed, and cups partially emptied of wine, forms the centre-piece of the scene.

Quiet voices murmur their conversation, occasionally punctuated by brief laughter, as two figures, groomed slightly more than usual, and scented slightly more than usual, stretch with feline grace on the scattered cushions, boots casually stretched out over the rugs, their wearers recalling past exploits and embarrassments with restrained but obvious relish.

The laughter subsides, and, momentarily, the conversation pauses. The room is quiet. Both men appear lost in thought; Averill with head bowed, deep in contemplation; the prince, head also bowed, but somewhat surprisingly, looking up a little, quietly observing his companion through shaded eyes.

Averill, to this point, enjoying the opportunity for a quiet, relaxed, convivial meal with the prince, is suddenly serious, opening his mouth to speak. Henry sees the movement and raises a finger to his lips. Averill remains silent.

No sound.

"Have you eaten well, Gregory?" the prince enquires.

"Indeed I have, my Prince."

Silence again.

"It seems we have only eaten a portion of the food," remarks the prince. "I do not feel inclined this night. But please, continue yourself. Do not let my inclinations affect your appetite, my friend."

"No, my Prince, I have eaten well; not excessively, but with satisfaction. And, as always, your hospitality is beyond reproach."

Henry smiles, and raises his cup in gentle salutation. Averill echoes the gesture, and both men drink briefly, quietly; their confident, informal camaraderie reflecting the mood of the night. A full moon, visible through the small arched window, highlights the soft, warm glow of the room with its own silvery hue.

A soft knock at the door intrudes upon the scene; impinging upon, but not piercing, the reverie. Averill looks up. "Shall I?"

The prince nods and Averill slowly uncoils himself, stands erect, and walks quietly toward the door. Henry lays back in quiet contemplation.

A serving maid, neat and tidy, with hair tied back and white apron spotless, enters carrying a tray and curtseys to the prince, awaiting his instructions.

Henry rolls onto one arm, addressing the maid, but is looking at Averill, a faint smile giving no clue as to his thoughts but reflecting his obvious good humour this night. "Please clear away the eaten food, but leave the untouched portions; I feel sure that Sir Gregory may well require further sustenance."

Gregory smiles with slight embarrassment, the maid curtseys again, and commences clearing and re-arranging the remaining food and wine on the table. Averill, still standing, watches her work. Henry rolls back onto the cushions again, surreptitiously watching Averill from under almost closed lids. Averill remains unaware that he is being observed.

The clearing done, the knight escorts the maid to the door, opens it, ushers her out, closes it again and returns to the prince's company. He sits again, but now, his body does not convey the easy relaxation, which marked the pair before the interruption. The urgency has returned. "My Prince..."

"How is Anthony?" asks Henry, eyes closed, and apparently oblivious to the earnest question Averill was about to ask.

Averill's regard for protocol is too ingrained for any reaction other than to answer the prince. "He is much better than I had expected, my Lord. He remains weak and very tired, but the pain, which had been with him for two days now, is lessened, and he breathes easier."

"Good, good," a drowsy tone.

Averill sits silently, weighing up the balance between his urgent need to talk to the prince about Mariel, and the apparent reluctance of the prince to let anything spoil the dreamy peacefulness of the night. He takes the now-refilled cup of wine from the low table, and drinks a little, his thoughts tumbling over each other in mild agitation.

Quietness descends upon the room, luring Averill back into relaxation.

A knock at the door, and Averill starts.

"Be still, Gregory."

Averill, with slight consternation, relaxes again. Unexpectedly, the prince rolls onto his elbow, then rises, stretches, and walks to the door. Opening it, he stands aside.

66

An elegantly dressed maid of the royal household, with braided hair and soft, pale clothing which rustles slightly as she moves, enters the room, curtseying to the prince. Not recognising her, Averill looks on with only mild interest.

The maid stretches out her hand toward the doorway.

"My Lady."

Another figure enters the room, with poise and grace, taking the prince's outstretched hand. A long, pale-green, floor-length gown with flowing lace sleeves accents a beautiful slim body. The translucent veil covering her face does little to hide her identity from Averill, who has bounded to his feet in surprise; followed immediately by alarm and confusion.

The embodiment of beauty and elegance and sensuality stands before him, and Averill can neither understand nor control his emotions. His head reels; he is both spellbound and traumatised by the sudden turn of events. Why is Mariel here? How did she come to be dressed so beautifully? Why is she holding the prince's hand? What is she to the prince? Has he lost everything he ever dreamed of even before he...? The thoughts are incoherent. Panic and fear clash loudly in his head. His stomach churns uncontrollably.

Slowly, deliberately, the trio advance toward Averill.

Prince Henry is smiling broadly, the maid demurely, but Averill stands rooted to the spot, trembling with conflicting emotions. Henry and the maid gently release the hands they have each been holding, and Mariel, with oriental grace born of a thousand years of civilisation, in one fluid movement, removes her veil, and curtseys, head bowed, soft hands and delicate fingers gracefully flexed, before her stricken knight.

The veil floats to the floor.

Averill remains rooted to the spot; agonised.

"You should take her hand, Gregory, or the poor girl will be forced to remain in that position all night."

The knight's heart pounds, the roar in his ears grows louder, and the trembling in his whole body threatens to topple him.

"Gregory, the whole world is waiting."

Slowly, uncertainly, Averill stretches forth his hand, and takes the beautiful, delicate fingers in his own. The vision before him arises, less than an arm's length away, her scent and her proximity overwhelming his senses. She looks up into his eyes. She is smiling; overpoweringly, radiantly, lovingly. He is weeping, as conflicting emotions subside and happiness beyond measure infuses his entire being.

A hand, which moments before had been leading a vision of beauty towards a passionately tormented young man, now rests upon the knight's shoulder.

"Stay here this night, Gregory; you will not be disturbed."

Averill's mouth moves, but no words emerge. The sound of the door softly closing makes no impact upon the man and the woman lost in each other's eyes.

★

Seated on a cushion by the low table, she has eaten with poise, drunk with delicacy, talked easily with her melodious, alluring accent, and smiled and laughed and caught his hand with such urgency, that Averill's grasp on reality is perilously close to lost. By contrast, after self-consciously banishing the tears, he has been alternately proud, humble, confident, abashed, boyish, knightly, and mute; unable to find any balance or consistency in his interaction with her. Every emotion is amplified to bursting point by the intimate presence of this wonderful creature.

Eyes meet once again, and suddenly the knight cannot breathe. She is not smiling now but looking at him, eyes wide, afraid of the growing intensity of her emotions. Her breathing is impacted by a shuddering inconsistency. His own heart is beating with such force that, momentarily, he fears for his life. Slowly, she leans back until her head rests upon a cushion; her eyes remain fixed upon his. Her hand reaches out towards him. She waits, arm suspended, fingers stretching toward him, lips slightly parted, breath coming in small gasps, eyes wide in fear of her own growing passion; losing control rapidly.

Averill's ability to command his actions deserts him. And yet, as if by magic, he is moving to her. Hands touch, fingers intertwine and arms draw the two beings toward each other. Unable to focus, the knight, the man, the boy inhales her scent, and closes his eyes. But still the magic persists as inch-by-inch his body transports him across the rugs to her. A wisp of hair touches his face. He stops. With one last drowning effort, he pulls his body close to hers, the soft pressure of her hair still upon his forehead.

Breathing returns, eyes open, and the man and the woman regard each other with neither smile nor voice, sustained through a moment in which time has ceased to pass.

Her hand slowly cups his neck drawing him down to her helplessly urgent mouth. Lips meet, muffling the soft, animal cries which burst forth, unbidden, but unrestrainable. Squeezing hands inflict exquisite pain and convulsing bodies grind against each other.

Hands tear at hair and flesh. Lips cover lips and eyes and nose and ears and chin and neck, as the entwined bodies thrash, then simmer, then lie dormant. Breathing returns in muffled sobs.

There is a moment for reflection, but no matter how deeply he peers into each corner of his soul, Averill can find no doubt, no wariness, no uncertainty.

There will be no other night like this; there will be no other woman like this; there will be no other reason for living than this; and there will be no life worth living, after this, if she should not be by his side.

The inexorable expression, of the burning, building passion in the bodies of the knight and the lady, commands attention. Averill rises to his knees, places his arms beneath her body, cradling her head against his shoulder, lifts and stands. She nestles securely in his grasp, arms about his neck, eyes closed, mouth pressed to him. He is amazed by her lightness. He remains still, not wanting to break the spell, and, without warning, is standing in a burning village, covered in sweat and grime, holding the battered body of a terrified young woman; her bruised and bleeding shoulder pressed against his own. But this time, there is no movement, no resistance, no flight. He remains transfixed as reality and dream compete, merging and separating over and over. And underlying the vision comes the realisation that, from the first moment he saw her, his course had been set.

The tiniest wiggle from the bundle in his arms returns him from the dream. As he looks down, she removes her mouth from his neck. "Bed," she whispers, smiles innocently, and resumes her attachment to him. Averill almost drops her, so suddenly does his heart lurch at the wantonness of her utterance. Her slight weight is not causing the trembling in the knight's limbs.

★

Soft, smooth, almost hairless olive skin appears to radiate its own energy as gently flickering light from the flames lighting the room passes through the translucent curtaining, now modestly closed, and infuses its gold-red hue into silks and blankets and flesh. The knight of Europe looks upon his first vision of Asia exposed. Head turned towards him, eyes closed, long black hair spread in glorious disarray across pillows and face, she lies, breasts rhythmically marking her slow, steady breathing. Averill stares in wondrous disbelief, observing every detail: her left arm is flung above her head, elbow bent, long slender fingers slightly curled in total relaxation.

He looks along her right arm to the hand resting on his bare thigh, unwilling to move lest contact be broken. He notices the relative lightness of his own skin under her hand, and stares in unchecked amazement at the beautiful dark red fingernails completing the exquisite hands. He lowers his face to hers, brushing her lips with his own. She runs her tongue along his partially open lips, and smiles, but does not open her eyes.

He nuzzles her neck and feels her squirm in delight. Now resting on one arm and leaning over her body, he begins to tease her nipple with his lips. Her back arches in response. A small sigh escapes her lips. The soft bud grows erect and firm. He pauses for a moment and looks down upon the dark, red, glistening centre of her breast, noticing that the gentle rise and fall of a few moments ago is now punctuated with small shudders. He cannot keep his hands from her, and runs his fingers from her underarm to her waist. Her body arches once again; a soft growl emanates from her throat; her eyes open wide, staring at him, then close again, but the breathing remains ragged. He is on hands and knees now, as the growing intoxication of the night erodes his composure. Her hand falls to the bed. She stretches it out, finding his thigh and runs her fingers slowly up, and down again. Now it is Averill's turn to inhale sharply, as the almost-but-not-quite sensation of imminent delight threatens to overwhelm him. She stops. He stops.

With delicate caution, he takes the blanket in which she is partially entwined and peels it back from her belly. Resistance; the blanket is caught between her legs. Gently, he grasps her hip and rolls her onto her stomach. The blanket falls free. Delirious, the knight stares in transfixed obsession, reality indistinguishable from dream. The rushing in his ears is thunderous. A hand, he vaguely recognises as his own, stretches forth and caresses first one then the other golden mound of perfectly formed flesh, as slowly, slowly, he leans forward and sinks his face into the cleft between her buttocks.

A slight movement and her legs part, just a little further. The warmth, the humidity, the scent: ecstasy; he does not move. Seconds pass; his hands slowly run down the firm backs of her thighs, and up again; a soft, muted growl. He lifts her hips. The intoxication of scent and proximity are overpowering; the slightest pressure and his mouth is absorbed into lips so soft they almost cannot be felt, warmth so inviting it is almost life-giving. He inhales her, consumes her, explores her, as her body begins to writhe in response; hands clenched to her mouth. A shuddering breath and she cries out. Averill withdraws, his tongue the only point of tenuous contact. But the boundary has been crossed, and smouldering passion ignited.

Aroused, she rises on hands and knees, and turns, releasing unchecked passion upon the knight. Hair flailing, tears unchecked, she throws her arms about his shoulders, and grinds her mouth to his in wanton, urgent abandon.

Hands run over bodies in bewildering, uncontrolled frenzy. Pain does not exist as teeth and fingernails deliver unsensed bites and scratches. For several moments, the passion of ecstasy is indistinguishable from that of wilful aggression.

Breathing in gasps, the lovers collapse back upon the bed, mouth to mouth, breast to breast, hands no longer inflicting sweet injury. Sanity returns by degree, but only in so far as the objects of pleasuring are now pinpointed: demure Choy Dip, gentle Choy Dip, ladylike Choy Dip works her man to straining hardness, whilst the knight finds his fingers lost in the exquisite warmth and insensible, wet silkiness of aroused womanhood.

Without thought, without plan, without conscious effort, hands move to buttocks, and the straining, swollen hardness of man is drawn into the life-giving warmth of woman. A moment of indrawn breath, and then the strong, rhythmic interplay of two bodies carrying their souls toward unsuppressible ecstasy.

Lost in each other, passions rise, until straining arms claw bodies together as the moment explodes in violent, guttural convulsion.

The wild animal slowly retreats: Choy Dip giggles. Her knight buries his head in her bosom. Minds float, returning to earth, momentarily, as lips meet; once, twice; and, some time later, for a third time.

A shudder, a sigh, and then, soft, steady breathing; nothing more.

★

Dawn's early light shines gently through the soft curtain.

Averill's eyes open. His left arm is partially hidden by the swathe of thick, scattered black hair, which also mostly hides the face of his beloved. His right hand is cupped around a soft, smooth breast, whose delicate fullness is sensed through the slight movement of his fingers.

He smiles, snuggles closer, and sleeps again.

★

In the courtyard below, knights and squires watch the nearby castle door with muted humour, aware that today's exercise in the surrounding hills is bound to be demanding, and likely to result in some nasty scrapes and bruises and, if they are not careful, something more serious. But it is not Averill who emerges, but Prince Henry.

"Your captain will not be joining you today, gentlemen. Something slightly more pressing has commanded his attention, so, I thought I might join your little escapade."

"We would be honoured, sire. We have planned..."

"Well actually, I thought I might, sort of, take it over a bit."

The prince turns on his heel and strides off. Gareth's jaw remains slack.

Looking back, the prince calls, "Well, come on. We have an army to raise."

Ever alert to an opportunity, Bryan strides past the gentle giant, reaches up and firmly pushes Gareth's jaw shut, ducking as the suddenly active big man cuffs the spot where his head had just been.

The spreading mirth portends a good day ahead, and a welcome break from the gruelling exercise previously planned for the day; though all know that day will come soon enough. But meanwhile, small mercies are to be gratefully accepted.

★

Elsewhere, in a beautifully furnished room far above the courtyard, where rough-hewn walls appear off-white in the diffused and reflected morning sunlight, a young woman lies nestled in the embrace of a sleeping knight. Her eyes are moist with emotion. Her heart is full of a love previously unknown.

She remembers a father, who, in travelling the world, decided to take her with him, and wonders how different her life might have been, had he decided otherwise.

She offers a silent prayer and places a finger of the sleeping knight into her mouth. She recognises the taste, smiles, then closes her eyes again.

CHAPTER TWELVE

From horseback, the view across the rolling downs appears calm and untroubled; nothing disturbs the serenity. And yet, the hairs on the back of Averill's neck are standing, and a sudden chill passes between his shoulder blades, causing him to shudder. Although all evidence is to the contrary, he senses danger, and is suddenly concerned for the safety of his small scouting party.

The others, including Anthony, on this his first venture since his period of convalescence, also sense the unseen danger and back their horses toward the covering tree-line. Only Averill remains exposed, but he too, after a moment's further scan of the grassy slopes, gently backs his mount into the trees. Only the occasional chink of metal on metal is heard above the steady rustle of wind through leaves, as unsettled mounts toss their heads in mild agitation.

A slight trembling of the ground and Averill turns in the saddle as the percussion of approaching hooves becomes intermittently audible. Hearts pump as the six knights look to their captain. A finger raised to lips and no-one speaks. The horses are backed a little further into the trees. The trembling increases, slows, then stops. Ears and eyes straining, the party remains silent and almost concealed, watching, waiting, alert to the possibility of attack from a quarter as yet unknown.

Snatches of muffled voices, apparently a foreign tongue, break through the steady rustle of the wind in the leaves. A horse suddenly neighs. The voice stops. Hands slowly withdraw swords; perspiration drips, blood pounds in ears. A moment's pause and the voice resumes. Seven held breaths are released as one; then held again as the sounds of men and horses crashing through undergrowth come ever closer.

Almost upon them now, the sound of swords hacking at creepers and vines suddenly ceases; replaced by the dull thuds of men dismounting. The voices continue in alarming proximity.

"*Cet imbécile nous fait tourner en rond. Je suis sûr qu'on va tous disparaître dans nos trous du cul. Eh merde, j'ai vraiment besoin de pisser.*"

Anthony chuckles, raising his hand to his mouth to prevent any sound from escaping. Gareth looks at him, uncomprehending, and then, as the others watch, a small rivulet of urine emerges from under the bushes and snakes its way under the legs of Gareth's horse. Now, all, except Gareth, have hands clasped to their mouths.

Averill is torn between the seriousness of the situation and the incongruous comedy of the unfolding events. Every sense tells him he should be alert, and vigilant and serious, yet the situation is so preposterous that it is impossible to remain unaffected by the humour pervading the entire bizarre scene. He raises his eyebrows to Anthony, who is now seriously in danger of falling from his horse as the comedic impact of the overheard conversation is exacerbated by the sight of Gareth, perched on his mount, straddling an ever-growing river of urine as the foreigners on the other side of the bushes relieve themselves of what has clearly been a long-retained burden.

And now, the serious, formidable knights of Averill's squadron, all within yards of imminent danger, are biting on their fists as they react not only to the sight of Gareth clearly displeased by the steaming stream passing beneath his horse, but also to the sight of Anthony, hand clasped to mouth, tears streaming down his cheeks, almost helpless with mirth at the unfolding situation.

Stifled laughter subsides, as the sound of men mounting on the other side of the bushes fills the air. Averill's hand is raised, and seriousness returns in general, although the occasional muffled chuckle breaks through. Within a minute, the band on the other side of the bushes has moved off. The knights relax.

"So, what was that all about?"

"Something about ever-decreasing circles and disappearing up their own arses," replies Anthony, still chuckling over the incident.

"Well, whatever is was, it was better than sitting over a river of smelly French piss, you bastards."

Howls of laughter now from the remaining knights. Averill turns away, grinning broadly, but still cautiously listening to ensure that the departing group is indeed moving further away.

"Come gentlemen, we need to follow and see where they lead. Perhaps we can gain some insight into the size of their force and its location."

They move off, just inside the tree-line; the group of fifteen armed and mounted Frenchmen now plainly visible about a hundred yards ahead, having ridden out from the trees, unaware of any other presence. The freshening breeze carries the sounds of the quarry to Averill and his knights, and lends comforting coverage to their own passage.

Anthony ranges up alongside Gareth. The pair ride on in silence for a minute, ducking occasionally as they pass beneath overhanging branches, until Anthony looks over and winks at the big man. Gareth opens his mouth to curse his companion, but in the end, it is an embarrassed smile which emerges.

"Bastards," he mutters.

★

74

Two blackened faces approach the crest of the ridge, as Charles and Robert inch forward in the darkness; elbows and boots scrabbling in the dirt. Flickering firelight from the other side of the rise causes the trees of the heavily-forested region behind them to cast giant, grotesque shadows. Looking back does nothing to calm the nerves as towering imaginary figures hulk and waver over the tiny bodies on the ground. The wind has freshened and the air is now unpleasantly chilly. The possibility of guards having been posted is uppermost in the minds of the brothers as they haul their way through the undergrowth and on up the incline.

The ridge is crested without incident.

Along the ridge, other pairs of eyes also reach their assigned destinations: a little to the left, Anthony and Bryan peer cautiously out from beneath large overhanging leaves of ground foliage, while further to the right Gareth and Thomas peer through the large clumps of thick grass which dominate the ground where the trees thin and the clearing begins.

The open space is approximately one hundred yards from side to side, enclosed on three sides by the ridge, but extending, apparently unbounded, into the darkness directly opposite the watching knights.

Averill slithers up into position alongside Charles and takes in the scene below.

The camp must contain at least three hundred soldiers. Some are building fires, some are eating recently cooked food, whilst others are digging with spades, creating hollows in the ground in which to sleep, protected from the biting wind. From time to time, men, individually or in small groups, disappear into the trees at the edges of the clearing; returning five or so minutes later, ablutions completed.

Here, hidden within the depths of the forest, an army is assembling. A combination of persistence and luck has brought Averill and his party here; persistence in the continued scouting sorties, which have become routine these past several weeks, and luck in finding this afternoon's lost party, almost at the edge of the forest, which provided them the opportunity to follow the enemy back to his hideaway. Averill is acutely aware that, without that element of luck, this assembling force may well have reached sufficient size to strike, without discovery; and the consequences of that are too frightening to contemplate: an unarmed kingdom against a foreign war machine, assembled and prepared for battle. Even now, the force is big enough to be a serious worry, and who knows at what rate it is increasing.

Another few minutes' observation and Averill has seen enough; he needs to get back to the king and report. He starts to slide back down the incline, then stops, alert to the faint, regular drumming of the ground. Cautiously, he inches his way back to the lip of the ridge, and waits, eyes straining to see into the darkness beyond the clearing, from whence, the faint vibrations seem to be coming.

A minute passes. Averill can just make out his six lieutenants, spread around the edge of the ridge; no-one moves. Then, second-by-second, the vibrations transform into the recognisable crunch of marching feet. A minute later and flickering torch-light becomes faintly and intermittently visible in the darkness beyond the clearing. Another few moments and ten, perhaps twenty torches can be seen, flickering as they pass behind trees now identifiable on the other side of the clearing. And now the full extent of the influx becomes visible as row after row of soldiers spill into the clearing. The sudden bark of French brings the new arrivals to a thudding halt.

A chill shiver passes momentarily through Averill as he realises that his party has stumbled upon the assembly point of a foreign force, well concealed within the depths of the forest; a force which is no doubt gathering strength for an offensive, which, from the numbers now arrayed before him, cannot be too far off.

A barely perceptible signal and the observers quietly slither back down from the lip of the ridge, melting into the grateful cover of darkness again, as the sounds of an army breaking ranks waft over the now-empty ridge and dissipate into the silence beyond.

Fifteen minutes later, at a location about two miles distant, the first blackened faces emerge from the trees into a small, intimate clearing. Charles places a reassuring hand on the flank of his nervous, skittish horse, steadying the mount whilst Robert, one-by-one, unties the reins of the remaining six mounts, and leads them from the cover of the trees where they have remained concealed, out into the clearing ready for the group's departure. Then, backing against a stout tree, the two knights watch and wait.

Over the next few minutes, six more faces materialise from the ghostly depths of the forest.

"Gareth, I need the situation reported to the king." Averill's tone conceals little; concern is evident in his voice, and none has any doubt as to why: the gathering horde has been an unanticipated surprise. Things are far more advanced and far more serious than any had realised.

The big man nods, aware of the responsibility, anticipating an unaccompanied dash through the night back to the castle. The risk of capture, and subsequent fate, looms alarmingly in his mind. This will not be pleasant.

But Averill has other plans. "Bryan, I need a second man to ride with Gareth; one man must get through."

Bryan's jocularity is curiously absent. "Yes, Gregory, I understand. Be assured, we will both get through." Then, unable to be resist. "Besides, he's too ugly to..."

Muffled chuckles momentarily break the tension.

Averill, focussed, does not even notice. "Anthony, I need to find the place where these troops are arriving. This will need to be done with haste, so a small, mobile party will be best; two men, no more.

"I know you've only recently recovered, but I need your language capabilities in case we overhear anything, or, a remote possibility, take a prisoner.

"Are you able to ride with me?"

Anthony nods, "Yes, Gregory, of course". He moves to take the reins of his horse from Robert.

And now, ticking off the items in the mental list he has been compiling, Averill turns to the remaining three knights.

"Charles, Robert, Thomas, I need to know what happens here come morning. I need eyes in the forest. I suggest you sleep now, but be in position before sun-up. You know the form; observe and remain undiscovered for the day, then make for home tomorrow night."

The three nod in brief, earnest assent.

Then, for a moment, there is silence as each man is momentarily lost in his personal thoughts; assessing the dangers, contemplating the likelihood, or not, of rejoining his companions two or three days hence. A scouting party is small and somewhat exposed, but the groups of two or three, into which they are now separating, are fearfully vulnerable. Each man knows that shrewdness, caution, and a sizeable slice of luck will be required if all seven knights are to meet again within the castle walls.

Gareth and Bryan mount. A quiet "God's speed" to each from Averill and they disappear, eerily, into the darkness.

The night seems colder.

Averill looks to Anthony: "Shall we?" then, one foot in the stirrup, turns to Thomas. "This is important Thomas, the picture will be much clearer in daylight; but, for God's sake, be careful."

"We're big boys, Gregory," Thomas offers. "You two take care, and we'll see you back at the castle within three nights."

★

A quiet, careful push through the dense undergrowth and trees to clear the vicinity of the assembling army, a few hours sleep deep within the cover of the forest, and the pale pink light of morning greets Averill and Anthony as they pick their way through the swirling mist, and on in the general direction of the coast.

"There's something oddly familiar about all of this," observes Anthony. "It's as if I've been here before, and yet, it's not like things usually are when you recollect them; you know? Usually you recognise a hill or a rock formation or a clump of trees, and you can put the picture together. But I'm struggling to get a grip on this; it's familiar but it just doesn't hang together the way it should."

"It'll come to you," remarks Averill.

The light has improved in the last few minutes and the riders urge their mounts into a canter. The steady drumming of hooves is the only sound made as the two knights ride on. Gradually, the view ahead becomes less obstructed as the trees thin. A faint track becomes visible and the riders find themselves moving under a discernible canopy of overhanging branches instead of pushing through the thick, irregular placement of trees hitherto encountered. The edge of the forest cannot be too far away now. Soon the cover, gratefully accepted so far, will give way to rolling downs and the two riders will be visible to searching eyes.

Without warning, Anthony's horse rears up, whinnying wildly and lurching sideways. Averill's horse crashes into the petrified mount, and both riders fall, entangled, to the ground. The men maintain a grip on the reins, and although tossed and dragged for some yards by the shying horses, are able to regain their feet and, at last, bring the frightened animals to a momentary halt.

Heads tossing wildly, eyes wide, nostrils flared, both horses remain alarmed and edgy, despite efforts to pacify them. The animals back away, pulling strongly on the reins being held by the knights, until they have moved some thirty paces from the point where the first horse reared. Here, at last, the animals become relatively quiet again. Averill and Anthony, for the moment ignoring the pain in their scratched and bruised legs, study the scene, looking for some clue to the totally unexpected and unannounced disturbance.

"Let me have a look further up," offers Anthony. "I still have that very odd feeling but just can't put my finger on it. I've been here, but I don't know when, or why. It's very odd, Gregory, very odd."

"Indeed; there's something very strange about this place; something the horses clearly don't like. Give me the reins."

Averill turns the two horses to face away whilst standing between their tugging heads, watching Anthony as he moves, cautiously, up the track again.

A moment later, Anthony turns into a clump of bushes at the side of the track. A few seconds later, he re-appears, falls to hands and knees and retches violently.

"Oh shit, Gregory, it's William."

Averill is torn between the need to maintain a hold on the skittish animals and the need to run to Anthony's aid. But Anthony holds up a hand. "It's alright Gregory, just give me a moment. Oh God, that's bloody awful."

Anthony regains his feet, and walks drunkenly back towards Averill, spitting the recently-risen bile from his mouth. He wipes the back of his hand across his mouth and spits again. "Oh fuck. Poor bastard."

"Tell me," urges Averill.

"It's William the bowman, or what's left of him. Now I know where I am. This is where we were being chased during my last scouting trip. I dare say if we continue down this track we'll find the overhanging branch that knocked me off my horse, and saved my life. Actually, I never saw it coming, so there's no chance I'll know it when I see it. But it was along here, I'm sure of it now.

"Oh God, Gregory, he's a mess. He's partly rotted, but it's pretty clear that they hacked into him before that. Poor bastard; I only hope it was quick."

"So now we know why they were so intent upon not letting you get away," notes Averill, rubbing his chin with the reins clutched in one hand. "You'd stumbled upon the route to their assembly point; clearly a cause for concern to them."

The two stand for a moment; Averill upright, holding the reins to both horses, Anthony bent, with hands on knees, still spitting the foul taste from his mouth.

"I want to bury him, Gregory. He deserves much more, but for the moment, that's all I can do for him."

"Of course," agrees Averill. "Let me help."

"No, I'll be fine; he was one of my men, and besides, someone needs to hold the horses and keep a lookout just in case any more of those bastards come along here."

Averill nods in agreement and watches as Anthony withdraws a small spade from his saddle, remarking, "The earth is quite soft, so this will be fine for digging," before trudging back to lay his faithful servant to rest in better circumstances than hitherto afforded him.

Averill slowly scans the surrounding trees and bushes and grasses, and notices a small, red squirrel, holding a nut in raised paws and looking directly back at him. The incongruity of the situation causes him to chuckle, and suddenly he wonders at his state of mind. Anthony is just up the track burying a faithful friend, yet he is here engaged by a squirrel. Has death and killing become so much a part of him that he is no longer moved by it? He thinks of his lieutenants and wonders how he would feel if it were one of them who lay hacked and dead at the side of the track. Or if it were the king, or Prince Henry, how would he react; and knows instantly, that he is not immune to feeling, for were it one of them he feels sure that he would not be standing idly by; he would be... But, he is not quite sure what he would be doing.

Would he be charging out in reckless isolation to wreak vengeance for his friends' lives, certain to lose his own? That has some romantic appeal. Or would he be coldly planning retribution; assembling an army of such scale as to strike terror into the hearts of those who committed the foul deeds? That also appeals.

And into this searching, inquisitive, receptive state, another thought enters: what if it were Mariel; what if it were Choy Dip? What if it were Odelia?

Shaken by the vivid and unexpected turn of his thoughts, the knight cries out and whirls around, ready to ward off the disconcerting images which have quickly formed. He struggles to regain perspective. The horses, already agitated, and alert to the slightest tremor, tug sharply at the reins, hooves stuttering at the ground in skittish alarm.

A moment's restraining effort, then peace returns; the animals quieten.

The squirrel has vanished.

But Averill is disquieted. He looks around. The scene rocks unsteadily as his head spins, then settles. A gentle breeze rustles the leaves in the trees. Nothing disturbs the peace of the glade, yet the knight remains shaken. What just happened? What is this feeling? What was this sudden, sharp horror which descended upon him, and where did the images come from; the images of the woman and the girl lying hacked and dead? And what of this growing awareness that, beside the king and the prince, whose protection is his sworn duty, there are other lives more important than his own? What is all this sudden upheaval of his hitherto stable world; a world in which he knew his place, but which now seems a little less certain than before? He has always been concerned about the welfare of his men, and prepared to die for the prince and the king; but this is different; this is a violent, gut-wrenching pit which opens up when he contemplates danger to his lady and her child.

He wants to take them in his arms and hold them and protect them. Suddenly, the world seems too dangerous a place, and Averill feels the growing need to shelter... to protect... to father. Ah, there it is, recognisable now. He is not going mad. He is not experiencing some irrational disturbance. For the first time in his life the contemplation of another's death has stirred a primitive reaction; fear, but not for himself; aggression, yes, absolutely; protection, just try me, by God. So, if this is what happens when one begins to love, then woe betide anyone who threatens his newly-formed family. Averill the warrior has found a cause which extends beyond his own person, a cause for which he knows he would die, and yet, a cause for which he knows he will do everything in his power to avoid dying, for his death would serve no purpose; would deprive the very persons he was protecting of the beautiful, private, little world so recently born.

And thus, through the contemplation of one death and the vivid imaginings of another does the knight recognise that everything which has gone before is as nothing compared with the effort he will expend in protecting his family. Averill the warrior has become Averill the father; the lion of battle has acquired a second persona; the wild beast when cornered; untested, no doubt, but undoubted, nonetheless.

A strange calm descends upon the knight. The horses sense the change and suddenly settle. Averill lets go the reins, which fall soundlessly to the ground, and the animals begin to graze. The knight looks up and is surprised to discover rays of early morning sunshine bursting through the trees, turning misty morning into the promise of glorious day.

By contrast and just returned from the gruesome task of burial, Anthony stands hands on hips, breathing deeply from the recent exertion, looking down towards the ground; thoughts elsewhere. Averill regards him quietly. A moment passes; Anthony raises his head to speak, but falters. Staring at his leader, Anthony is suddenly unsure of himself; feels momentarily off-balance, but certain that, in the time it has taken to bury William, something remarkable has happened to his captain.

"What has happened here, Gregory?"

A flame burns in the champion's chest; a flame which will not be extinguished. In this most incongruous of places, in these basest of circumstances, has come a moment of epiphany. He takes the few paces required to reach his comrade and places his arm around his friend's shoulder. "Come Anthony, you have honoured William as well as any man could in the circumstances. Now, we have a task to fulfil, you and I, and the day waits for no man."

Somehow, Anthony feels uplifted. God knows he shouldn't, having just buried poor William, but somehow, there is something new in Averill; a serenity, and a fierce confidence, which cannot be denied. He shakes his head, sure that he will never understand the strange, complex being beside him; but thankful that he is beside him and not opposed to him.

The two knights mount and head toward the thinning trees which mark the edge of the forest, and the beginning of open ground. Anthony turns in the saddle, searching for something, anything, to shed some light on the events of the last few minutes, but finds nothing.

They pass the recently completed grave of William the bowman. A red squirrel stands erect upon the freshly turned soil, watching their passage.

★

The smell of sea air is discernible now, and the soft thunder, which from time to time punctuates the air, is the crashing of a not-so-distant surf. The trail has been clear enough; the movement of several hundred men has left wide, muddied tracks, which have become encrusted under the day's warm sun. The steady crunch of the horses' hooves provides a rhythmic, hypnotic background to the passage of the two knights.

Clearly, the route had been scouted beforehand; passing, as it does, well to the west of the villages which dot the route to the coastal fishing and market village of Brighthelmstone.

Twice now, the riders have come across peasant folk making their way homeward in the late afternoon, and twice the knights' questions have been answered in the same manner: numbers of torches have been seen during the night, moving in the distance, but the peasants have preferred to stay indoors, not wishing to learn the nature, or the origin, of those who carried them. On one occasion, a large fire was seen in the distance towards the coast, but beyond that there has been little out-of-the-ordinary to report. And, in the mornings, fresh tracks have been clearly visible as the sun's early morning light has swept slowly over the rolling hills.

The riders continue on in silence, certain now that they have found the landing point of the foreigners, but not sure what inspecting the beach will achieve. Yet, Averill has determined that they must complete this last task before tuning homeward.

His thoughts turn to the groups of knights he has despatched; to Gareth and Bryan, and their dash back to the castle to warn of the assembling of foreign troops; to Charles, Robert and Thomas whom he commanded to stay behind in the vicinity of the presumed enemy. He wonders if he has consigned any of them to their deaths, and, if so, how many. He thinks of Anthony and of William the bowman, and is confused by his mixed thoughts of sadness for William, and for his family, and relief that it wasn't Anthony who suffered William's fate. This is a messy business; nothing is clear, nothing is as it seems when two armies line up against each other. Here there is doubt, here there is uncertainty, here there is the strong possibility that he and Anthony will have ridden to the coast to find nothing of value, no information to assist in whatever preparations are required for whatever action is about to unfold. Averill is beset by doubt, and consumed by worry for his scattered knights.

The pleasant warmth of the day is fading and the gusting, spray-laden breeze buffets the two knights as they dismount and walk the last few yards to the edge of the sharp incline which leads down to the waves crashing against the dark, glistening rocks a little way below.

The two men stand at the cliff edge and watch. Below, a large, smooth bed of yellow sand is revealed each time the waves recede, small circles of dryness quickly spreading outwards as the water seeps away, until, once again, the waves roll in and crash furiously against the dark, wet rocks. At a lower tide, this would almost certainly be an expanse of beach sufficient to land an army; especially if transported in a number of smaller batches of men.

A moment's pause as he surveys the situation, and then Averill turns to Anthony, mouthing words unheard above the roar of the waves, and points downwards. Another moment to collect his balance and then Averill is lurching from rock to rock down the face of the cliff, making his way towards a point where the coast disappears back behind a headland. Anthony, still on the grassy ground at the top of the cliff, matches his captain's progress towards the point, the two horses following behind, tugged along by the reins now in Anthony's firm grip.

The point is reached and Anthony peers over. The area appears to be a large bay, but the darkness of the rocks and the shadows of the late afternoon combine to render its features indistinct. Averill's progress is considerably slower as he hauls himself from rock to rock, grazing hands on the rough texture of the higher rocks as he grips tightly for purchase. Twice he slides painfully downward as his boots slip against the spray-dampened slime of the lower rocks. Anthony cannot hear the curses above the crash of the waves, but knows Averill well enough to be in no doubt as to the colour of the language in use as the king's champion, totally out of his element, makes his way, precipitously around the point.

Respite.

Averill rests against the rock-face, gasping for breath. He looks around, but like Anthony above, is foiled by the darkness of the rocks and the shadows. And, to make matters worse, he has no idea what he is seeking.

Frustration. Disappointment.

A few moments longer then he will retrace his steps. He scans the bay and the surrounding rock face, but can make out nothing of significance. Reluctantly, he turns, reaches out to grasp the next rock, misses, and slithers down one, two, three large rocks, coming to rest as his right leg smashes into another black shape, which, upon impact, crunches and splinters into a wet, messy pulp. Anthony, on the cliff-top above, watches helplessly as Averill suddenly doubles over.

Wincing from the sharp pain, Averill reaches down and takes the shape in his hand. The outer portion collapses under his grip into a mushy black mess; however, the object retains its inner structure. Looking around, Averill now sees more of these strange objects; in fact, the cliff at this level appears to be littered with them. The pain is forgotten as he reaches out and retrieves another. Once again, the outer third disintegrates under his grip, into the same black mush, but the inner structure remains intact. Realisation dawns, and Averill sinks back against the cliff-face.

Anthony watches intently as his leader makes his way along the rock-face, retrieving, brandishing for Anthony to see, then discarding two more of the long, black, gracefully curved objects. Another few minutes and Averill has almost made his way back to the top of the cliff. His hands and forearms are streaked with blood and the black stains, yet gripped tightly in his left hand is one of the curved black objects.

Anthony reaches down to pull his leader back onto the firm ground at the top of the cliff, but is rewarded instead with the black object. Seconds later the head, then the torso, and finally the legs of a grimy, but clearly focussed Sir Gregory Averill finally emerge to stand atop the cliff.

"Well, what do you think?" pants Averill.

"I don't know. What is it? It looks like a burnt piece of wood."

"Exactly; a burnt piece of wood. There are more of them down there, all burnt and charred."

Anthony appears mystified. "I'm sorry Gregory, but I don't see the significance of this."

"These are the ribs of boats."

"But why are they burnt?"

"I'm not sure, but they're all the same. I suppose it's possible that they landed in rough weather, and the boats were damaged, and, rather than just leave them, they burned them to minimise the chance of discovery."

"Sounds plausible," concurs Anthony. "So, you think this is where they landed?"

"Yes, I think it might be," replies Averill. "There are enough of these to represent a fair number of boats; probably enough to carry several hundred men.

"The thing that worries me," continues Averill, "is that we don't know how many other boats landed men here, then returned undamaged."

"Yes, I see," replies Anthony. "So, do you think there's anything more we can do here?"

Averill turns and scans the cliff and the rocks again, then shakes his head. "No, I think we've found what we were looking for; so I guess it's time to head back and let the king know."

"Can you ride?" asks Anthony.

"Of course. I'm a bit scratched and bruised; and I'm covered in this wet, mushy ash, but that will soon wash off."

"Then I agree. We had probably better get moving and deliver this information to the king."

"We'll ride to the forest, camp, eat and sleep, then continue on in the early morning. We should be back by the following night."

Anthony considers the situation. "This just got nasty didn't it?"

"No," replies Averill, inspecting the charred beam in his hand. "It's always been nasty. We just didn't know how nasty until now." Then, looking up at Anthony. "I believe that army which Prince Henry was rounding up is going to get bloodied much sooner than we anticipated. And, I'm afraid to say, I don't think we're ready for this. I think we could have a battle ahead of us, and I'm not sure we can handle it."

"Surely, you're not serious" counters Anthony.

"On the contrary," replies Averill, now regarding Anthony intently through narrowing eyes. "Just think about it: We've only recently finished one campaign, all of our foot soldiers have been released to go back to their lords, our archers are back tending their sheep or whatever they do, half our knights have ridden off to the far corners of the kingdom with their new brides, and we're now about to face an army we didn't even know about yesterday. I don't think things could get much worse; do you?"

Shocked by Averill's intense and coldly measured assessment of the situation, Anthony considers, but, for all his efforts, is unable to draw another conclusion.

Under his cloak, hastily thrown over his spray-sodden clothing, Averill shivers as the pair depart. A cold wind is at their backs as they ride from the cliff, and inland towards the distant tree-line marking the edge of the forest. The setting sun casts long thin shadows across the broad, undulating land.

Above the riders, the evening sky is inappropriately glorious.

CHAPTER THIRTEEN

Bedraggled and cold, the two riders approach the grey foreboding walls of the castle, ramparts tipped in pale orange in the slowly fading evening light. In other circumstances the image may have appeared beautifully surreal, but Averill's worsening fever betrays the legacy of yesterday's soaking on the rocks, and Anthony's recent illness has left him exhausted by the long ride home.

Another few minutes and they pass under the portcullis and on into the courtyard, already lit by braziers. Eager squires take charge of the horses. Nor has their approach gone unnoticed in the castle: Gareth, whose gruff and rugged appearance belies a constant gentle concern for the welfare of his leader, is already bounding down the stone stairs, anxiously looking from face to face, as he reaches the wretched pair.

"Welcome home Gregory, Anthony. Bryan has gone to alert Prince Henry of your return. How was it?"

Charles and Robert, rugged thickly against the evening chill, and Thomas, whose long, dark cloak flaps slowly in the cold, swirling breeze also reach the bottom of the stairs and emerge into the flickering half-light. Averill scans the group, relieved to see their faces again, and smiles, albeit wanly.

"Let's go inside and we'll tell you all about it when Prince Henry arrives. But, we have a little problem, I'm afraid. Thomas, can you get us something hot to drink; I fear that we are not as well as when we were together last."

★

Prince Henry, seated comfortably near the fire blazing steadily in the hearth, leans forward in alert informality, elbows on knees, hands clasped loosely together, and directs his remarks to his champion.

"Gareth and Bryan returned late yesterday and informed me of the existence of the forest camp. And this morning Charles, Robert and Thomas arrived to fill in further details. I will let them tell you of the situation in their own words, but first, Gregory, I want to hear what you have encountered."

There is a short pause as food arrives, and hot drinks for all. As they eat, Averill relates the story of the ride to the coast, mentioning first the discovery of William's body, then secondly the finding of the burnt-out shells of the invading army's boats.

"I see," nods the prince. "So, we know where they landed, but have no idea how many other boats arrived with men, and then departed safely."

"Exactly," replies Averill.

"How many do we think are now in the forest camp?" the prince continues, looking directly at Thomas.

Thomas looks to Charles and Robert before answering confidently, "About seven hundred, my Lord."

The other two knights nod in confirmation.

The muted sounds of eating echo within the room as the prince contemplates the picture compiled from the reports of the returned parties. Averill has warmed a little from the hot drink, but has eaten very little and sits with head in hands as his fever takes further hold. Anthony is faring not much better, as his exhausted body begins to fail in the battle to remain awake. The prince, alert to the need to deal with the growing threat, yet aware of the obvious need of his knights for recovery, decides that, for tonight at least, there is nothing more which can usefully be achieved.

"Gentlemen, thank you for your reports. I propose we all sleep upon these matters and re-assemble tomorrow morning to plan our course of action. Pray, continue here until you have eaten adequately. But, for now, I will bid you goodnight."

"Gregory, I suggest you wrap up well; this does not look like a trivial cold. Take care, my friend."

Wall hangings flap softly in the swirling breeze of the prince's departure. One-by-one, the knights finish their supper and retire to rest. Gareth sits quietly by as Averill forces himself to eat a little more, then together they depart; the big man draping has arm carefully around the shoulder of his leader, aware that this last day has cost much in terms of his captain's health.

★

The concerned face staring down at him breaks into a faint smile as Averill opens his eyes.

"So, you're back with us at last."

Light headed and disorientated, the knight lies still, looking up at his prince, still not quite able to focus, but aware that the strange muffled sounds which have accompanied the throbbing aches in his head and behind his eyes, have receded now. The words he is hearing are crisp and clear.

"You are a very fortunate man, Gregory. I don't believe I have ever seen a woman so devoted as your lady. She has nursed you for the past three days now. She is one in a million my friend, just as you said she was.

"I shall leave you now; I have matters which require attention, and I know that you are in good hands. I just wanted to drop by and see how you were progressing. But I am happy, now that you are back with us again."

The prince pats his champion softly on the shoulder, then rises from the edge of the bed, and quietly departs.

Averill closes his eyes again and rests. A faint movement of the air announces another presence. He recognises her scent as she settles down beside him. Her hand strokes the roughness of his unshaven face, her lips lightly brushing his own. His eyes remain closed, but slowly he moves his hand to cover hers. She licks his ear, whispers to him, then snuggles closer. He smiles, and the world retreats once more.

★

The tone of the light tells him it is late afternoon. He dares to move his head and finds that the throbbing is no longer there. She is looking at him; hunger in her eyes. He smiles; she raises her head from the pillow and slowly lowers her lips to his, kissing him; first softly, then urgently, passionately. He senses her exquisite agony and cups his hand behind her neck, pulling her to him. Her eyes widen with anticipation and, for a moment, she struggles with her clothing, then snuggles in beside him.

The blankets provide a sensual warmth to their embrace. He attempts to rise but finds he is still weak. Gently, she pushes him back; he submits and lies still, looking up into her smouldering eyes as she moves her hand down his chest, then slowly twirls her fingers through the soft hair of his belly. Slowly, tantalisingly, she lowers her head and breathes hotly onto his nipple, then bites tenderly before running her tongue over the now erect bud. Her hand moves again, and his breath becomes ragged as another, more heightened pleasure overtakes the first. Slowly he hardens as her fingers work steadily at him; gently at first, then with increasing urgency. For a moment he opens his eyes, and sees her staring at him with wild intensity. Abruptly she turns, slowly trailing her wet tongue from his chest to his belly and beyond. Her legs now straddle him as she, on hands and knees, takes him in her mouth. Her darkly swollen, parted flesh glistens with moisture only inches from his face; her scent pungent and overpowering. The whimpering sounds she makes as she gorges herself are coupled with an increasingly regular movement of her hips.

Unwilling to submit too soon to the exquisite ecstasy she is generating, he grasps her thighs and draws her buttocks to him. She moans in ecstasy as his tongue dips into her, savouring the delicious nectar now flowing thickly and freely from her. Absorbed in animal passion, she grinds her quivering flesh against his mouth. Her hand still grasps him strongly as she shudders in waves.

88

Unable to resist the mounting pleasure, she releases her hold on him and turns to face him once again. Without a pause, she slides hot and dripping down over his belly until her parted legs straddle his hips. She pushes further and he slides easily and quickly into her.

Reaching up he grasps her swinging breasts and begins rolling her swollen dark red nipples between his fingers. Her hands on his chest, she rides him hard; her fingernails digging into his flesh in exquisite agony. Mouth open, eyes wide, pupils dilated, she tosses her head violently from side to side, her long black hair flying in great arcs in time with the violent thrusting of her thighs.

Averill, too, has lost all awareness of his surroundings as he stares without blinking and with desperate focus at the wonderful creature now impaled upon him. She thrusts harder and faster; panting animal sounds from deep in her throat emerge, uncontrolled and unrestrained.

No longer capable of thought, he releases her breasts and clasps the full, soft flesh of her hips. He is about to burst.

She screams a long shuddering wail in sensual harmony with the unsteady guttural cry from her knight. Their bodies convulse in uncontrolled rhythmic release as orgasmic spasms debilitate the two lovers.

Whimpering, shuddering, panting, she collapses, exhausted upon his heaving chest. A minute passes, two minutes, then the slightest giggle. He smiles, still bathed in the warmth she has generated. She wiggles her hips to feel him inside her again, and, with head still lying upon his chest, stretches her arms up to cup his neck in her hands. Then slowly she pulls herself along his body until her mouth reaches his. She kisses him, long and deep and sensually.

"I love you, my beautiful man, I love you so much," she murmurs. Wrapping his arms around her body he finds himself unable to respond. She lifts her head to look at him, then moves her hand to wipe away the tears from his eyes.

"I know, my love, that's how I feel too... forever."

He smiles, but the tears continue. Strange thing, happiness.

CHAPTER FOURTEEN

The king and Prince Henry lean over a table strewn with maps. The prince is half a head taller than his father, exuding a soft, easy confidence as he listens to the king's words. By contrast, the king appears gaunt; worried.

A shaft of crisp morning light from the window angles across the room striking the beautifully decorated pitcher sitting prominently upon the sturdy side-table. Scattered reflections create a scene of incongruous, surreal beauty which belies the gravity of the situation.

A page enters and bows, announcing a visitor. "Sir Gregory Averill, Your Majesty."

The king, still leaning solidly on the table, looks up momentarily but otherwise does not move, as Averill bows and advances. By contrast, Prince Henry, grinning broadly, strides purposefully across the room, arms outstretched.

"Ah Gregory, it's nice to see you on your feet again."

Clapping his companion on the shoulders, the prince looks intently at Averill. "Are you alright again now? Are you ready for this?"

"Over here, you two."

The two young men respond to the rasp of their king's voice, and stride swiftly back to the table.

"We've had these drawn up since you returned," continues the king. "You'll find the position of the encampment indicated as accurately as our cartographers can determine from the information provided by your knights. Please look carefully and let me know if anything seems amiss."

Averill focuses on the task, remembering landmarks, recalling times taken to travel, and estimating distances covered. His finger glides along the map as he traces the circuitous outward path taken by the group and then the more direct return path he followed with Anthony.

"My recollections of our outward journey are clear and I do not disagree with the dispositions indicated here, Your Majesty," Averill responds. "However, my recollection of the return ride to the castle is much less clear, and hence, I am afraid I can neither verify nor correct any of the features indicated here, I'm sorry."

"No matter, Gregory," replies the prince. "Anthony's input has already been incorporated, and we are confident of his recall, as I'm sure you are.

"Two scouting parties are out as we speak; just watching, hopefully unobserved. And we're also making enquiries through our network of 'friends'. But, we're not ready for battle just yet."

The king straightens, looks darkly at the two younger men, then walks slowly toward the window, hands clasped behind his back. A moment's pause as he gazes out over the courtyard of a castle stirring, reluctantly, into wakefulness; then speaks. "Indeed, Gregory, as Henry says, we are not yet ready for a battle."

"Nevertheless, I fear one is coming, and its timing may not be up to us."

Still looking over the blithely innocent scene outside, the king continues. "In your absence, Henry has begun the task of raising a new army, and although some progress has been made, we are thwarted by the wide scattering of knights and men which occurred at the end of our last campaign. We are, therefore, building from our weakest for a long time... and this new threat was not anticipated. I fear we will be caught underprepared."

The younger men wait, uncertain which way the king's mood will lead.

Silence; broken only by the alternate clasping and unclasping of the king's hands behind his back, as he looks out the window, seemingly oblivious to all about him. The strong, once handsome features are now etched and lined from the worries and the battles, both military and political, of a reigning monarch, compounded by the skin affliction which has blighted his later years. And, as he ponders the situation, the shoulders sag; just a little.

He turns, takes a moment to regain his focus, then, looks from his son to his champion... and back again. He smiles and nods, as much to himself as to the two young men waiting on his words. "But then, this is what we do best, isn't it? Backs to the wall, odds against us; Crécy, Poitiers... I suppose we wouldn't have it any other way, would we?"

A pause stretches time, as the words sink in.

Then clearly, confidently; a king once again: "So then, let us gather ourselves; let us assemble this rag-tag army of yours, Henry, and let us exercise these few brave knights of yours, Sir Gregory, and let us see just what we can put together by way of a fighting machine.

"We may be rough, and we may be unready, but we are England, and none shall deny us that, be we ever so ragged in our appearance."

The two young men stand, inspired by the quiet intensity of the king's words. Once again, the king has transformed the situation from one of pending despair into one of unrestrainable pride. And once again, the prince recognises the enormity of the challenge he faces to fill his father's boots, when the time comes.

The king smiles again. "Come, let us walk among our people; our minds are now cast, and our presence will give our people confidence that all is well in God's world.

"After you, Henry."

The prince turns and strides from the room, heart beating strongly with the pride infused by his father's words.

The king does not follow, but turns to Averill. "My son is a sometimes wayward and sometimes petulant young man, Gregory. And he does cause me grief from time to time with his ill-thought comments and his eagerness to impress. But he is also smart, and has become very competent in battle. And, one day, he will be king."

"Yes, Your Majesty."

"Never let him down, Gregory." Intensely.

"Your Majesty, I would never..."

"I know, Gregory, I know."

A pause, as the king regards his champion. "But, as I said, my son is as impetuous as he is brilliant, and I need to know that someone unafraid to speak his mind will be beside him, Gregory."

Then quietly: "Henry tells me you have found your woman."

"Oh," a smile, a blush, a stammer, "yes, Your Majesty, I believe I have."

Another silence, as the king continues to look into the now unwavering eyes of his champion.

"Never let her down either, Gregory. Never take her for granted."

Averill opens his mouth to answer, but the king holds up his hand, then turns and looks quietly out the window again. Softly: "I remember my first queen... so beautiful... so majestic. I was the king... but she was the majesty. I loved her so much... so much."

Averill is moved by the king's quiet strength. "I remember, Your Majesty. I remember how you looked at her. And I remember how lovely, how soft, how serene she seemed; although I was only young."

"Only young?" barks the king, swinging to face the younger man again. "You're still 'only young', you colt." He smiles, then continues: "Your father would have been proud, Gregory... very proud."

Then, staring out the window again; quietly, softly, reflectively: "Yes, indeed; we remember, don't we? Such a lady... such a wonderful, wonderful time.

"Don't you ever take your lady for granted, Gregory. They are such delicate creatures... here one minute, gone the next. Cherish every moment you have with her; these days will only come once in your lifetime.

"And one day, you will look back, as I do now, and ask 'Where did the time go? Where did all those beautiful moments go?'

"Life; it rushes by so quickly... so quickly."

The king turns back again, places his arm around Averill's shoulder and starts toward the door. "But come, Gregory; Henry is far ahead, and we are losing ourselves in..." then stops and reflects again. "In something worth losing ourselves in, my boy."

Momentarily, he regards his champion again, then tousling the young man's hair, he turns and strides ahead.

But Averill remains standing, watching, striving to absorb the lesson just delivered. He knows he has only grasped a modicum of the wisdom dispensed, yet feels an inexplicable mixture of pride and sadness; as if his future had just been foretold. There was something there; something he should have grasped, but it eludes him. And then, his thoughts turn to Mariel, and the lesson fades. He shakes his head, smiles, and moves to follow the prince and the king.

The dust settles, and the sound of boots recedes as the trio, one-by-one, pass from the castle out into the courtyard... to walk among the king's people.

CHAPTER FIFTEEN

Averill's breathing is ragged as he stumbles over the irregular ground, brushing through the waist-high grass, reaching out and almost catching the large pink bow on the back of the party dress bouncing in unsteady fashion on the young figure scampering across the ground not three feet ahead of him. She slows, turns, then shrieks with surprise as she spies the knight almost upon her, and charges off again down the nearby slope; arms flailing as she strives to retain her balance; the sound of vibrant laughter filling the air. Averill resumes the chase with valiant endeavour, but within another minute calls a halt and falls breathlessly to the ground. Another figure, bare-footed, panting and laughing, dress hitched above her knees, long black hair waving and glinting in the afternoon sunlight, catches up and, happily, falls upon him.

Odelia is beside herself with gaiety and turns once again, this time to see the knight and her mother locked in embrace, laughing uncontrollably and rolling down the slope towards her. At once, she charges back up the incline and completes the picture by falling on top of the rolling tangle of arms and legs, thereby making the chaos complete.

Slowly, breathlessly, the three bodies, shaking with mirth, disentangle themselves; but it is the smallest figure which stands first.

"Come on, Daddy, let's do it again," she shouts as she begins the struggle up the incline again.

"Oh, Odelia; it's time for a rest," her mother pleads, and Averill nods in muted assent, laughter still preventing any more coherent response.

The little girl is insistent. "Can we go to the maypole, Daddy... please... can we?"

Knowing his inability to refuse her plea but also aware of the absolute futility of his becoming involved, the chuckling knight seeks an honourable exit. "Perhaps Mummy can take you; after all, it's the ladies who are best at the maypole, isn't it?"

"Oh yes, can we please Mummy... can we?"

With whispered words in the ear of her man, promising sweet retribution at the appropriate time, Mariel accedes to her daughter's request and the pair link hands and dance off toward the tall pole, already adorned with colourful ribbons, and around which a small crowd of eager would-be participants is beginning to gather. The spruiker and the musicians complete the picture of engaging summer jollity, as the bells of morris men further afield bring additional clamour to the joyous afternoon.

Eyes closed, Averill lies back upon the sloping ground and relaxes.

"Daddy," he muses. She says it so easily, as if nothing in the world were more natural, and it affects him so powerfully. It is a sweet surprise for which nothing had prepared him. And yet, now that he has heard it, there is no going back. She is his, just as much as her mother is his. And he would not have it any other way.

A moment later the ground shudders as a new arrival falls in barely-controlled collapse to the ground next to him. Averill has no need to open his eyes.

"Lazy git," rumbles the big man as he stretches out his legs.

"Peasant," responds the knight, then shouts in mock agony as a large fist imparts a muted blow to his upper arm.

Instantly on his feet, Averill is shaping to respond to the erstwhile attacker, when a young voice pierces the unfolding scene. "Touch him and you'll have me to deal with, you... you... you big bully."

"And me," chimes in another, distinctly feminine tone.

Recognising defeat, Averill drops his arms in mock surrender. "Alright, come on, do your worst."

At once, a sinewy flash, topped with red hair, and about five-and-a-half feet tall, launches itself at the knight. Averill is knocked off his feet, and, within seconds, is once again rolling down the slope locked in struggle.

Gareth looks on, shouting encouragement to his son as the pair battle for supremacy.

"Give it to him, James," laughs the woman clinging to Gareth's arm, as she watches her boy, inch-by-inch, being forced into submission. The struggle continues for a few more minutes, then, with a sudden twist, Averill pulls the boy to his feet, and in one lightning-quick movement, has him pinned, immovable, arms crossed in front of him.

Struggle is futile. The boy arches his head back and looks directly up, into the eyes of his captor.

"I will beat you, Sir Gregory. One day, I really will, you know."

"Yes, my boy, I know you will... one day," the knight replies, graciously. "But until then, let's make sure that we're always on the same side, shall we? After all, when you become as big as your dad, I really don't think I'll want to be fighting you."

A look of self-conscious pride passes over the young boy's face, as Averill releases his arms, and tousles his hair.

"And as for you, Wendy Littlewood," he turns to the strong, smiling woman, still clutching Gareth's arm, "well, if I had a wife as proud of her men as you are of yours, then I would be as happy as that ox standing next to you now... and rightly so."

The ox, with one arm around his wife, embraces his leader with the other and grins the silly smile of one pleased beyond measure with the situation, and not in any mind to change it.

A pause, then attention turns to a slight, disconsolate figure stumbling unsteadily towards the group. As she approaches, her eyes can be seen flicking from side to side, as the dizziness slowly recedes, and gradually her balance returns. Behind her, Mariel holds her hand to her mouth, stifling laughter, as she observes the effects of her daughter's recent encounter around the maypole.

"Daddy, the boys ruined the maypole."

"Oh, sweetie, what happened?" asks Averill as he leans down and sweeps the downcast little creature into his arms.

Arms flung about his neck, she rests her head on his shoulder, for just a moment, then animated once again, continues. "Oh Daddy, those boys, they are so annoying. Honestly, I don't know why they can't do things properly."

Now Averill cannot contain his smile. Mariel reaches him and places her arm around his waist. "And whose words are they, my love?" she enquires with gentle, but unconcealed delight.

"Alright," admits Averill, abashed that one of his stock phrases is being used back at him, yet delighted that it is his little girl who has picked it up, and moreover, is using it with all of the emotion of an indignant young lady. What a change has been wrought in this ragged little orphan. And how like her mother she is becoming, before his very eyes.

"Well then, why don't you and Mummy and I go back and do it right?" offers Wendy. "And we'll only have girls this time."

"Oh, yes please, Auntie Wendy," Odelia replies, wriggling free as Averill gently lowers her to the ground. "Can we Mummy, can we?"

In fact, resistance is not an option as the little girl, focussed upon her quest, has taken both Mariel and Wendy by the hand and is tugging them both back toward the maypole, where a jolly crowd is engaged in a hilariously uncoordinated attempt to untangle the result of the previous dance.

The knights remain standing, Averill, hands on hips, watching the departing trio, and Gareth, arm resting carelessly on his son's shoulder, watching his captain.

"So, Gregory, life brings its own surprises?"

"Indeed, Gareth, indeed," responds the knight, thoughtfully. "I could never have imagined this; not in a thousand years." He shakes his head in continued disbelief. "It's humbling, actually, for one sees one's own vanity. I wanted the perfect woman; flawless, untouched by another man, a virgin, the most beautiful creature of the kingdom.

"And then, in the most brutal of circumstances, in the most pitiful of situations, God reveals his angel. She was well hidden, mind, but from the moment I saw those eyes, I was utterly captivated; I could not get her out of my mind."

"Ah, yes," chuckles the big man. "We remember the circumstances quite well. We knew we'd lost you; we just didn't know why. However, it soon became apparent." A pause. "But, you're still a lost cause, you know, Gregory; totally smitten; absolutely useless to man or beast."

Averill opens his mouth to protest, but then, recognising both the jibe and the fundamental truth behind the comment, smiles, nods quietly and acquiesces. "Yes, Gareth, you are, of course, quite right; totally smitten, totally useless… and happier than I ever thought possible."

Gareth moves to respond, but Averill interjects. "But, what really scares me is the intensity of what I feel. And what really surprises me is that I feel it for both of them; Mariel and Odelia. If I had to save one or other, I don't know what I would do; I couldn't choose. By God, I hope I never have to face that decision; I don't know how I would live with myself afterwards, having let one of them die. I think it would ultimately consume me."

"Believe me, Gregory" replies the big man, "It is a situation we husbands and fathers all face; I, also, could not make such a choice."

Abashed, Averill retreats. "I'm sorry, Gareth, that was callous of me. Of course, you understand what I'm talking about; you have Wendy and James; and, of course, you would face the same impossible choice. Indeed, your love for your family is already a number of years more advanced than mine, and yet, here am I, lecturing you on the subject. Pray, forgive me."

"No, Gregory, you were not callous; you were just experiencing the awe that we all feel when we love, and when we become responsible for another's life. Oh, certainly, we have responsibility for the king and the prince, and for each other on the battlefield, but this is different. This is a protective responsibility, sweeter and more painful than any other you are likely to encounter. Mark my words, Gregory, from this point on, this love of yours will direct the course of your entire life."

A silence envelopes the two knights, as each man, slightly embarrassed by the outpouring of emotion, reflects upon the words which have passed between them. Uncharacteristically hesitant, Averill stands, with hands on hips, looking toward the maypole in the middle distance. The musicians are playing the first bars of a lively melody, and Mariel, Wendy and Odelia, each with a ribbon in hand, are beginning the intricate dance around the pole, alternately under and over the ribbons held aloft by the other dancers.

"You're a good man, Gareth."

A large hand falls gently upon Averill's shoulder. "I'm very proud to serve under you, my captain."

★

Sprawled casually across the plush, thick blankets covering the bed, back resting upon soft maroon cushions, Averill allows his fingers to play delicately through Mariel's long, soft, black hair. He smiles, and bends to kiss her head as she continues her story in soft, accented tones. Odelia, lying between them, breathes steadily and deeply. Partially covered by a beautiful damask blanket and with one arm flung carelessly across her forehead, she lies exhausted.

Thrilled and excited by her day's activities, she has talked without ceasing ever since arriving back at the castle two hours ago; re-living every exciting moment of the afternoon; from the early frustrations with the boys who wouldn't do things properly, through to the later triumph of a glorious maypole dance with her mother, Auntie Wendy, and the other women and girls who had been so determined to achieve perfection. But now, sleep has overtaken her and her boisterous and animated contributions to the conversation have slowed, and ultimately, ceased. Mariel's right hand, protectively stroking her daughter's shoulder, slows, then stops, resting quietly on the sleeping child's arm.

"I wish you could have seen the waves," she continues, "sometimes higher than these castle walls. And when they came, the captains had to turn the big ships so that their bows would slice through the waves as they came crashing over us. On one terrible occasion, I saw one of the ships in trouble; her captain had been so busy securing the cargo that he had not left enough time to turn his ship. It was awful. The waves were so enormous that they poured over the sides of the huge ship, and she started to roll from side to side; huge, slow rolls, each one further than the last. We watched, helpless, from about four hundred yards away; but there was nothing we could do. It was an enormous ship, and yet we could hear the timbers cracking; just occasionally at first, but then more frequently. And gradually, the cracking gave way to what seemed like a long, low groaning, and the ship began to break up. There were families and cattle and horses and fresh water on that ship. It was late in the afternoon and the sky was dark. The rain came down more heavily, and the wind drove the huge waves over her. We last saw the ship leaning heavily to one side, with that awful groaning becoming louder and louder.

"By morning, the storm had passed, and although our own ship was covered in broken timber from the masts, and torn cloth from the sails, we were still unharmed. In the distance we could see ships scattered across the ocean, and over the rest of the day, the surviving ships managed to sail

98

towards each other and become a ragged formation once again. But, we never saw that ship again. One hundred families lost. It was terrible. There was much sadness on our ship for many days. All of us had known families on that ship; many of us had lost friends that night. And, some of us began to wonder whether we had embarked upon a fool's journey.

"I tell you, my love, I know of nothing more frightening than nature gone wild. There is nothing that can make you feel so helpless as wind, or sea, or fire out of control. I have seen all of these things during my time travelling with my father, and sometimes I tremble just remembering how close we came to not surviving."

Reaching up, Mariel clasps Averill's neck and pulls him down.

"Hold me, my love. Hold me, and never let me go; I feel so safe with you. I never want to leave your side. I want to be with you until we are old and grey together, I want to have a home together, and stay in one place together. I have wandered far enough in my time, and now I have found you, I do not want to wander anymore."

Averill places his arms around his soft, delicate woman and gently hugs her to him. Rocking slowly back and forth, he comforts her until the moment passes. She smiles, and wipes away the hint of a tear.

"I'm alright now, my love. I haven't remembered that night for such a long time. I'd forgotten how terrifying it was."

"Tell me more about your father," probes Averill, carefully steering the conversation away from the terrifying images of violent, uncontrolled nature.

"Ah, my father," murmurs Mariel. "He was our guide, our light, our direction; he was the star we followed... and I was 'Choy Dip', his little butterfly." She pauses, smiling to herself at remembered images of far-off times in far-off places, then, returning to the moment, she continues.

"We had a happy little family. My mother was warm, and gentle, and pretty, and played such beautiful music. Her favourite instrument was the erhu."

"What's that?" interjects Averill.

"What, the erhu? Oh," answers Mariel, tossing her head back and stretching one graceful hand out to trace the shape of the imaginary instrument in the air. "It's a wooden instrument, with a hollow base of six or eight sides, and a long neck. There are two strings made of many fine threads of silk, which run from the base to wooden pegs at the top of the neck. And over the ends of the base is stretched snakeskin, which makes such a beautiful sound as the strings vibrate. There's another long wooden piece, a bow, which has horse hair stretched very tightly from end to end. As you play the bow back and forth across the strings, it makes such a beautiful sound. You move your fingers up and down the strings, and the sound changes; just like your lute, except that with the erhu, the sound sort of slides from one note to the next. It is a different sound from your music, but, for me, it is just as beautiful; perhaps even more so. I can hear it now."

"It sounds quite amazing," remarks Averill.

"Yes," replies Mariel, "it is; it really is.

"If only you had heard my mother playing," she adds. "Sometimes, her music was so beautiful it made you cry. I wish I could let you hear it. I learned a little. I was never as good as my mother, but I think, with practice, I could have played quite nicely."

Averill is entranced. "Perhaps one day, my love, we will be able to journey back the way you came, and maybe find a traveller who knows where to find such an instrument. And then, you can play for me... and perhaps even teach Odelia to play."

Mariel's eyes are glistening as she lifts her face and pulls her lover's head down towards her.

"Oh, yes, my love; to journey with you across the lands that I have seen, would be so wonderful. There are sights you cannot imagine; you would be amazed; utterly amazed."

"What happened to your mother?" asks Averill. "Is she still alive?"

"No," replies Mariel. "She died when I was about sixteen years old. She was having another baby, quite late in life really, but something went wrong.

"One morning, I awoke to find my father in tears, just whimpering. He was sitting on their bed, with my mother in his arms, rocking her back and forth. I did not know what had happened, but I could see that she was not responding. Her left arm was just hanging down. And, as he laid her back on the bed, I saw the blood. There was a lot of blood; something to do with the baby. I never found out exactly what."

Silently, Averill holds her to him, as she buries her face in his chest. He feels her slight shudders as she cries softly, re-living times long past, from a life and a place of which he has no knowledge, no understanding.

Under the blanket, Odelia stretches and turns onto her side. Mariel reaches out and gently strokes her daughter's arm. Slowly, quietly, the little girl resumes her deep, steady breathing.

"There's just us now," whispers Mariel. "Just me, and my daughter... and my wonderful man."

She looks up into Averill's eyes once again, and smiles. "I have never been so happy, my love; never."

Averill smiles back. "You haven't told me about your father," he gently prompts.

"I will, my love," she replies, "I will... but not tonight. We have had such a wonderful day and I need you to hold me now; I just want to snuggle down and let the world pass us by. Can we do that?"

"Just a moment, then," replies Averill, standing and lifting the small bundle, blankets and all, from the bed, and placing her just three feet away on the second bed, prepared especially for her in the corner of the room. He covers the exposed arm then returns to Mariel, who has disappeared beneath the blankets. The dress she was wearing lies on the floor beside the bed.

CHAPTER SIXTEEN

Daylight has not yet broken, but the bustle around the castle is gradually intensifying. In the distance a cock crows, then another, and soon there is a cacophony of crowing and cackling as domestic fowl in pens scattered across the castle herald the approaching dawn. A single ray of sunlight pierces the gloom; long shadows crystallise from out of the darkness; the voices of the fowl become sporadic, then silent again. Within minutes, the night is receding and the preparations of the hunting party and its noble spectators become clearly visible.

The king, concerned at the growing anxiety spreading through the castle, occasioned by the possibility of an unwanted battle, has once again applied his talent for surprise and ordered a hunt, and, in the process, hone further the fighting skills of his men-at-arms. Although just a hunt, all involved know the dangers presented by a cornered and enraged boar, and those who finally despatch the beast will have to overcome their own fear as well as the powerful, slashing tusks of the enraged animal in the process. More than once has a wild boar impaled upon a spear driven itself along the shaft toward its attacker. And more than one of the king's men bears the scars of deep tusk wounds delivered by a dying wild animal which refused to capitulate.

For Mariel, the occasion is an astonishing mismatch of vacuous and high-spirited fashion against the preparations for the deadly pursuit of wild boar hunting. The ladies, herself and Wendy included, are decked out in gaily-styled skirts and blouses. Brightly coloured ribbons adorn their hair, and cloaks of hues as various as the rainbow catch the eye as the ladies of the court run, unselfconsciously, between the privies and the milling, wheeling horses tended by the squires and grooms of the court; taking last-minute opportunities to make themselves comfortable for the longish ride ahead.

Averill has left his lady, having placed her in no uncertain terms in Wendy's care for the day; and having been told, decorously, but also in no uncertain terms, that he would do better to mind his own skin than worry about the Lady Wendy's ability to protect his lady.

Gareth is still chuckling as the knights approach the king and Prince Henry.

"Your Majesty," says Averill bowing in greeting; the others following suit behind him. "It looks a fine morning for the hunt."

"Indeed, Gregory," replies the king. "I do believe today's little jaunt into the bush will rid us of much of the bitterness which the recent focus on training and rumour has allowed to infest our people."

"I see Mariel is with us, Gregory," remarks the prince.

"She is protected by my wife," offers Gareth, wincing momentarily as Averill's elbow finds its way into his ribs.

"As Gareth says, my Prince," continues Averill. "She is taken under the Lady Wendy's wing for this, her first hunt, my Lord."

"Very good, Gregory," replies the prince. "I trust she enjoys it."

"Well then, enough of this banter. Let us be off." And, wheeling his horse toward the raised portcullis, the king trots off. Prince Henry digs in his heels and quickly ranges up alongside his father. Taken off-guard, Averill and his knights sprint back towards their horses. Meanwhile, around them, mild pandemonium breaks out as almost-ready knights, beaters, buglers, dog handlers and grooms realise that there is no more time for preparation and run in flustered disarray towards horses or the castle gate. Gradually, the diverse and scattered throng of mounted and foot collects itself into a semblance of order and makes its way through the opening and out into the beckoning countryside.

The hunt is on.

★

The angle of the sun, low, from south of east, suggests about eight of the morning. Averill and Prince Henry stand slightly apart from the rest of the gathering, boots and legs bathed in sunlight, upper bodies shaded by the leaves of the wide-spread branches of the chestnut trees, under which the party has stopped to enjoy a welcome draught of ale, and the opportunity for a quiet stroll into the adjoining bushes for a comfort break.

Averill's left boot traces a repetitive path in the sparsely-grassed ground, as, momentarily lost in thought, he savours the brew. Prince Henry, similarly, enjoys his ale, but unlike his companion, is alert to his surroundings, and observes with interest Averill's withdrawal into his thoughts.

"For goodness sake, Gregory," exclaims the prince in mock exasperation. "Spit it out."

Slightly startled, Averill looks blankly at his prince, then, with a sudden slight shake of his head, returns to the here and now.

"I'm sorry, my Lord, I was miles away."

"Yes, indeed," agrees Henry. "I could see that."

"It's just that... well, I have something I need to say," replies Averill. "And... I guess now is as good a time as any; isn't it?"

"I don't know, Gregory," answers the prince. "Is it?"

Averill looks intently at his prince, as if trying to break through some invisible barrier. But, the only barrier is in his own mind.

Henry waits patiently; a slight smile playing around his lips, enjoying the minor discomfort which seems to be consuming his friend.

"Gregory, I've known you long enough to know when something's bothering you. And, I also know that these things are invariably trifles which you have blown into major issues in your mind. I don't understand how you can be so cool and focused and terrifying whenever the situation is one of extreme danger, and yet you become a nervous wreck when it comes to women. It's about Mariel, isn't it?"

Averill is momentarily speechless; unaware that his plight is transparently obvious to the prince. A moment's hesitation. "Well, actually... yes, it is.

"You see, we, um..." an embarrassed pause, then, "well, we love each other."

"Yes, Gregory; I and every other knight of the court are well aware of that fact. But the question is, what are you going to do about it?"

Averill stands mute; a sheepish grin on his face. The prince inclines his head in patient question.

"Ah, yes. Well, you see, that's just it. I've actually... well, I've asked her to marry me."

"And?" Exasperated.

"And?" Querulous.

"And, what did she say?"

"Oh, I see. Um... 'yes.' She said 'yes', actually."

A wide, boyish grin breaks across Averill's face. The prince takes a pace forward, wraps his arm around Averill's neck, draws him close and claps him heartily on the back. Then, standing back, hands on Averill's shoulders, he surveys his compatriot of a hundred wonderful adventures, both sensual and savage.

"So, the mighty Gregory Averill has been captured, at last. The last bastion of independent manhood has been subdued; and by a princess from the East... and about time too."

Then, turning on his heel, the prince departs, striding purposefully back to the main group gathered at the centre of the grove of chestnut trees. Averill turns away and stares out over the field, silly grin still on his face, relaxed now that he has made his confession, and thoughts on the precious creature whose arrival has captured his heart, totally, and turned his whole world on its head.

Moments pass; a hand slides lightly around the knight's waist, and a head rests gently upon his shoulder. Neither Averill nor Mariel speaks; the moment is precious and neither wishes to disturb it.

And thus the pair of lovers remains, snatches of sunlight catching their faces, the rest of their bodies shaded by the overhanging branches, quite unaware of the drift of knights and ladies towards the tree under which they are standing.

The king's voice is close, and powerful. "My Lords, my Ladies…"

Startled, Averill and Mariel swing around to be confronted by the king, and behind him, the assembled knights, ladies and gentlemen of the court.

Prince Henry, at his father's side, is grinning broadly. The rest of the assembly, unaware of the reason for the gathering, is now talking in hushed tones, curious to learn the reason for the king's call to gather at this point.

Holding one hand up for silence, the king continues, "We have among us one who, for as long as I can remember, has distinguished himself by his dedication and commitment to the causes of our community. However, he has singularly disappointed us over the years when it has come to women."

A slight chuckle ripples through the gathering as they begin to catch the mood of the king, and understand the reason for the assembly.

The king continues, "Not that the women with whom he has been linked have in any way been unsuitable; far from it for me to suggest that. Indeed, most of them have appealed to me, greatly."

Circumspect laughter.

"But… and here's the thing… none of these women has ever been able to hold onto him. He has remained wild, untamed some might say, and totally beyond the reach of those who would possess him."

A murmur of confirmation from the knights and several ladies within the assembled throng.

"But now, it seems, the situation has changed, and one whom we have only had the pleasure of knowing for a relatively short time, has done what most of us wished for, but had begun to despair of ever seeing.

"I have been advised, by a source in whom I place great trust," and here the king looks to his son, "that Sir Gregory Averill has asked the Lady Mariel to wed him. And I suspect that, after the usual amount of dithering which we have come to associate with Sir Gregory in his dealings with women, he would have approached me to seek permission for this match."

Averill shuffles, uncomfortably, but Mariel holds him tightly, gazing up into his face, smiling hugely, enjoying the moment, confident in its course.

"Well, my people," continues the king. "I have no time for such dithering, and so," and here the king turns from the crowd and faces the knight and his lady, "Sir Gregory Averill, do you have anything you wish to ask me, or… am I ill-advised?"

Averill looks from the king, to Mariel, and back to the king again. And then, as on so many occasions before, the shuffling, slightly embarrassed young man, upon whom the court has long depended for its continued safety, now draws himself erect, and prepares to answer the challenge of his king.

"Your Majesty, I cannot deny that your words are indeed true. I have, over the years, engaged in encounters with the beautiful ladies of our court, and on more than one occasion, I have come close to seeking a match. But always, there has been an underlying doubt that I could give myself truly to the woman of the moment. Always, I felt that I would not live up to the expectation of either the lady in question or the court of Your Majesty. And so, as you have rightfully said, I have declined these sweet opportunities.

"But, what I did not know, and what I now commend to all of you who hear me this day, is this: you do not choose love; love chooses you. Never before did I understand that it was not I who was in control, but love. Never before did I understand that this is not a course which one chooses, but a course which, I suspect, is laid before one by God himself. Never could I have even begun to piece together the strange and beautiful circumstances which have led to this moment. And never could I have begun to imagine the total devotion I would feel for a woman that I have felt these past months.

"And so, if it pleases Your Majesty, I would like to follow the course which is now laid before me. I do, indeed, wish to wed the Lady Mariel, and would be most humbly grateful if Your Majesty were to bestow his blessing upon us both, and accede to this request."

Cheers, applause and prolonged whistling are subdued as the king raises his hand again for silence.

"Gregory, my boy, there is little I need to say. It has been clear to those of us who know you, that, for some time now, you have been totally smitten by this woman. And Mariel, I do not think it untrue to say that you have been equally enamoured of this knight; although I must say that you have handled it with significantly more aplomb than our young hero here, who has forgotten his duties, let his fellow knights run amok, and generally lost his way, during the course of his realisation that his life should be sweeter than it has been hitherto."

A knowing chuckle emerges from the closest of the gathering.

"But, if you will accept the wisdom of an old man, let me counsel you as follows: there are three things in this world which define a man and a woman; your faith in God, your obedience to your monarch, and your devotion to each other. To your faith in God, I will let our bishop speak on another occasion. In obedience to your monarch, I have nothing more to add. Sir Gregory has demonstrated this so many times that it will never be in question. Regarding your devotion to each other, I have only this to say: my queen was the making of me. I was like you, Gregory, and like Henry, my son, and one day, your king. Yes, I was brave; yes, I was handsome, although you might not think so now; but I was not... humble. I did not see what my eyes were showing me; I did not hear what my ears were telling me, I did not recognise that even the least among us has a part to play in this world. I did not understand how a king must serve; until I met my queen. It was she who opened my eyes and unstopped my ears; it was she who taught me how to lead; it was she who showed me what it is that makes a man.

"And so, Gregory and Mariel, when you look into each other's eyes, when you hold each other, when you lead your children through this world, understand that it is in serving that you become fulfilled. Leadership is vital, but compassion is everything. Your men will love you for it, your children will adore you for it, and the imprint you leave on this sometimes sad and brutal world will be defined by it."

A pause; no boisterous response now, but a quiet melancholy which spreads through the assembled crowd; a memory of younger, happier times. The king surveys his people, then taking Mariel's and Averill's hands, he joins them in his own and grants the request: "Lady Mariel, Sir Gregory Averill, you, indeed, have my blessing for this union."

And, as Averill sweeps his bride-to-be into his arms, and spins around with her clutching his neck, the king re-casts the mood, shouting above the gathering. "And now... to the horses. We have a hunt to pursue, and the day draws on."

And then, quietly, turning again to Averill and Mariel, he continues, "Although this unexpected interlude has, indeed, been worthwhile, and made the day memorable in the extreme."

Then, quietly, to himself, as if an afterthought, "So nice. To remember has been... so nice."

★

The horses are cantering now. The hounds have disappeared ahead and in the relative distance a hunting horn sounds its stark, repetitive note. The pace is quickening as the king, Prince Henry and Averill lead the pack of boisterous, eager knights, following the sounds of the horn with growing excitement and sporadic outbursts of bravado. At the rear, the cluster of gaily-coloured ladies are talking less now and concentrating more on the difficult business of trying not to get left behind as the dangerous but exciting passage through the forest gathers pace.

Staccato tones burst from the distant horn; the quarry has been sighted. Blood rises, spurs dig in and caution is forgotten as warriors, so long constrained by delicate scouting, soul-searching worry, and long, tedious preparation for the castle's defence, now find themselves unleashed in pursuit.

No quarter is asked and none given. The king, fine horseman that he has always been, leads the charge, with Prince Henry and Averill challenging closely. Behind them, several knights, including Charles, Robert and Anthony, are starting to pull away from the pack and almost ranging up alongside the prince and Averill. The ground under-hoof is soft yet firm, and speed increases. Neither Averill nor the prince is prepared to yield to the closing knights; nor is the king prepared to yield to either Averill or the prince.

The three leading riders now form an arrowhead of man and beast, charging headlong through the forest; the snorted, hot breach of the following coursers almost alongside.

Within minutes, a pack of six forms the lead group; Averill's three lieutenants having now broken away from the peloton of riders behind. The ground begins a gentle climb upward, and the six riders collectively hunch forward, urging their mounts up the incline.

Cresting the slight ridge, the pack thunders left as the trail sweeps around a large moss-covered rocky outcrop and begins a gentle descent.

The pace quickens yet again.

Averill is now level with the king; his right knee brushing against the king's left leg. On the other side, Henry is a foot behind and closing. A low-hanging branch forces the pack of six to duck collectively as it slashes past. The king looks sideways and grins fiercely at Averill. Henry sees the momentary opportunity, seizes it, and drives his horse alongside his father's. The three are now abreast, charging down the incline and beginning a slow wheel to the right as the track resumes its original direction. At their backs, Anthony and the brothers form a second tier of fury.

A moment later, the lead riders barely have time to register the fallen tree-trunk rushing toward them. Averill and Henry wheel left and right respectively, crashing crazily through undergrowth, horses shrieking and tumbling, prince and knight thrown to the ground, skidding head over heels through bushes and nettles, blood spattering the leaves as they crash through the undergrowth. The king has nowhere to go.

Silence; then the pathetic sound of injured horses struggling to rise, and the hoarse, muted gasps of winded men. The gay, staccato notes of the hunting horn, now close by, are ignored as the larger group of riders now rounds the bend and ploughs into the carnage.

Horses wheel and rear upward as riders come to a chaotic halt and dismount in confusion. Gareth lumbers toward the slash of colour lying crumpled beyond the fallen tree-trunk. Two more figures run up behind him. Quickly, the big man kneels, then gently turns the king over. A dark stain is spreading beneath the skin at the king's throat. Gareth bends closer, looking into the king's face, seeing unfocussed, sightless eyes, and noticing the slow drip of bright crimson blood from the king's open mouth. Sitting back on his haunches, the big man raises his hands to his face and cries out in disbelief.

A few feet away, Anthony is on hands and knees, dazed. Beside him, Charles stands, staggers unsteadily toward his brother, then falls to his knees again. Robert is lying on his back, staring blankly upwards, trying to gather together the threads of his mind and remember what has just happened.

The pack of ladies on horseback now arrives, galloping headlong into the confused and milling scene of injured knights and terrified and broken horses. Several of the ladies fall heavily to the ground as horses crash into each other. Others dismount, clumsily, and run to their aid.

Mariel sees Gareth beyond the tree-trunk, and, heart in mouth, she lifts her skirts and runs towards him. She finds the big man, still on the ground, with hands covering his face. Anxiously, she tears at his hands, squeezing them in anguish. "What has happened, Gareth? Where is he?"

The big man looks blankly back at her and mumbles, "The king."

Slowly, the horror of the incident dawns upon her as she recognises the still form on the ground beside Gareth. Bending close, she looks into the sightless eyes, sees the dark, angry, spreading bruise at the throat, and the small pool of now darkening blood on the ground at the king's mouth. Stunned, she continues to gaze at the lifeless form, noticing the delicacy of the placement of the king's arms beside his torso, hands trailing, palms uppermost. One finger appears to have been broken.

She stares, impassive, as gentle words echo, over and over, in her mind: "... the imprint you leave on this sometimes sad and brutal world..."

Then, gradually, a new imperative forces its way into her consciousness. "Gareth," she says, "Where is Gregory?"

No answer.

Mariel grasps the big man's shoulders and attempts to shake him. "Come on, Gareth, where is Gregory?"

Still no answer.

The knight is staring at the body of his king, still locked in a realm of disbelief.

Mariel rises, desperately looking around, but sees only confusion; knights tending to knights, women tending to knights and other women. She now notices that the prince is nowhere to be seen, either. She runs to Anthony.

"Anthony, Anthony... where is Gregory; and where is the prince?"

Anthony is struggling to his feet now, and Mariel places her arm around his shoulder in an attempt to help. However, the knight is taller than she, and eventually she succeeds in only holding his waist, as he finally stands upright.

He looks around, recreating the scene in his mind. Carefully, he pieces together the sequence. "We were charging down this trail... rounded that bend... and then, I don't know what happened. I saw Gregory's horse take a sudden turn to the left, and, I think the prince went right; but I'm not sure. It all happened so quickly."

But Mariel is no longer there. Rushing into the bushes to the left of the fallen tree-trunk, her skirts become torn and her hands scratched as she forces herself deeper into the undergrowth. And then she sees him, sitting on the ground, scratched and bloody, but otherwise unharmed. He looks blankly at her; nothing registers. Urgently, she rushes to him, falling to her knees and cradling his head in her arms. "Oh Gregory, my love."

Several moments pass, and then, a hand caresses her head. "I'm here, my love; I'm here."

Then, as memory returns and realisation dawns, "But what of the king, and Prince Henry? Have you seen them?"

"Oh Gregory," she wails. "I have not seen the prince, but I fear the king is dead. I was with Gareth, who is with him, just a moment ago, but I fear the worst. And Gareth is beyond reach. I think he also knows the king is gone."

Averill's senses, battered by the fall just taken, struggle to assimilate Mariel's words. Rising to his knees, he takes her head, roughly, in his hands. "What did you say about the king?"

Shocked by the ferocity of Averill's grasp, Mariel stammers her response. "I f-f-fear he is dead, my love. He was lying on the ground... n-n-not moving. His eyes were open, but I swear they were seeing nothing. There was blood on the ground, from his mouth. And Gareth was with him, but mute.

"Oh Gregory," she wails, again. "What has happened here?"

Stunned by the situation, and shocked into awareness by his own ferocious treatment of his lady, Averill suddenly clasps her to him. "I'm sorry, my love, I'm sorry. I did not mean to harm you."

Then, kneeling on the ground, holding his lady to him, Averill is at last able to begin assessing the situation. If the king is dead then Prince Henry is now king. But, if Henry is also dead, then God only knows what will happen with his brothers not having been preparing for the role. And, with an enemy force assembling in the forests this is no time for division within the castle.

He needs to know whether the prince is safe, or not.

Gently this time, he takes Mariel's head in his hands and looks directly into her eyes. "I have to find the prince, my love. I have to find him. Do you understand?"

"Yes, of course," she replies. "Of course."

"Then help me up. I am a little unsteady at the moment, but will be alright in a few minutes."

A moment later Averill and Mariel emerge from the bushes; he, focussed and hurting, clinging to her as he limps out. Mariel is looking, frantically, for the prince.

"There he is," she exclaims, pointing to where the king's body lies, and Averill stops sharply, taking in the shocking sight confronting him.

"Come on, quickly," he urges, and together they hobble toward the small but growing crowd of knights and ladies who surround both Gareth and the prince; the latter kneeling with one arm around his father's shoulder, face pressed close to the now pale face lying motionless on the soft earth.

Averill kneels, and places his arm around the shoulder of his prince. "Your Majesty."

The prince does not move, but continues to look into his father's face. Tears fall silently to the ground. "He is gone, Gregory." The words are slow, soft, and gentle. "My father is gone."

Then looking up into the eyes of his friend: "His last words were about love, Gregory; about love... and compassion; and about my mother.

"He rarely spoke like that. He was always worrying about plots and rebellions, and arguing with parliament, and, I think, regretting the actions he took so long ago with respect to his cousin Richard. But today, just for a moment, he was happy again; I know it, I heard it in his voice. He was happy because of you and Mariel and your plans to wed; and he thought of the woman he loved... he thought of my mother."

There are no words which Averill can utter in response; no words appropriate to offer a prince beginning to grieve the sudden and tragic loss of his father.

Moments pass in silence, then the prince rises to his feet. Averill rises with him.

"Please take him home, Gregory."

"Where do you wish him laid, Your Majesty?"

Henry is silent for a moment, as thoughts come slowly. "My father always talked of dying on pilgrimage to the Holy Land, but never had the opportunity to make that journey. Take him, therefore, to the Abbot's house at Westminster Abbey, and place him in the Jerusalem chamber. This is where I wish him to lie whilst we prepare for his burial.

Suddenly aware of the new order, Averill takes a pace backward, kneels, then rises and turns to seek assistance. The gathered knights and ladies, watching in silence now, recognise the gesture, and, collectively and unbidden, fall to one knee before their new king.

All except Gareth, who has risen and now stands facing Averill, eyes still red from weeping beside the body of his dead king, shoulders uncharacteristically slumped; impassive, bereft of direction.

"You are unhurt?" Averill asks.

"I am unhurt, my Lord."

Averill searches Gareth's face, seeking confirmation of the big man's well-being. "Are you with me, Gareth?"

"With you, my Lord; I am whole again."

Averill places his hand on Gareth's shoulder and gently commands: "Then take some men, select two horses, and fashion a litter between them, that we may carry the body of our king back to Westminster."

A moment's silence as Gareth looks pleadingly into his captain's eyes, wishing that things did not have to be as they are, yet knowing full well that time cannot be undone. Then, with the barest nod of his head, he acknowledges the order given. "Aye, my Lord."

★

Odelia's breathing is deep and steady as she lies snuggled beneath her warm blankets.

The light has faded, and now, inside the castle, as twilight gives way to night, the agonies of this tragic day seem to multiply with each passing moment.

On the larger bed close by, Averill lies, looking up at the ceiling. The beautiful dancing patterns made by the flickering shadows from the braziers around the wall fail to penetrate his trance-like state. In the crook of his outstretched arm, Mariel's head rests, her tear-stained face also staring upward. The back of one wrist rests on her forehead, her other hand tightly clutches her lover's forearm. The steady rise and fall of her breasts is interrupted, from time to time, by small shudders which tell of her distress.

Minutes pass; the only sound is that of Odelia's strong, steady breathing.

There are no more words; they have talked sadly, forlornly, despairingly, about the day's senseless unfolding. They have railed against the fates which conspired to cause a king to die so pointlessly. They have remembered the happiness and the serenity of the morning, and offered to sacrifice it all if he could be but brought back. And they have lapsed into prolonged silences as every word uttered has seemed to reinforce the extent of the tragedy.

The fragility of life has been starkly exposed, and Averill's senses reel, as if he is drifting in a sea of isolation. Still looking toward the ceiling, seeking something firm to grasp, he murmurs, "Tell me about your monk."

Nothing disturbs the sound of Odelia's steady breathing, as Mariel's mind at first rebels against the new request, then slowly acquiesces, and gradually begins shifting focus from the events of this day to those of other days so far in the past.

"Um..."

112

So hard to let go of today.

"He was..."

Nothing; then faint images... and the smell of the sea... and the sounds of sea-gulls... and steep, jagged rocks... and those great, round turrets; the first thing you saw... and the arches; those beautiful stone arches.

"He was... kind... and gentle... and he cared for me and my baby for so long... in that place... in the hospital."

"Where was it, again?" asks Averill, still staring at the ceiling.

Mariel is quiet for a moment, dragging distant memories back into focus. "It was called Rodos," she whispers.

Silence; neither speaks. Averill waits, mind hovering now between the fateful images of today, already becoming dulled by too much grief, and the imaginings of another place; this 'Rodos'.

Mariel has mentioned it before, but they have never actually talked in detail about those times, about what happened, about how she came to be there, and how she came to leave, and about what happened to her father. Perhaps this is not a good time... perhaps no time will ever be a good time... or perhaps here, tonight, it is the right time to talk about those events; the right time because she has already poured out her emotions, and perhaps now, she will talk, already drained, and not be consumed by further grief. Perhaps now she can at last reveal, without holding back, what happened during those 'missing' years; those years between the start of the sea voyage with her father and her rescue with Odelia from the village attack, almost a year ago.

"Tell me how you came to be there, my love," prompts Averill. Turning on his side, he softly strokes her shining black hair.

"There were only about twenty ships left of the great fleet which set out from home; from China."

Averill continues to stroke her hair, watching...

"We had been sailing for more than a year, I think. Along the way, we had stopped in many places, seen many strange sights, collected many strange things. And, often, when it came time to sail again, some sailors could not be found. We frequently had to spend weeks in one place while repairs to the ships were made, and I think that, often, the sailors found women there and decided to run off with them, rather than face more long months at sea.

"I always went ashore with my father; he was a trader, and so he was always keen to meet the people where we landed and see what he could pick up from them. Of course, he had many fine silks and beautiful vases to trade, so he could always obtain wonderful and amazing pieces in exchange. He was also quite a good artist, and spent much of his time drawing the strange birds and animals we encountered.

"After one long stay in a place where the vegetation was thick and the trees very tall, we had stocked the vessels until every space was filled with food and water and collected treasures; then we commenced a new phase of our journey. We had travelled south for many months, then west, and then north through huge seas, but now, for the first time we began travelling east; I thought we were starting our journey home. But after several weeks, I noticed that the seas were not so huge, and the weather had changed from storm after storm, to days of sunshine and beautiful breezes. Certainly, there were storms, but not continuously as before; now, they came and went in a few hours. It seemed as if we had entered paradise."

Mariel stops talking now and Averill, still stroking her hair, watches to see if she is about to break down again. But, surprisingly, she turns her face toward Averill and looks intently at him. "I became pregnant here, my love."

Averill's stomach lurches. He should have known; he should have expected it; it had to have happened somewhere.

"Do you want me to continue... or, don't you want to hear about it?" she asks.

Quickly over the shock, Averill has no hesitation. "My love, these are the pieces of your life which are hidden from me. Yes, I want to hear. I want to know everything about you."

Mariel reaches over and pulls Averill's face to her own, kissing him long and deeply. "I love you, my love," she whispers. "Today has been so awful." Then quietly: "He was so happy, just this morning."

A moment's reflection, then she asks, "How is Henry?"

"I left him at the chapel," replies Averill. "We had talked a lot, and sat in silence a lot. The bishop arrived and led us in a long, gentle, very reflective prayer. It was so moving. Then Henry said that he wanted to be alone, so I left him there.

"He is strong, my love, but the affairs of the court will not permit him much grace, so he will need time alone, and also time with his closest friends over the next few days. I will visit him again in the morning."

Then, after slight consideration, he continues, "But, perhaps, that may not be so easy now; for I suspect that, from now on, I will be granted audiences rather than having the immediate access I have enjoyed to this point. The world has changed, my love; the world has changed...

"As did your world... I want to hear more; pray tell me... I love you so much, and I want to hear..."

Mariel releases the gentle grip on her lover's head and falls softly back onto the bad. Averill similarly lowers his hand from his lady's hair and rolls backwards. Both are quiet, looking upward. The flickering shadows on the ceiling now register, and, for a moment, both are immersed in the magic.

"There was a sailor; actually there were several, and there were several of us girls on the ship. We had been together for all of the months of the voyage, and, although we weren't supposed to talk with them, sometimes we did.

"Often during the long afternoons, the sailors would stand at the front of the ship with us, and point out the clouds; their shapes, which ones brought rain, which ones meant strong winds. I learned to read the weather quite well, and could tell when a storm was coming, when I should go below to safety, and when I could stay up top. I also learned about the sun; simple things like where it rose and where it set, but also more interesting things like how it moved north and south and how the seasons changed as it moved. And at night, I learned about the stars; the way they moved and the creatures they were said to represent.

"On other afternoons, I spent time with my father, watching him drawing his birds and animals, trying myself, but not doing very well. But he always laughed and encouraged me. He told me a lot about my culture, about our emperors, about the battles our country had fought. And he taught me how to write beautiful Chinese characters; I loved this, and would spend hours practising.

"One night, it was so glorious, you had to be there to experience it; the sun had set but the glow above the horizon was still pink, the breeze was gentle and the big ship was moving so beautifully, with just the steady swish of the water as we cut through it. Three of us were standing in the near darkness, watching the water below. I was so alive that night, as if all of my senses were on fire. And then three of the sailors joined us, so quietly, and the boy I had seen before was one of them. He gave me his drink to share, and stood behind me, very close, looking at the beautiful pink glow as it gradually faded."

Mariel is silent; tears roll softly down her cheek as she looks over at her man. "I'm sorry, Gregory; it just happened. It was like I was floating and didn't want anything to stop. I did not know myself and the intensity of my responses until that night.

"There was no other night like it, for within a few days my father had fallen ill. The physician on the ship had many herbs and made many drinks for my father, but none could make him better; he spent most of each day sleeping, and often had a fever. The physician said that he needed fresh fruit and fresh vegetables, but there were none on the ship.

"But, we were lucky. We were passing through an area where we saw many small islands; but our ship's captain was looking for a larger one, so that we could stop and take on fresh food and water, and make repairs. About five days after my father fell ill, I awoke and heard the sound of seagulls. I rushed up to the top and saw that we were approaching land; but the sight amazed me, for there, right before us was the entrance to a harbour, and on each side of the entrance was an enormous grey stone wall, and within each wall was a huge round building; a tower, with what I now know to be battlements at the top. And further inland the ground rose to a giant rocky hill, and, built at the top of the hill was a magnificent white, stone temple. It was so unexpected; it was a building of the size I had not seen since I left home; and yet, it was different; a different style, but just as magnificent as anything I had seen before. It was as if I had come home, but to a new home."

Averill is now sitting cross-legged, looking down at his lady, shaking his head slightly, trying to create an image of the scene Mariel describes. She too is now immersed in the story and rises to sit, cross-legged, facing him.

"It was Rodos, Gregory," she exclaims, eyes shining, "or 'Rhodes', in English. It was the most amazing place I had ever seen."

For a moment, the magic has worked; the tragedy of the day has been supplanted by another story; a story so far from the here and now that Averill is totally absorbed, as is the story-teller, as she relives the events of so long ago.

"Go on," says Averill, gently. "Go on."

A pause, as Mariel gathers her thoughts, then: "What was most amazing of all, was that, here, at Rhodes, the most important building was... a hospital. I did not know it as we approached the harbour, but the hospital was to become my life for the next nine years. It was the most beautiful building I had ever seen, with high vaulted ceilings, and angular stone columns joined by exquisitely-carved arches; and yet, it was also the saddest; it was filled to overflowing with the injured and the dying; the pilgrims to the Holy Land. Over time, I became accustomed to the sadness of it all and learned to hold on to life as a God-given blessing; but on that first day, as we approached the harbour, I felt as if my life were taking a new turn, a new direction. I just knew my father and I were going to leave the ship; and I was excited... and afraid."

Averill stretches out his hands, and holds Mariel's face in them. "I love you, so much... so much," he says, with tears in his eyes. "How did I ever find you?"

Mariel smiles, blushes, then continues, "We could not understand what the people on the shore were saying, but when we carried my father from the ship, they understood, and several of them led us along the dusty paths to the hospital building. We were taken in and my father was placed on a bed near an arched window set into the thick stone wall. Several men came to tend to him, and I sat with him for the rest of the day.

"Later, in the evening, another older man came to me and indicated that I should eat, so I went with him. During the meal, he pointed to my belly and made a 'round' sign with his hand. I nodded, and he just placed his hand on my head and smiled a sad sort of smile. It was so gentle, I cried. He held my hands, and when I looked up, he smiled again and nodded. I don't know how, but we understood each other; and, for some reason, I once again felt as if I had come home."

"This was your monk," says Averill, nodding in understanding.

"This was my monk," replies Mariel, "Father Eustace... he was English."

"Later, I brought some of our possessions from the ship," continues Mariel. "Not many; just a few small pieces of pottery, some beautiful silk scarves, and several of my father's books with his drawings. Father Eustace kept them for me. He would look at them often, and smile a lot; but he always made sure I knew they were still mine.

"Our ship sailed a few weeks later. Father was recovering, but slowly, and I did not want to return to the ship; I knew my baby would be coming later, so we stayed. I stood outside the hospital the afternoon our ship left, and watched as it sailed out through the harbour entrance. I did not quite know what I felt. It was as if I was consciously choosing a new path for my life; a new adventure."

Averill waits; Mariel is clearly immersed in her thoughts. Moments pass, then she begins again.

"My father died before my baby came. He had become well enough to walk again for a time, and we often sat outside in the beautiful warm weather and watched the birds. He started drawing again, but was quite weak, and could only draw for short periods of time. Of course, he was angry at first when he learned that I was pregnant, but over time he came to accept it, and, I think he was even looking forward to becoming a grand-father. But, sadly, that didn't happen. At some point, the sickness returned and day-by-day he became weaker. Father Eustace spent much of his time with my father, caring for him right until the end."

A pause.

"There are some beautiful trees on Rhodes; trees which provide shade in the afternoon sun; trees which made me feel cool and refreshed when the days were hot. We buried him at the edge of the hospital *cimetiere*, under the shade of one such tree."

Mariel lifts her head, to look into Averill's eyes. "One day I would like to visit Rhodes again... to see my father's tree..."

"We will, my love," comforts Averill, taking her hand in his. "We will."

"I began helping in the hospital, and started to learn more about the people who lived and worked there; and Father Eustace started teaching me English. Within the community, there were milites, and cappelani and servientes armourum; Father Eustace was a cappelani. These were 'les Chevaliers Hospitaliers'. They had started their mission four hundred years earlier as the knights of St John of Jerusalem."

A sudden pause as wide-eyed, Mariel looks at Averill and jokes. "But you know all about milites and cappelani; about knights and chaplains, don't you?"

"Yes, my love, I know of them," replies Averill. "But of their lives, and their ways, I know very little; pray continue. I am learning English history from my little Asian butterfly."

Demure and abashed, Mariel continues, "My baby came in the late autumn. She was born before the Christmas festivities began. By now, I knew a little English and asked Father Eustace to help me with a name for her. He actually named both of us," she says, smiling at the memory.

"I had told him that my name was Choy Dip, but it wasn't until later that I could tell him what it meant. He called me 'Mariel'; a little English, a little French. He said it was elegant, and reminded him of the two most beautiful countries he knew. And, together, we chose 'Odelia' for my baby. It seemed appropriate for a little girl starting her life in Rhodes, for there were a number of little girls there with names that sounded similar, but this one was the most pleasant to my ear.

"The main language in the hospital was French, so, as time went on, I began to pick that up too. One could not help but become proficient in French. But, always, it was the English I wanted to learn. I would look at the pennants flying on the towers, and at the coats-of-arms on the walls of the great halls. The fleurs-de-lys were beautiful, and Father Eustace told me, later, that they came from the tears of Eve as she left Eden. But it was the lions of England which stirred my imagination, and, I think, my passions. I vowed that, one day, I and my daughter would see the country that Father Eustace spoke of with such love and tenderness.

"And so, for the next nine years, this is where I lived, with my daughter. Father Eustace taught me etiquette; how to behave in an English court, and in a French court, too; how to curtsey, how to dance; but most of all how to serve, with grace and humility.

"And I taught Father Eustace how to read the clouds and the wind, and at night, how to read the stars; how the pole star is always in the same place, and how the other stars move in a circle as the night progresses, and how the sun travels from north to south and back again as the seasons change. He said he had noticed it, from the changing shadows on the ground, but had never seen it through a sailor's eyes. I said that I was not a real sailor, but he just laughed and said that I would do until a better one came along.

"And Odelia began to speak French and English, and Father Eustace began to teach her Latin, and I showed her Chinese characters, and silk painting, and her grand-father's drawings of his beautiful birds."

"She has inherited his talent," remarks Averill.

"Yes, I have seen," says Mariel. "Her drawings are so beautiful, and the details she includes are so fine. I am very proud of my daughter; she has been the centre of my life for a long, long time now... and now she has a daddy."

"Yes, indeed," agrees Averill, nodding quietly. "She does."

The mood is pensive as Mariel and Averill, facing each other, hands joined, reflect upon all that has been talked of this night. And around the edges of thought, the tragedy of the day flutters, awaiting its inevitable return to be dealt with.

Averill lies down again, and pulls his woman with him. Gently, he kisses her eyelids. "How did you come to leave Rhodes?" he asks.

A moment's thought, then, "It was time," Mariel replies. "After nine years, it was time. And Father Eustace had decided to return to England. He was getting older, and had told me he had been thinking more and more about the deep woods and green fields of England, and wanted to see them once more before he died. And so, we decided that we would make the journey together.

"The Grand Master was sad to learn that we were leaving, but said that he understood and blessed all of us before we departed. The priors put on a small banquet for us, and there was much laughter and much drinking, but, in the end, there was also much sadness. We had all been part of a family, and now we were leaving Rhodes; Father Eustace forever. It was especially sad for him.

"The next morning, we left on one of a dozen ships travelling to Venezia. The ships were so much smaller than the one on which I had arrived all those years earlier. They were actually fighting ships with fewer than one hundred men on each; but the Hospitalier ships were feared on the seas. This was Odelia's very first sea voyage. An extra tent had been built into one of the ships for us, so this was rather special treatment. We travelled without incident, and arrived in Venezia after about ten days. Father Eustace told me that, from here, we would travel overland to France, and then on to England. It was, just as it had been all those years before; exciting and yet frightening."

Mariel is quiet for a few moments, then continues, "Father Eustace did not reach England."

Another pause; reflective. "We bought two quiet, old horses in Venezia, then started north-west, towards Trento. It was here that the mountains started. After three more days we reached Merano and turned west into a beautiful, wide, green valley between the mountains. We travelled for about six hours each day; it wasn't difficult, and gradually we found that we could manage longer and longer between rests. A few more days' travel and the valley had become narrower and the mountains even higher; it was amazing; almost overpowering. After another three days we were through the mountains and then the lakes began; some of them were huge, stretching for kilometre after kilometre. A day and a half later we reached the edge of a new lake, and passed beside it for the rest of that day and all of the next day. In the evening we reached the end of the lake and we had arrived in Zurich.

"We rested for two days in Zurich, taking some time to explore the city, but mainly resting; then we set out for France. Father Eustace told me he had heard of a beautiful cathedral in Amiens, Cathédrale Notre-Dame d'Amiens, and that was where we were heading. We passed through the southern part of Germany, and then, within two or three days, the language changed and we knew we were in France.

"With the mountains behind us, we were making good progress and on about the sixteenth day we entered Reims. We knew it was now just a few days to Amiens and I could see Father Eustace smiling more as each day passed.

"We reached Amiens late on a Saturday evening and found simple lodgings near the edge of the town. The next morning, Father Eustace woke us early and we walked the last few kilometres to the cathedral. Oh Gregory, I can't begin to tell you how beautiful it was. There were three huge arches at the entrance, and, as we approached, we could see that each arch was about eight layers deep. Each layer was filled with carved figures, saints and angels, and all painted in the most beautiful greens and blues and reds and yellows. I had never seen such beauty. But it was as you entered the cathedral that the true majesty struck; it felt as if all of the air had been knocked from your body; the arches, the windows were like nothing I had ever beheld before; and the ceiling was so high... so high. All three of us were speechless; even Odelia, who as you know will chatter almost all the time, was lost for words. We knelt and prayed. We stayed for a long time; we did not want to leave. Father Eustace met the abbot and they spent all of the afternoon together, while Odelia and I explored Amiens.

"I don't know what happened to Father Eustace after that. It seemed to me that, in his mind, all the different parts of his life were becoming mixed together. He would look at Odelia and me and smile, but in a way which showed that he didn't know who we were, and he would talk to us about things which had happened long before we knew him. Then, at other times, he would know us, and where we were, and remember that we were heading for England. I think something happened to him at Amiens; something which affected his mind, but something which, for him, was beautiful. It was as if his life had become fulfilled and nothing he did now would ever change that.

"And then he was gone. The night before we were to leave, he asked Odelia and me to pray with him. We knelt and he placed his hands on our heads, and blessed us, and for some reason, I felt that this was the last time we were going to see him. I was crying and looked up at him, but he just smiled at me, so lovingly, and said 'Be still, my child... tomorrow is a new day.' Then he also knelt on the floor and took Odelia's face in his hands and said to her, 'Remember this night, Odelia. Remember this place and what you have seen here. This is the work of the Lord. And remember: He is with you... always.'

"We went to bed, but I couldn't sleep, and during the night I got up and listened outside his door. There was no sound, so I went in. He was still warm, and his face had that same gentle smile I had seen earlier that night. I will never forget it, Gregory; it was as if he had become an angel."

Mariel stops momentarily. Her brow is furrowed as she ponders, once again. "How the abbot knew, I will never know; but he did. He came the next morning.

"We left Amiens a few days later, but had little money and no means of making the crossing to England. Eventually, after almost a week, we were taken in by *les païsant*; some peasant folk, who gave us food and shelter in return for work. When they first saw us, they were very wary, because of our Chinese features. But when we spoke French as well as they did, they accepted us, and after some weeks, they even became a little friendly.

"Gradually, over the months and seasons that followed, we became peasants ourselves; a mother and her daughter with no man to provide for us, so we worked in the fields when we could, and begged at the roadside when we had to. I would look at Odelia in her ragged clothes, her face covered in dust and dirt, and think back to our life on Rhodes, and curse myself for taking all that from her. At night, I would cry myself to sleep, thinking about my home in China. But then I would remember that I had no-one there, and besides, it was pointless to even think about finding a way back.

"And that is how we were when you found us, after the village had been attacked and burned."

Averill's mind is racing, putting the pieces together; but now, her story completed, Mariel lies exhausted, looking over at her daughter sleeping soundly and safely beside her.

A tear trickles down Mariel's cheek as she turns back to Averill. "Oh Gregory, I am so fortunate to be here. And, I have seen so many places... and have known so many people... I should feel privileged. But, so many of the people who have been part of my life are now gone; my mother, my father, Father Eustace, and now the king. Why is it like this, Gregory? Why do we have to lose the people we love most?"

And now the tragedy of the day, coupled with the memories revived this night, take their toll upon the soul of Choy Dip, the Lady Mariel; and she begins to sob; helplessly. Averill holds her to him, brushing his hand gently across her temple. His eyes remain open though, as thoughts of huge ships and stone hospitals, of towers with lion pennants flapping in the breeze and knights in far-off lands waging war on land and sea, of valleys between giant mountains and lakes a day's march long, of cathedrals... and a village... and a mother and child huddled together in the corner of a burning hut, pass through his mind in serial confusion. And then, overtaking them all, come the sad and vivid images of a close, fierce grin, and a broken king.

A muffled sigh comes from Odelia as she turns in her sleep, then steady breathing resumes. Slowly, silently, sleep descends upon the rest of the room.

Sometime later, the candles in the braziers on the walls begin to sputter and die. The fantastic moving patterns on the ceiling fade to nothing. No-one notices.

CHAPTER SEVENTEEN

The chapel is cold and Averill shivers a little as he peers in. In the subdued light within, the hunched form of Prince Henry is visible; kneeling, head resting upon clasped hands.

Softly, quietly, Averill moves down the aisle of the chapel, then gently falls to his knees beside the prince. Brothers in arms, brothers in joy, brothers in pain; the pair remain motionless together. Breaking sunlight gradually lightens the interior of the sad, intimate location as the pale light of dawn slowly gives way to day.

The prince turns a gaunt face to his long-time companion; long-wept tear stains now appearing in salty outline. Placing a hand upon the knight's shoulder, the prince slowly raises himself to his feet and gently commands, "Walk with me, Gregory."

A lark sounds a singular trill to the day, and then disappears into the distant sky, as the subdued pair emerge through the timbered doorway in the grey stone wall. The garden into which they emerge is breathtaking in its greenery. In the pond to the right of the doorway, a goldfish swims lazily by, and, for a moment, neither man breathes; unconsciously held by the beauty of the scene.

"Life continues, Gregory," remarks the prince, "life continues."

Then, gaze wandering slowly around the garden, he adds, "All of those things which, yesterday, were part of the future, are today upon us, my friend; upon us far sooner than I had ever expected."

A moment's thought, then, turning to his companion the prince continues, "My God, Gregory, there are so many decisions to be made; decisions about embalming, the funeral, a coronation, and..."

"Your Majesty," interrupts Averill. "Pray, forgive me, but these are not things to trouble your mind with at the moment. You have an entire court at your disposal now, and a father to mourn. There will be time for these things soon enough, and good men to take care of them too. But, for the moment, the affairs of the world can wait a little longer, my Lord."

Henry looks, studiously, at his companion, and asks, almost lightly, "And where did you acquire such wisdom my old friend; this is not the Gregory Averill I knew but yesterday. Have you grown so much in one night?"

A slight pause, a strained, embarrassed smile, and Averill responds, "Aye, my Lord, I believe I have."

The prince waits for further explanation, but none is forthcoming as Averill silently reflects upon the long, intimate conversation of the preceding night.

Then Averill continues, "I remember my father. Actually, that's not true; I remember how I felt when he was with me, more than I remember him. I remember that everything was possible, and that no-one could harm me; I remember that his face was always rough when he hugged me, and that I liked it being so. I remember that my mother never smiled as widely as when he came home to her, and the house never carried as much laughter as when he was present."

A pause. "And I remember how quiet it all became when he was no longer with us.

"These memories warm me, my Prince; they are important, and I am so glad that I have them."

"I understand, Gregory," replies the prince.

"No, my Lord," continues Averill, undeterred. "The point I wish to make is this: do not let these days be overtaken with worldly affairs. These are days which you will remember again and again; mark my words. Take time to honour your father, to recollect the many wonderful times you had together, to impress his memory upon your mind. For soon enough, there will be urgent forces calling upon you, and this time will not come again."

Then, somewhat embarrassed by his unsolicited outburst, Averill continues, "I apologise, my Lord. Sometimes my tongue takes me places..."

"Gregory, Gregory," interrupts the prince. "Do not apologise, for yours is counsel I value most highly. You speak from your heart, and almost always without weighing the consequences of your words; and for this, I am most grateful.

"I gratefully accept your advice, and will, indeed, spend the day in quiet contemplation of things which have been, and things which are yet to be achieved."

A moment's silence, then the prince continues. "But there is another matter which also requires our earnest attention, Gregory; and although I will spend the day as you have urged, I have some advice for you in return.

"I fear we are about to enter a state of uncertainty; perhaps even of emergency. There are foreign forces in our land, and battle of some form is very probable. And so, we must put our affairs in order, perhaps more quickly than we would otherwise have chosen. There will be a period of mourning, for my father, and a coronation, for me. These things are unavoidable... and appropriate, and must be planned and executed with circumstance and dignity.

"But, in addition, there is your wedding to the Lady Mariel, Gregory. It must go ahead. For although the affairs of state must proceed, so must your wedding. My father made his feelings known full well, yesterday, and I dare say that he would not have wanted the tragic turn of events to delay this happy event.

"Therefore, my friend, while I take some time to reflect upon the past and contemplate the future, I would be most pleased if you would also make plans for your future."

"Aye, my Lord, but this is not..."

"Enough, my friend, enough," admonishes the prince. "I know your intentions, and I am grateful for your concern and for your advice. But go now, and make your plans with your lady, for I require some time to myself, and this garden is where I wish to be."

Averill bows in acknowledgement. The prince, momentarily, places a hand upon his stalwart companion's shoulder, then turns quietly away, to walk toward the edge of the garden; quiet, pensive, solitary.

★

"... and thereto, I pledge thee my troth."

"... and thereto, I pledge thee my troth," repeats the knight.

"Arise, Sir Gregory. Arise, my Lady Mariel. In the sight of God, and before these witnesses here gathered, I now pronounce you man and wife."

The bishop is uncharacteristically gentle this day, for today has been a day for much reflection. Earlier, in the morning, he heard the confessions of Averill and the Lady Mariel as they prepared for this day of matrimony. And, later in the day he spent time with Prince Henry, taking the prince, once again, through the protocol of the forthcoming coronation, and, along the way, recounting a number of the discussions held with the prince's father, in years gone by; little-by-little, exposing the prince to the oftentimes painful moral and legal dilemmas which confront a king.

But now, in the chapel by the garden where Averill and the prince walked solemnly some three days earlier, the bishop is, himself, uplifted, as he ministers the rites of Christian marriage to a knight, who still seems a boy to the priest, and a beautiful young woman who has emerged from the East to satisfy the longings of the serious, and often lonely, young man. Brilliant, orange-red shafts of light from the setting sun stream in through the open doorway, framing the knight and the lady as they rise from the velvet cushions upon which they were kneeling, and turn to face the small but distinguished assembly.

The smiles on the faces of the couple are radiant as they gaze at each other, lost, and unaware of the other glowing smiles being reflected back at them. Prince Henry approaches, coughs quietly, and Mariel is momentarily abashed.

125

"Your Majesty, I... I apologise," she stammers, curtseying in the same single, gracious movement.

The prince smiles as he extends his hand and gently lifts Mariel to her feet again.

"Dear Mariel, please do not apologise, it is I who should apologise for seeking to take your attention from your new husband for a few moments."

And, beside the prince and Mariel, Lady Wendy has flung her arms around Averill's neck, hugging him tightly, tears flowing feely down her cheeks.

"Oh Gregory," she cries. "This is so wonderful. We have wished for you to find someone special for so long, but I could never have imagined a match such as this."

The heavy slap on the back and the gruff, "Well done, Gregory," confirm that Gareth concurs with his wife's heartfelt congratulations. Averill beams at them both, almost convinced that his feet are no longer touching the ground, and beginning to wonder how much more enraptured he can be.

Then, as sunset slowly fades to evening, and the sixteen assembled guests move in happily-chattering twos and threes out into the candlelit garden for the small but memorable banquet, the prince takes his leave. He has attended the wedding, he has shared the joy which is due his boyhood friend and ally of countless adventures, he has kissed the bride and offered her his warmest wishes for a long and happy life with her man. But now there are affairs of state to consider; now there are matters of protocol to review, and now there is a force gathering somewhere in the forests to the south of the castle which can no longer be ignored. And so, he leaves, to continue the task of acquiring the mantle of kingship, even though the coronation is still some few days off.

He turns and, momentarily, looks back. The candlelight from the garden casts flickering shadows on the walls of the castle, and the sounds of soft laughter fill the air.

"Be happy, Gregory," the prince murmurs. "Be happy." Then he turns again and walks inside. Kingship will have its glamour and its pageantry, but it also has its price.

★

The scent.

It is the scent which arouses him every time. The scent of a woman becoming aroused herself.

His hand slides softly over her breast, as he himself floats dreamily through the images of the wedding banquet: happiness subdued by the king's

126

recent death, gentle camaraderie in place of boisterous fun; speeches of love, and honour... and death.

And, somehow, he feels that this wedding has been unique. Somehow, it would have been more fun, but less poignant, in other circumstances. Somehow, it would have been a grander affair with the whole court present, but less memorable. And, somehow, this wedding will live on in everyone's memory as the most beautiful, the most romantic... the most tragic.

Mariel lies, unmoving, left arm draped carelessly across her forehead, eyes closed, steady breathing punctuated by a slight shudder as his hand continues down over her belly.

The wine has gone to his head, but just enough to induce a dreamy blissfulness. The long wet kisses, the giggles, and the slight unsteadiness in her walk, until he took her in his arms and carried her to the bed chamber, tell Averill that his bride is similarly affected.

Tomorrow, and thereafter, she will be his wife; tonight she is his bride. His fingers trace a slow circle around her belly, then gently move down to caress the soft, black hair.

Another shudder, and this time her hand stretches out until it finds what she is seeking. Averill utters a muted groan of pleasure and buries his face in her breasts. The rushing in his ears begins; his head begins to spin. Without any conscious thought, he runs his fingers through the soft hair and finds the full, rippled flesh surrounding the hardening bud.

Eyes suddenly ablaze, Mariel gasps, and pulls him to her. He lifts his head sharply in exquisite agony, amazed at her strength in moments of passion, and is forced down again as she grinds her mouth against his.

The words are incoherent but the intent is clear.

His fingers enter the slippery nothingness of aroused woman; her legs part as caresses become more urgent. Dreamy gentleness gives way to blind, mounting ecstasy. Sweat glistens on bodies gyrating in the warm candlelight.

He lifts his head, meaning to probe her with his tongue. Violently, she grasps him in her two hands and shakes her head. "No. I want you now."

He sinks easily into her as her legs and arms wrap tightly around him; limpet-like. For a moment he cannot move as waves of ecstasy course through Mariel's body. She cries out; long and ecstatic. One touch has been enough.

As she relaxes he begins to move; slowly, gently, deeply. Her tears fall softly onto the pillow. She looks intently at him; her smile radiant through wet eyes.

The smile does not waver as he continues to thrust. Then, as all sensation converges to a point, she pulls his head tightly against hers and whispers to him. The knight's body convulses; once, twice, three times; his hoarse cries muffled in the pillow. Slight shudders continue for a short time. She holds him to her, caressing his hair.

Turning her head to one side, she allows her gaze to wander about the room, taking in the ornately-carved torch brackets, the rich carpets and the cushions of various reds which adorn the room. The images are blurred by her tears, but it does not matter. Her sigh is long, gentle, heartfelt.

She turns back, closes her eyes and wraps both arms around her knight, holding him tightly to her.

"My beautiful, beautiful husband."

CHAPTER EIGHTEEN

The table is still strewn with maps.

Another shaft of morning sunlight angles across the room and once again the beautifully decorated pitcher sitting prominently upon the sturdy side-table scatters reflections of surreal beauty.

The king's favourite room – 'the map room' he called it – is occupied by a solitary figure, leaning upon the table, back bent as he studies the maps; and Averill, as he bows and enters, is overcome by a sudden feeling of loss.

Sensing as much as hearing another presence, the prince looks up and stares intently at Averill. Silence, for several heartbeats.

"Can you feel him, Gregory?"

Averill is finding it difficult to respond, and walks slowly to the window, looking out onto the courtyard.

"He stood here, Your Majesty... then took us with him to walk among his people; to give them hope and encouragement."

"I remember," says the prince, nodding slowly, then continuing suddenly. "But I can feel him, Gregory; I can still feel him... here... his presence is so strong."

"I imagine you will always feel him here, Your Majesty," replies Averill, softly. "This room was a favourite of his, and he often called us here."

"Yes, indeed," responds the prince. "I suppose it's to be expected, isn't it?"

"Yes, Your Majesty," concedes Averill. "I believe it is."

A pause as the prince reflects a little longer, then he straightens.

Brusquely, as if having shrugged off a cloak: "Gregory, I have a task for you, which will take you away during the coronation. I apologise for this, but I fear that our information on the enemy movements is now seriously out-of-date, and that we are risking too much if we let that situation continue. I am concerned that he may already be marching upon us, and I need you to find out."

"Of course, Your Majesty," Averill replies. "I will assemble a small scouting party and we shall depart as soon as you wish."

"I'm sorry, Gregory... about the coronation."

Averill chuckles; the prince looks bemused.

"Your Majesty," continues the knight. "You, of all people should know my allergy to pomp and ceremony."

Then suddenly aghast. "I'm sorry, Your Majesty, I did not mean to imply…"

And now Prince Henry is laughing; the first time in quite a few days.

"Dear me, Gregory," he chuckles, "what a pair of fools we are. I think I am depriving you of a royal occasion, only to find that you would rather be charging through the forest with the wind in your hair, and you suddenly think you have offended me, when, quite frankly, I would give anything to be there beside you.

"Oh dear," he chuckles again, "what a pair we make."

"Indeed, Your Majesty," replies Averill; wry smile on his face. "I suspect that I will never really grow up; and it is comforting to know that you, when you can forget your responsibilities for just a moment, have similar thoughts.

"We have seen much of life together, Your Majesty, and I am honoured that you still choose to share some of your more frivolous thoughts with me."

The prince stands, hands on hips, shaking his head slowly as the chuckles subside. "Memories, Gregory," he confides. "Lots of memories, we have."

Then purposefully again: "But now, pray be on your way. I have matters to attend to here and I am anxious to know what is happening outside our gates."

Averill bows and turns to leave.

The king's whispered voice in his ear stops him abruptly. He whirls around, but sees only the prince, bent over the maps one more.

The prince looks up. "Was there something else, Gregory?"

"I thought I heard…" He pauses, then, "No, it was nothing, Your Majesty. I am on my way."

He surveys the room one last time, then turning again, walks toward the doorway. The whispered voice is now a presence all around him, and he slowly recognises it for what it is; a strong, benevolent, inspirational ghost of yesterday, come to say 'Farewell.'

"Farewell, Your Majesty," he whispers.

★

Little boys playing tors in the dirt scatter, screaming excitedly and flattening themselves against the rough stone walls, as the seven great horses thunder through the narrow street, and charge, in a hail of flying stones, beneath the raised portcullis of the castle.

Released from the intensity of the past two weeks, the knights revel in the outpouring of pent-up energy; following days constrained at first by shock and sadness, then by ceremony, and finally by boredom.

Once through the gate the riders fan out, none prepared to lag behind the others, and charge across the gradually dipping plain surrounding Windsor's wall. Lightly armoured and helmetless for the moment, the seven thrill to the rush of the wind through their hair and the unrestrained power of their mounts beneath them. Pounding hooves throw clods, torn from the earth, behind them, as the riders put distance between themselves and the castle.

But gradually, the exhilaration of the moment subsides, and the group slows to a canter as the trees of the forest approach.

The mission is simple: find the enemy force, assess its disposition and progress, and report back. However, the execution may prove a little more difficult, since in the intervening period since the enemy presence was first discovered, the castle has been initially unsettled by the realisation that the greater portion of its fighting force has been released and is now dispersed across the countryside, then rocked by the tragic and untimely death of its king; and now unnerved by the consequent, forced transition of leadership as a coronation is arranged, and an untried prince is about to take on the mantle of kingship, and, possibly, even conduct a war.

And, Averill's words of the morning left no doubt in the minds of his lieutenants that this was a mission of both extreme importance and extreme folly, since the events of the preceding two weeks have now left them absolutely blind to the recent build-up and movement of the enemy forces. And yet, to a man, they had all thrilled to the words, had recognised the seriousness of the situation and the dire predicament in which they now found themselves because of lack of intelligence, and had, unreservedly, voiced their eagerness to be a part of the mission to redress the situation. But then, Averill had expected nothing less, for these were men born to action, like him. And, as much as the love of woman, and the tenderness of embrace, and the pride of service were sweet and joyful and rewarding, it was ultimately action which defined his being, his fulfilment, his *raison d'être*.

Or so he believed.

The plan, like the mission, is simple: travel to the hidden encampment discovered by good fortune these few weeks past, and, should the enemy be no longer there, then follow what trail remains to discover his whereabouts. In theory, this should not prove difficult, since the movement of such a mass of men would leave considerable evidence of their passage, and potentially, of their health. Nevertheless, the mission is risky, in that they might come upon the French when they least expect to, and will then be massively overwhelmed and can expect to perish together with no word of what has transpired ever getting back to the castle. So, a certain amount of caution is required to ensure their own safety, and yet, time is of the essence since every day which passes brings confrontation closer. A delicate balance, and one which is beginning to occupy Averill's thoughts.

The knights sense the swing in their leader's mood, and gradually the high-spirited activity and banter of the morning's preparation and departure give way to the more-focussed concentration of men, who know what to do and are good at what they do, getting on and doing it.

★

The scattered remnants of the empty encampment confirm what they all had expected: the French have moved on. But, although the cinders of the several large campfires are cold to the touch, there is sufficient evidence in the moisture in the discarded fruit scattered through the refuse to deduce that it is only a few days since the force departed.

The equation is simple: a thousand or so men on foot, seven knights on horseback. They should come upon the enemy force during the next day.

A brief scout of the forest surrounding the enclosed clearing reveals no evidence of any of the sicknesses, which often befall a large group living in close proximity. From this, Averill concludes, unhappily, that the strength of the enemy is not in decline.

Two distinct trails mark the passage of a large number of men. The knights, from their previous mission, recognise the one along which the enemy arrived, and, accordingly, the party prepares to move out along the second.

Tension is ratcheted up a notch.

Within the first mile, Thomas leans from his saddle and vomits his most recent meal onto the ground below. The others chuckle, with the total absence of sympathy common in comrades of long standing.

"Fuck, Thomas," remarks Gareth, feigning distaste. "You're supposed to put them off; not us."

"I've been waiting for that," remarks Anthony. "So now, we can get on with it, confident that we are all now fully prepared to deal with these bastards. Isn't that right, Thomas?"

"As you know," replies the knight, unsteadily, trying to wipe the foul taste from his mouth with the back of his hand. "This is my customary preparation for battle; so, yes, you could say I'm now ready to face anything they throw at us."

Momentarily, the mood lightens, as all recognise the bond which they share; a bond born of battles fought, of flaws understood and accepted, of fears overcome, when lesser men would have turned and run.

Averill urges his mount into a trot. The others follow, and the small party heads down the trail, acutely aware that the critical point in their scouting mission is approaching.

★

For an hour now, the riders have been passing sporadic indications of fighting; crushed and slashed foliage spattered with blood, ground churned up by melees of hoof-prints; and yet, up until now, they have encountered no dead or wounded. Averill, unable to make sense of the signs, is agitated, but pushes on since time remains a factor.

The suddenness of the encounter is not what makes it surprising; although that certainly adds to the impact. One moment, the small scouting party is cantering along the trail, apparently alone, anticipating that sometime soon they will hear the sound of marching feet, and have time to approach the mass of men on foot with some degree of preparedness and an appropriate level of caution, not to mention, camouflage. Then, in the next second, the seven riders are starkly silhouetted as they crest a rise in the trail and come face to face with a group of more than a hundred men, with weapons drawn, crouching silently on either side of the trail.

The shock is palpable... on both sides.

In the fraction of a second that it takes to react, the men face each other, eyes wide with surprise, as reeling minds struggle to assimilate the scene. And, in the same fraction of a second, the forest behind the crouching warriors erupts into mayhem as a score of roughly-clad horsemen, with swords flailing, charges across the trail, scything through any individual unfortunate enough to be within striking range. The crouching men in front of the knights leap to their feet and turn towards the skirmish, leaving Averill and his knights doubly shocked, but not so stunned that they cannot recognise the opportunity to cheat death. A short, sharp, barked command, and an instant later, the riders have roughly wheeled their mounts and are charging back along the trail, hearts pounding, lungs burning as they gasp for breath through fear-constricted chests.

A few minutes later, Averill leaves the trail and leads the party into the cover of the forest trees where they halt, breathing heavily.

"What the fuck was that?" explodes Gareth, drowning out identical questions from Charles and Robert. "What the hell were they all doing there?"

They look to Averill, whose mind is blank as he struggles to piece together the scene just encountered.

"It seems to me," remarks Thomas, "that we might have a larger and more complex problem than we first thought."

"Yes, I'm beginning to think likewise," agrees Anthony, whose mind has also started to piece together the elements of the scene.

"Well," mutters Gareth, still smarting from the sudden descent from relative serenity into stark chaos, "It still beats me. Would one of you two smart arses mind explaining?"

"I think Gregory might have the picture," ventures Thomas.

"Indeed," replies Averill. "I think we may all be coming to the same conclusion.

"It seems, Gareth," he continues, "that there might be two enemy forces at our doorstep; one, the French, which we have known about for a little while now, and one which, until a few moments ago, was completely unknown to us."

"Oh, shit," is the muted reply, as the big man ponders the consequences of this assessment, which appears to have dawned upon more than one of the group.

"And," adds Anthony. "It seems, from the way the French were waiting in readiness, that this second force has been harrying them for some time, and that, their impact has been significant enough to have them worried."

"I agree," remarks Averill. "Those men we came upon were taking things very seriously."

A moment's thought and then Averill continues: "Gentlemen, I see the situation as follows: one, we now have two foreign forces on our soil; two, we have no idea how large the second force is; three, we have no idea whether these two forces will distract each other from their initial purposes, which we must surmise was to attack us, or whether they will join forces and wipe us off the map; four... I can't think of a four. However, I think those three are enough for us to deal with at the moment."

"I'd feel much less uncertain if we knew more about the second lot," responds Gareth.

"Agreed," says Averill. "But, we also need to get this new information back to the castle as soon as possible."

"Then, we split," suggests Robert. "Charles and I can scout this area for the new lot, to see if we can determine their size, and where they're heading; and hopefully determine where they're from."

"Yes," nods Averill. "I agree that we need to split our attentions."

Then, after a moment's consideration, "I'd like Thomas to accompany you; I'd appreciate his perspective on what you encounter."

"Of course, Gregory," volunteers Thomas.

"Yes, absolutely," confirm Charles and Robert, in concert.

"Then let us be off," commands Averill. "Robert, Charles, Thomas, be careful. The information you bring back will be critical, and we cannot afford for you to be captured. Fortunately, there is enough chaos here, for the moment, to give us a little breathing space; a little, but not much.

"I need to see you again before sunset tomorrow. So go, and... God speed."

The trio raise their hands, then, wheeling their mounts away from the others, head deeper into the forest; meaning to circle around to pick up the trail of the riders who had carried out the sharp, brutal attack on the French.

"And we," continues Averill looking from Anthony to Gareth and then to Bryan, "will make for the castle, with all haste, to advise the prince of this latest development."

"Actually, Gregory," remarks Anthony, with a slight smile. "I believe it is the king we will be advising."

"My God, yes," chimes in Gareth, "it will, indeed, be the king. In all of this excitement I had forgotten that the coronation is today."

"Then we will not be bearing happy news for our new king," Averill responds, "for I see troubled times ahead. But we will first need to understand this complex problem which confronts us. Much as I love Henry, how I wish his father's experience were available to us now. This is a time for wise old heads, and we, none of us, possess that at the moment.

"Come, we must be on our way."

And with that, the four also push further into the forest, away from the French soldiers, no doubt, by now recovered from their disarray. The four know that they will encounter another trail within an hour or so, and from there they can make their way, speedily, back to the castle to deliver their critical but unsavoury message.

Averill's mind is churning; the possible outcomes are many, but the one which consumes him most is the potential alliance of the enemy forces. He knows from first-hand experience that this could mean death to most of the castle's fighting men. But more worrying still, he is acutely cognizant of the brutality which engulfs many of the young women of a besieged castle, and the violent and bloody end which many of the children suffer.

Aghast at the thought, he suddenly spurs his horse into the undergrowth ahead. The others, caught off-guard, respond, and the pace quickens.

CHAPTER NINETEEN

They are awake again as the first shafts of sunlight sweep across the ridge which has kept the knights hidden overnight. Morning light reveals the nature and extent of the small hollow which has served as their forest sleeping space. The bracken and ferns which they sensed in the darkness have provided good cover, and the collection of fallen and broken tree-trunks through which they picked their way has provided additional deterrent against discovery by either of the foreign forces.

A quick, light breakfast, then attention is turned to the horses. Within another thirty minutes they are ready to move off.

"We should reach the castle before midday," says Averill; largely to himself, although the others are listening. "We can report our findings this afternoon, and then complete the picture when Charles, Robert and Thomas arrive this evening."

Averill looks up to see the three knights watching him.

"Sorry; just trying to get a picture clear in my head."

"We understand, Gregory," replies Anthony, "and I'm sure we all agree. We will, indeed, be much better placed by nightfall to understand what confronts us and to begin planning a response."

"Indeed," remarks Averill. "So then; let us be on our way."

★

The pace has been steady all morning, with occasional stops for personal comfort and to allow the horses a breather. But now, with the castle just one middle-distance hill away, the natural eagerness which accompanies the end of a journey is beginning to take hold and the riders are pushing just a little harder.

The forest is thinning and soon they will be breaking out into the exposed plain which surrounds the castle. For years, men have commented upon the magnificent defensive advantage the plain has afforded. There has been no hiding place for enemies, and the slight incline leading up to the castle has meant that defending troops have had the distinct advantage of riding down upon an advancing enemy; usually with spectacularly gruesome results.

The four press on for several more minutes, then the last of the canopy of trees flashes by and the riders are suddenly pounding across the open plain.

The heat of the late-morning sun instantly begins to warm the knights and momentarily Averill feels a burst of insane happiness. And, try as he might to keep his mind on the serious task at hand, the image of Mariel and the sound of her soft, accented voice fill his mind.

Yet, within a heartbeat, all thought is banished as another group of ten or so riders emerges from the forest, ahead and several hundred yards to the right. The group is riding equally hard towards the castle, and even from this distance it is clear that these are not locals, for their armour is foreign, as is the decoration of their horses.

Without command or comment, Averill and his three knights spur their horses forward, but the hope of catching the other group is faint as both groups are now riding hard and the castle is just over the next hill.

Averill is struck by the distant lead rider and his horse. In other circumstances, the huge, sleek, shiny, black beast would be considered magnificent, and the rider's intensity remarkable, but now, in foreign colours and uncertain circumstances, they appear malicious, and Averill is unsettled by the potential danger they represent.

Conversation is difficult, but Gareth ranges up alongside his leader shouting, "Do you recognise them?"

"No," roars back Averill, "Do you?"

Gareth shakes his head and Averill looks left towards Anthony. Anthony also shakes his head.

They are beginning to make an impression upon the distance between the groups, when suddenly one of the riders ahead turns and sees the pursuit. The warning cannot be heard by Averill and his knights, but they clearly see all of the riders turn to look back, momentarily, then hunch down and spur their mounts ahead even harder.

The foreign group crests the hill and disappears beyond it. Now temporarily blinded to their progress, Averill hunches forward and pushes harder. The others follow suit, and then, suddenly, the crest of the hill is before them.

Another rasp of breath and the four thunder over the rise.

Before them now spreads the panorama of castle and plain... and women and children.

Averill's heart lurches sickeningly and he screams a long, guttural, "No-o-o-o!" as the unfolding scene bursts upon his senses. The group of riders ahead has reached the bottom of the dip in the plain and is about to start up the incline towards the castle wall. Their hard riding for their own reasons, plus the even harder riding to remain ahead of Averill's group, coupled with the descent from the hill, has caused the pace of the lead group to increase frighteningly. There is no way now that they can, or apparently even wish to, divert from their path directly toward the main gateway in the castle wall.

Averill's eyes are fixed upon Mariel, running desperately to protect Odelia, still playing blissfully with a group of children at the edge of the wide track across which the riders are now spread. Children look up, petrified by the terrifying sight of the foaming horses charging towards them. Some start to run, but others remain rooted to the spot, overcome by terror. He sees Odelia suddenly look up as if she has heard a voice she recognises, and realises that Mariel has almost reached her daughter.

The boot in the stirrup raking the flank of the huge, glistening black horse, now swings out, striking the desperately running figure with the long black hair with such force that she is lifted from the ground and hurled through the air before crashing to the ground again in crumpled disarray. One hundred yards behind, Averill's agonised roar is unheard above the thunder of hooves as the horses of the lead group plough, mercilessly, through the mass of children. Two further small, broken bodies lie still on the ground as the riders flash by. Another two flail desperately on the ground where they have been flung by the impacts.

Mariel has not moved.

★

Heart pounding, hands shaking, sweat dripping from his face, Averill kneels beside the slight, still form of his lady and listens closely. There is a breath; shallow and unsteady, but a breath nonetheless. Gently placing his damp, dirty hands on her shoulders, the knight slowly turns her over until she is laying on her back, looking up at him.

"Oh, my love, my love," he cries in anguish, holding her face in his hands and bending his head close to hers.

The soft voice responds in dreamy disconnection from reality: "My darling; you're here."

"Yes, my love, I'm here.

"Do you hurt? Where is the pain? What can I do for you?" The questions tumble from the distraught knight's lips.

"I feel nothing, my love. What happened? I'm so happy you're here. Where is Odelia?"

The question forces Averill into sudden awareness of his surroundings; of Gareth and Anthony and Bryan also on their knees beside him. Still holding Mariel's face in his hands, he looks around desperately, and sees the little girl, standing alone, wide-eyed and fearful with hands clasped together beneath her chin. She looks from her mother to Averill and back again.

A woman runs shrieking toward them, hands outstretched, hair flying behind her. Gareth suddenly stands and catches his wife as she collapses into him.

138

"Marie-e-e-l!" she screams, looking down at the still form.

Shrugging herself free from her husband's grasp, she drops to the ground on the other side of Mariel and begins stroking the prone young woman's hair; confused, not knowing what to do, but needing to do something.

Turning back, Averill softly answers the question: "Odelia is well; she is here beside you." Then turning again, he gently calls the little girl's name. Hesitantly, she moves to him, still staring intently at her mother's face.

Mariel smiles. "Come here, Odelia. Mummy wants to talk to you."

The little girl kneels beside Averill and asks, "What has happened, Mummy? Will you be alright?"

Mariel coughs and immediately whimpers in agony. The dribble from her mouth is flecked with red. Averill stares, fear now mounting, mind blank; unable to put the picture together; unable to move forward from this point. Desperately, he looks from Anthony, to Gareth, to Wendy, to Bryan; seeking some glimmer of assistance as his overloaded mind refuses to function, but no-one in the group is performing any better.

A further frozen moment passes, then a breakthrough: the mission. There was a mission, he recalls; and they have a report to deliver. Not the important issue, but something to get his mind functioning again. He speaks. "Anthony, you must take Bryan and go to Prince Henry. We need to advise him of the situation. Pray go now and complete this task for me. I must remain here a little longer."

"Of course, Gregory; of course."

Anthony and Bryan quickly rise, then, turning to Gareth, Anthony places a firm hand on his shoulder. "Don't leave him, Gareth."

Gareth nods. "Definitely not."

Mind now working again, Averill turns back to Mariel. "What can I do for you, my love? Shall I lift you up and take you inside?"

Odelia is stroking her mother's forearm and staring intently at her face, as if willing her to become whole again.

Mariel's eyes are closed, her breathing shallow. Words come slowly and softly; Averill bends his head to hear her.

"Where is Odelia, my love; I can't see her."

"She is here, beside you. Can you feel her stroking your arm?"

"Ah, yes, I can feel her.

Mariel turns her head. "Odelia, can you give Mummy a kiss?" The voice is weak, but gentle.

The little girl smiles, hopeful now, and leans over to place a kiss on her mother's lips. She looks up at Averill and asks, "Daddy, will Mummy be alright?"

The knight lifts one hand from his wife's face and draws the little girl towards him. "Let's wait and see, shall we? Mummy has had an accident."

"Is it late?" asks Mariel. "It seems so dark."

And, suddenly, Averill knows; knows that a life is slipping away; knows that a dream is ending; knows that all of their plans for a future are fading.

And in that same instant he recognises that his strength is now needed; strength to ensure that his beloved feels no fear; that the moments left to her are warm, and gentle, and loving... and unafraid.

"Perhaps it is late, my love," he responds; voice unsteady with emotion. "Perhaps the day has moved on a pace, and we have been too in love with each other to have noticed it."

"Gregory, I'm frightened; I can't see anything."

Averill struggles to control his voice as the lump in his throat becomes almost unbearable. Tears fall from his eyes onto Mariel's now ragged dress.

"Don't be afraid, my love; I'm right here with you. I'm holding you close to me; can you feel me?"

Mariel smiles, unseeing. "Yes, my love. I can feel you. It's so nice to be in your arms. I always feel safe in your arms, my love; do you know that?"

Unwilling to look away from his wife's face, Averill blindly holds out a hand to Wendy, whose sobbing is now continuous. He feels her fierce grip and knows the pain she is enduring. A minute passes, then the grip relaxes.

Averill withdraws his hand and places his arm around Odelia's shoulders, drawing her even closer to him now. She continues to stroke her mother's limp forearm.

"Mariel, can you hear me?" asks the knight through his tears.

Silence.

"Mariel?"

No words... no breath.

★

Averill is oblivious to the piteous stares of the peasant folk lining the track, as he carries the still form of his lady toward the castle gate. No thoughts impinge upon the blank mind; overloaded and shut-down now as stark realisation transitions into grief. Each step occurs without volition; one foot placed after the other without thought, without will.

Behind him, huddled groups of parents and friends shed tears of relief as smaller forms, lying on the ground, begin to move again, and, one-by-one, look up into concerned eyes. One little boy will walk with a pronounced limp from this day forward, but the others, once scrapes and bruises heal and fade, will be only a little worse for their terrifying ordeal.

The Lady Wendy has already departed, taking Odelia with her, to focus upon flowers, and songs, and little animals, in an effort to soothe the hurt and confused young mind.

Gareth walks with Averill, one hand resting comfortingly upon the distraught knight's shoulder; comforting for Gareth, who needs something, anything, to do; but unseen and unsensed by Averill.

The sad, pathetic progress continues; under the portcullis and into the dusty streets where, days before, seven knights had roared their excitement at being unleashed into action again; up the wide, grey stone stairs, where Anthony had once lain, battered and bloodied, after he had escaped from ambush, and William the bowman had not; along the hallowed halls, where the footsteps of a king, and a prince and a captain, had echoed in forceful unison, in times which would come no more; on, without reason or intent, until they stop before the door to the bedroom in which all of Averill's dreams of grace, and commitment, and love, had been so perfectly fulfilled.

Unbidden, Gareth opens the door, and stands aside; unwilling to cross the threshold into Averill's private enclave. But the grief is suddenly too much for the stricken knight, who falters and cries out in sustained anguish, "Oh God, why-y-y-y?"

And, as Averill begins to crumple, the giant at his side clasps him with gentle strength, and, supporting both the knight and his burden, half-carries, half-drags the entwined pair to the large, soft bed, where he gently lays them down.

Then, as a thought takes root, he bends down again and lifts the dazed knight from the bed and carries him to the adjoining chamber, where he once again gently lays him down; watching carefully as Averill slips, emotionally spent, into sleep.

The big man quietly leaves the room.

★

Averill starts as he wakes, and the terrible reality comes crashing in upon him again. Rising giddily, he is confronted by Gareth's close, concerned stare.

"Gregory?" asks the big man; but then, there is nothing to follow; no question which makes any sense; no comment which can serve any purpose.

Averill, momentarily disorientated, looks wildly around the room then turns urgently back to Gareth. "Mariel?"

"She is here, Gregory. Come with me." And gently, the big man takes his captain about the shoulders and walks him slowly into the bed chamber.

Wendy, hairbrush in hand, looks up as the pair enter, and, wiping tears from her eyes, steps back a pace. On the bed lies the earthly form of the beautiful creature who was Choy Dip, the Lady Mariel; now washed clean and clothed in her favourite embroidered, white silk dress; lying still upon the bed, hair brushed and shining, face soft and peaceful, hands crossed delicately over her breast, beautiful bare feet visible below the dress.

The knight is unprepared for the exquisite beauty of the scene, and slumps momentarily in Gareth's arms. The image is surreal, and Averill struggles to assimilate it. But, piece-by-piece, he recognises what has happened; what Wendy has done for him, and how much he has taken for granted Gareth's continued presence.

He places his free hand on Gareth's shoulder and hauls himself erect, looking directly into the big man's eyes. The understanding is mutual and Gareth nods in response. Then, turning slowly, Averill walks the few paces to Wendy and places his arms around her. No words; just the sound of Wendy's sobs, muffled in his shoulder. She raises her hands to hold Averill's face, then, lifting herself on tip-toes, kisses the knight; with the love she holds for him and for the loss she feels for them both.

Quietly, Gareth and Wendy retreat, leaving Averill standing alone, looking down upon the form of his beloved.

Then, gently, as if not to disturb her, he lays down on the bed; his face only inches from hers. The comfort from having her near is overwhelming; the bottomless despair which had been consuming him, recedes. Even in death, her presence has the power to heal. He looks at her; nothing more, just looks at her; close, beautiful; his Choy Dip.

Slowly, his fingers begin to trail over every exposed part of her body; her lips, her nose, her ears; as if just by touching her, he can absorb part of her into himself. There is no urge to kiss her; the eyes are not aflame with passion. The feeling is of love; pure and limitless. He gently lifts a slim, delicate finger, just slightly, and notes that it is now becoming resistant to movement. He notices that she has become more pale. And, little-by-little it dawns upon him that she is becoming like the beautifully carved marble statues he has seen in Westminster; statues which, until this moment, had seemed too smooth, too pale, too perfect.

And then, as his insight deepens, he recognises that this is the image he will carry with him from this time forth; not an image of flesh failing, but rather one of flesh transforming into the smooth, white stone; capturing forever the exquisite form and beauty of the woman he loved so dearly. The realisation is profound; overwhelming. He lays his head beside that of his beloved and holds her to him; and sobs uncontrollably.

Time passes; a tiny piece of reality intrudes: he cannot stay here forever... and nor can she. But the thought of leaving, of breaking the contact, is too hard to bear. He knows he must, but he cannot. He knows that the time will come, but is desperate that it not be now. And so, he closes his eyes once more and traces the outline of her cool, slender fingers under his own.

★

He wakes, not knowing how long he has slept, and notes that someone has been in to light the candles around the wall. The room is bathed in a soft, warm glow. She is cool to the touch... and paler now. The image of beautifully carved marble is even more compelling, and he is strangely comforted by this. But he also knows that the time has come to say goodbye. However, the thought is too painful to bear, and so he tells himself that he can see her again tomorrow, and that perhaps this parting is just goodnight. Slowly, he rises from the bed, his fingers lingering on hers, then... contact is broken; and so is his heart.

At the doorway he turns and looks back at her; so beautiful, so peaceful; so much the only woman he ever wanted. The image shimmers as the tears drop silently to the floor.

CHAPTER TWENTY

"I have no words, Gregory; no words which come close to expressing what I feel in this moment."

The king, kneeling, hugs the shoulders of his closest friend, his favourite knight, his ally of a thousand adventures, or so it seems; his mind refusing to accept the reality that Mariel is gone; and rebelling against the knowledge of the further devastating news he has yet to impart.

Suddenly, he stands, and swinging away in violent rage, grasps a drape adorning the window and ferociously tears it from its railing, shouting in agonised vehemence to the disembodied fates which have conspired to produce this day. "This is not supposed to happen. This is not the way this ends.

"My God," he cries. "Why have you abandoned your bravest... and your loveliest? Why have you allowed this to happen? Why have you permitted this calamitous day to ever dawn?

"Why?" – ferociously.

"Why?" – agonised.

"Why?" – pitifully.

Emotionally drained, the king allows the rent fabric to drop to the floor.

Averill, momentarily startled by the outburst, looks towards his king; but then, with nothing penetrating the protective barrier his subconscious mind has established, he drops his head into his hands again, and remains so; impassive... silent... broken.

And now, anger building again, the king paces past the window... and back again, then looks out; furious at the action he is about to take; railing against the fates which have brought him to this point; unable, now, to separate the agony he feels for Averill from the outrage he feels for himself.

He is still grasping the window ledge, as, little-by-little his breathing subsides, little-by-little his mind settles, little-by-little his thoughts clear again. He looks deep within himself, searching for another way to deal with this, searching for something which will spare his lifelong friend from the inevitable torrent of despair which is about to be unleashed. But the path ahead remains stark and unchanged; and now there is no further putting it off.

Henry kneels again, this time in front of his knight, and, taking the damaged man's hands in his own, he commences: "Gregory..."

No response.

"Gregory… there is something which has happened; something which you need to know…"

Averill raises his head slightly, but the eyes remain distant, unfocussed. A slight nod of the knight's head signifies that he is listening, as well as he is able; and so, the king begins.

"I have received several visitors, Gregory…

"And Anthony and Bryan also came to see me… with news of your mission…

"And, an hour ago, Charles, and Robert and Thomas returned, bringing me news… of the mission with which you tasked them, Gregory."

The king's voice is low; his words are gentle. He is acutely aware that he is picking his way through the shattered mind of the distracted knight.

"Do you remember, Gregory?"

Averill looks into the eyes of his king, and nods, absently; uttering his first words since the king arrived. "Yes, Your Majesty, I do remember."

"Well, Gregory," continues the king. "You were right. The forces you encountered are both foreign; and both are intent upon our destruction. This is, they were, until they encountered each other.

"But now, as I believe you foresaw, there are several possible ways that this situation can play out: one way sees us overrun and destroyed. Another sees us survive…"

And here, the king takes a deep, shuddering breath. Here, he falters, for here it is that he will begin the destruction of his friend and champion.

"But there is a price, Gregory," he continues. Then, absently, to himself, "Such a price, that I scarcely believe I have paid it."

A moment's silence as the king assembles his thoughts; searching for the right way to deliver the devastating message; and finding, still, that there is no good way.

"We can establish an alliance, Gregory. We can establish an alliance between our forces and those of the French who landed on our soil these weeks past.

"The other forces are Welsh rebels, and the French fear for their own survival if they oppose them. But they also fear for their own survival if they join them in fighting us; for after that battle is won, after we are defeated, as we surely will be, then the French themselves believe they will become the next victims.

"And so, Gregory, they have come to us with a proposal of alliance; a proposal which may well save our homes… and the lives of most of our young men and women…"

And here the king pauses again; looking intently at the knight, searching for any sign that he is beginning to comprehend.

145

But there is no reaction, no movement, and so the king continues, "And, I have accepted, Gregory; I have accepted their proposal."

Then, with deepening anguish, he approaches the raw heart of the message.

"But, as you well know, Gregory, our army is still being drawn together; whereas the French forces are already assembled. And, as you also know, Gregory, although our army will ultimately be larger, it will be relatively untrained; whereas the French force is battle-ready."

The king knows, full well, that he is skirting the issue, seeking to buy time, trying desperately to lead the knight to see the inevitability of the outcome, and thus, perhaps, to lessen the severity of the blow when it comes.

But, there is no more time; there is no recognition by Averill of what is to come; and so, the king plunges on.

"Gregory, the condition of the alliance is that the captain of the French army is to be the captain of the combined forces..."

Then, making the point unambiguous: "There is no position for a king's champion, other than this one..."

And now, bringing the message into brutal, stark relief: "There is no longer any position for you to hold."

The words hang in the air of the silent chamber.

Neither man speaks.

One man looks, heartbroken, into the eyes of the other. The other man continues to stare, unblinking, into the distance.

Then, as if emerging from a dream, Averill stands and walks slowly to the window, looks out, and in a harsh, cold voice, asks his question.

"Who is their captain?"

And this is the question the king knew was coming. This is the question he wanted to avoid. This is the question, which when answered, may well cause the final destruction of his companion's already fragile mind.

"You know him, Gregory.

"He is the knight who led the group of riders to our castle this day. He is the knight who..."

And here the king falters; here the king does not wish to go; but go, he must.

"He is the knight who took the life of your wife, Gregory. His name is Sir René Bijou."

Silence.

A long moment, then Averill turns his cold, drained face toward his king, and in a dull, emotionless voice, quietly asks for solitude: "I beg your leave, Your Majesty."

Then, slowly, he turns to the window again.

Behind him, a king stands; agonised by what he has done. It was the correct decision, of that there is no doubt; the survival of the castle is assured, the massacre of hundreds, perhaps thousands, is avoided.

Surely, this justifies the sacrificing of one knight?

But the king knows that it does not; and he looks in growing pain at the slumped shoulders of his former champion, as the latter grasps the window ledge and looks out, blankly... over the courtyard of a castle... whose king he once used to serve.

CHAPTER TWENTY-ONE

It must have been a ferocious battle.

As Thomas tells it, the combined forces of the English and the French marched forth two nights after the alliance was sealed. At the same time, scouts had reported that the force of Welsh rebels was approaching the castle from the west; having eschewed the direct route in favour of one which avoided the widest portion of the plain surrounding the castle.

And so, on the morning of the first Sunday of autumn, battle was joined in the marshy land west of the castle.

The rain had been sporadic on the Saturday, and the king had contemplated waiting for a finer day. However, the new champion was confident that the combined forces could gain an element of surprise if they were already in position when the fine weather came.

And so it proved.

Two thousand men had departed under cover of darkness and rain. Cloud had covered the face of the moon, and the vast number had managed to cross the plain unobserved to take up position at the tree-line of the forest.

The English archers and French crossbow-men had complemented each others' capabilities quite admirably, whilst the knights and men-at-arms of both nationalities had learned to act, if not in unison, at least with sufficient common purpose to allow the strategic initiative to be pursued without massive loss of life on their side.

The Welsh, for their part, had the numbers to match those of the combined forces, and the added advantage of an unrestrained ferocity which threatened, at one stage of the late morning, to render the defenders impotent, as the ruthless mob, wielding clubs and axes and maces of horrifying potential, charged time and again upon the lances and shields of the wall of soldiers.

But, ultimately, it was their lack of discipline, their inability to out-think the combined forces, which began to see the repeated charges of the attacking forces settle into bloody, thrashing melees, which gained no ground, and only piled-up dead on both sides.

As the late afternoon sun broke through the thinning clouds, and as the wall of defenders had not surrendered even an inch of ground, it became apparent to all that the attack was faltering.

The sun was dipping towards the horizon, and the stand-off had lasted an hour, as both sides watched and waited and considered the course the day had taken. From opposing ends of the now churned up mud, extending one hundred yards from the tree-line, in which the blood and shit and vomit of dead and dying soldiers now mixed, both sides watched fearfully, as leaders plotted strategies.

And then, quite suddenly, it was over. The Welsh rebels, in unison, raised their swords and shields and roared out another sustained, violent and blood-curdling scream; and all who opposed them prepared for another onslaught. But instead, they then turned and trudged from the field of battle; ignoring the cries of their wounded, and forsaking their dead completely.

The king immediately sent scouts into the forest to run parallel to the departing horde, in order to ensure that this was no feint, which would ultimately see the defenders besieged from another quarter. However, by the time dusk had arrived, the reports coming back confirmed that the enemy was, indeed, heading back north and away from the castle.

The day was won.

CHAPTER TWENTY-TWO

The group sit in muted contemplation, staring into the bright, burning coals of one of several fires blazing in the courtyard. Other knights are grouped around other fires arranged around the courtyard. Inside, the feasting and revelry continues, as knights, both English and French, re-live the day and drink to drown the inevitable sadness which will descend when, tomorrow, they start to tally the cost of today's encounter.

But each of the six now gathered outside has, one-by-one, felt the loneliness of the night and been moved to rise, bow towards the king, then walk silently from the noisy, boisterous assembly, out into the courtyard adjacent to the feasting hall. And from there, as if under the same invisible spell, each has found his way to the fire set at the furthest corner of the courtyard, seeking isolation and contemplation, but finding, upon arrival, that his like-minded brothers are similarly affected.

Bryan sits quietly; the last of the six to arrive, and notes that the sombre mood inexplicably matches his own, and wonders what powers are at work to affect him, and his companions, so.

"Come on, chaps," he begins, trying to raise spirits a little. "It's not as if..." but then stops, as the awful poignancy of what he is about to say breaks over him.

A minute's silence; two; three.

"It didn't feel right; he should have been there," broods Anthony.

"He should have been bloody leading the charge," spits Gareth.

"I doubt if he was interested in leading the charge," replies Thomas; "after what's happened..."

Then quietly: "After what they've done to him..."

Another long pause as the knights stare in detached, hypnotic silence, into the fire before them.

Suddenly, Gareth can contain his anger no longer: "Look, I know Henry had to accept the proposal, otherwise we'd all be dead by now; or, at least, preparing to die... along with our women and children... so, I know he did the right thing. But why did he have to go and make that French bastard champion? Especially when we know what he's done. I just don't get it."

"It's politics," remarks Anthony. "It's all bloody politics. It doesn't matter if you're French, or English... or Spanish, or whatever... it's all the same; they do what they have to, and bugger everyone else."

150

"Well, I just don't get it," mutters Gareth. "But I guess I never will. It's just makes me so fucking angry."

"Such a waste," echoes Charles.

"More than a waste," retorts Gareth. "It's a fucking disgrace... is my opinion."

"Amen to that," adds the cloaked figure now standing quietly at the edge of the gathering.

All six look up, then abruptly stand, preparing to kneel again.

The king waves them up.

"Your Majesty," responds Gareth. "I apologise for my intemperate words."

"Not so, Gareth," replies the king. "It is I who should apologise. It is I who need to seek forgiveness. May I?" he gestures.

A pause as the king sits, then slowly, quietly, reflectively: "I need to be here. I need to be here among those most loyal to him; those who will never desert him as I have done; to seek your forgiveness. Not for what I have done, because I know, and I believe you know, that it had to be done. But to seek your pardon for driving a knife into his heart, when one had already been driven in by the fates which conspired to create the blackest day I have yet known."

The king pulls the hood of the dark cloak over his head and leans forward, fingers rubbing at his temples, staring at the ground. "I would remain here, in your company, if I may... away from my court... and consider what has transpired these few days past... and contemplate what is now before us... in the strange new world of... 'alliance'."

Six pairs of eyes stare, hypnotically, into the flames of the still brightly burning coals. One pair continues to stare at the ground.

"Has anyone seen him?"

"No, Your Majesty."

★

Two still, silent forms kneel side-by-side, heads bowed in prayer. The swish of the bishop's evening cassock gradually fades as he leaves; slowly, solemnly.

The chapel is now empty; save for Averill and Odelia.

Two candles, lit earlier in the evening at the start of the vigil, have almost burned out.

Odelia has bravely knelt with Averill and uttered the words of the liturgy, with apparent understanding and, remarkably for one so young, without any hint of complaint.

Tomorrow there will be a funeral, but tonight, the body of the Lady Mariel lies only a few metres away; pale, silent, beautiful beyond compare.

151

At last Averill rises, and holding out his hand, assists the little girl to stand. Then, together, hand-in-hand, they walk the few paces to stand beside the still form of Choy Dip, the Lady Mariel.

The pain in Averill's breast is almost unbearable as he looks upon her; the eyes, almond-shaped, but closed now; peaceful; the lips, paler than in life, but beautiful nonetheless; the slender, delicate hands crossed upon her breast, over the long, white, oriental silk gown, so exquisite in its simplicity. She could be sleeping, so beautiful is she now.

He struggles to take in the vision before him; to imprint it upon his mind, so that it will never be forgotten; knowing that, after tomorrow, the opportunity will never come again.

The little girl looks up, and, with heart-rending tenderness, reaches up to touch his brimming eyes.

"Don't cry, Daddy..."

PART 3

CHAPTER ONE

Winter has all but ended; the last snows now a receding memory. Daylight hours are lengthening, and, from time to time, as the year progresses, the countryside awakens to the chilly, crisp, cloudless mornings which transition into the lovely, mild spring days for which England is noted.

And, although the hour is early, the morning already promises such a day.

A horse meanders slowly through the forest; its rider sits half-slumped in the saddle. The reins hang, untouched; the animal chooses its own path. Occasionally, the dishevelled and disinterested figure on the horse looks up, but generally, his eyes are downcast. He shows no interest in his surroundings, nor, apparently, in his destination.

And yet, for all his raggedness, there is something about him which suggests that perhaps it has not always been so; something, not quite tangible, which suggests that once the eyes might have sparkled, and once the figure might have sat proud and upright in the saddle. He still sits the horse well; unconsciously moving as if an extension of the animal. But, for the moment, the hints of what he might have been in a past life remain just that; hints.

The sun has burnt through the early morning mist as horse and rider emerge from the thicker trees of the wood into a small clearing, surrounded by yet more forest.

For a moment the horse continues, unchecked, then, with just the slightest murmur, the rider utters a soft, single syllable. The animal is beautiful by anyone's standard, and responds, instantly, to the rider's soft commands, coming to a halt. Awkward, ragged saddle-bags complete the strange picture.

The horse stands, head erect, flanks occasionally quivering, but otherwise immobile. The rider sits, also unmoving, just sitting, as if lost in a distant world; present in body but clearly absent in mind; faded glory in a sad, pathetic coat.

Minutes pass; the horse lowers its head and begins to graze. The rider continues to sit... motionless.

Then, slowly, as if waking from a dream, he lifts his head and gazes around; apparently taking in the clearing in which he now finds himself; observing the ring of trees to the right, and the slight grassy rise ahead, from which a single, solid oak tree rises impressively. And there, just to the left of the rise, about twenty metres further on, a discernible gap in the continuing ring of trees.

Slowly, he dismounts, and still loosely holding the reins begins to trudge toward the gap. The animal obediently follows behind.

Shambling on, the man reaches the gap... and passes quietly through. The horse follows.

Several more shuffling, unhurried paces and he comes to a stop, dropping the reins, and for the first time appears to register what he is seeing. He turns, slowly, full circle, then reaches over and absent-mindedly strokes the mane of the silent animal. Once again he looks around, and once again he turns full circle, taking in the scene before him.

The beauty of the glade in which he now stands begins to impinge upon his mind: the stream which gurgles and splashes as it flows over the low rocky outcrop which spans its path; the same rocky outcrop which culminates in two flat boulders, one behind the other, not two metres from the stream; one, knee-high and flat, the other, shoulder-high and upright, forming a wide, natural seat under the still sparsely-leafed early spring boughs of a tree whose trunk stands on the other side of the stream. The scene is serene... and idyllic.

A strange relaxation comes over him; a feeling of... peace. The agony which he has fought to keep at bay, which has debilitated him month-by-month, recedes a fraction. A tiny piece of the wall which has built up around the damaged mind, cracks and falls away, and a tiny portion of the beauty before him breaks through to register, ever so slightly, upon the broken psyche which has lain dormant for such a long time.

Hesitantly, he moves towards the rock seat, and, standing before it, slowly runs his hand over the stone; feeling the sharp, rough texture where the sun now strikes, then noticing how it changes to become a soft, spongy moss at the side where the shadows persist. He bends his head and peers closely at the phenomenon. A spark of interest; not much, but a spark nonetheless.

He turns and sits on the stone base and, for the first time in many seasons, actually feels warmth, as the sunlit rock gives up a portion of itself.

Eyes closed, he relaxes, and as the warmth begins to spread through him, the forlorn expression which has been etched into his face for so long now, eases just a fraction. A lock of hair, bearing the first wisps of grey, falls across his forehead and for just a moment, before he brushes it aside, a rakish, youthful carelessness hints, again, at the man he once may have been.

CHAPTER TWO

Wendy looks up as the slow, hesitant footsteps approach, but Odelia has already begun clearing away her play-things in anticipation of Averill's arrival; exactly as she has done for the past three nights at this time. The day has been sunny; another of those lovely, crisp spring days, which turn into mild warmth as April moves into May; and Wendy and Odelia have spent most of it outside. But, as evening approached and the sun began dipping toward the horizon, they returned inside, and Odelia has spent the past hour dressing and re-dressing her various rag dolls.

The gentle knock at the door has been expected for the past five nights. Odelia jumps to her feet, and, with girlish eagerness partially muted by ladylike decorum, half walks, half runs, to greet the visitor.

"Hello Daddy," she breathes, reaching out to clasp him around the neck.

"Hello, my beautiful young lady," comes the quiet, melancholy reply, slightly muffled by the embrace she has flung around him.

Lifting her head, she retains her hold upon him, but searches his face earnestly. She stands taller now; almost to his shoulder. The innocent cuteness of childhood is beginning to give way to the embryonic beauty of young womanhood. He looks back at her, and, for a moment, his eyes moisten.

Shaking his head to break the spell, he looks toward Wendy.

"How are you, Gregory?" she asks with forced casualness; unwilling to reveal her concern for his welfare; a concern which has been steadily mounting during his absence.

"Fine, thank you Wendy," he replies, slowly, "just fine."

"Did you travel far this time?" she continues, not believing a word of his previous response.

"An interesting ride," he responds, avoiding the real question. "Some of the old trails; some new ones."

"Did you see anyone?"

"No... I wasn't really looking, and... well, I don't really need anyone these days.

"Where's Gareth?" he asks, changing the subject.

"Oh, they're on a hunting trip," she replies. "They left yesterday morning, so I expect they'll be back some time tomorrow."

"Ah... I see," he responds, slightly deflated. "It would have been nice to see him again."

Odelia takes his hand. He smiles at her, and runs his fingers slowly through her hair. "So beautiful," he murmurs, almost to himself, "so beautiful."

Then, looking suddenly away, he continues, "Sometimes I miss those days. Sometimes..."

But there are no more words. He has disappeared within himself again, lost within a world, at whose nature those about him can only guess.

"Come and sit down for a while," prompts Wendy. "I was just getting some food ready for Odelia and me, so it would be lovely to have you join us."

But he appears not to have heard. Odelia leads him to the soft seat by the window, and sits beside him for several moments, stroking his forearm, just to ensure that he is comfortable, then rising, she turns to Wendy. "Shall I prepare the table, Auntie Wendy?"

"Yes, pet, that would be very helpful," Wendy replies; and cannot help smiling at the re-emerging self-confidence which has clearly weathered the terrible blow it had been dealt.

However, her concern for Averill remains; his return to his former self seems as hopelessly distant as ever, and she can only guess at the pitiful state of his mind.

★

"Thank you, Wendy," says Averill, at the doorway, kissing her gently on the cheek. "It was very kind of you to look after Odelia whilst I was away, and very kind of you to provide dinner for us this evening."

"Gregory, it's my pleasure," she replies. "You know that Gareth and I are always here if you need us, and that Odelia is always welcome.

"In fact," she continues, "there will be a market in the square in three days' time, and I could use some help from Odelia in preparing for it. Would you mind if she came here again tomorrow?"

Odelia looks expectantly at her father, whilst Averill ponders the matter. For both Wendy and Odelia, the outcome is obvious, but for Averill, the conundrum of not knowing how to make the days happy for his daughter, weighed against the feeling of imposing upon Wendy yet again, are a significant dilemma.

"She would save me such a lot of effort, Gregory," Wendy continues. "I'm sorry to ask again but it would really help."

"Oh," replies Averill, now understanding in his slow, affected way. "In that case, I'd be very pleased to let her come over again."

"Good," concludes Wendy, "that's settled then.

"I'll see you tomorrow morning, pet," she adds, kissing Odelia.

The young girl's wan smile speaks volumes. At once pleased at the prospect of spending another fun day with Wendy, she is also moved by the sad decline in her father, whose mind appears to be struggling to deal with the realities of life as it now is. She takes his arm, turns, waves briefly to Wendy, then, together with the only father she has ever known, walks slowly down the hallway towards the wing of the castle which, for one glorious season, provided the idyllic retreat in which she and her mother had come to love this strong, gentle, but now broken man.

It has taken a long time, but she has now reached the point where she can think of her mother without breaking down; without dissolving into the unconsolable little girl she was for so much of that first winter.

She wonders what it will take to bring her father back again.

★

The muffled hooting of the soft, white owl, which haunts the trees just adjacent to his window, conveys so many feelings that he cannot instantly separate them. As a boy, the sound had always filled him with excitement; hinting at mysterious quests and distant adventure. And, as he had grown into a young man, the owl had become his personal inspiration; wise in its preparation for attack, clever in the use of its natural weaponry, and ruthless in its execution; qualities which he had endeavoured to bring to his own persona.

But now, overlaying all those features, are the attributes which Mariel had discerned; the solitary beauty, the defensive alertness, and the softness when tending its young; characteristics which had not been apparent to him, until she had enhanced his awareness with her untrammelled love.

And now, in this shadowy half-world which he inhabits, he recalls her tender descriptions of the creature, sees her excited, smiling eyes as the falconer placed first the owl, then later the peregrine, upon her slim, leather-encased arm and encouraged her to carefully remove the hood, whilst keeping the jesses lightly but firmly grasped in her fingers.

Another soft hoot, then the briefest of flaps and the owl is gone. The reverie is broken and Averill is starkly aware of the emptiness beside him. He reaches out to where she would have been, to where her head would have lain, to where those dark eyes, shining in the moonlight would have looked back at him, enticing him to be a man to her woman yet again.

The overpowering agony of that first winter has abated, but the sadness remains. The nights when he didn't sleep at all, and stood for hours at the window until the pale light of dawn transitioned into the dull gloom of another dark day, then fell exhausted onto the bed and wept until sleep mercifully came, are not so frequent now. The days spent in the stables, compulsively sweeping the floor until not a spot of dirt remained, or brushing the soft hide of a horse until silky smooth, or in the armoury, hefting swords for some totally un-remembered purpose, aware that those around him were addressing him, but hearing little and understanding less, are almost behind him now. He knows he is still uncommunicative, but also knows that Anthony and Gareth and the others now accept his strangeness, and look at him with less concern than they used to. He knows that Wendy worries over him, but cannot quite grasp why; after all it's not as if he's going to kill himself... is he?

A sudden swish and flutter; the snowy owl has returned, no doubt with a skilfully despatched kill. Oddly, it feels better with her back; as if, although the world will never be complete and beautiful again, at least, with her outside, there is one small piece of the puzzle as it should be. It feels almost... comforting.

He lies, motionless, looking out at the moonlit sky. His mind wanders. Images of midsummer frolicking, overlaid with the sounds of soft, feminine laughter, gradually give way to other images; a line of solemn, slow-burning candles, and a chapel, and a beautiful, unreachable figure in white, lying peaceful, and silent, and still.

He recalls that first meeting after Mariel's death. Strange how he observed the king's rage as he tore the long drape from its railing, but felt nothing. Strange how he sensed that the talk of 'alliance' was leading towards disaster, yet could not even begin to guess at its form. And strange how the king's pained announcement that there was no place for him anymore, although like a kick in the guts at the time, was, ultimately, so... right. Nothing mattered anymore; nothing stirred his interest, nothing could command his attention. Protecting the realm, leading men into battle, fighting to ensure a population's survival; none of it mattered any more. He was no longer part of that world.

And strange how long it took him to recognise that there was another soul affected, even more than his, by the tragedy. She was only twelve years old then. She had never known the man who gave her life, and now she had lost her mother as well. He had tried to comfort her, but knew that he was failing, and falling apart. And, as it took place, he sensed that their roles were interchanging, and that it was she who was holding him together; it was she who had wrapped her arms around him, and hugged him, as only a daughter can, and had told him, not once, but so many times, the only thing she wanted from him: "Don't cry, Daddy." She had wanted to see him once again in control of their lives; had wanted his gloom and despair to lift; had wanted him to smile and be happy once more. All things he could not achieve for her.

He had known, instinctively, that he needed to try to maintain a routine which would provide her with some stability, some boundaries which stood firm, some framework for a world which approximated the one to which she was accustomed. And, to an extent he had been successful, for a time. He had, mechanically, done the things which needed to be done, had been there for her morning and night, had provided food and love and shelter.

But, one-by-one, the demons had come, and gradually, the carefully constructed lie that he was living began to crumble, and, day-by-day, he became less capable of holding himself and his world together.

He recalls the conversations with Gareth and Wendy, his worries that the world which Odelia inhabited was becoming a world of loneliness and sadness. She needed friends, young girls of her age, women to teach her the things her mother would have taught her; happiness, laughter; all the things a girl needs as she grows into a young woman.

And so he decided that separation was necessary for her to experience the richness of life that maturing young girls needed, and for him to find the solitude to deal with his demons, the only way he knew how; alone. Wendy, of course, was as accommodating as anyone could have been; she had loved Mariel like a sister, and she now loved Odelia with the same tenderness that her mother would have shown.

That was when the wanderings started; the days and weeks when he would ride out, with no knowledge of where he was going, but with a driving need to go; to ride hard, to pound the tracks and trails through the forests and the villages; to come to the end of the day, somewhere, anywhere, alone and consumed by exhaustion, which rendered the grief impotent. But gradually, the absence of communication with any living thing had its impact upon his mind, and as the months passed, the need to ride himself into the ground began to dwindle, and then, ultimately, disappear, and the wanderings became dispirited, detached sojourns to nowhere.

His thoughts return to the king; to the strained relationship which now exists between them. The monarch has suffered too, from the circumstances which were thrust upon him. And yet, as Averill recognises, the king has not been able to simply walk away from his responsibilities, as he has. The king has had a realm to govern, and a people to lead.

There has been a mighty campaign in France which Henry has conducted with commitment and passion and bravery; an echo of his great grand-father's campaign at Crécy; a campaign for the 'just rights and inheritances' of the English monarchy in France. He has heard the stories of the siege, the destruction, and the final capitulation of Harfleur; and he has heard the story of the wonderful victory in the fields by Agincourt, where a few thousand tired and bedraggled English bowmen and men-at-arms completed the rout of the massed French army; how the flower of French nobility was decimated by the commitment and the unswerving bravery of the king and his happy few. All these things the king has achieved, and returned home in spectacle and glory, whilst he, Averill, has tried, and failed, to find a purpose to his life again.

There have been a few meetings between them; difficult meetings, for the king still carries the scars of the actions he was forced to take that afternoon so long ago. His heart still goes out to his once favourite knight; his and his kingdom's champion; the man he was forced to abandon to save the realm. But Averill also knows that he has not been gracious in his treatment of the king; not through any malice or unkindness, but simply because there are no feelings; only emptiness. He knows that, once, they were close; apparently, his memory tells him, like brothers. And yet, he looks into his king's face in the same way he looks into all other faces, and all other aspects of life; with disinterest.

And so, the meetings between them have become sporadic, only occurring when their paths cross, either because it cannot be avoided, or, more often, just by chance. The words are brief, the sentiments distorted.

"Ah Gregory, it is good to see you, my old friend. How goes it?"

"The days pass well enough, Your Majesty."

Except for the day when the king and his retinue had rounded the corner of the street, and run headlong into Averill returning from another pointless sojourn into the forest.

"Ah, Gregory, how goes the day?"

"The day goes well enough, Your Majesty."

But the kindly, innocent words of the monarch, and the bland response of his subject, had been overshadowed by the presence of the sinister figure beside the king; the figure of a knight whose callous boot had, in an instant, brought Averill's world to an end. No words had passed between them for full ten seconds. Averill had stared into Bijou's eyes, hatred burning his gut with such intensity that the bile had been rising in his throat when the king had taken him by the shoulder and turned him aside.

"Walk with me, Gregory," he had said. And Averill, shaken by the confrontation, had not had the presence of mind to either accede or decline. What they talked about, or for how long they talked, he still has no recollection. The only memory he carries is that of the overpowering hatred which Bijou's close presence had engendered in him. And the recollection that, on that day, when the embodiment of evil become so personal, he had vowed to kill the man for taking the life of the most beautiful creature he had ever met; the woman who had loved him without reservation; the woman who had shown him how beautiful life could be, and without whom, life was now utterly desolate and pointless.

Suddenly he feels overpowered; tired beyond reason by the anguish of the memories brought to the surface again.

162

He turns onto his side now; arm resting across his forehead, his other hand stroking the bed where she should be. The sounds of soft, steady breathing come from the other side of the light curtain which divides his sleeping space from Odelia's. He listens, reassured, and wonders whether he would have survived had she not been here; ponders whether he would have killed himself, or whether his mind might have snapped completely if there had been no daughter to keep him from retreating totally into the otherworld of memories; memories as vivid as his Choy Dip now here beside him; her voice, whispering in his ear; her eyes, smiling, laughing; her hair brushing his face now as she straddles him; the sweet scent of her breath as she whispers her love to him; her kisses, long and deep; her embrace, tight and urgent as her breathing become ragged...

The arm around his shoulder is more urgent now; gently shaking rather than caressing.

Pale light fills the room as Odelia, kneeling in her nightdress beside the bed, looks, smilingly, at him.

"Good morning, Daddy."

The vision begins to fade; the dream gradually giving way to the reality, and, little-by-little, the haunting love, which has brought him through the night, is overlaid with another; gentler, more protective. He lies in the half-world between dream and reality; abandoned, desolate, yet still clinging on. He vaguely remembers the man he once was; indistinctly recalls the energy which used to course through his body each new day; remembers briefly that he once believed life to be sweet; once believed happiness to be there for the taking; then, with heavy heart, realises, once again, that this world in which he now walks is a world of shadow and darkness.

The last soft, mystical veil falls away; the dream is no more. He recognises his surroundings, becomes aware of the growing morning light, then turns his head and looks into the smiling, almond-shaped eyes regarding him with quiet expectation.

"Good morning, sweetie," he answers, looking into the young, beautiful, oriental features, so much the image of her mother, then turns away to hide the tears.

A young hand strokes his forehead. "I love you, Daddy."

CHAPTER THREE

The man sits quietly upon the horse, just as he did the last time; the day he came upon this place.

The ring of trees is just as he remembers it, and there, up ahead, the slight grassy rise with the single large oak tree; a crowning centre-piece to the beauty and the solitude of the location. And, to the left, the slight gap in the trees which he noticed last time, but which now seems somewhat less obvious. Springtime is advancing, the leaves becoming thicker on the branches. Soon, perhaps, the gap may disappear from view, and only be known to those who chanced upon it during the wintertime.

Silently, he gazes at the scene, as if waking from a dream; appears to be taking strength from the beauty and the tranquillity which pervade the area. The horse remains motionless, as if also sensing the latent energy of the surroundings. A few more moments, then the man slowly dismounts. The reins drop softly to the ground.

Slowly, hesitantly, he walks towards the central oak, then stops, his gaze momentarily directed towards the gap in the trees; memories of the alluring glade filtering into his mind. But then, a short shake of the head and he continues on. The glade can wait a little longer.

Standing beneath the oak, he gazes up at its branches, impressed by the sheer size of the trunk and limbs. He leans forward and rests his head against the cool trunk. Something stirs in his mind. He ponders, but the image remains out of reach; a memory, an activity; something from his distant past; something he feels he should know, but, for the moment, cannot recall. He looks around, searching for a clue, but nothing makes an impact, then slowly, he lowers himself to sit, cross-legged, on the soft grass in the shade of the magnificent old oak.

He remains there; mute, withdrawn, unmoving. The sun gradually rises higher in the sky as the morning advances. The grazing mare loses interest in her surroundings and walks slowly to the tree. She nudges the hunched form still seated on the ground. He looks up, startled by the intrusion into his private world, then begins to piece together the scene; the horse, the clearing, the shade of the tree, and, ah yes... there was a glade.

Stiff joints and tired muscles resist as he hauls himself upright, then turns and starts down the gentle slope of the mound, emerging into the bright sunlight. A short, sharp whistle and the mare looks up expectantly, then trots the few paces between them, slowing to a walk to follow obediently behind him as he makes his way toward the gap in the trees.

A few more paces and the man, and then the horse, disappear into the shadowed wall of greenery, to emerge a moment later, on the other side of the natural barrier, in the small, sun-dappled glade, carpeted in lush, green grass. As before, the man stops in the centre of the glade and turns, full circle, taking in the comforting, protective surroundings. The sound of the gurgling stream, and the splash of water tumbling over the rocky outcrop lend the scene a light-heartedness not palpable on the other side of the trees. He notes the sunlit rock seat and recalls, from last time, the warmth when he lay upon it.

He walks to the seat again, then, on a whim, takes a further step to the edge of the stream, and bending down, cups his hands and tastes the cool, clear water. Squatting, he takes in his surroundings, noting again the strange angle of the trunk of the tree on the other side of the stream, whose branches overhang this side.

For a few moments, he trails his fingers in the stream, watching the eddies they create in the swiftly flowing water, which breaks and dances its way around the obstacles before tumbling over the low, rocky outcrop in the middle of the flow.

Shaking his head to break the hypnotic spell, he stands at last and stretches, then, recalling again the warmth of his last visit, turns back to the seat and, once again, stretches out upon the sunlit rock. Looking up, his gaze follows the overhanging branches back to the trunk, then down to the dark, rich earth on the other side of the stream. He notes that the leafy coverage is much thicker now than on his last visit.

The warmth from the stone surface beneath his back begins to work its magic. Interest in the immediate surroundings gradually fades, to be replaced by... dreams.

★

He wakes, and stretches. The sun is high overhead now and he notes, vaguely, that he is both hungry and thirsty. He continues to lie on the flat rock seat, but struggles with the emerging realisation that he cannot remember feeling hungry before. Until now, nothing has penetrated, not hunger, not pain, not heat, not cold. He holds his hands up in front of his face and studies the scratches and bruises, but has no idea from whence they came.

Slowly, he swings his legs off the seat... and stands. His back aches from the time spent lying on the hard surface. Strange: he cannot remember noticing his back aching before. In fact, he cannot recollect noticing anything much at all before.

He sways, unsteadily. His sudden awareness is disconcerting and he is uncertain of its cause, or its consequences. He walks to the horse, seeking reassurance, and strokes its mane tenderly. He breathes deeply, and slowly, the rising panic is contained.

The rough, worn saddle-bags, which look so comically out-of-place on the sleek beast which has been his travelling companion for so long, contain a varied assortment of apples, bread and other pickings from along the way. He opens one, and, within a short time, both man and animal are munching contentedly upon the liberated items of fruit and bread.

And, as the afternoon sun traverses the sky, its light momentarily strikes the wet rocks, over which the stream is tumbling, at just the angle to reflect the sparkling pattern into his face; the face of the man seated cross-legged on the grass at the feet of the sleek, white mare.

He looks over at the rocks, dazzled by the rapidly changing patterns which shimmer and dance and break and fold before him.

He gazes, mesmerised, and then... smiles.

Another small piece of the wall encasing the fractured mind breaks away. A chink appears. Sunlight and beauty stream in...

★

Perhaps the lost and haunted look, which has been etched on his face for so long, seems a little softer now; or perhaps it is the softening of the sunlight as it passes through the delicate shade of the canopy overhanging the glade.

And perhaps the stoop in his bearing, as he now sits on his horse, seems a little less pronounced than when he arrived earlier in the day; perhaps.

Gently, he wheels the mare around and takes in the view of the glade, one last time, then, with the slightest pressure of his heels, urges her forward, toward the gap in the trees.

They pass through and emerge on the other side, back in the clearing which abuts the secluded, protected glade. They continue on, skirting the oak tree, and heading toward the track which leads back into the forest. But, the uneasiness remains; something he should know; something he should remember. He halts the animal and looks, once again, at the oak at the centre of the clearing.

What is it? What is it that he remembers? What is it that a single, isolated tree in the middle of a clearing keeps bringing to the edge of his mind? Has he been here before? He thinks not. Has he encountered such a tree before? Possibly. But where? When? Under what circumstances?

He stares, intently, at the tree, willing it to reveal its secret, but to no avail.

He prepares to leave.

A hazy memory shimmers, solidifies, then finally reveals itself. He chuckles as he recalls: the quintain; the one they constructed as boys; the one they would run at, with wooden lances tucked under their right arms, pretending to be knights, intent upon striking the target suspended from the overhanging branch of the one big tree in the centre of the clearing. The chuckle dies away, but the smile persists.

He stares at the tree; no longer confounded by its secret. An idea forms; embryonic, but persistent.

Abruptly, he digs his heels into the mare's flanks, and hauling on the reins, turns her away from the tree. A little canter to the tree-line, and they turn again, man and beast, in a fluidity which belies the hesitancy of a few moments earlier and hints at a partnership of trust and understanding which is clearly not new.

His hands are slightly sweaty as he grips the reins. A strange yet almost familiar tightness grips his chest as he considers the distance to the overhanging branch. Then, in a heartbeat, they are moving, gathering speed. The mare responds with an unexpected energy and the man is suddenly alarmed and quickly reels her in. They stop, not half-way to the oak. His legs are trembling, his mind spinning. He recognises that it was fear that caused him to stop, but there was something else; a release, an excitement... a familiarity.

He breathes deeply to steady himself, then, once again, they turn; beautifully, fluidly, in tune with each other; and retrace the ground to their starting point. They turn. He stares hard at the tree, breathing deeply and steadily, then, with an abandon not felt for a very long time, he launches the animal into motion.

This time there is no alarm, this time there is no slackening, this time there is nothing but driven, focussed energy as the combination of a man and a horse charges towards, and then under, the overhanging branch of a magnificent oak atop a slight rise at the centre of a clearing. And, as they rein in, the man is hunched over the neck of the horse, clinging desperately to the reins, but laughing deliriously at the reckless sensation which has just infused his body, and his mind. For the first time, the mare appears frisky, and the man is having trouble controlling her. And yet, as he battles the energetic animal, the smile on his face remains undimmed.

He sits upright in the saddle, patting the neck of the mare, contemplating another charge, but decides against it. There is a strange clarity to what he sees as he looks around. The clearing seems bright and airy, the suffocation he has been experiencing for so long now appears to have lifted; at least for the moment. He notices, for the first time, that the sky today is not grey, but blue... and wide... and high; and wonders if, perhaps, just perhaps, the demons are beginning to depart.

He considers his next action; then decides. "Home," he murmurs.

The smile persists.

CHAPTER FOUR

Wendy, slightly out of breath from the pregnancy which is beginning to show, trails behind Odelia as they make their way under the portcullis and out into the clearing surrounding the castle. It is early afternoon and the pair have spent the morning industriously preparing the cheeses which Wendy will display at the market later this week. The cheeses are boutique; a range which Wendy has gathered from a succession of merchants who have passed by, and through, the castle with their wares. Her nose is sensitive and refined and over the recent months her stock has become quite delectable. And now, she feels, it is time for her to reveal her new-found passion to the other ladies of the court, and to encourage them to join her in this rather eclectic pursuit of fine food; and to introduce the soirées she has learned about, also from the passing travellers. Time it is, she believes, to bring a little more culture from the continent to the English court.

But now the pair, backs and arms tired and aching, have decided that an afternoon of fresh air and fun is in order. Odelia is fascinated by the slight bulge which has become noticeable in Wendy's body and has been asking questions almost non-stop, during the morning, about the phases of pregnancy and the issues surrounding child-birth and the subsequent care of babies. And Wendy, for her part, has enjoyed the excitement which her announcement to Odelia, earlier this morning, has generated. The pair have become close over the almost two years since the death of Mariel, and the prospect of a baby has drawn them even closer together.

The basket of food and the folded thick, multi-coloured blanket are evidence of the picnic which is about to ensue. And the pair are not alone, as several other groups of women and girls are already scattered about on the grass within a hundred metre arc from the castle gate; and a number more are making their way out to take advantage of the bright sunshine that has turned this gentle morning into a brilliant warm afternoon just made for frivolity.

"Odelia, come and sit with us."

"Odelia; over here."

"Hello Odelia. Where are you sitting?"

The chorus of invitations is impressive, and Wendy laughs at the perplexed look on the young girl's face as she attempts to respond to all of the calls upon her, without favouring any one over another. Eventually, they choose a spot to lay their blanket and unpack their basket; however, within minutes, the boundaries between the groups have disappeared as the girls congregate to chatter, then break apart to visit other friends.

And so the afternoon continues; from time-to-time broken to allow for breath to be taken, food and drink to be consumed, and laughter and games to ebb and flow with the rise and fall of energy levels among the girls. And mothers, relieved of the burden of care of their individual daughters, also gather in small groups to talk excitedly about the latest comings and goings within the castle, the latest liaisons both public and private, and generally, to exchange the gossip which has been accumulating during the long winter months now being consigned to yesterday in the sunshine which spring has brought to the land.

An hour passes, then two, and a slight chill in the air heralds the approach of evening.

But then the excitement mounts again, as a group of horsemen crests the ridge between the forest and the castle.

At once, Wendy, skirts lifted, begins to run, slightly awkwardly, towards the returning hunting party, and, as one, the group turns towards her. Other women follow, quickly outstripping their pregnant sister, running, gaily, to greet their returning men-folk. The atmosphere is one of extreme jollity.

The girls all feign disinterest for a few moments, but, gradually, the lure of reunion with their returning fathers overcomes their attempts to appear 'grown up' and, one-by-one, they break from the group and charge, squealing towards the now dismounting riders.

Big, strong men lift breathless ladies from their feet into passionate embraces moments before smaller figures crash into them, demanding attention. The reunion of families is wonderful to observe.

The last of Odelia's companions finally abandons her pretence at indifference and charges towards the hubbub of chatter, rising in volume as mothers and daughters compete to be heard above each other.

Only Odelia remains; alone. She watches the excitement for a moment, then, solemnly turns and sits, facing away from the excited, chattering, re-united families, and starts to pick at the pieces of chicken left over from the picnic. The tears, hidden from the others, drop silently to the grass as the despair which, from time-to-time, engulfs her still-fragile mind, takes hold once again. She keenly feels the absence of her mother, and sadly reflects upon the broken shell her father has become. Suddenly, it is all too much and, overwhelmed, she falls forward, head in hands and sobs in abject loneliness.

Minutes pass, then firm hands grasp her shoulders and gently pull her upright. Soft, strong arms wrap around her and hold her close as Wendy enfolds the abandoned child in her embrace; a vibrant young woman as often as she is able, but, deep within, a child, when the cold, harsh winds of reality blow hard.

Gareth kneels beside the pair and, in a despairing effort to do something useful, runs his fingers through the young girl's long, dark, shining hair.

"Shhh," croons Wendy as she rocks the girl backwards and forwards, flooding her with warmth and love. Odelia's face remains buried in the older woman's bosom.

In the distance, at the crown of the hill, a head appears, followed, a moment later, by the upper part of a horse. Then, the rest of the rider and the mount come into view as they crest the rise and make their way slowly down the track toward the now dispersing group of re-united families. Gareth touches his wife on the shoulder and nods in the direction of the hill.

Wendy looks up and sees the figure, then bends her head and whispers, "Look, Odelia, Daddy's come back early."

The young girl looks up in the direction indicated by Wendy, and through her tears and shuddering breathing, manages a wan smile. She looks back at Wendy. "I should go to him, Auntie Wendy, he may need me."

And now it is Wendy's turn to weep softly, as the heartbreak of one tragically deprived child, preparing to ignore her own pain and tend her damaged father, brings forth, yet again, the anguish of that day almost two summers ago, when the most beautiful creature she had ever met was taken from them all, by a callous act of violence which still makes her blood boil when she thinks of it.

Odelia stands.

"Thank you, Auntie Wendy," she says, as Wendy rises too. She kisses Wendy, then reaches up to Gareth and kisses him, lightly, also.

"I'll go and get my dad," she continues, then turns and begins the slow walk towards the rider in the distance, who has reached the broad hollow between the hill and the castle, and is now commencing the long, gentle climb up the slope towards the castle wall. Gareth stands silently behind Wendy, arms around her shoulders, hands folded over the plumpness of her pregnancy. They both watch the progress of the young girl, so apparently alone, and wonder in what condition she will find her father on this occasion.

★

The distance between the pair decreases, step-by-step, as Odelia, on foot, walks down the track towards her father, and Averill, on horseback, makes his way up the slight incline.

This meeting has occurred many times before, as Averill has returned from his strange sojourns to God only knows where. And always, the result is the same; the agonised, distracted former knight, aware of his daughter's presence, yet seemingly unable to recognise her pain; to comprehend the love

170

which brings her here, time-after-time; or to respond in any manner which might give the young girl hope that, in time, life might return to the happier times they once knew.

The distance between them closes. Uncharacteristically, he stops, dismounts, then, reins still clutched in his hand, resumes the gentle climb on foot.

They approach... and meet; on the harsh, dusty track worn into the green spring grass, under a bright blue late-afternoon sky.

"Hello Daddy," she begins, searching his face; eager to determine if there is any degree of awareness. He bends down, and on one knee places his arms around her shoulders and gently hugs her to him.

"Hello princess," he answers.

Surprised that he has actually responded, Odelia wraps her arms around him and leans her head, lovingly, against his. "Welcome home, Daddy."

He continues to hold her and gradually she realises he is weeping. He holds her for a moment longer, then, releasing his grasp just a little, he lifts his head and looks directly into her eyes. "I seem to have been missing you for a long, long time, sweetie," he says, softly.

A sudden intake of breath as the impact of his words hits her. She looks into his eyes; eyes which are no longer blank and distant, but are now alive with the torment of his pain and his happiness. And suddenly she knows; knows that this is no longer the empty shell of a man who used to be her father; knows that somehow a piece of the magic which used to infuse his being has returned.

The two lost, lonely souls stare into each other. Then, through his tears... the older one smiles. The younger one's bottom lip quivers in her attempt at bravery. She fails; gloriously, beautifully; and bursts into tears of happiness as she recognises that her father, as she once knew him, has returned. She flings her arms around him, crushing him with the intensity of the pain which is now streaming from her body.

They embrace, long and tenderly, father and daughter; and, little-by-little, the shudders consuming her frame begin to recede. Her breathing becomes steady once more.

Averill stands. "Come here, sweetie," he says; then, in one strong, fluid motion, he sweeps her up and into the saddle of the horse standing quietly by. He looks up at her, still smiling, then, taking the reins again, he begins to lead the animal towards the castle.

A slight chuckle. He turns his head and smiles up at her, but continues on. Another giggle. He smiles to himself, and keeps walking. But, a burst of laughter causes him to stop and turn. "What is it?" he asks, bemused.

"Oh, Daddy," she laughs. "Why do you still have these funny old saddle-bags? They're so... huge; and they look so funny on Damsel."

And this time, it is Averill who begins to chuckle, as the incongruity of the enormous and ragged saddle-bags, bouncing back and forth, on the beautiful, silky white flanks of the mare, penetrates his mind for the first time.

"They do rather spoil her beauty, don't they?" he replies, actually taking them in for the first time. "But then, they do carry a lot," he continues, "and I've needed that."

She is still laughing. "Oh, Daddy; they're awful..."

He considers. "Perhaps I should change them." Then looking up at her, smiling. "Well, maybe later..."

Odelia looks down at him; dark brown, almond-shaped eyes smiling back, long black hair shimmering in the breeze. Her heart is singing. "Whatever you want, Daddy," she coos. "Whatever you want."

The man turns, and, reins in hand, starts walking again; no longer stooped, no longer distracted.

Up ahead, a man and a woman stand at the side of the track, apparently awaiting the arrival of the pair. Averill waves.

The woman buries her head in her companion's chest. "Oh Gareth," she whispers. "What has happened?"

The big man wraps his arms a little more tightly around the soft, warm body of his pregnant wife. "I think, my love," he replies, "I think our Gregory might have just found his way home."

★

Nothing changes. Bryan is in full flight, describing the intimate charms of a young lady of the court, Charles and Robert are ribbing him mercilessly as the fantastic details emerge, indicating, without any pretence at subtlety, that they believe not a word of the story and challenging him to offer some evidence which can support the fantasy, whilst Anthony and Thomas talk quietly between themselves, unprepared to be drawn into Bryan's fanciful account.

The approaching footsteps are measured and steady; two pairs. The story-teller is too engrossed in his account to be interrupted, and the brothers are enjoying the challenge of bringing him down too much to notice. It is Anthony and Thomas who suddenly cease their conversation and look up. The subtle absence of their murmured background causes Bryan to falter mid-sentence.

In the doorway stands Gareth, beaming with pleasure at the surprise he has brought, and beside, him, shuffling uncomfortably, is Averill, looking from face-to-face around the group seated at the rough wooden table.

"My God, it's Gregory," exclaims Charles, still animated from his verbal jousting with Bryan.

"Hello Gregory," from the thoughtful Thomas. A pause. "It's very good to see you again."

"I wasn't sure about coming here," responds Averill, his words slow and careful.

"But I dragged him along," interjects Gareth. "Said it would be good for him. And besides, it's time he visited the people who miss him most."

Averill smiles, self-consciously.

"You're looking well, Gregory," adds Anthony, more kindly than accurately.

"You never were a good liar, Anthony," is the slow, gentle reproach. "But thank you for saying so, anyway."

A few, muted chuckles. The conversation is difficult, but no-one is walking away.

"It's been a long time, Gregory," says Thomas.

"Indeed," responds Averill. "Things were... difficult, for a while; for quite a while, in fact."

"I expect so," replies Thomas. "So, how are you feeling?"

Averill appears to consider before answering, "Quite well... I think, is the answer.

"And, I'm not sure I could have said that a week or two ago," he adds.

"Is that so?" replies Anthony.

"It's hard to explain," continues Averill. "It was as if I was in the world, but couldn't actually become part of it. I would see people around me, and know that they were talking to me, but nothing made any sense, and I didn't really know how to respond. So, I didn't. It was just easier that way.

"I imagine I've appeared quite strange for some time now," he adds.

"Oh, you always were strange," chips in Bryan, only to receive a friendly cuff from Robert sitting beside him.

"Would you like to sit down for a while?" asks Anthony. "We're just having a bit of a chat after eating; we can easily drag up two more chairs."

"Actually, I think I might just say 'no' for the moment," replies Averill, backing away slightly. "I'd like to get back to make sure Odelia is alright. I'm sure she is; she's with Wendy, and they always get along," he adds, smiling.

"I'm afraid I've let her down for quite a while now," he continues, "and I'd like to be with her again, for a time; really with her, I mean; listening to her, answering her questions; you know, being a father again instead of a stranger. I think she must have found things very difficult... for a long time now."

"I'll come with you," says Gareth, turning to leave.

"No, Gareth," says Averill, raising his hand to the big man's shoulder. "Stay here with the lads for a while; I'm sure you have things to discuss. I'll be alright. I can find my way back quite well. I'll just thank Wendy for looking after Odelia again these past couple of days, then we'll go.

"Goodnight, gentlemen," he adds. "I may well see you again soon. We'll see."

He smiles, half-waves, and leaves. The six look at each other as the slow footsteps fade.

"Well, what do you think?" ask Gareth.

"Oh dear," remarks Thomas. "There's certainly something there now, but, gee, there's a long way to go, Gareth."

Gareth nods. "Anthony?"

"Well... I've seen him a few times over the months, and, as he said, he just wasn't with us. But, at least now we can talk to him.

"I think it might take a while, but I'd be prepared to say that I think the worst might be over."

"I agree," replies Gareth. "He and Odelia ate with us this evening, and although he didn't say much, he was certainly in the room with us; and that's something that hasn't happened for a long, long time. He seems, somehow, to be at peace with himself again.

"And you wouldn't believe the change in Odelia," he adds. "She was as bright and happy as I've seen her for a very long time; almost like she used to be.

"It was rather wonderful, actually."

A pause, as they reflect upon the recovering shell of the man they have just witnessed.

"Do you think he'll ever fully recover?" asks Charles.

Anthony and Gareth look at each other, but it is Thomas who answers. "I remember the Gregory we all knew; the strong, disciplined, fearsome individual who carried everything before him. And I can't even begin to imagine the anguish which has left him in this state. But, underneath, it's still the same Gregory; it's still the same man who surmounted every obstacle that ever came his way, and I don't see why he won't surmount this one."

"Time will tell," remarks Anthony. "By God, I hope you're right, Thomas, but time will tell."

"Indeed," adds Gareth. "But the first step was today. And I, for one, want to be there when it happens."

"Amen to that," replies Thomas. "Amen to that."

CHAPTER FIVE

The muscular arm makes light work of the bellows which, with strong, regular breath, encourages the flickering flame to spread through the underlying coals of the rapidly heating forge. The strengthening glow begins to illuminate the area immediately surrounding the forge; however, the rest of the workshop remains in darkness. Dawn has barely broken, and although most of the castle are now awake, somewhere between ablution and breakfast, few have ventured out into the crisp morning air.

"That's a nice even spread you're getting, William," offers a slow, restrained voice from the shadows.

"Holy Mother of God," is the startled response, as the blacksmith whirls to confront the intruder. "Who's there? Show yourself, by God, or there'll be the devil to pay."

A figure leans forward until head and shoulders appear, barely illuminated, in the shaft of pale sunlight passing through the workshop.

"Oh my God, Sir Gregory," is the amazed response. "I thought you were... that is, they said that..."

"What, that I was dead?" asks the visitor.

"No, Sir Gregory, not that," replies the blacksmith. "They said that... well, they said that I would probably never see you again; leastways not here, Sir Gregory."

The figure moves out of the shadows and slowly walks toward the recovering blacksmith. He stops, a pace or two away, and leans upon the large, cold anvil. "Well, William," drawls Averill, looking down, thoughtfully, "perhaps they were right."

Then, as he lifts his eyes, gaze moving slowly around the walls. "It's been a long time since I thought about workshops, and forges... and axes and swords..."

"We all knew that something bad had happened, Sir Gregory," interjects the blacksmith, "that your lovely lady had suffered some terrible fate. And then you just disappeared... and no-one told us anything much about what had happened. And I guess the stories just grew. Some said that you'd gone away; some thought you might even have died from a broken heart; some said that they'd seen you riding on a white horse in the early mornings or late at night; some said that it didn't really look like you anyhow, and that, maybe, it were your ghost.

"There were lots of stories, for a while, Sir Gregory; lots of stories. But then the winter came and, well, you know how it is in wintertime, Sir Gregory; everyone thinking about his-self, and his family, and keeping warm, and, well, I guess we all just forgot about you.

"And that was more 'n a year ago now; and we've 'ad another winter since that one, so it's been a long, long time since you was on anyone's mind, Sir Gregory.

A slight pause as the blacksmith draw breath, but he feels compelled to continue. "So you could have knocked me over with a feather when you poked your face out into the light here this morning; knocked me over with a feather you could have, Sir Gregory."

Silence, then Averill prompts, "You'd better not forget your forge, William."

"Oh my Lord, you're right, Sir Gregory," replies William. "You've certainly addled this old brain; 'scuse me, Sir Gregory."

And, turning his back to Averill, the blacksmith begins steadily pumping the bellows again.

Pale sunlight gradually reaches the remaining corners of the workshop and over the next few minutes a steadily increasing roar begins to accompany each stroke of the bellows as the coals begin to glow.

"I'm here for a reason," remarks Averill, suddenly.

"I may be an old fool," replies William, composed again, "but I didn't think you were here for your health, Sir Gregory."

He turns, eyes moist. "By the Lord, it's good to see you again, Sir Gregory.

"And I'm sorry for all them words, just now. I just couldn't stop, you know."

Averill smiles. "Yes, William, I do know.

"We've spent a lot of time in this workshop, you and I... and the king... when we were young."

"Yes, we have," agrees William, brushing the back of his hand across a damp cheek. "Yes, we have."

Averill looks around the workshop; the tools of trade neatly arranged on the walls, the main forge in one corner, several smaller braziers, anvils of various shapes and sizes, shadows appearing and disappearing as William works the bellows, but intermittently now; the coals are burning brightly; familiar heat now radiates from the forge. And, despite the strenuous, noisy work which is usually carried out here, there is a calm, peaceful spirit at work in the workshop this morning.

"And what is it that you would be looking for, Sir Gregory?" asks William, hefting a mallet, spinning it in his substantial hand, then turning to face Averill again.

"I need a sword, William."

"You have a sword, Sir Gregory."

"Too heavy, William; too heavy," replies Averill. "I've lost a lot of strength over this past couple of years, and will need to regain it piece-by-piece. I need something I can wield comfortably for a while. Can you find me one?"

William nods, now understanding. "Of course, I may just need a little time."

"And I need an axe."

"An axe?"

"A woodsman's axe; I have some trees which need cutting."

The burly blacksmith stands, arms folded, looking directly at Averill, then smiles. "You're not going to tell me what you really want it for, are you?"

"I just did."

"Well, no matter," chuckles William turning away. "I know better than to ask you what's on your mind. You'll tell me when you're good and ready."

Averill says nothing, but surveys the workshop one more time. The blacksmith becomes aware of the silence. "Are you alright, Sir Gregory?"

"Yes, William," is the slow, melancholy response. "I was just remembering; remembering when we were boys... the king and I... how we would arrive here on cold winter mornings, and you would have warm milk waiting for us; and a set of hammers lined up for each of us. I remember how many times we tried to make our own swords, and how many times you threw the terrible results back into the forge.

"I grew up in here, William; here, and in the stables, where good men like yourself showed us what it meant to be men; what it meant to treat your fellow man with integrity; how to carry our badges of rank with dignity and with compassion."

"Ah, Sir Gregory," replies William, "you're placing too much store in those times; we was just doing what our king expected of us. He was a grand man, our king what was, and we, all of us, was proud to serve him. And if that meant dealing with little bastards like you, and like the prince what was, then we was happy to be of service, Sir Gregory; happy to be of service."

A pause as William considers some more, then, "We've all seen some good knights, Sir Gregory, and we've all seen some bad. But it's the good 'uns that we remember best... like your father, Sir Gregory; he was a good 'un; a real good 'un."

A pause, as both men reflect upon private memories. Then Averill straightens and starts towards the doorway. "I'll be back tomorrow morning, William. Is that enough time?"

"Should be, Sir Gregory; should be."

Averill suddenly stops and turns. "It's been good to talk William; it's been a long time.

177

"Oh, and no-one needs to know I was here this morning," he adds, as he finally departs.

"Were you?" is the innocent response of the blacksmith, facing the forge again and wiping the back of his hand across the other damp cheek. "Big girl," he mutters to himself.

The rhythmic roar of the forge increases. There is an uncharacteristic energy to the blacksmith's pumping of the bellows.

★

Three grey days of rain and blustery wind have swept the land, forcing activities indoors and rendering travel virtually impossible. But, today, a bright morning sun shines from a clear blue sky, warming the soft, damp earth and drying the foliage of the forests.

A sleek white horse canters from the shadow of the trees and out into the sunlight of the clearing. The rider sits easily in the saddle, moving as one with the horse. However, his face is expressionless; remote; but not to the same extent as on his previous visits to the clearing. This time, he is more clearly aware of his surroundings, and, with a little effort, one could almost imagine him having a purpose.

A soft murmur and the horse slows to a walk. Beast and rider continue moving around the tree-line at the edge of the clearing; the rider looking into the forest with apparent interest. After a few moments he gently tugs the reins and the horse obediently stops. The rider dismounts, leaving the reins trailing, and walks into the trees. After a short time, he emerges and, returning to the horse, reaches into the long leather pouch attached to the rear of the saddle.

The woodsman's axe which he withdraws glints in the sunlight. Holding the neck of the handle, he runs his thumb across the edge of the blade and notes the fine roll of dusty skin which is delicately scraped off. He nods, smiles, lets the axe slide through his fingers to the ground, then removes his shirt, rolling it into a ball and stowing it inside one of the two unwieldy saddle-bags which again dangle over the horse's haunches.

"They're still really handy," he says to himself, chuckling slightly at some thought associated with them.

Then, stooping to pick up the axe from the ground, he walks on into the trees.

Within a few moments, the silence of the forest is interrupted by the rhythmic sound of chopping, each stroke accompanied by myriad small echoes from the surrounding trees. And, only moments later, comes the cracking sound of splintering wood, following by a dull thud as timber hits earth.

Averill emerges, backwards, hauling the mid-sized felled tree behind him. His face is dripping, his arms, back and chest covered in sweat, and the band of his trousers dark with moisture from the unfamiliar exertion.

Reaching the horse, he drops the tree to the ground, and turns, chest heaving, to stand with both hands resting on the saddle.

"My God," he mutters to no-one in particular, "this is going to be so hard; I'm not sure I really want to do it."

Moments pass, then, with hands on hips, Averill begins to walk, in a circle beside his horse, gradually bringing his breathing under control. A few times around, and the evidence of his footsteps begins to appear in the trampled grass.

Recovered, he returns to the tree, collects the axe from the ground where it had fallen when he dropped the tree, and begins the task of removing the larger branches from the trunk. From time-to-time, he stands groaning, and, hands on hips, rotates his pelvis to relieve the pain and the ache of the continuous effort for which his body has long since lost its capacity.

After a few more periods of activity, interspersed with spells resting on folded arms on the saddle, the tree is devoid of branches. Then, with a final, straining effort, he raises the axe and attacks the trunk. Within a short time, the trunk is trimmed to about nine feet in length. Averill sinks to his knees, then, slowly, rolls forward until he lies, exhausted upon the soft, warm earth.

"My God," he mutters to himself. "How can I be so weak?" And, inwardly, he wonders at the sense of the task he has set himself; the task of recovery. And yet, as he lies shattered upon the ground, he knows that, painful as it may be, this is the only course of action open to him, if he ever wishes to re-enter the world; and the brotherhood which he held so dear, so long ago.

Strange, he muses, how his mind seems to be clearing; how this one task he has set himself, seems to have brought with it a clarity of purpose which he has not known for such a long time. He recognises that it is a pitifully simple task, one which, in the past, would have been dealt with without a second thought, but a task which, right now, is absolutely consuming him. But he feels a strange, light-hearted confidence that once he achieves this objective, then he will be that much more capable of addressing the next challenge he sets himself, and then the next, and so on.

A few more minutes then, rolling on his side, he rises onto hands and knees, and, with a final herculean effort, raises himself to a standing position. Aching, screaming muscles cause him to cry out in pain, but gradually the agony recedes and, once again, he starts to gingerly walk the small circle, now trampled into the grass, which brings movement and relief to his protesting body.

He looks down at the roughly trimmed trunk each time he passes it, but, eventually, decides that further useful effort today would be impossible. And so, disappointed that he has to abandon his plan so early, but committed to return as soon as possible, he starts the painful, bent-backed walk towards the point in the tree-line where he knows the entrance to the glade is hidden. A short, sharp whistle, and the white mare lifts her head, then begins to trot after him.

The prospect of fruit, cool sparkling water, and a warm rock bed upon which to stretch out, momentarily banish the pain from aching muscles. The man walks on, slowly and gingerly, but with an unmistakable determination not previously evident in his bearing. The healing may have only just started, but that is has started, there is no doubt.

★

The exit from under the canopy of trees and out into the broad expanse of open land heralds a mixture of emotions. Up until this point, the dense forest has provided a sense of comfort; the rich, green foliage incorporating soft, waving ferns of various hues; the occasional red deer skittishly crossing his path; the ever inquisitive squirrels, standing still, tempting him with their insolence, then vanishing in a flash, but always, he imagines, with a wicked smile; the occasional flutter of birds breaking cover when the sound of the approaching hoofs becomes too much for them to ignore.

But then, the trees thin, the dappled sunlight begins to infiltrate, and moments later, the cover and protection he has felt to this point, are gone. Beneath him, the mare canters on without effort or concern, but, in an instant, he is transported from the deep, comforting womb of the forest out onto the wide open expanse of the plain.

The rise to the hill ahead is familiar, as is the dip which he knows will follow; down to the broad hollow which then becomes the long gentle rise to the gate of Windsor Castle. All of this, he knows, all of this has filled his nights, and his nightmares, for longer than he wishes to acknowledge. Yet over the months, his mind has pushed it aside, has chosen to not acknowledge his surroundings, any surroundings, but especially those associated with that tragic day. And, on this basis, he has coped, has existed, has managed to pass each day and each night, without sense, without happiness, but without pain.

But now, by some strange power associated with the beauty and the tranquillity of the glade, he is becoming re-absorbed into the world; is recognising that life goes on and that he has a part to play in it.

But what he hadn't been prepared for is the return of sensitivity; the renewed awareness of things, both good and bad. And so, as he approaches the scene of the tragedy, his stomach churns, his hands begin to perspire, and the composure which he has striven so hard to achieve, begins to falter and crumble. His posture in the saddle becomes ragged. His hard-won serenity starts to desert him.

He had been so pleased with today; pleased that he had found a direction, pleased that he been able to work towards the goal he had set himself, even if his body had groaned and ached and ultimately failed him, and he had only managed part of the task. But now, he wonders if he has really made any progress at all. The demons, which seemed to be departing, are suddenly back. The day which had promised so much, appears to be slipping back into the dark vale of despair in which he has existed for so long.

He is at the bottom of the broad hollow now, just starting up the long, gentle incline to the castle gate. He knows exactly where it happened, exactly where Mariel's life ended and his torture began. It is burned into his mind. He forces himself to look ahead to the spot, in an effort to bring the growing despair under control... and sees... something. Too far away to make it out clearly, he puzzles at the strange multi-coloured shape on the ground at the side of the track.

As he approaches, the shape begins to move; to become more upright. A minute later he can make out a face looking toward him... with hand raised to shield her eyes from the dipping sun. The young girl lifts her other hand to wave to her returning father, and waits, sitting demurely at the side of the track, as he closes.

He dismounts, and she, standing now, rushes into his outstretched arms. "I missed you, Daddy."

"Where's Wendy?" he asks, momentarily alarmed at finding Odelia here, alone, outside the castle walls.

"Up there," she replies, pointing. Averill looks up to see another figure, sitting on the grass beside the castle gate, waving to him.

"It was too far for Auntie Wendy to come," explains Odelia. "She's pregnant, you know, Daddy."

Averill waves back to the figure, and laughs at the same time, buoyed by the admonishing tone of his daughter. He really should have known better.

"Oh Odelia," he remarks. "It is so nice to find you here, and yes, you're right, Auntie Wendy is pregnant, and I should have known that, even if she were not right by your side, she would be watching over you, somewhere close by.

"I apologise," he chuckles, ruffling her hair.

"Can I ride Damsel?" she asks, mind already dismissing the previous conversation and moving forward with the apparent unlimited energy of youth.

"Yes, of course you can," he responds, lifting her easily into the saddle.

He takes the reins and begins walking up the slope to the castle gate, and the waiting Lady Wendy.

★

Once again he has been thwarted by the weather; it has rained ceaselessly for two days. But this morning has dawned dry and slightly warmer with a cover of low, grey cloud to accompany him on his journey. The ground will be soft, and, for that, he is thankful, since although his strained muscles no longer scream in protest, he knows, full well, that there is only so much they will achieve before reaching exhaustion once again. He recognises that his recovery will be a step-by-step process and is eager to begin.

The tree-trunk lies exactly where he left it.

He dismounts and looks casually around for the right spot; somewhere where the ground is not too uneven, somewhere far enough in from the tree-line that he can approach the pell from all angles.

Finding the spot, he marks the ground with his heel, stamping down onto the broken earth until a deep imprint remains, then turns and walks back to the mare and her baggage. He withdraws a short-handled spade and returning to the spot just marked, bends his back to the task of digging the deep, narrow hole which will be required to hold the tree-trunk upright and stable.

Spadeful by spadeful, the mound of displaced earth beside the hole rises, and despite occasionally stopping to stretch his aching back, and ultimately completing the task on hands and knees, he achieves his objective in less than an hour. The hole is ideal; an arm's length deep, round, with vertical sides; exactly what was required.

He stands to survey his work, and, feeling rather pleased with himself, drops the spade near to the mare and then turns his attention to dragging the felled and trimmed tree-trunk to the hole before somehow manoeuvring it upright. Nine feet of tree-trunk is not easy to move, and the temptation is to take a rope from the saddle-bag and let the mare haul it. And, it might just come to that; but first, there is the belief that he can move it himself, to test.

Effort and stubbornness are applied with equal persistence, where common sense ought to have prevailed. And, moments later, he laughs at the basic stupidity of what he has done, but is elated by his success, even though he is once again on hands and knees, panting with exhaustion. The end of the trunk is at the hole. Now all he has to do is lift it upright.

One last effort.

He stands, and, hands on hips, rotates his pelvis once again, banishing the stiffness and the pain. Then, bending one last time, and with a straining, full-throated roar, he lifts the end of the trunk furthest from the hole and holding it over his head, staggers step-by-step towards the hole pushing the trunk upright. The ground shudders with a resounding thump as the end of the trunk drops to the bottom of the hole. He has his pell. The task of filling around the post and tamping the earth tight will be trivial by comparison. But it will need to wait a little while, until he arises from where he has slumped onto the ground, shattered, but chuckling with delirious delight.

★

Enough is enough. The pell is now secure in the ground; ready for the training which he has been rehearsing in his mind since that first day.

Overhead, the sky is clearing; patches of blue now showing through the thinning clouds, and sunlight filtering through, drying the ground, and warming the man and the horse.

He tries to remember: what was it like to be a knight?

★

With the Lady Wendy's pregnancy advancing, Averill, at Wendy's suggestion, has called upon the young woman who was Mariel's maid, offering her the role of maid and companion for Odelia. The young woman has accepted the offer with tearful delight. Mariel's passing had left her bereft of a loving mistress and companion. Her commitment to Odelia had been well recognised, but Averill in his frail mental state, had failed to take any action, and Wendy had stepped in to take charge of Odelia's welfare whilst her father's mind descended into nightmare. But now, Averill is again capable of rational thought, his realisation has caught up with that of everyone else, and the slight which he had innocently delivered to Sarah has been righted. And Odelia, re-united with Sarah, is already showing signs of becoming the vibrant young girl she had once been.

And so tonight, for the first time since taking Mariel into his life, Averill sleeps alone in his room. Odelia has moved from the space she occupied first beside their bed, then later in her own curtained enclosure, into one of the adjoining rooms, and Sarah into the other. The day has been filled with laughter and excitement as the girls have moved both Odelia's and Sarah's possessions into their respective rooms, and Averill has been relegated to the background by the domestic activities of Wendy, who came to lend a hand, and the two girls. But now, the day is over, the meals consumed, the frivolity of bath-time completed, and silence has descended upon the household.

183

Averill lies quietly on his bed, lonely from the absence of the familiar, steady breathing of his sleeping daughter, but at the same time, content that he has made the right decision for their futures. He recalls the scene just an hour ago in Odelia's room, when he knocked and entered, to find Sarah brushing Odelia's long, freshly-washed, silky black hair, and the girls giggling contentedly as they swapped stories. He had stood at the door for only a few minutes, but it was enough. Sarah had looked over and smiled at him whilst continuing to brush his daughter's hair, and Odelia had laughed and commented that it was, 'So good to have Sarah back again.'

He lies, quietly, thinking; of how much his daughter has grown during the time he has been absent, and how much the sparkle of her personality reflects that of her mother. He is not sure what it is, but something of the Orient infused Mariel, and now infuses Odelia, with a softness and an elegance and an energy, which makes them unique in this drab, western world.

His thoughts are interrupted by the low, soft hoot of the snowy owl outside his window, and he rises and walks quietly to the window to look out at her. There she sits, lit by moonlight, all fluffed up, and, for all intents, looking back at him. He suspects that it is only illusion, but it is an illusion which is hard to shake, and so, he doesn't try. He feels the connection; as if she is now the guardian of the love he will always feel for his lost wife, and the love he feels for his daughter. He stands at the window, looking out, just thinking, about everything and about nothing. A sudden flap of wings and she is gone. He returns to his bed and lies down again, peacefully; knowing she will return; knowing that the connection is broken only temporarily; knowing that it will be re-established very soon... one day... somehow... somewhere... because love never dies, merely changes form.

All is quiet, and, gradually, the silence is overlaid with the sound of deep and steady breathing.

And later still, the dreams come; soft dreams, beautiful dreams; nightmares no more.

★

What was his name?

Boris. Yes, that's it; Boris.

Boris had said, "Slowly lad, train your muscles to make each thrust slowly and accurately. Speed will come later, but first, we need accuracy. You'll never take a man down if you can't hit the right spot."

Sir Boris had been his father's choice of battle tutor. His father had said that fathers training sons was a recipe for argument and falling out, and had sent him, with a swift but friendly kick in the pants, into Boris's gruff care.

Boris must have been good, because the king had made the same choice, and he and the prince had found themselves growing up together, striving for supremacy between themselves, but generally becoming harbingers of mischief together. And Boris had regularly delivered them to the blacksmith's workshop and told William to try to make something of the useless pair. And just as regularly he had taken them by the ear and dragged them, yelping, to the stables and pitched them inside, shouting to someone to teach them how heavy a hundred shovelfuls of horse shit were. And they had plotted and schemed and determined how to get even with Boris; and never once had they managed to get the better of him. And Boris had cuffed them about the ears, and kicked them in the pants, and worked them until they dropped, and gradually, they had taken shape and learned the lessons of combat, and grown in stature and in strength, until, eventually, there were few in the court who could stand up to them. And Boris had laughed and told them they were still a pair of girls, but deep down, they knew he was proud of them.

But that was many years ago, and the young man who trod that path is no longer here. Today he is replaced by an older, but wiser man; one who remembers effort, and pain, and exhilaration, and success, but also knows loss, and despair, and loneliness; but one who is determined to tear aside the veil which seems to cling to him, making every step an effort; one who is determined to make his maturity an advantage and not a weakness; to concentrate on the task at hand with a dedication that his youthful self could afford to spurn; to progress from pitiful old man to worthy warrior, perhaps even worthy enough to be called 'knight' once again, more rapidly and more comprehensively than when he last travelled this path.

And so he takes the stance: shield arm raised, wrist of sword arm locked ready to take the impact, and begins playing the routines in his mind again. Then slowly, carefully, painstakingly, he steps, raises and thrusts, directing the sword-point to the charcoal crosses drawn on the pell at the thigh, the waist, the breast, the neck and the eye of the imaginary opponent. Over and over he repeats the exercise, and over and over he watches as the strikes miss their target; correcting and repeating, correcting and repeating. Perspiration drips from his eyebrows, his elbows and his wrists, but nothing interrupts his concentration. Forearm and thigh muscles scream from the abuse of repetition, but the mind, for so long imprisoned in grief, is now concentrated upon this single task; and concentration is something Averill has always had in abundance.

The effort continues, until, eyes glazed from concentration and arm unable to lift the sword again, he falls to his knees, then slowly rolls onto his back. The sword falls from his open hand as he lies, panting, on the ground.

Staring up at the sky, his mind opens to the memories which are starting to flood back.

Boris had perished the same day his own father had died; both sacrificing themselves for the kingdom. Battle had already been joined when a third force arrived on the scene, opening a second front on the king's army. All knew that two fronts could not be supported, and that time was required to deal with one and then the other. And so, Sir John Averill and Sir Boris had swung their combined forces towards the second front, to give the king the time he needed to despatch one enemy, before coming to their aid. And they had almost carried the day, but for the weather. It was cloudy and blustery, although the charge across the open ground had begun in sunshine. They had smashed through the enemy line on the charge and were re-grouping to force their way back again. But within minutes, the heavens had opened and driving rain had turned the ground into a quagmire. The horses had struggled to make way and the knights had been unable to break through again to reach friendly forces. Isolated, they had been surrounded by the enemy foot soldiers. The king had seen what was happening, and despatched Sir Richard's and Sir Warwick's forces to assist, but they had still been hacking their way toward the encircled knights as the last of them was dragged from his horse and disappeared under the combined mass of enemy foot soldiers.

The king had completed the massacre on the first front and ridden hard behind Richard and Warwick, bringing the main force with him and decimating the remaining enemy. The time bought by Averill and Boris had been sufficient to ensure the victory, but they and their men had perished.

Averill knows the story well. It was told to him and his mother, personally, by the king. And the king had told the Lady Amelia that her son would not be left untrained and unguided, for such deeds as were performed by Sir John Averill that day would never be forgotten as long as the king lived. And so Gregory and Prince Henry had continued their education together, and become inseparable as friends. Yet Averill always knew that if ever the day came that the prince had to choose between kingdom and friendship, then, painful as it might be, there would be no contest.

He lies, still, on the ground, breathing becoming more controlled. Gradually, the feeling returns to his right arm. He stands again, flexing his fingers and breathing slowly and deeply. He picks up the discarded sword and begins walking his customary circles, encouraging his body to move, and banishing pain to the back of his mind. He pauses, hands on hips, and looks down; summoning the resources he needs to continue, then takes the stance again, raises the shield, locks his wrist and slowly, deliberately thrusts towards the pell.

The first strike is wayward and he chastises himself for the continuing errors. The second is better, but still some way adrift. On the third, the tip of the sword is flecked with charcoal as it buries itself into the wood.

CHAPTER SIX

The courtier had knocked softly at the door, and when Averill answered, had delivered the simple message, "His Majesty would like to see you, Sir Gregory."

Averill had been momentarily stunned by the unexpected summons, but his response had been automatic. "Yes, of course. Where exactly?"

And the courtier had duly delivered the remainder of the king's message. "The king says you will know where to find him, Sir Gregory."

And so, a short time later, Averill finds himself walking a corridor he has not walked since before his world disintegrated. As he walks, he passes through shafts of early morning sunlight slanting in through the beautiful Gothic arched windows; familiar, yet somehow surreal. He continues, as if in a dream. The boundary between reality and the dream becomes indistinct. Images and voices from the past fill the corridor.

"Don't you ever take your lady for granted, Gregory. They are such delicate creatures... here one minute, gone the next."

He stops, startled by the image, feeling suddenly faint; and steadies himself against the timber-panelled wall, stunned by the impact of the elder Henry's words; words he had forgotten until now; words brought to life again by being here in this corridor of memories; words which he had absorbed in all seriousness at the time, but which, he now knows, he had never understood at all.

He drops his hand from the wall and continues on again, trembling slightly, senses heightened, aware of feelings which have been subdued for an age, it seems. Whether he intended it or not, the king, by summoning him here, has opened a window which Averill had not even realised had been closed, and now, little-by-little, the man of grief and pain is learning to immerse himself in this sensation; which he is beginning to recognise as life, itself.

He pauses at the threshold of the map room and breathes deeply, steadying the trembling which followed the vivid recollection of the old king's words, and heightened by the anticipation, or is it trepidation, of the meeting with the king.

He knocks and enters.

The room seems more spacious than he remembers, and Averill recognises that the large and always-cluttered corner desk, where the king had often sat, is no longer present; replaced by a newer, more elegant piece, carved and polished, with three drawers each side. Yew, he thinks; perhaps a reflection of the order the younger Henry wishes to create within his domain. The map table remains the centre-piece of the room, and, along with it, the almost forgotten smell of parchment and ink and leather bring an unanticipated feeling of belonging.

Henry is standing looking out of the window to the courtyard, but turns, immediately, and walks purposefully over to where Averill stands. Clasping the knight by the shoulders, the king looks into his eyes, and, with gentle gaze, asks, "How are you, Gregory? Are you well?"

The gulf between the two men remains unbridged.

"I believe I am well, Your Majesty," Averill responds, evenly.

The king maintains his grasp upon Averill's shoulders, looking intently into his old friend's eyes, trying to discern something of his state of mind; but there is nothing in the returning gaze to help him. He turns away and walks back to the window, and looks out again. Averill remains unmoved, but uncertain; unsettled by the unexpected familiarity of the room against the strained relationship with the king.

"I spoke with Anthony only a day or so ago," ventures the king. "He said that Gareth had brought you to visit your knights, and that you seemed well."

"Yes," replies Averill. "I did see them. It was one evening, after we had eaten. It was good to see them again, although I can't quite remember what we talked about. But I do remember it was good to see them."

"And, I hear that Odelia is growing into a beautiful young lady," adds the king.

"Yes, my Lord," replies Averill, "she is, indeed."

An awkward pause.

"What are you doing with yourself, these days, Gregory?" asks the king.

"Not a great deal," replies Averill. "I seem to spend a lot of time thinking... and riding."

A slight pause as he recollects, then: "I have recently visited a number of villages within several days' ride of the castle; places I never knew existed before... with craftsmen capable of the most beautiful work... in wood, and leather, and silver..."

Another longer pause; and then the words begin to flow. "I have been impressed by the scale of small achievements which are made across this land, Your Majesty. I had never really appreciated what talent we have in this country; but there are artisans who create, and merchants who trade, and women who sew and knit; all of whom seem to contribute to what I would call..." And here he pauses for a moment, searching for the right word. "... a 'fabric', I think I would call it," he finally decides, "which seems to hold their small communities together, but which, as I have seen, exists in town after town and village after village, and appears to actually hold the entire land together."

He stops; suddenly aware how much he has spoken.

"I apologise, Your Majesty, he adds, with a slight, embarrassed smile. "I have not spoken so many words at once for a very long time. It is most unlike me."

"No, Gregory," replies the king, gently. "It is perhaps unlike the man you have become. But, I remember another man, a knight I recall, who, from time-to-time, felt compelled to speak his mind, when his prince or his king became too engrossed in their own pursuits, and failed to lift their eyes to see the world about them; especially to see the beauty around them."

He looks directly at Averill. "I would value the counsel of that man, if he were to return," he adds. "I would value that counsel, very much."

"Your Majesty does me an honour I fear I do not deserve," replies Averill. "I have no great recollection of what has happened these past years, but I know that I have not been of much use to anyone during that time.

"I believe I have abandoned…"

"No, Gregory," interrupts the king. "You have abandoned no-one. If anything, it was we who abandoned you; it was we who left you in the cold when you needed comfort."

Once again, he walks to Averill and takes him by the shoulders, speaking directly to him. "I have learned a great deal since taking the crown, Gregory; a great deal. My actions were callous. I could have handled things much better than I did."

He looks directly into Averill's eyes, trying to determine how his words have been received, but finding nothing, he turns away again.

"And I have felt pain, Gregory, and watched the gulf between us widen for too long now; and I wish it to end. Do you think it can end, Gregory?"

Averill looks down. "I know nothing of the gulf you mention, Your Majesty," he replies. "I know that I have not been approachable; but that has not been anything to do with feelings between us. Even those I love most, my daughter especially, have been unable to bridge the gap to reach me these past two years. I'm afraid I have been lost to all who cared about me, my Lord, and that is something I regret greatly."

The king is silent for a moment, weighing the words, then, "You have had your pain, Gregory, which I could not possibly begin to comprehend; and I have had mine. But it seems to me now, that perhaps it was my guilt, for what I had done to you, that imagined a barrier between us which, perhaps, did not exist at all.

"As I listen to your words now, it seems that you bore no grudge, and perhaps, if I had been at all sensitive, I would have realised that your withdrawal was caused by grief and not by anger.

"I would be very pleased, Gregory, if our separation could be ended."

"Your Majesty," replies Averill, "I am hopeful that my separation from all who love me is now ended. I seem to have but blinked and my daughter has grown into a beautiful young woman, the Lady Wendy has become pregnant, and my king, who was a dashing prince, as I last remember, has become a man of wisdom and humility.

"I have been away too long, Your Majesty. It is time I returned."

The king offers his hand. "Welcome back, Sir Gregory; you have been sorely missed."

Averill clasps his hand in friendship. There is no smile, but a small nod is sufficient to convey the feelings of the moment.

And, as the tension in the room begins to fade, the king finds a subject more befitting a lighter occasion: "The tournaments will be upon us soon, Gregory. Will you attend?" he asks; adding, "To observe, of course."

"I cannot say, Your Majesty," replies Averill. "The tournaments always interested me when I was a boy, and later of course when I participated. But I'm not really sure how I feel about them at this time. I'm afraid I need a little more time, Your Majesty; not all things are clear yet. Perhaps I will know, in time."

The king smiles, and nods in understanding. "Of course, Gregory; of course."

There is no more to be said, and much to be absorbed.

"Thank you for visiting today, Gregory," says the king. "I think perhaps we might now be facing in the same direction. Perhaps, one day, God willing, we may even ride the same path again, my friend."

At last Averill smiles; just a little.

"Go now, and enjoy your day," continues the king. "I will attend to mine more contented than I have for some time.

"It was good to see you, Gregory... and good to talk, once again."

Averill bows. "Your Majesty." He turns and leaves.

As he walks down the corridor, there are no words ringing in his ears, no images from the past; it is the present which occupies his mind. The king's words were kind and gentle. He feels a strange sensation, which he thinks might be the beginnings of... contentment.

His grip on reality feels a little more secure.

★

"I thought I would return this to you, William," utters a voice from the shadows.

The blacksmith jumps with fright. "For the love of God, Sir Gregory, will you stop doing that? You know this old heart of mine won't last forever, and, if you keep that up, it might not even last the day."

Placing the sword upon the anvil, Averill ignores the blacksmith's response and continues, "It has served me well, William, but I believe you know why I am here today."

"Oh yes," replies William, "although I actually expected you several days ago."

"Did you now?" enquires Averill. "It must have been the weather."

"Ah, yes," concurs William, "the weather. That's good, Sir Gregory; I would never have thought of that."

"Well, that's why you're a blacksmith, and I'm a..."

The banter suddenly stops, as Averill baulks at uttering the word.

"... Little boy who needs a bigger sword?" offers the blacksmith, leaning on the anvil, looking closely at Averill.

"Something a little heavier," continues Averill, back on safe turf.

"So where is it?" asks William.

"Where is what?"

"The pell you've set up; or is it pells?"

"You always were sharp, William," remarks Averill. "Yes, there have been several to this point; but I've only just started."

"And, how's the aim, Sir Gregory?"

"Tolerable," replies Averill.

"Ah, that good?" replies William, feigning surprise. "So you haven't lost your touch?"

Averill chuckles, remembering. "You wouldn't have said that if you'd been there the first week, William; very ordinary."

"Indeed?" asks the blacksmith, leaning forward on the anvil, face inches from Averill's.

"Indeed," replies Averill, also leaning forward, returning the blacksmith's stare.

The pair remain in mock confrontation for a moment, then William breaks away. "Well then," he mutters, turning to open the rugged metal cabinet beside the anvil, "you'll be wanting something nicely balanced, I imagine. Something a little like..." Reaching in he draws out an old, grey, oiled sword, holds it upright in one muscular arm, carefully inspecting the blade, then turning, passes it to Averill, who takes it from him... and winces.

"Bastard," he mutters, but loud enough for William to hear.

"You said 'heavy'," replies William.

"You never did have any sense of proportion," counters Averill.

"Then give it back."

"What, and have you tell the world I couldn't hack it; not bloody likely."

"Suit yourself," replies William, turning away, a self-satisfied smile on his face.

"Bastard," mutters Averill, again.

"And don't bend it," shouts William over his shoulder, as he returns to his interrupted task at the forge.

"Shit," says Averill, testing the sword in the air; then to himself: "Well, there'll be no half-measures now, my son."

He walks out into the early morning air, bemused, determined, and slightly overawed by the task he has set himself.

★

The first tournament of the season is now only two weeks away, and wherever one goes there is talk of it. And although he has been unable to avoid hearing about it, Averill has, up to this point, been able to remain separate from any involvement. However, as he now ambles down a backstreet of the village market, looking variously at tubs of apples, onions, sides of lamb, trinkets, weaving, and made-to-measure garments of dubious origin and quality, his solitary sojourn is interrupted by the crump of marching feet, and the passage of knights across his field of view, at the crossroad up ahead.

He continues to meander on down the shaded street, stopping to inspect, and test, and then purchase an enticing red apple. But stirrings of interest are subconsciously gnawing away, and, a few moments later, as he reaches the intersection, he unconsciously turns left toward the still faintly discernible sound of marching feet.

There are many more people on this street, mainly peasants to whom his face is quite unfamiliar, so he continues on in his preferred state; anonymity. The street is dry and dusty; typical of early summer. The sky is bright, and, without thinking, he gradually makes his way across to the sunny side. A group of urchins forms beside him, for a little while measuring their steps against those of the tall, willowy stranger, but none speaks to him, which suits him perfectly. Idle chatter was never one of his strong points, and these days, that is true even more so. The urchins mimic his walk for a few more moments, then, laughing brashly, run off to find a more responsive target.

He rounds the next corner, slowing his leisurely pace even further, then stops. The ground slopes away slightly, and about fifty yards ahead, opens up into a roughly circular grassy space, in which a number of knights and their squires are now busy, readying themselves for what is obviously going to be a little pre-tournament practice. Slowly, Averill edges closer, keeping to the side of the street, until he feels at a comfortable enough distance to keep an eye on proceedings without the risk of becoming involved. A number of the peasant folk have also stopped and are standing around nearby, interested to see what will eventuate. After a short while, a couple, in the midst of work errands, cannot wait any longer and, muttering discontentedly about the time it takes a knight to get ready, pick up their loads and move on again. But others with less pressing engagements remain, hopeful of seeing the knights in action.

It is not long before lightly-armoured knights are flexing their arms and shoulders, and stretching calf and thigh muscles in preparation for what promises to be an entertaining little workout.

They begin.

The clash of swords and the grunts of the knights, as they strike and hold and push off each other again, mingle with the 'oohs' and 'aahs' of the crowd as they gradually become involved in the spectacle. Occasionally, there is a muffled cheer as one or other of the combatants makes a good strike, and, as the pace intensifies, the crowd begins to applaud the efforts.

Averill suddenly realises that he is not alone. Two of the spectators have gradually moved closer, and now stand with arms folded on either side of him.

"I don't think they're very good," one comments.

Averill ignores the remark and continues to observe, quietly.

"No, I think they're pretty average," concurs the other.

No response from Averill.

Moments pass, then the big man leans down a little and speaks quietly into Averill's left ear, "Although they're probably better than you are."

Still no response from Averill.

A longer pause as the three continue to watch the contest.

"Yes, they're definitely better than you are," adds the other in the right ear.

Without taking his eyes off the action, Averill responds, "Well, we'll never know, will we?"

The two look at each other, smile conspiratorially, then the big man turns his head a little further to look at Averill. "That's entirely up to you, Gregory."

But, before another word can be uttered, there is a ripple of movement in the crowd nearer the field, as they back away from the entrance, allowing several young squires to pass through, followed by a retinue of knights surrounding a tall, well-built man, wearing light armour.

Averill stiffens, his eyes instantly glaring hatred, as he recognises the form of René Bijou striding into the clearing.

He turns to leave, but a strong hand on his shoulder holds him back.

"Watch him, Gregory," says Gareth. "Help me learn all about him; I am drawn against him this tournament and it would please me greatly if I could take him down."

Averill stops, turns again to stare at the hated man; hesitates a few more moments, then his shoulders slump.

"I doubt I can assist you, Gareth," he replies. "It is a long time since I have held a sword..." he hesitates, "... in anger."

Neither Gareth nor Anthony notices the slight pause in Averill's response.

"Nevertheless," continues Anthony, "your insights would still be appreciated."

Averill looks from one to the other, then bows his head.

"I'm sorry," is all he says as he turns and starts walking slowly up the slight hill to the market again. Behind him, Gareth and Anthony look crestfallen.

They return their attentions to the encounter about to begin. Gareth is particularly interested to study Bijou's form.

At the top of the street, before he turns into the market, Averill pauses and looks back toward the field. Bijou has already begun sparring with one of the knights of his retinue. Averill continues to observe, with a fascination borne out of hatred, and, even from this distance, it is apparent that Bijou's greatest attribute is his strength. His timing is not perfect and his motion is not fluid; each thrust and parry does not lead smoothly into the next. But all of that is made irrelevant by his sheer strength. Averill's hatred of the man increases yet again. Not only is he not a talented swordsman, nor a graceful combatant, but his strength is such that it doesn't actually matter. He is evil, a murderer, but added to that, he is an imposter, masking his deficiencies through his bludgeoning strength; and that also rankles Averill deeply.

He turns on his heel, and walks back into the market-place, heart beating appreciably, hands perspiring and trembling, thoughts racing through his mind. He should just walk away: the bastard has caused more grief than Averill ever wished to know. He should just forget him and move on with his life, such as it is. But there is a persistent core to Averill's being, which will not let go, which seeks retribution, somehow, somewhere... someday. He stops. Peasants brush past him as they carry on their business in the market, probably wondering why this tall, solitary man is just standing there, lost in thought.

He shakes his head; the idea is preposterous. True, he is working at regaining some semblance of proficiency with the sword, but that is just to prove to himself that he can do it. And, true, he did enjoy the rush as he charged at the imaginary quintain under the tree in the clearing, but that's what it was, imaginary. But to consider actually entering a tournament again; now that's a different thing altogether; that's dangerous, and probably very,

very foolish. What is there to be gained? Why would he even consider it? And yet, the memory of the rush of excitement he experienced when he let himself go for just a moment, coupled with his disgust at the obscene strutting of Bijou, and the underlying churning in the pit of his stomach every time he even thinks of the bastard…

He shakes his head again, and walks on. Foolish! Absolutely foolish!

But a seed has been sown, and from such seeds…

★

The sleek, white mare and her rider emerge from under the trees at the edge of the clearing and canter out into the bright sunshine. Behind them, the powerful, dappled brown stallion carrying the squat, barrel-chested man with arms like tree-trunks, and the smaller grey carrying his wiry, ginger-haired companion, also bustle forth into the clearing.

Noticeably absent from the mare are the awkward saddle-bags which have been present on previous occasions. She looks sleek and fast; a thoroughbred. By contrast, the other two horses seemed loaded to the hilt with all manner of bits and pieces which are apparently the accoutrements of their riders.

The two companions wheel their horses around, surveying the scene. William whistles as he counts, "One, two, three," then quiet muttering, until, "nine; I make it nine."

"Yes, nine," agrees the ginger-haired man.

"Well, you have been busy, Sir Gregory," remarks the blacksmith. "Have you tried the new one yet?"

"Over there," says Averill, pointing to the ninth pell, which already bears several scars marking the impact of the point of a sword.

"I see you still have some work to do," remarks the blacksmith, noting the errant strikes. "Arm a little tired, Sir Gregory?"

"You should know," Averill replies. "It's your lump of lead."

"I take offence at that remark," comes the grinning reply. "After all, it was you who said you wanted something a little heavier."

"Give me time, William," counters Averill, "just give me time. I'll be on the marks within a couple of weeks, I promise you."

The blacksmith looks around at the eight other posts standing erect in the ground, noting how the distribution of cuts and slashes has inched closer and closer to the charcoal crosses, until on the eighth pell, there is no charcoal to be seen; all having been obliterated by the repetitively accurate sword strikes.

"Indeed, Sir Gregory," he concurs, "I believe you will."

"So, where do you want it?" interjects the ginger-haired man.

"I thought over there, Joseph," replies Averill, pointing in the direction of the large oak tree at the centre of the clearing.

"Why not on the flat, away from the rise?" asks the carpenter.

"Too easy," replies Averill. "I want to be working uphill. The extra effort and the changing terrain will make things more difficult. And that's how I want it."

Joseph smiles. "You're serious, aren't you?"

Averill smiles.

"You know," Joseph continues as he dismounts, "when William came to me and told me what you were planning, I thought this might all be just so much fancy. After all, you've been gone for nigh on two years now, and we, none of us, thought to see you again, Sir Gregory; heard all sorts of stories about you.

"But I see here something which I could not have imagined in a thousand nights of dreams, Sir Gregory. I see the secret training ground of a man on a quest. And I, for one, Sir Gregory, would not be betting against you succeeding."

"Shall we begin?" asks Averill, slightly embarrassed by the carpenter's heartfelt vote of confidence.

"You said the logs were ready?" queries the carpenter.

"Indeed," says Averill, leading them to the side of the clearing where two tree-trunks lay, already stripped of branches and bark.

"You did all of this yourself?" asks Joseph, incredulously. "Cut them down, dragged them here, and stripped them?"

Averill just smiles.

"Fit bastard, aren't you?" remarks William.

"Getting there, William," replies Averill, "getting there."

The blacksmith's 'Hrmphh' says it all.

"Well then, let's get into it," says Joseph, opening one of his saddle-bags and dropping a small axe, an adze and several boring tools onto the ground. "This is going to take a while, so we'd better get our arses into gear."

★

The late-afternoon sun shines obliquely down on the three men, sitting quietly on the grass of the clearing, drinking ale and sharing stories from yesteryear.

"It's just like when you were a boy, Sir Gregory," says Joseph, chuckling. "But back then it was all promise; it was all what might be, and we could only wait and watch and see how you and the prince was going to turn out."

He pauses to take another draught from the mug; one of three which appeared, magically, from William's saddle-bags when the work was completed.

"Right little rascals you were too, the pair of you," continues Joseph. "But I think we always knew you was going to make it, Sir Gregory. Aye, and the prince too, God bless him."

"Looks good, Sir Gregory," comments William, looking in the direction of the sturdy quintain now standing, firmly embedded in the mound, under the overhanging branches of the central oak tree.

"Could be tricky, though," he continues, "what with that slope, and them branches and all."

"Yes, indeed," replies Averill, "it will be perfect. And, thank you again, gentlemen; I could only do so much on my own, and, as you know, this is not something I want known at this time; so your assistance and your discretion are both greatly appreciated."

And, with that, he jumps to his feet and walks to the mare, returning moments later with two small purses.

"For your efforts, gentlemen," he says as he drops a purse in front of each.

"Not on your life, Sir Gregory," protests William. "This is not something for which I require payment; it is my honour to do this for you."

"And mine also, Sir Gregory," adds Joseph.

"No gentlemen," replies Averill. "This is fair recompense for your efforts, which, I know were offered freely, and which I appreciate. But," he adds, "if you do not accept payment today, then I will never be able to ask you to do anything for me again, for fear of falling further into your debt.

"So you see," he continues, smiling, "it is actually for my benefit that I need to pay you."

William and Joseph exchange glances, then both smile, graciously.

"You're a good man, Sir Gregory," says William. "It is my honour to serve you... and to accept your payment. I thank you."

"As do I," adds Joseph, "... a good man indeed."

Averill nods, graciously.

"I'm itching to try it," he continues, looking again at the sturdy quintain. "It looks so good; so well-built. Thank you Joseph, it's outstanding."

"You'll be needing a lance, Sir Gregory," comments Joseph. "When will you bring it here?"

Averill smiles.

"Already here, Joseph," he replies. "In the undergrowth, wrapped in protective hides, just waiting...

"I brought it from the castle yesterday; just before daybreak. Oh, and before you ask, there'll be no practice runs while anyone else is here. After all, it's going to be pretty ugly for a while."

"I doubt it," mutters William. "I seriously doubt it."

"Well, I don't," replies Averill, laughing. "I have no illusions about just how big this next mountain is going to be to climb."

"Indeed, Sir Gregory," replies Joseph. "But, by God, it's good to see you climbing them again, my boy."

★

Averill had bidden goodnight to William and Joseph as they passed through the castle gate, and had continued on alone to the eastern stables. The sun was setting, and the evening was becoming cooler. Two of the squires at the stables had been pleased to take Damsel and assure Averill that she would be well watered, fed and stabled for the night. And so, satisfied that the last task of the day had been adequately addressed, Averill had left to walk back to the castle.

But even before he reached the wide stone steps which, brooding and dark in the twilight, led the way up to the reception hall of the castle, the laughter floating down from the open window high in the wall had told him that Odelia and Sarah were already at home, and probably engaged in some form of mischief.

And moments later, as he strode in through the doorway, he found the pair, rolling on the floor, beside themselves with mirth, over some story which Sarah had heard in the market earlier in the day. But, before Averill could determine the cause of the hilarity, there had been a knock at the door and Gareth had entered, without waiting for an invitation.

"She's in labour, Gregory. She's with the midwives. I've been turfed out, and I'm not sure where to go or how long this is all going to take."

Averill, hands on hips, and a slight smile on his lips, looks back at the intruder. "My God, Gareth," he replies, "you're no better now than you were when James was born."

The big man looks back at Averill, slightly stunned. Although flustered himself, he was not expecting such an in-control response from Averill. He stands open-mouthed, trying to gather his thoughts.

Averill turns to the girls, still struggling for breath on the floor.

"Have you two had dinner?" he asks

"Yes, Sir Gregory," replies Sarah, desperately trying to stifle the continued giggling. "Miss Evelyn prepared a lovely meal for us. We weren't sure when you would return, Sir Gregory, so I thought it best that we eat at the normal time."

"It was absolutely lovely," adds Odelia. "I'm sure there's more there if you would like some. Shall I ask Evelyn, Daddy?"

"No thank you, sweetie," replies Averill. "If you two have eaten then I think I'll walk with Gareth for a while to see if we can settle him down a bit. And I want you bathed and in bed when I return.

"Sarah," he adds.

The instruction is clear, and neither of the girls object, but as they turn to look at each other, the laughter bursts forth again.

Averill shakes his head in mock despair, then, wrapping his arm around the big man's shoulder, offers, "Come on, Gareth. Let's see if we can get you through the next few hours."

Gareth is still nonplussed by Averill's apparent command of the situation, and, given his own precarious state of mind, submits, meekly, to whatever the other man has in mind.

★

They have drunk a little and talked a lot; well, actually, Gareth has talked a lot, and Averill has listened, patiently, to the disjointed outpourings of Gareth's preoccupied mind.

And, shortly before midnight, the sound of running feet has interrupted the meandering conversation as both Sarah and Odelia have rushed into the room, for Odelia to announce, "Auntie Wendy has had a baby girl."

Once again, Gareth is non-plussed, and sits looking totally bemused as Averill, Odelia and Sarah, all wrap themselves around him in a rolling group hug.

The girls untangle themselves and Odelia continues, "Isn't it wonderful; a baby girl. I wonder what she'll call it?"

"I think Uncle Gareth might have a say in that," replies Averill.

"Oh no, Gregory," he replies. "If it's a girl, I wouldn't know what to think. I'll love her for sure, but I'll leave the naming to Wendy."

"Can we go and see?" asks Odelia.

"I don't know," replies Averill. "What do you think, Gareth?"

"Um, well, yes, I suppose so," replies Gareth. "I'm not really sure about these things. So let's go and see, shall we?"

"Goody!" shout the girls in unison, and together they haul Averill and Gareth to their feet.

"Now quietly, please," instructs Averill. "The rest of the castle is probably asleep, and won't want to be listening to your shrieking."

"Sorry, Daddy," replies Odelia, "but it's so exciting."

The party heads off down the corridor, the girls in front, talking excitedly, Averill and Gareth following behind.

"A daughter," muses Gareth. "Who'd have thought I'd have a daughter?"

"I think your troubles have only just begun," offers Averill, placing a consoling hand upon Gareth's shoulder, then laughing, heartily, at the big man's sudden look of alarm.

Gareth is confused. He is a father, and Gregory appears to be in control of the situation. These are both unexpected developments.

But now he is about to see his daughter; his daughter! And all other thoughts evaporate in the growing bliss.

★

Wendy's hair is wet and lank across her forehead, but the weary smile on her face is radiant as she cuddles the small bundle beside her. Gareth is surprisingly delicate as he turns down the cover ever so slightly to gaze upon the face of his new daughter. The girls are standing either side of him, cooing unrestrainedly, and Averill is standing at the foot of the bed observing the scene. A sudden pang of regret touches him as he realises that this is a scene which he will never experience. But, with an effort, he dismisses the thought, determined to not let anything spoil the moment for Gareth and Wendy.

After a few more moments, he decides that perhaps they have visited the weary mother for long enough.

"Come on Odelia, Sarah. I think it is time for us to leave now and let Aunty Wendy and her baby get some rest," he suggests.

"Oh, but she's so cute," insists Odelia.

"Well, I'm sure you're going to have plenty of opportunity to see her over the next twenty years, young lady," replies Averill, gently but firmly.

The girls stand.

"Goodnight, Auntie Wendy," they chorus, and Wendy smiles delightedly; pleased at having been chosen an honorary aunt by not just Odelia, but Sarah as well.

"Goodnight Odelia, goodnight Sarah," she replies. "Thank you so much for coming to see our baby. Please come again tomorrow; you may get to see her with her eyes open."

Averill and the girls turn to leave, but Wendy interrupts. "Gregory, can you stay for a moment?"

"It's alright, Daddy; we'll see you at home," says Odelia, as she and Sarah link hands and depart, chattering excitedly once again.

Averill sits on the side of the bed, as Gareth, smiling quietly, stands beside his wife, holding her hand. The bed is located centrally in the room; a wooden headboard and small overhead canopy providing a homely backdrop for mother and daughter resting peacefully now. Light from four torches on the side walls bring a warm glow to the scene. On a small table beside the bed stand a pitcher and a bowl; still slightly warm from the hot water they held earlier.

"Gregory, I have a request," begins Wendy, cautiously. "Gareth and I have talked it over, and we agreed that if it was a girl, we would ask you."

"Ask me what?" replies Averill, with quiet interest.

"Gregory, we were wondering if you would allow us to name our daughter Mariel?"

The gasp from Averill betrays his unpreparedness.

"Don't answer now, Gregory," continues Wendy. "I understand that it might be a bit of a shock for you, and I'm sure you will want some time to think it over. And," she continues, "please be assured that we will accept your answer, whatever it is."

Averill's mind is reeling; focussed thought is impossible. He looks from Wendy to Gareth and back again, unable to identify his own emotions. Recovering a little, he stands once more, and offering a quiet 'Goodnight', walks unsteadily from the room.

Wendy looks at Gareth. "Oh dear, Gareth; I'm not so sure, now."

"Don't worry, my love," replies Gareth. "We knew it wouldn't be something he could answer immediately. It will take a little time."

★

As he walks back along the corridor, breathing becomes progressively more difficult until he has to stop, and, leaning against the panelled wall for support, he forces himself to breathe slowly and deeply until the panic passes. He thinks, perhaps, he should feel overjoyed at Wendy's desire to name her daughter after Mariel; but he is not. In fact, he is totally unable to comprehend what he is feeling; there are too many memories, too many conflicting emotions; too much of him wanting his Mariel to be the only one.

Head still spinning, he reaches the doorway to his residence and enters. Quiet but excited chatter from Odelia's room tells him that the girls are still discussing the new arrival.

He opens the door and looks in, but remains silent as the girls stop their talking and look expectantly at him.

A long pause; until Odelia asks, "Daddy, are you alright?"

He nods, but is still unable to find the words. Eventually he manages a brief sentence, "I think it's time for bed for all of us now."

The girls acquiesce, and, as he leaves Odelia's room, he is aware of Sarah walking toward the door to her bedroom, and Odelia pulling the bed covers up to her chin. But beyond that, he has no perception.

In his room he stands at the window, searching for the owl; seeking comfort, but she is not there. He is alone.

It may have been minutes, or it may have been hours, but eventually he realises that he is feeling chilly. The night sky is clear and bright from a full moon, and the temperature has been steadily dropping.

Exhausted and confused, he turns away from the window, walks to his bed, and slowly eases himself down, and then, moments later, falls flat on the bed, head still spinning.

Anger is the dominant emotion now; anger that he cannot have Mariel to himself; anger that someone else should feel her loss as he does, and want to honour her memory. She is his, only his, and he wants her memory to himself... forever.

He knows that if he says 'no' then Wendy and Gareth will spend the rest of their lives devastated that he stood in the way of the tribute they wanted to pay to Mariel, and, worse still, every time they address their daughter, a regret of his making will be on their lips.

And he knows that if he says 'yes', he will live the rest of his life hearing a name that belongs to only one person in the world, being used by another; and he is not sure if he could take that.

And so, in turmoil approaching grief yet again, he tosses and turns on the bed, hammering his pillow in frustration, unable to accept any of the alternatives before him. But gradually, the effort of the day takes its toll, the pounding of his pillow becomes less agitated, and, some time later, his deep, steady breathing is the only sound in the room.

A swish and a flutter outside and, unheard by Averill, the owl returns.

Pale morning light is softly illuminating the room as he opens his eyes. Immediately, the thoughts of the previous night crash in upon him, jolting him awake. But then, surprisingly, the turmoil begins to recede, and over the next few moments, a gradually spreading peacefulness descends upon him. He lays quietly, almost serenely, then turns his head and looks out the window to where the tops of the trees are visible, beginning to show green in the early morning light.

There is a hazy image in his mind, gradually crystallising; of a passageway in a castle, and a young woman, head erect, long black hair flowing, right hand raised to wipe away the tears; a picture of injured beauty and fierce pride. He recalls almond-shaped eyes, soft oval face, lips rich and full, skin smooth, a slightly olive complexion; on her right cheek, a smudge of flour where a hand has wiped at tears, adding a stunningly attractive adornment to the vision of beauty. The image fades as it is replaced by another; of a maiden, standing silently in the courtyard of castle, pail and milking stool on the ground beside her, head back, eyes closed, swirling a soft silk scarf above her head; for a moment, oblivious to everything around her. Suddenly startled, she opens her eyes to stare directly at him. The scarf, not yet tied, falls softly to the ground. He recalls that words are exchanged, although he does not hear them. He recalls taking her dusty hand and placing it against his cheek. He recalls her smile breaking through, encompassing eyes, cheeks, lips, outshining the morning sun and lighting with it, every fibre of his being.

He does not hear his own words, but he knows the response. It has been with him, constantly, since that day: "My name is Mariel... from the other side of the world... My Chinese name is Choy Dip; it means 'beautiful butterfly'."

And there the conundrum is resolved; there the angst ceases to exist; there the path ahead becomes clear. There can be more than one Mariel, for that was a name chosen by a kindly priest for a young woman, alone and pregnant in a foreign land. But there is a more fundamental identity for his lost love; from the moment she was born, she was Choy Dip, Beautiful Butterfly; and there is no demand for this name to be shared, no requirement for him to acknowledge any other when all he wants is to acknowledge his beloved; no images other than those he holds most dear which will come to mind when that name is uttered.

And so now, as he lies on his bed, he knows that Wendy's baby will, indeed, be named 'Mariel' with his blessing; knows that Odelia will now have the opportunity to love and care for a little girl who carries her mother's name, and carries it to honour her; and knows that his own memories of his beloved will not be diminished: there will only ever be one Mariel who was 'Choy Dip'.

A soft hoot from outside his window is the final piece in the puzzle. His owl has been present throughout the revelation; and it seems right that she should have been there. She has been his comfort and his reassurance for several seasons now. She has sat with him through long, lonely nights and cold wintery days, keeping faithful vigil with him, without complaint.

He rises, stretches, and walks to the window to look at her. She sits, all fluffed and contented. And as he gazes, he is sure she is looking back at him.

Today will be a good day.

CHAPTER SEVEN

So, this is it; the last big step.

He looks down at the lance which he has just unwrapped from the hides protecting it. He knows it well; old, rather battered, but beautifully balanced. He bends down and picks it up, suddenly realising the difficulty he is going to have with no-one here to pass it to him when he is mounted. A moment's thought and the problem is solved. He will rest it upright against the boughs of one of the many trees at the clearing's edge. From there it will be easy to manage.

He has held it before, including when he brought it here to the clearing, but this is different; today he means to use it. His excitement is compounded by the knowledge that he has managed to keep his activities secret from everyone; except, of course, William and Joseph. No-one knows how much he has progressed these last couple of months. He has felled trees, dug holes, stripped branches and bark, lifted and dragged trimmed trunks into position, hauled them upright, refilled holes, tamping down the soil to produce solid, immovable pells; back-breaking work, all of it. And, as a consequence, his body is as hard and as supple as he can recall it ever being. The weeks of practice, first with the light sword to rejuvenate muscles which had long been dormant, followed by work with the heavy sword to stress those same muscles well beyond the levels required for actual combat, have brought a smooth, satisfying precision to his movements.

There is still one phase of work remaining with the sword; but that must wait a while. Today, the focus shifts to the lance, and the challenge it represents.

Placing the lance upright against a suitable tree, Averill walks back to the mare, mounts, then guides her back to the tree-line. He stops, wanting to savour the moment.

And, as he sits, his mind momentarily turns to the glade, where the healing began; where the journey, which has brought him to this point, commenced. He will go there again in a little while; to immerse himself in the soothing, refreshing, uplifting balm it always provides. But right now, he is revelling in his returning strength and the clarity of purpose he feels. He stands in the stirrups, arms spread wide, and roars his jubilation, just for the sheer pleasure of experiencing life itself. Then, slowly, deliberately, he reaches out, wraps his fingers around the lance, and lifts it from the ground. The thrill is unbelievable. Here he is, on a competition mare, lance in hand, quintain in view...

And then he laughs, almost dropping the lance. Yes, he is on a competition mare, lance in hand, quintain in view... and he is about to make a real mess of it. For he knows full well, that the lance, of all weapons, is so difficult to control, to aim, to steady, to hold in position, that it will be some considerable time before he will be able to split the target of the quintain with the point of the lance.

"Well, my boy," he mutters to himself, "we'd better get started. This could take some time..."

★

The first pass was awful. Only half-way there he knew he was going to have to abort. The muscles, which he had built up during practice with the heavy sword, were of absolutely no use with the lance. The weight distribution was different, the pressure to be applied was from a different direction, and sitting an eager, galloping mare was quite different from standing with feet planted firmly upon the ground. It was a disaster. He had expected that it would be difficult, but, in reality, he had forgotten just how difficult it is to master the lance. Nevertheless, he had persisted, as of course he knew he would, and although he never actually got the point of the lance anywhere near the target of the quintain, at least he was now able to complete a pass, and keep the lance roughly horizontal.

A quiet afternoon in the glade had relaxed him after the strain and concentration of the morning. The brilliant summer sun had been quite intense and he had spent a most enjoyable time, boots off, wading in the gurgling brook. For her part, the mare had clearly enjoyed the respite after the repeated exertions of the morning and had lain down in the dappled shade of the glade.

But now, as the afternoon advances, Averill decides that one more tilt is required before they set off home again.

He aches from head to foot; arms, chest, back, thighs; all have worked in new and unfamiliar modes, and although this is activity which his body once knew well, it has been so long, that the memory of the muscles has dimmed appreciably.

A crisp whistle and Damsel struggles to her feet. Averill also rises, painfully, from where he has been laying on the grass, and, taking the trailing reins in his hand, he leads the mare from the glade, pushing through the densely leafed gap and back to the clearing.

Still holding the reins, he breaks into a stumbling trot, forcing the mare also to break out of her easy walk. A few more circuits around the central oak and then, without stopping, he hauls himself up into the saddle. Now, they canter a wider circle around the clearing, warming up both man and beast until he feels mentally alert, even though the body still feels heavy.

"One last tilt," he mutters to himself and directs the mare to the tree where the lance rests upright.

He hefts the lance and allows the head to come down, rotating the weapon until the hilt is couched comfortably under his right armpit. There is a little chafing and he suspects a little bruising as a result of this morning's efforts, however, it is not too bad, and will no doubt survive one more pass.

And so prepared, he looks intently at the quintain in the distance, then digs his heels into the mare's flanks. She accelerates, not with the tearing energy of earlier this morning, but certainly with enough to cause the point of the lance to wobble alarmingly. Averill strains, correcting his aim as they rush towards the target. Within seconds the line to the target drifts away wildly as they reach the mound and commence the climb. Correcting furiously, Averill hunches down even further as the overhanging branches loom closer, knowing that the impact from one of them could crack his skull.

Point of the lance coming back toward the target, pounding from the saddle being accommodated by tight grip, but relaxed elbow and shoulder. The scenery flashing by becomes a blur as he focuses acutely upon the point of the lance relative to the approaching target of the quintain.

Impact!

A glancing blow; the quintain swings wildly, and the tip of the lance shoots skyward.

"Gotcha!" he says, breathing hard; unable to get any more words out. But the smile says it all.

They slow, come to rest, then turn back towards the oak.

That will do for today; a good note to end on. No point even thinking about any more work; both man and beast have done well today; better than he thought they would, but still an enormous gulf away from where he wants to be.

★

He is approaching the wide door to the eastern stables, leading Damsel, as the gaggle of knights emerges, chattering animatedly.

"Woah, Gregory," exclaims Bryan as he crashes into him. "Sorry captain," he continues, "I didn't see you at all."

Averill smiles, slightly embarrassed. "Well Bryan, it's been a long time since someone's called me that."

The group has now got over the double shock of rounding the corner and finding someone in their path, and then finding it to be Averill.

Anthony looks carefully at him. "You're looking well, Gregory."

"That's what you said, last time we met, Anthony," Averill reminds him.

"Maybe," replies Anthony, "but this time I mean it. You must have been out and about quite a bit to get that suntan," he adds.

"Not really," counters Averill, "there's just more sunshine this time of year."

"So, what have you been doing this last couple of weeks?" continues Anthony, seeking some hint as to the obvious improvement in Averill's appearance and demeanour.

"Riding, actually," replies Averill, innocently. "Quite a lot of riding."

Thomas, standing at the back of the group, starts to chuckle. Anthony turns to stare at him. "What?" he demands.

Thomas shakes his head. "It's no use, you know," he replies, still chuckling. "You won't learn anything." Then, clearly delighted at the transformation he sees in Averill, he continues. "You'll only find out when he's good and ready to tell you, and not before. Don't you remember what Gregory's like?"

Anthony turns back to look carefully again at the tall, willowy, sun-tanned figure in front of him, and, suddenly the penny drops: this is no longer the pale shadow of a knight they once knew; this could almost be him again; not quite, but almost.

"Can I take Damsel, Sir Gregory?" a voice enquires.

Averill looks around to find James standing beside him.

"Yes, of course," replies Averill, handing the mare's reins to Gareth's son. "You look taller in the sunlight, James," he comments.

The young man beams with pleasure and turns to lead the mare into the stables. Gareth tousles his hair as he passes. "Look after her well, James," he instructs. "It seems to me she's been worked pretty hard today. Isn't that right, Gregory?"

Averill smiles as he ignores Gareth's probe. Thomas shakes his head again, and this time laughs out loud. "You're wasting your breath, Gareth."

"I know," replies Gareth, smiling, "but it was worth a try. Might have caught him off-guard, you know."

"No," replies Thomas slowly, looking directly at Averill. "No, I think we're beyond that now. Aren't we Gregory?"

"I wouldn't know, Thomas," replies Averill, smiling innocently. "I wouldn't know."

The light-hearted banter is cut short by the sudden commotion inside the stables; a commotion which suddenly bursts out through the doorway as two bodies, struggling ferociously, shouting abuse and raining punches upon each other, fall heavily to the ground, where they continue to roll and scrabble and punch and swear until Gareth's roar brings the violent quarrel to an abrupt halt.

Averill and Gareth each drag one combatant upright by the collar. Both boys are choking from the constriction of their throats.

"What the hell do you think you're doing, James?" shouts Gareth at the dishevelled, red-haired, ragged mass of torn clothes and scratched flesh, hanging from his grip.

"And you. Who the hell are you?" shouts Averill at the similarly-dishevelled wiry youth with the curly black hair, dirt-stained face and bloody arms.

James, large-framed and strong like his father, breathing furiously, tries to talk. "He's a little shit, Dad... he really is... he's always angry... always trying to pick a fight with somebody."

The other boy, a couple of inches shorter than James, is defiant. "Well, you, and all your spoilt mates, all think you're so fucking high and mighty. It makes me sick. I'll take you down any day, Littlewood."

"Not bloody likely," spits James back at him, before Gareth intervenes. "Enough," he shouts looking at each in turn, "enough."

"How did this all start?" asks Averill, quietly.

"Who the fuck are you?" asks the dark-haired youth, looking up at him with wild eyes.

Gareth raises his hand to cuff the youth, but Averill raises his own hand in restraint.

"My name is Averill," he replies. "Gregory Averill."

The youth sneers. "Ah, the broken down Sir Gregory Averill. My dad told me about you... told me you were something special... you don't look so special to me now."

This time Gareth gets the cuff in before Averill can save the boy. "Watch your manners, you little shit."

The youth stares back defiantly.

"It's alright Gareth," Averill decides. "He's right..."

Then looking directly at the boy, he continues, "It's true; I'm not the man I once was."

Then, bringing his face within inches of the boy's, he adds, "And you're not the man you could be, my son."

The boy glowers back at him, but then, in the face of Averill's steely gaze, the bravado suddenly collapses, and the young man lowers his head.

"Look at me, boy!" roars Averill, and the youth visibly wilts under the vicious onslaught, but lifts his head to look into Averill's burning eyes.

Passers-by have stopped; shocked by the ferocity of the interaction between the two. No-one speaks.

"Who is your father, boy?" hisses Averill.

"William," is the quiet, sullen reply. "William, the blacksmith... Sir Gregory."

Averill straightens. "Ah, William," he repeats. "Yes, I know him; good man... good man." Then leaning closer again, and with the cold, cruel precision of a stiletto, "So what happened to you, boy?"

Movement again at the periphery of the encounter, as the passers-by recover, and depart to go about their business.

Bravado banished by the sheer intensity of Averill's questions, the boy looks directly at Averill and replies, "I didn't turn out that well, Sir Gregory."

Silence; and Averill is not inclined to break it. The youth continues to look, uncertainly, at Averill.

Then, with icy intent, Averill continues, "So now... all I have to do is decide whether you're worth wasting any time on... or not."

He ponders, then decides. "I think you'd better be on your way, boy."

"You too, James," adds Gareth, quietly. "Go and finish grooming Sir Gregory's horse; then you can get cleaned up."

The two chagrined ex-combatants slink away; sullenly refusing to look at each other.

Averill looks at Gareth. "Interesting..." is his somewhat unexpected assessment.

★

"I met your son yesterday, William," comes a quiet, disembodied voice from the shadows.

"Jesus, Mary and all the saints!" explodes the blacksmith. "When are you going to stop scaring the bejeezes out of me, Sir Gregory?"

"Sorry," answers Averill, moving forward into the pale, early morning sunlight slanting in through the open doorway.

"Which one?" continues William, holding a hand over his still thumping heart.

"Wiry, about five foot five, dark curly hair, bit of a temper."

"Ah, Rupert," replies the blacksmith. "Come late that one, he did." A pause. "Not sure what I'm going to do about him, Sir Gregory. Not like the others, that one; seems to need more... I don't know what it is he needs, Sir Gregory, but it seems I'm not man enough to give it to him."

"Seems to have got in with the wrong crowd, he does," continues the blacksmith. "And now all I hear is, he's been in another fight, or he's been seen hanging around with some of the young ruffians I wish he didn't know, quite frankly."

Another pause. Averill waits patiently as the blacksmith gathers his thoughts again.

"The other boys were big and strong, like me, but Rupert, he takes after his mother more, I think; lighter built. And quick? My goodness, Sir Gregory, he could run like the wind when he were younger. Still strong mind you, but different. More... I don't know, more..."

"Subtle?" prompts Averill.

"Not quite sure what you mean there, Sir Gregory," replies William, slightly embarrassed. "That's not a word I know a great deal about."

"Sorry," replies Averill. "What I meant was, perhaps his strength was more hidden; there, right enough, but not quite so obvious."

"Aye, that's it, Sir Gregory," replies William, nodding thoughtfully, "that's exactly it. It weren't there in-your-face, like."

"And he were always asking questions," he continues. "The other boys was quiet, and easy to look after; knew their place like. But young Rupert; he always wanted to know everything there was to know. He were too much for an old blacksmith like me, Sir Gregory."

Another pause, then William continues, "But them days are long gone, Sir Gregory; days when I would look at him and be proud of my boy. Nowadays, he brings me nothing but sadness. I wish it were otherwise, Sir Gregory, but it ain't so."

"I've made a few enquiries about him," remarks Averill, manoeuvring the conversation in a new direction.

"Oh aye," is the downcast reply.

"Seems he often follows the squires and watches them when they're training."

"Fat lot of good that's going to do him, Sir Gregory," retorts the blacksmith, with feeling. "He'd be a damn site better off putting his back into a trade, like the other boys."

Silence. Averill watches quietly. William leans despondently upon the anvil, not inclined to start anything productive at the moment.

"Has he ever held a sword, William?" asks Averill.

"Oh aye," replies William. "He often used to take an old one that I'd let him have, and pretend he was a knight, like, Sir Gregory. But there wasn't nothing I could teach him. I can make 'em, Sir Gregory, but I can't use 'em."

"Pretending he was a knight, eh?" repeats Averill, watching for William's reaction.

"Oh, nothing serious," protests William. "He never assumed he was above his station, Sir Gregory. It were all in fun like; back in those days.

"He knows he can't be a knight, Sir Gregory," the blacksmith adds, concerned that he may have overstepped some invisible mark. "He knows he's not high born."

"He's quick, you say?" asks Averill.

"Oh, yes, Sir Gregory, he's quick alright; when he wants to be," replies William.

"And strong?"

"Like I said, Sir Gregory, it isn't a huge strength like that the other boys have, it's more... how did you say... more settle?"

Averill chuckles. "Indeed, William; more subtle."

The blacksmith smiles in slight embarrassment. "Sorry," he says, then adds "... my turn," with a broader smile.

Averill is standing, arms folded, leaning on the edge of a work-bench. He chuckles quietly at William's reference to the 'sorry' theme, which has laced both their responses.

"And he's certainly not afraid of anything much, is he?" remarks Averill, seeking only notional confirmation.

"Aye, that he's not, Sir Gregory. There's very few'd cause young Rupert to cower in a corner. I just wish he'd put all those talents to good use. It disappoints me so much, Sir Gregory; so much."

"Perhaps he's just not been challenged by anything life has brought him yet," suggests Averill.

"Well, Sir Gregory," replies William, "you don't get too many challenges when you're a blacksmith's son."

"No, I suppose not," concurs Averill.

Silence again, as both men withdraw to their thoughts.

"I suppose I'm going to need a squire," remarks Averill.

The blacksmith's heart lurches at what he thinks he has just heard. He says nothing.

"Someone quick... and persistent," continues Averill, "... and subtly strong..."

Still no comment, but the twitching of the blacksmith's jaw muscles reveals his suppressed agitation. A moment's further hesitation. "Wouldn't do no good, Sir Gregory. Squires become knights; and Rupert can't be a knight, now can he?"

"Explain?"

"He's not high-born."

Averill regards him through narrowed eyes, then, quietly and unequivocally, "Believe me, William: if I say he can be a knight, he can be a knight."

The blacksmith remains resting on the anvil, looking at the floor, not yet daring to believe the opportunity being laid before him.

"I suspected he might have the talent when I saw him yesterday," continues Averill, "and everything you've said this morning only strengthens that view.

"So; would you allow him to become my squire?"

There is a hush in the workshop as William absorbs Averill's words; then, looking up into the knight's eyes, "That would please me, Sir Gregory; that would please me a great deal."

"I would work him into the ground."

"It's as you say, Sir Gregory," concurs William looking directly back at Averill. "It's work that he needs; something to take his mind off all this fighting; something to make a man of him.

"I've tried, Sir Gregory, but, as you see, I'm not much of a man meself these days."

"He may fail," adds Averill.

"Aye, that he may," concurs William, nodding slowly.

"He may not be good enough," continues Averill, pushing the conversation to its limit.

"Well, Sir Gregory," replies William, standing upright, displaying a pride and confidence he has not felt for a very long time, "if he don't try, he'll never know now, will he?"

"No William, he won't."

The blacksmith nods. He looks around the workshop, becoming aware again that there is work to be done... but not just yet. He feels a need to understand the sense of enormous and unexpected pride he is feeling for his youngest son; a misguided son, for whom, until a few moments ago, he felt nothing but despair; a lost son, for whom he had, unknowingly, been pining since those first few years of promise, so long ago; a 'different' son, in whom he had placed great hopes, only to see them reduced to dust as the boy grew into a callous, misguided youth. And now, out of nowhere, a chance of redemption has been offered him.

"You'll be needing to find that light sword again, William."

Gazing at the floor, keeping his emotions in check, the blacksmith nods. Words seem a little difficult to come by just at the moment.

Averill turns to leave. "Oh, and William..."

"Sir Gregory?"

"If I ever fight again, I will want you for my armourer. You're enough of a man for an old warrior like me."

A cup already full with unexpected bounty, begins to overflow. The blacksmith drops his head and leans forward on the anvil again. A hand falls gently upon his shoulder. "What do you say, William; two old, broken men refusing to lie down. Think we could do some damage?"

"By my word, Sir Gregory," replies William, damp eyes looking up into the bright, clear eyes of a knight rediscovering his direction. "We could take on the entire French army, and there'd be a goodly number in paradise before us, I wager."

Averill nods, and looks back at the blacksmith. "That's why I want your son as my squire, William." Then, poking him gently in the chest. "This is the man I want him to become."

★

The blacksmith is still staring out the doorway, where Averill departed. His shoulders shudder slightly. It is a long, long time since tears have rolled down these cheeks.

CHAPTER EIGHT

"My father said to bring this to you."

Averill pauses in his task of cinching the girth strap around the chest of the sleek, white mare, and, still bent, turns to look at the owner of the voice.

The blacksmith's son stands at the doorway to the stable, proffering the light sword and scabbard.

Averill turns back to his task. "It's not for me," he mutters.

Rupert remains at the doorway, early morning sunlight illuminating one half of his body; a long shadow cast across the floor of the stable.

Averill continues preparing the mare.

"So I should take it back to him, then?"

Averill stops, and once again, turns to look at the young man. "No," he replies. "That wouldn't help at all."

He returns to his task, with apparent disinterest, leaving the young man, slightly agitated and confused.

"So what the fuck am I supposed to do with it?"

And now, Averill straightens. He puts down the brush he has been using on the mare's mane, and walks slowly over to the young man, stopping directly in front of him. Hands on hips, he looks down at the blacksmith's son, some six inches shorter.

"I beg your pardon?"

The chill in the quiet words carries a menace beyond anything the young man has experienced in his arrogant, undisciplined interactions with the ruffians whose company he has been keeping. His heart is beginning to thump.

He hesitates. "What should I do with it?" he asks, fighting to keep his voice even.

Averill's eyes continue to burn into him.

The young man's eyes waver slightly; but do not shrink from the challenge of returning Averill's gaze. Moments pass, then, "What should I do with it... Sir Gregory?"

"I suggest you strap it around your waist," replies Averill still looking fiercely into the young man's eyes. "We have a lot of work to do."

And with that, he turns and walks back to the mare, to resume brushing her mane.

"Are you fucking joking?"

214

Averill ignores him.

A pause, then, "Are you serious, Sir Gregory, or is this some kind of joke?"

"No joke, boy," Averill replies without looking at him.

"What do you expect me to do with it?" he asks, starting to unwrap the belt of the scabbard.

"I expect you to learn to use it," replies Averill. "And learn to use it well... Rupert."

The blacksmith's son looks up, abruptly. "I d-didn't know you knew my n-name, Sir Gregory," he stammers, now wildly off-balance.

"I make it my business to know the people who work for me," comes the unexpected reply.

And now, the young man's mind is racing; fear mounting.

"I'm n-not sure I want to w-work for you... Sir Gregory," he stutters; foolishly, but bravely.

"I'm not sure you have a choice," retorts Averill, once again staring blackly at the young man for a long moment, before returning his attention to the mare.

Rupert's stomach is now churning. A drop of perspiration runs down the side of his eye. Angrily, he brushes it away. He turns his attention back to the scabbard, but his shaking fingers refuse to thread the belt through the buckle, and suddenly, through the mounting anger of a disorientated and trapped animal, the trauma of the moment becomes too much.

"Shit!" he shouts, hurling the sword and scabbard to the floor. "Why the fuck do you want me? Why don't you go and get one of those fancy fucking pansy boys to do your work? Why pick on me? Why don't you just leave me alone?"

Averill whirls, and strides towards the enraged young man. And, for the first time in his life, Rupert is afraid enough to raise his hands to ward off the blows he fears are about to descend upon him.

But Averill stops less than a pace from the now quivering young man, and, in a voice dripping with malice, he leans closer to reply to the young man's questions. "Because, you little bastard, you've broken your father's heart," he hisses, "... and that offends me, deeply."

Rupert is shocked; staggered; his mind reels.

Here is a man whose demeanour, when relaxed, is beginning to appear like that of a caged lion, and who, when angered, carries a malice, which, frankly, scares the shit out of him. And such a man is concerned about his father's feelings. What fucking madness is this? How can his own father, a broken down old blacksmith, even be noticed by such a man, let alone be important to him?

He opens his mouth to protest, but Averill turns abruptly, and walks back to the mare.

"But perhaps you're right. Perhaps, this would be too much for you. Perhaps you should just crawl back into that hole you came from and we'll forget about the whole idea of you working for me."

Averill picks up the brush again, walks to the side of the mare's rump, and begins brushing her tail.

Rupert, bewildered, angry, fists clenched by his sides, almost screams in frustration. He didn't want the opportunity when it was offered; in fact, was shit scared of what it might entail. And now, suddenly, before he's had a chance to even think about it, it's being taken away.

He screams, giving vent to the poisonous, accumulated anger which swirls and contorts within his sixteen year-old mind. Life is so fucking unfair. Everything that's ever come his way has turned sour. He even started life as a blacksmith's son; how pathetic is that? So, what fucking chance did he have anyway? Why does he think that life could ever be anything more than standing in front of a roaring furnace, smashing the shit out of a piece of glowing metal? Why does he even bother watching the squires training; what is it that's inside him that makes him torture himself by noting their clumsiness and believing he could do better?

He stomps angrily to the door of the stable, kicks the thick wooden post, and breathing heavily with anger and frustration, stands, hands on hips, looking out.

The squawk of chickens and the muted voices of passers-by provide a benignly incongruous background to his wild and angry thoughts. Once again, life has given with one hand, then immediately taken back with the other. A familiar black gloom descends upon him.

A close, quiet voice behind him, "Beautiful morning..."

He whirls around to find Averill standing there, looking out over his head at the early morning sunshine slanting down across the courtyard of the castle, bringing into half-lit relief the trappings of the market being assembled for trading later in the day.

"Well, what's it to be?" asks Averill, quietly, still looking out.

The young man looks intently back at the knight. The turbulent mind begins to settle. He takes a deep breath...

"I'll stay."

"I'm sorry?" Averill is still looking out over the courtyard.

"I'll stay... Sir Gregory."

Averill lowers his gaze from out into the courtyard, to look directly at the young man. "Then understand this, boy: if you stay, I will work you harder than you ever thought possible. And, if you work for me, then I doubt you'll regret it in the end. But I assure you, you'll regret it more than once along the way. Is that clear?"

"Yes, Sir Gregory."

"Well?"

"I'd like to stay, Sir Gregory."

A long, long pause, as Averill looks into the young man's eyes, searching for the shiftiness he fears he may still find in them.

"Then, so be it."

★

The two horses and their riders canter out from the trees of the forest and into the clearing; Averill on the sleek, white mare, once again bedecked with her cavernous saddle-bags, Rupert atop a slender, brown, gelding which Averill has made his for the day.

Neither speaks. An air of uncertainty surrounds the pair; an air which is reflected in the sidelong glances the younger man, from time-to-time, surreptitiously casts toward the older, and further reinforced by the feigned disinterest the older man shows for the younger, whilst secretly watching his every move like a hawk.

As the horses slow to a walk, Rupert looks around, taking in the strange, uniformly spaced features around the edge of the clearing. Averill observes a slight change as the young man straightens a little from the slouched posture he has adopted throughout the journey to this point.

"I've seen those things," Rupert comments, with just the slightest trace of interest creeping into his tone. "I've seen the squires training with them."

"Pells," remarks Averill. "They're called pells."

The young man continues to take in the scene, his gaze traversing the cut and slashed posts, moving further right until he is looking at the large oak tree at the centre of the clearing. He stares at the unexpected structure under the shade of the tree, then pointing, and with yet another slight increase in interest level, he ventures, "And that one over there; that's a quintain, isn't it? I know that one. I've seen the way it comes 'round and knocks you off your horse if you don't ride through properly."

Averill regards him impassively.

The new squire's gaze continues around the clearing, but finds nothing further to remark upon. He looks back to Averill, and finds the older man looking directly back at him, expressionless.

"What?" he asks, unsettled by the smouldering intensity of the older man.

217

Averill's eyes continue to burn into him, then, "You're older than most boys when they become squires. So, you've a lot more work to do to catch up... if you're to be any good."

Once again Rupert is unsettled; unsettled because his usual response to criticism is anger and violence. But he is well aware of the foolishness of such a response with Averill. He remains seated upon his mount, but the agitation persists.

"Why me?" he suddenly asks.

"I told you," replies Averill. "You've broken your father's heart. His dreams, his hopes; you've destroyed them all."

The temptation to lash out at Averill, to throw his assertion back in his face and follow up with a foul-mouthed tirade, is almost overwhelming. But the young man is no fool, and instead he turns away and breathes deeply in an effort to control the turmoil within. The gelding beneath him snorts, and shakes its head, but otherwise, remains placid.

Moments pass then Rupert, still battling the swirling anger in his head, looks back at Averill. "What's my father to you, anyway?" he asks. "Why do you give a shit about him? He's just a blacksmith."

Averill draws a slow, deep breath. "Ah yes," he replies, "just a blacksmith."

Then, with unexpected gentleness, he continues. "I was once like you, Rupert; faster than everybody else, stronger than most of the other boys, good at everything I tried; a real pain in the arse, I imagine."

Rupert is caught off-guard by the unexpected comment, and laughs despite himself.

Averill continues. "But I was luckier than you. I came from a family already in the king's service. My father was a knight, beloved by His Majesty, and my path ahead was laid out long before I embarked upon it.

"I looked up to my father. Who wouldn't? A warrior, a commander in the king's army, a man to be reckoned with."

Rupert's interest begins to wane. This has nothing to do with him, after all.

"But," continues Averill. "It was not my father who made me the man I am today."

Suddenly Averill is quiet. Rupert looks up to see the older man staring into the distance, and is strangely affected by the look on the older man's face; a faraway look which has transported him to another time and place.

Moments pass, then Averill notices Rupert again and smiles a small, sad smile. "The man I am today? No, that's quite a different story. What I meant was: it was not my father who made me the man I was... when the world was at my feet."

The young man looks blankly at Averill.

Averill observes the young man's confusion, and, with an effort, forces himself to focus on the tale he wishes to tell.

"Two young boys, Rupert; a knight's son and a prince; both bright, both strong, both completely unaware that their lives were more privileged than those of almost everyone around them; but with fathers sufficiently wise to recognise that their boys would become insufferable boors if they were not taught some fundamental truths: that prowess comes from sheer bloody hard work, that righteousness comes from compassion and integrity, that greatness comes from sacrifice and humility."

Averill looks directly at the young man. "These are strange bedfellows, are they not, Rupert?"

The hitherto coarse, misguided young man struggles to make sense of what is being said to him. He has heard the words, and has a tenuous grasp of what they might mean, but is still struggling to understand how they might relate to himself, or more to the point, to his father, who was, after all, the original subject of the conversation.

"In order to lead, Rupert," continues Averill, "we first had to serve. Along with the gentler aspects of court life, which, by the way, you will have to learn, we were trained in the art of warfare; in the care of our horses, in the fashioning and the use of our weapons, but most of all, in the importance of every man-at-arms, every archer, every knight; even the boys with the luggage who would accompany us to the battlefield."

Averill looks steadily at the young man, to see if the words are making any impression, but then presses on regardless.

"But these are not things which a knight can usefully teach a squire with any real impact, Rupert. These are things which can only be taught through example, by honest and common men; men whose days are spent crafting wagon wheels, breaking and shoeing horses, forging hot metal into weaponry, and a myriad other back-breaking tasks. It is only by becoming one with the common folk of the land that a young squire can begin to earn the respect of the men he will one day command in battle. For without such respect, Rupert, a knight is just a solitary oaf who will fail alone, and fall in battle alone.

"These were the lessons I had to learn Rupert; long, painful lessons; lessons which turned all of my ideas, of who serves whom, on their head; lessons which I learned whilst shovelling horse shit, learning to string a bow, and trying desperately to forge glowing metal into something which resembled a sword.

"I thought I was shit-hot, Rupert: I was a squire among common men. I was going to be a knight; they weren't.

"But what I learned was that I didn't really understand what shit-hot was, until I spent time with men who really were shit-hot; men who could cut and splice and fashion lengths of yew into bows which bent and strained and sprang back with a power beyond imagining; men who took raw logs and stripped and shaped and joined them to form structures that could withstand the strongest storms this land produces; men who could heat metal to just the right temperature and wield hammers which I could barely lift, and pound and grind the metal into the most fearsome and deadly weapons I had ever beheld; men who were shit-hot at what they did, and who eventually made me, a young, arrogant, privileged squire of noble birth, with an over-rated opinion of himself, understand that it is not a man's birth which determines his value, but his willingness to acknowledge that all honourable men, whether high-born or no, are deserving of recognition and respect."

Then, quietly, "Your father, Rupert, for some reason I never knew, took me under his wing, and taught me all that. He encouraged me, harangued me, chastised me, laughed at me when I complained that life was too hard, kicked me in the breeches when I was too slow or too lazy, and loved me like my own father until those layers of arrogance and privilege were scraped away, to leave a humble young man worthy of his time and his effort and his love."

Averill is staring into the distance again, lost in the memories of another time and another place. He muses, almost to himself, "And only then, did my father consider that I was worthy to become a knight."

In the silence which follows, a long forgotten feeling stirs deep in the core of Rupert's being, and the young man recalls another time and place; when he listened to a man he loved telling stories at bedtime. A man who to Rupert, then, was everything he needed in the world, before he fell among those who would mock the old man, make jokes about his dirty, grimy appearance and his slow, affected speech, and tell the young Rupert that the old man was just like their own parents; useless, out of touch, worth no more than the pigs in the pens outside.

The wetness and the stinging which Rupert suddenly feels in his eyes usually accompany the blind, unfocused rage which takes hold of him when the affairs of the world do not go his way. But this time, the feeling is different: he sits a little taller in the saddle, looks about him without any need for the bullying and the bluster which has become so much a part of his persona, and begins to re-assess his views of the old, broken knight, and the dim, pathetic blacksmith; views which had been so convincing only this morning.

Beside him, Averill returns to the here and now, and abruptly dismounts from the mare.

"So then, young Rupert; we'd better get our arses into gear, hadn't we?" he grins, and opening the saddle-bags withdraws two woodsman's axes and drops them with soft thuds to the ground.

By contrast, Rupert's dismount is more cautious and uncertain. A strange conflict between trepidation and excitement works away within him: work is still a foreign concept, and yet he is somehow unable to resist this man, and the small steps which are starting to carry him away from the angry, pointless existence which has been his lot to-date.

"What do we do with these?" he asks, with subdued petulance.

"Oh, I think you'll find out soon enough," replies the older man, already striding into the forest.

"Do you expect me to carry both of these?"

The sound of muted footsteps... fading.

"Fuck."

The young man has an axe slung over each shoulder as he stumbles into the forest.

CHAPTER NINE

"Oh Daddy; it's such a beautiful day," chirps Odelia, hugging Averill as he stares out of the window over the soft, green landscape, bathed in bright early morning sunshine.

"You're up early, missy" he replies, wrapping his arm around her shoulder as she cuddles into him.

"Of, course," she replies. "It's the fair; and we're going, aren't we?"

"Oh. Are we?"

"Daddy, don't be silly; you know we are," comes the earnest reply. "You promised."

"Ah yes. So I did. Well, I suppose that settles it then, doesn't it?" he laughs.

"But, won't it be a bit boring for you?" Odelia asks, concerned that the day might not prove as exciting to her father as she knows it will be for her.

"No, certainly not," replies Averill, without hesitation. "Gareth is entered in the joust this afternoon and I intend to watch him."

"Why don't you enter, Daddy?" comes the enthusiastic response. "You used to be so good."

Averill hesitates. Memories tumble over each other; but they seem so remote, so distant; so much a part of another life.

"Ah, Odelia," he replies. "That was a long time ago. Times change, people get older..."

"You're not old, Daddy", she counters. "In fact, I think that you could even beat Gareth if you really tried."

"Do you think so?" laughs Averill, warmed by the confidence his daughter shows in him.

"Of course," she replies, with conviction. "I remember what Mummy said. She said that if all the knights entered the tournament at the same time, and fought each other until there was only one left standing, it would be you."

Averill is quiet. Unbeknown to them, he had overheard the conversation between Mariel and Odelia. He can still picture the scene: he had looked up from his preparations to see Mariel brushing her daughter's hair, the little girl asking why Averill was getting his armour ready, Mariel explaining that there was to be a competition, Odelia asking her mother if it wasn't dangerous, and Mariel offering her glowing opinion of her man's prowess.

"Yes, she did, didn't she?" he replies, gently.

Odelia looks up at her father, aware that she has touched him with her innocent comment. "She was right, Daddy," she continues. "You were the best of them all. I remember."

These are the times that all of the successes he has achieved in dealing with the sadness and moving forward, come tumbling down; the times when the gentlest words manage to penetrate the defences most poignantly, and bring back into stark relief, the magnitude of the loss which still exists at his core.

For a moment, as he blinks back the tears and stares intently out of the window, the room is quiet. Two young hands clasp each other around his waist, and a young head rests lovingly upon his chest.

Little-by-little, as he strokes the soft, black hair, the anguish subsides.

"Perhaps you're right," he concedes. "Perhaps it is something I could do again... one day."

Odelia looks up at him again. "I would cheer for you, Daddy," she promises.

"I'd be very disappointed if you didn't," laughs Averill through the tears.

The smile and the hug are worth everything; absolutely everything: so amazing that such happiness can exist side-by-side with such sadness.

"So, shall we get ready?" he asks.

"Yes, Daddy," she replies, standing on tip-toes to kiss him. "I'll wake Sarah."

He turns back to the window, listening to the patter of bare feet skipping away, and searches idly for his owl; but is not surprised that she should not be there. His mind is serene with the after-glow of emotional release. It really is a wonderful day.

★

"I don't like this, Gregory."

"Well, I don't believe he will actually get hurt, but I think he has a difficult job ahead of himself."

"Oh well, at least if he gets knocked off early, we can get on with the drinking."

Anthony is worried, Thomas philosophical, and Bryan irreverent, as ever.

"I hope he smashes the bastard," says Averill, with quiet malice. "He's a fucking animal."

There is a long pause as all in the group wrestle with the same unspoken thought. Eventually, and unsurprisingly, it is Thomas who finds the way to frame the question. "Do you ever think that, one day, you might pull on armour against him, Gregory?"

Averill's stance is one they have all seen before: standing, hands on hips, looking at the ground, left foot tracing a small arc backwards and forwards in the dirt as his mind wrestles with the problem.

"No, I don't think so," is the considered reply.

Images of the clearing, and the pells, and the quintain, tumble through his mind. But now is not the time. His own views are not yet well-formed. There is too much uncertainty that he can even reach the pitch that will be required to return to competition. And, to be truthful, he has not let his mind dwell on the prospect of exacting vengeance against Bijou, in any specific form; other than the desire to tear the bastard's heart from his body. But that is just raw, unfocussed hatred.

No; a decision to pursue Bijou, for the chance to destroy him, would require him to admit the man into his mind, and that is something he is not prepared to do, for fear of being consumed, yet again, by the depression he knows it would bring.

Emerging from his thoughts he asks, "Has anyone spoken with Gareth this day?"

"I saw him, this morning," replies Thomas, "and Charles and Robert are with him this afternoon, for the preparations."

"And?" queries Averill.

"And... I thought he seemed well enough," continues Thomas. Then cautiously, he adds, "He carries your anger, Gregory, and he is determined to unseat him, and to inflict as much harm as he possibly can. But he is not driven by the same depth of feeling as consumes you, Gregory; and, as a result, he is not reduced to a state of nerves by the event."

"He will do his best, Gregory," adds Anthony, gently. "And I believe he will acquit himself well. But, I pray you, do not lay any greater expectations upon his shoulders. He already offers you his unquestioned loyalty and support."

"Thank you for your salutary words, gentlemen," replies Averill, smiling back at them. "As always, your assessments are spot-on. It is good that he is not affected by the prospect. And, with a little luck, he will inflict some serious damage during the event.

"So, shall we go and see what transpires?"

★

"May we sit with you, Gregory?"

Averill looks up as Wendy, Sarah and Odelia, the latter two chattering excitedly as usual, slide in to occupy the remaining cushions of the wooden bench upon which the three knights are already seated. Odelia's long hair is braided with multiple coloured ribbons, whilst Sarah has acquired a more demure necklace of plaited flowers. Momentarily, Averill's attention is distracted from the forthcoming joust, as he regards the ladies with undisguised pleasure. The three knights rise, and, with gentlemanly grace, bid the ladies welcome.

A rough young face among the crowd, at the barrier which separates the spectators from the course, turns and looks back toward the box in which Averill and his companions sit. The young man's heart beats a little faster and his breathing becomes a little ragged as he takes in the form of the youngest of the females. Such an unusual appearance; such amazing eyes; soft, deep complexion; so beautiful. Clearly, she is foreign. But how is it that she sits in a group with Averill?

He continues to gaze until the blast of the nearby trumpet causes him to swiftly turn back to the course, where two knights, on horseback, begin their gentle progress to opposite ends of the tilt. He recognises the flaming red hair of Gareth's son, as the latter walks ahead of the horse of the closer knight, and wonders what it must be like to be the privileged squire of a knight participating in a contest. It is a small step for the imagination as he becomes the knight on the horse, about to face a gallant opponent for the hand of the fair maiden.

He turns again. The young, beautiful, dark-haired creature is standing, laughing and applauding the big knight as he makes his way to the end of the course. The young man's breath catches in his chest once again.

The general hubbub of the crowd becomes hushed as the steward at the centre of the course raises his flag. The young woman sits, excitedly, and Rupert's attention is drawn back to the joust.

The flag drops, and in an instant the two chargers are tearing at the ground as they accelerate towards each other. Both lances begin their downward arc as the riders tuck them tightly under arms and raise shields for the impending clash. The ground is shuddering now as the heavy beasts, bearing fully-armed knights, thunder toward each other. Both riders lean forward; each intent upon threading his lance past the protection of the opponent's shield and onto the breastplate behind.

Rupert is half standing with excitement. Never has he been so close to the action; never has he felt the thunder and the noise of the contest pounding his chest before. Hitherto, his standing with the group of ruffians who have been his companions for so long, has compelled him to disinterest in the tournaments, as the group has wandered aimlessly between the tents, pulling pegs from the ground, kicking over bins and generally creating as much nuisance as they possibly could. But today he has slipped away from them and has found an out-of-the-way vantage point to watch the proceedings, unmolested.

The crash of splintering wood is sharp and shocking. Rupert's ears are not accustomed to such violence. A fist on flesh is one thing, but the sound of two lances striking their targets at the ferocious closing speed of the charging beasts is a level of intensity which he has never before experienced. He winces, gasps, and finds he cannot hear from the thunder of blood pounding in his ears. He realises he is standing, fist raised in the air, screaming along with the scores of men and boys beside him, and wonders how he came to be so.

Averill also winces, Odelia gasps and clutches Sarah's arm tightly, as the young maid cries out in fear and holds her hands to her mouth. Wendy utters an uncontrolled shriek as Bijou's lance crashes through Gareth's shield and into her husband's breastplate. The big man is flung against the high back of the saddle, as is Bijou from the sheer inertia of Gareth's strike, which, although not penetrating the defence of the shield, has, nevertheless, pounded his opponent's shield back into his armoured ribs, causing the knight to grunt in pain as the breath is torn from his lungs.

The splinters from the two shattered lances rain down upon the course as the horses charge through the debris, both riders now hauling upon reins to bring their mounts to a halt.

The first pass is over, and both knights remain, slightly battered, but still mounted.

The full-throated roar of the crowd which accompanied the clash dies away to an excited, continuous babble as men and boys re-count the action, and women fan their faces from the heat of the blood which has rushed to their cheeks.

Rupert's hands are still shaking from the impact of the thunder and the noise and the ferocious intensity of the clash. Why, oh why has he allowed his life to-date to be so misguided by the callous fellows to whom his grudging loyalty has been given?

No more.

He turns again to look back toward the box where Averill and his party sit. The young woman is examining her companions arm and appears to be laughing apologetically. Her face is flushed so brightly that the beautiful, deep complexion appears to almost radiate. Rupert's mind reels from the combined effects of the acute violence he has just witnessed and the staggering beauty he beholds. Momentarily, he loses balance and cries out as he almost falls from his seat.

"It wasn't that hard a hit," laughs the large man next to him. "Just you wait for the next one; that should be really interesting."

Embarrassed, the young man apologises and steadies himself once again.

Gareth shakes his head to clear the fug clouding his brain, as he wheels his horse around and starts back towards James, waiting at the other end of the course with a new lance. Much as he hates Bijou, he acknowledges that the man has strength, and is no slouch when it comes to battle. He has seen the strength close up before, but has never been on the receiving end of it. However, he is comforted that he also saw Bijou's head flung forward as the shield crashed into his ribs, and so, is confident that he is hurting no more than his opponent.

Odelia has her arm around Sarah's neck and is laughing and apologising together. In the excitement of the clash, she has dug her fingernails into Sarah's upper arm, drawing blood. Sarah, equally excited by the clash has not even noticed until Odelia's gasp of horror at what she had just done.

"Are you alright, Wendy?" asks Averill.

"Oh Gregory," she replies, breathlessly. "Yes, I'm fine. I know how these contests go, and I know that Gareth is big enough and ugly enough to look after himself. But I still cannot help it. Every time I see him hit, my heart jumps and I want to run to him and make sure he is unhurt."

Taking the lance from James, Gareth smiles.

"Well, I think we just gave our Monsieur Bijou a little tickle for his troubles," he remarks lightly. "What do you think?"

"Yes, Father," smiles James in relief. "I think he knows there are two out there. But how are you?"

"Fine, my boy; just fine," replies Gareth, not commenting upon his surprise at Bijou's strength.

Once again the flag is raised. Gareth settles, hefting the lance slightly into a more comfortable grip. Averill hunches down, focussing upon the big man, not prepared to look at his opponent. Rupert takes one quick glance at the beautiful creature in the box behind him, then rapidly turns back to look first at Gareth, then at his opponent, trying to weigh up the advantages each might possess. Wendy closes her eyes, offering a little prayer. Odelia's eyes are wide, her heart racing; this is so exciting; better than she remembers from when she was small.

The flag drops. Two chargers strain and tear at the ground as their riders dig in spurs and hurl their weight forward.

Within seconds the thunder of hooves resonates in Rupert's chest. He holds tightly onto the wooden bench as the knights converge. The mighty crash of the first pass is repeated, but this time, Gareth's aim is fractionally amiss. Bijou's lance strikes Gareth's shield, shattering as it slams the shield back into the opponent's breastplate, whilst Gareth's strike scuttles off the top of Bijou's shield. The lance does not break.

Score to Bijou.

The disappointment in the box is palpable. Wendy's 'Oh' is the only comment she makes. Having seen Gareth take the strike on the shield, she knows he is not hurt; but disappointment still hangs over her. Averill curses softly and looks at the ground.

Anthony shakes his head. "Big job now," he comments.

"Indeed," remarks Thomas, watching as Gareth returns; ensuring that the knight appears uninjured.

"Are you alright, Father?" asks James as Gareth arrives.

"Yes, I'm fine," the big man replies. "Not very happy with that, though," he continues. "Just an inch. That's all there was in it; a bloody inch."

A pause as he looks over at the box, to see Wendy looking concerned. He waves, she smiles; then, looking down at James. "Well then. Let's see if we can't knock him into next week, this time," he laughs.

The boy looks up at his father with love, and pride, and admiration. "Yes, Father; let's do just that."

The flag drops.

The ground shakes as the beasts thunder towards each other. Lances level and tucked in tight, shield arms cocked ready to take the strikes, horses sweating, straining, nostrils flaring; shredded grass and soil flying; impact!

Armoured bodies hurled backwards in saddles, wild grunts as air is expelled from lungs, splintered debris raining down upon the spot two horses occupied barely a second ago, both knights drop the shattered remains of their lances.

The crowd stands as one and applauds as both knights turn to leave the field. The next two combatants are waiting to enter.

The steward makes the customary announcement. "The winner, by three lances to two: Sir René Bijou." And Bijou walks his horse to the podium to receive the garland.

"Drinking time," remarks Bryan, but Averill remains sitting, staring out over the field, unsettled and uncertain of his emotions.

"You go on ahead," he remarks, at length. "I think I'll stay here for a little while."

"I'll take the girls with me," offers Wendy. "I think we'll go and see how my boys are doing."

"Thank you, Wendy," he replies, looking up.

"Are you alright, Daddy?" asks Odelia; highly perceptive to Averill's moods.

"Of course," he replies. "Just give me a hug and I'll be even better."

She obliges; and a young pair of eyes, close to the field of combat, stare back in deepening confusion.

"Wendy," calls Averill, suddenly.

She turns back to him.

"Yes, Gregory?"

"I'm sorry, Wendy," he offers. "I meant to ask. How is little... Mariel?"

A moment, as they look into each other's eyes, then the lady wraps her arms around Averill's neck and hugs him to her. "Oh, Gregory," she whispers. "Thank you so much for asking. She is wonderful."

Averill nods, unable to speak further.

"Dear, dear Gregory," continues the lady. "I am only just realising how hard this is for you; how much it costs you to say her name. It's a difficult thing to want to honour someone Gareth and I loved so much, when it causes you so much pain."

Averill lifts his head and smiles through the tears. "No Wendy, it is I who should be grateful to you for wanting to honour her so. I think that, with time, it will become easier."

Gently, she wipes a tear from his cheek and smiles back. "Yes, dear Gregory; I hope so."

★

The roar of the crowd erupts from time-to-time as the jousts continue, but Averill has long since left the box where he and his companions watched Gareth's valiant but unsuccessful attempt to unseat Bijou. The big man was certainly not disgraced, maintaining his seat just as securely as did the king's champion; and, in the end it was a just matter of inches. But, at the end of the day, as Averill had known deep down, something special had been needed, and it hadn't been found.

He wanders past the gaily coloured tents, chuckling from time-to-time at the comedic phrases of the various spruikers, energetically attempting to part fools and their money, and half-listening to the chatter of the peasants and artisans and townsfolk as they enjoy a pleasant afternoon of banter and relaxation. But his mind remains unsettled, with partially formed thoughts and an underlying uncertainty about what life holds for him from this moment on.

For the first time in a long time, he allows the questions to form: *Who am I? Where am I going?* And finds that he has no answers.

He stops, and, as is his want in these situations when he withdraws from the world to reflect, buys an apple to munch on as he walks and ponders.

Once I was a knight, a captain, a leader of men; but no longer...

Once my life had a purpose; a king to serve; an army to lead. But now... now, I don't know anymore.

His thoughts naturally turn to the clearing... and the pells... and the quintain. *Yes, I can regain some of my former skills; and yes, I can think about entering some tournaments again; but to what end?*

And then he allows the wider issues to come into focus. *Of course, I have a daughter to care for, and there is no doubt that that is a task of the utmost importance... and the utmost joy...*

But even in that, he realises, *the need becomes less day-by-day. Odelia and Sarah have become close, and grow more and more capable of looking after each other. And Wendy makes sure that they do not get into trouble.*

I sometimes think that...

The self-pity about to be formulated dies on his breath as a pitiful, battered and bloody form staggers around the corner and into his path.

It takes a moment for the apparition to make sense. "My God, Rupert!" he cries, rushing to grasp the crumpling body. "What happened?"

The dark matted curls are caked in blood, as are the boy's scratched and swollen hands. Dark bruises are visible through the rent sleeves and body of his jerkin. His bottom lip is cut and swollen, and, from head to toe, the young squire is caked in mud.

A small crowd gathers as Averill kneels, holding the semi-conscious youth in his arms. "Move away," he commands, gently. "Let him have some air."

The peasant folk do as bidden and the light, cool breeze brings some slight relief to the injured boy.

"Rupert?"

The eyelids flicker slightly, but then are still. No answer.

Carefully, Averill places his arms under the shoulders and knees of the boy, picks him up and starts back toward the castle. His mind recalls the last time he carried such a burden back to the castle, and threatens to undo him. But shaking his head quickly, he banishes the image. He will not permit his mind to admit that occasion at the moment.

★

Now bathed and cleaned up, Rupert lies, eyes closed, upon the bed. Sarah has made broth and is sitting beside him, encouraging him to eat. Odelia stands, holding Averill's arm, watching as the young squire coughs and splutters through the process; but gradually, the young man begins to synchronise his actions with the proffered spoon and, little-by-little, the bowl empties.

The eyes open and look out from the bruised and swollen face.

Sarah rises to leave, and Averill moves to sit on the other side of the bed, reaching out to place his hand behind the young man's neck. "What happened?"

"My friends..." utters Rupert, hoarsely. "They don't like that I've become your squire."

Averill nods, and immediately realises the foolishness of his belief that he could just pluck the boy out of his rough and underprivileged circumstances, without there being any consequences. And yet, he knows that, if the boy were to be saved, if he were to be given an opportunity in life, then plucked out he needed to be.

He ponders the situation and, piece-by-piece, begins to realise that there was no simple way of extracting Rupert from his surroundings without angst of some form.

"Well," he replies, partly to himself, "it's done now; it's out in the open."

And... the path ahead is clear. Averill's earlier doubts are, for the moment at least, banished to the background. There is work to be done; a squire to be educated in the arts of self defence, and after that, in something a little more dangerous to those who would accost him.

He smiles, and Rupert, through painfully swollen lips, whispers his response, with predictable lack of humour, "What's so fucking funny about this?"

Averill chuckles. "Ah, not so damaged, after all?" And then, "I'm sorry, my boy. I wasn't smiling at your current predicament, for that is nothing to smile about. No, Rupert, I was thinking about the next time your 'friends' meet you."

"I'd rather not," comments Rupert.

"Believe me, my boy," replies Averill. "It will be a very different story. And now, young man," he continues, "do you think you can walk?"

★

Only once during their slow and stilted walk back to the blacksmith's house, did Rupert raise the subject.

"I saw someone sitting with you this afternoon, Sir Gregory."

"Did you, Rupert? I didn't see you. Where were you?"

"Down by the fence. I wanted to see the joust, but didn't want my friends to find me.

"Didn't work, did it?" he adds.

"No, it doesn't appear that it did."

"But I saw you, and... there was someone sitting with you."

"There were several people sitting with me this afternoon Rupert," replies Averill.

"Yes," replies the young man, now displaying an earnestness not previously seen in his character. "But this one was in your room again, where you cleaned me up."

"Ah... yes, she was," says Averill. "And one day I might tell you a little about her. But for now," he continues, voice bordering upon unpleasant, "I suggest you forget her."

Rupert is stunned by the unexpected severity in Averill's tone; and equally, Averill is shocked at his own response.

Silence, as they slowly walk on, each lost in his own thoughts; the older man struggling to recognise the acute pang which passed through his heart as Rupert encroached upon what had hitherto been his private world. For the first time, he recognises that his daughter has become... desirable. And this shocks him, firstly, because he has always regarded Odelia as a little girl, and, secondly, because he had not seen it coming.

He lengthens his stride, forcing Rupert to hurry his struggling gait, to keep up. The young man does not utter a word of complaint. He has seen the change of expression on Averill's face and once again is overawed by the presence of the man. Broken down old knight? Not fucking likely.

CHAPTER TEN

The routine has become well-established now; training in the mornings, individual practice in the afternoons.

A few days after Rupert's encounter with his former friends, he and Averill had left the castle and ridden off into the forest, arriving at the clearing less than two hours later. The morning had provided a rude awakening for Rupert, when, as soon as they had dismounted, Averill had taken him by the neck and landed him flat on his back, then roared at him to get up and fight, as if his life depended upon it.

Hurt and angry, Rupert had scrambled to his feet, and in blind fury launched himself at Averill, only to find himself immediately back on the ground with a mouthful of dirt, and Averill standing over him. Then, surprisingly, the knight had held out his hand and hauled Rupert to his feet.

"Cold, Rupert," he had admonished. "You must stay absolutely cold. No anger, just a deep, burning intention to take the head off any man who comes at you.

"Now," he had continued, "we start like this; it's called 'the weighing scale', 'wag' for short. It means being well-balanced, with your weight low and your knees bent, so that your opponent cannot knock you off your feet." And with that, the two had locked arms as Averill demonstrated.

Over the next two hours, the moves had followed: the grasps, the draws, the jerks, the transferences of weight, the leg hooks, the hip throws, the recoveries. And, slowly, deliberately, the young squire had begun to feel the power which leverage generates; had learned how the point of balance affects who gets thrown and who remains standing; and had begun to enjoy the thrill of the combat, so different from the un-disciplined thrashing and scrabbling which had previously been his way when fighting. No, this was something different, this felt powerful. This felt as if he could actually take control of a situation.

And then, as if to reinforce the size of the task ahead, and to keep the gradually swelling head from believing in itself too much just yet, Averill had once again sent the young squire sprawling into the dirt.

"That's where we start tomorrow," he had said, and Rupert had momentarily hated the man. But then, the gradually maturing Rupert had surfaced, and swallowing his anger with uncharacteristic control, he had nodded, and held out his hand to Averill. "Then pull me up; I'm stuffed."

The knight had generously agreed and bent to haul the young man to his feet, whereupon he had found himself on the wrong end of a leveraged grapple, and falling backwards toward the sparse turf.

"You little shit," he had uttered, almost involuntarily. "I can't believe you did that."

"Must have a good tutor," Rupert had replied, now on his feet and walking toward the horses.

Rising to his feet, and brushing the grass and dirt from his clothing, the knight had shaken his head and smiled to himself. *So much like someone I remember. Sir Boris called me a little shit, too.*

★

There are thirteen pells now, and Rupert has felled, stripped, sunk, and raised three of them. The pale, pimply skin and rather shapeless form which were previously his have become firmer and more tanned and, although not yet hard, the signs of a wiry, athletic body are beginning to appear.

This morning has been an introduction to the teachings of Fiore de'Liberi da Premariacco, the Italian master, whose manuscript *Flos Duellatorum*, which translates as *The Flower of Battle*, has impressed Averill with its detailed coverage of both armed and unarmed combat. And now the squire is conscientiously taking the stance, advancing, and slowly and carefully wielding the sword through the prescribed arcs, to land on, if at all possible, the charcoal crosses drawn on the pell at the vulnerable points of a human target.

By contrast, Averill is working at another of the pells with the new sword, which William and Joseph have fashioned between them. This one is made of whale bone; is not quite as heavy as the previous monster provided by William, but is almost indestructible; a necessary characteristic since Averill has now embarked upon the final phase of his swordsmanship recovery, where speed is paramount, and is attacking the pell with little restraint.

From time-to-time, Rupert pauses and watches with undisguised awe as the knight begins to close in upon his own set of charcoal targets.

The young man returns to his task, and raises his sword, ready to advance once again. He remains, statue-like, as his mind reflects upon the scene: here he is, with the knight who was once the captain of the king's army, and who, for some reason he is yet to uncover, was apparently abandoned by all who revered him. And he, a callous, underprivileged ruffian from the streets, is learning the art of wrestling and being tutored in the arts of warfare, with the prospect of one day becoming a knight, by that very same man of mysterious past glory. And all of this is being done in secret, away from the training ground of the other squires, away from the castle and the courtyards, and the onlookers. Such a scene that it scarcely bears believing; and yet, there is no doubt it is real.

He turns slowly, with almost dance-like grace, sword still raised above his head, and gazes over at the quintain. *And this*, he thinks, *not even touched yet. Oh, imagine, the feeling of sitting on a warhorse, charging full-tilt towards the target, lance held firmly under the arm, wind whistling through the hair, thundering across the open space...*

And, in the same trance-like state, with the same surreal dance-like grace, he completes the turn to face the pell again, and in one fluid motion, slowly and deliberately brings the sword down with an angular strike at the neck-mark on the wooden post.

A charcoal-streaked chip of wood flies off, and, in continuing the follow-through he comes face-to-face with Averill, standing, sweating, watching his young charge's progress.

"Lucky," remarks the knight.

Rupert smiles; there is no bluster. "Jealous," he replies, turning gracefully back to the pell and flowing into a new stance.

Averill watches with his own mixture of admiration and pride. Even after such a short time, Rupert is exhibiting traces of that grace which is the defining characteristic of outstanding swordsmen; a grace which, he recalls, Bijou does not possess.

His disdain for the man gnaws away inside him, once again.

★

Quiet, solitude; the soulful world which Averill inhabits from time-to-time, when the world of man is not the place he wants be. This other world, this world of dreams, of what once was, of love and warmth and beauty... and sadness... is the refuge to which he returns when deeper matters trouble his soul; as if he is a more complete person when immersed in the memories of his beloved than when working at being the recovering knight of the daylight hours.

He stands at the window, looking out over the moonlit scene, gazing into the trees where he knows the owl sits. And, because he knows where to look, he finds her there; quiet, unmoving, seemingly staring back at him. Her occasional slow blink is like a heartbeat between them, renewing the connection, over and over again.

What to do?

The question rolls around in his mind, touching so many aspects of his being; and yet he does not wish to address it directly. This should be a logical decision based upon the facts which are clearly evident: he is an older, slower man than when he commanded the king's army. He is a less driven individual than when he commanded the king's army. He is an out-of-touch combatant working valiantly to regain some of the skills he possessed when he commanded the king's army. And yet, he somehow knows that it will not be a logical decision which he makes. And gradually, piece by minute piece, he comes to know that it is within his private world, where feelings hold sway over logic, where emotion makes reason subservient, where the impossible is rendered impotent, that he will learn the course to follow.

Images form and fade, and as they do the trickle makes its first hesitant splash on the way to becoming a torrent. He sees Bijou's bludgeoning strength, which Gareth could not master, and slowly recognises the hitherto unconscious desire to conquer it. He sees Rupert's growing grace with the sword, which Bijou does not possess, and becomes aware again of the disdain he feels for the man who lacks the artistry and the beauty of execution which, to Averill, is so much a part of being the king's champion. He sees the image of his beloved as he holds her close and remembers her last, soft words to him, "I always feel safe in your arms, my love; do you know that?" He hears the voice of his young daughter as she sought, so recently, to comfort him, once again, "She was right, Daddy. You were the best of them all. I remember."

And somewhere, deep within his psyche, a shift occurs; an uncertainty fades, and as it does, the ever-present gnawing with which he has been living for so long, quietly ceases. He continues to gaze out of the window, but feels a stillness within; a peace and a calmness which he had forgotten, but now finds familiar once again. He recognises a clarity of purpose which has hitherto been missing, and, although he has made no actual decision, he knows, nonetheless, that a decision has been made and the path ahead made clear.

In a tree outside, as if freed of her responsibility of watching over the ruminating knight within, a white owl stretches, launches herself into the air, and disappears into the night... to hunt.

CHAPTER ELEVEN

"How much further?" asks Gareth, as the four canter through the lush summer foliage of the forest. Shafts of dappled sunshine slash through the leaves, whipping irregular patches of light and shade across the figures on horseback as they pass.

"Not long now," replies Averill.

Rupert and James ride easily behind the knights; not overtly antagonistic, but still not exhibiting any degree of friendship.

Several moments pass in silence as the four continue on, then gradually the forest canopy begins to thin. A few more minutes, then suddenly the knights and the boys burst from the trees into a large clearing.

"Holy shit. What's been going on here, Gregory?" asks the slightly incredulous Gareth as the four rein to a halt.

Averill and Rupert exchange glances, but neither comments. Averill has instructed the lad to give nothing away, and, in evidence of his growing discipline, Rupert has remained tight-lipped throughout the journey.

Gareth turns in the saddle as he counts, "... fifteen, sixteen, seventeen."

Then, as the pieces begin to fall into place in his mind, "You've been training, Gregory; away from all the prying eyes of the court, you've been training."

Then, slowly, the light dawns.

"My God; you're going to take him on, aren't you? You're bloody going to take him on.

"By all that's holy, Gregory, I never thought..."

But now, Rupert has lost the thread of the conversation. "Who are you going to take on, Sir Gregory?"

"He's bloody taking on Bijou, that's who," retorts Gareth. Then, as the potential consequences start to impinge. "Are you sure about this Gregory? The man's an animal; strong as a fucking ox, and as mean a bastard as I've ever met. And don't be fooled, Gregory, he can wield a sword as well as any man I've met; even if he isn't the most graceful on the field."

"That's the knight you fought, in the last tournament, isn't it Sir Gareth?" continues Rupert.

"Yes, it is," chimes in James. "I don't like him at all."

Rupert turns abruptly and stares hard at James. Then, turning back to Averill, and with a smile unseen by James, adds, "Well, I don't think I like him much, either."

Then, to the surprise of both knights, he turns again to face James and adds, "Come and I'll show you what we've been doing here."

Rupert strides off toward the ring of pells, with James in his wake.

"Remarkable," comments Gareth. "I cannot believe it's the same young lad, Gregory. How have you done it?"

"William's a good man, Gareth," replies Averill. "I've known him for a very long time. Any boy of his just had to turn out well, if he were only given the opportunity. All I did was provide that opportunity; and a few swift kicks up the backside, which always moves things along a bit."

"You've taken him as your squire?" queries Gareth.

"Indeed," replies Averill. "He's a natural, Gareth; smart, quick, and absolutely unafraid; still rather rough around the edges, mind you, but I'm beginning to think I could back him in a tight corner. He's a fighter, Gareth."

"Yes, I've seen that," replies Gareth, recalling the last time Rupert and James met, and the effort involved in separating the pair.

"We need to keep the youth coming through, Gareth," continues Averill. "A few more like James and young Rupert there and we'll be in good stead."

"Amen to that," replies Gareth, watching the two lads examining the pells, running their fingers across the cuts and slashes, noting where the charcoal marks have been struck and where they have been missed.

"But now, back to this little escapade of yours. I don't believe you've brought me out here to admire your ring of pells.

"And, I see there's a quintain over there under the tree. Rather dangerous isn't it? I can imagine a few split skulls from those low branches there."

Averill looks over toward the structure, and, as is his habit when thinking, begins to trace his left boot in a small arc on the ground.

"Well, I've had a couple of practice passes and it's not too bad. I'm going to start on it in earnest pretty soon. I wanted to make sure that it wasn't too easy; you know, a bit of uneven ground to challenge the aim, and something to focus the mind. I just thought that the possibility of knocking your brains out was a reasonable way of achieving that."

Gareth is suddenly torn between the humour of the response and the deeper recognition that the broken knight is, piece-by-piece, regaining much of the essence which made him such a great friend and outstanding leader.

"Where have you been, Gregory?" he asks. "You've been gone for so long. It's wonderful to have you back."

Averill shrugs, still looking at the ground. "It was a long way down, Gareth; a very long way down. I'll never ever be able to forget. The love will always be there... and the sadness." Then looking directly at Gareth. "I'll never forget her, Gareth; never. But now, I feel an urgency to move forward; to do something worthwhile again.

"Rupert was the first step. And, surprisingly, it was the way he started to change which inspired me. I don't know what it was, but seeing him grow, day-by-day, into a better and a more focussed young man, somehow rubbed off on me; convinced me that, perhaps, I should have a go, too.

"And that constant gnawing feeling in the pit of my stomach, every time I thought of that bastard, had just become too much. I had to do something about it."

Gareth nods, then places his hands on Averill's shoulders. "So, where do we start?"

"Right here," replies Averill, leading Gareth to the edge of the clearing. Bending down, he pulls out the wrapped skins which had been placed under the foliage the previous day. "Just some light work today, I think," he adds as he peels the skins back. "Choose."

Gareth is shaking his head and smiling hugely as he selects a sword. Then looking at the ring of scarred pells, he adds, "I hope I'm ready for this."

"Me too," replies Averill, hefting the sword and twirling it in his hand; tip of the blade not six inches from Gareth's nose.

The big man looks hard at Averill. "Bastard."

The two young squires pause in their examination of the cuts and slashes of the pells; looking over to where the two knights stand, swords brandished, facing each other.

"Oh shit," exclaims Rupert. "I've been waiting to see something like this."

"I've seen it before," replies James. "This is going to be fucking incredible."

Rupert looks, surprised, at James. "Shit, I thought you were a goody-goody; but, you swear too!"

"Abso-fucking-lutely!"

CHAPTER TWELVE

The change in routine has allowed Averill to spend days with Rupert, days alone, and days with Gareth. This has worked well for all concerned, since, as Averill recognised, there was going to come a time when Rupert needed to be exposed to the wider circle of squires, and to start taking in some of the courtly etiquette required of a budding knight. And so, with the friendship between Rupert and James blossoming at a surprising rate and the imperative of preparing himself for a tournament, Averill has accepted Gareth's offer to take Rupert under his wing in matters conducted at the castle. Averill, meanwhile, has continued his periods of work, alone, with Gareth, and with Rupert, away from the castle and its prying eyes.

The initial clash with Gareth had been instructive. He had known that the stationary pells would be good for re-training the muscles and gaining strength and precision in wielding the sword. But, the degree to which he had lost his battle-craft when dealing with a moving target disturbed him. Gareth was no slouch when it came to swordplay, and Averill quickly became aware of just how much effort was going to be required to regain anything approaching his former prowess.

Two more sessions had followed and although Averill was close to exhaustion at the end of each, Gareth had commented that they were starting to pick up the pace again. Just how much of the comment was encouragement and how much was realistic assessment, Averill was unsure. Nevertheless, in his mind there was no doubt: He had to be ready when the time came. And that time was not too far away. Already the strong heat of the middays was behind them, as the year progressed through the summer. The final tournament of the season was still some six weeks away, but those weeks would pass in no time, and there was still a minor mountain to scale. Averill was in two minds: was the timescale he had set himself so foolish as to be unachievable; in which case he was setting himself for serious embarrassment, as well as potentially serious injury? Or was the approaching deadline just what he needed to focus the mind and concentrate his efforts? There was, of course, no way of knowing which was true, and so, with characteristic single focus, he had chosen to lower his head and plough on with the training.

And now, sitting astride the sleek, white mare, lance upright, he trots towards the edge of the clearing, stops, turns, and breathes deeply as he views the undulating ground between himself and the quintain, and notes with a little concern that the overhanging branches are a little lower than he remembers from the first excited passes he had made a few weeks ago.

Another breath, then, tucking the lance under his arm, he gently spurs the mare and starts towards the quintain at a light gallop. The tip of the lance wanders alarmingly as they approach. Hanging leaves slash his face as he passes under the lowest branch. The pass is over, and the unmoved quintain mocks his effort.

And thus the afternoon continues. Time after time he returns to the edge of the clearing, and time after time, he and the mare gently gallop in over the undulating ground, up the slight incline, under the spreading branches and past the quintain. And time after time, the quintain remains unmoved; sometimes the miss is by a hair's breadth, sometimes it might as well be a mile.

Memories of such practice from years past return, when as a young squire he would charge back and forth cursing himself, and the quintain, and all those who relentlessly pushed him to do better. But this is a much older Averill now; one who understands frustration, one who knows the effort that is going to be required, one who has suffered so much that this frustration is but a flea-bite in the scheme of things. And so, he continues, even though perspiration impedes his vision and at least once causes him to graze his head on the lowest branch as it flashes by; even though shoulder muscles scream with the agony of maintaining the lance horizontal, and thighs ache from the effort of clinging to the mare as she charges across the irregular turf.

And, late in the afternoon, with the sun dipping to the west in a cloudless sky, the sweat-drenched knight calls a halt to the agony. Today has not been a day for revelling in his achievements. But, he knows from long experience, that he has been setting a platform for the next session, and the ones after that; knows that every muscle that aches today is better prepared for tomorrow, and knows that had he abandoned the work hours ago, when it would have been easy to do so, then he almost certainly would not be ready when the final tournament of the season came around.

The glade remains his private sanctuary; unknown to Rupert, or to Gareth and James. And so, at the end of the torture, he slides gratefully from Damsel's back, and leaning heavily upon her flanks, rests for a few minutes. Then, taking the reins in his hand, he starts towards the line of trees where he knows the entrance to the glade is concealed by the thick summer foliage.

Time for rest... and recovery.

★

Three weeks remain.

The inter-play between Rupert and James has become strong... and competitive. Averill and Gareth spend the mornings working with the boys, repeating wrestling holds, basic leg hooks and hip throws, over and again; and working the variations which are derived from these fundamental grappling positions, requiring the young squires to emulate them precisely. The youths' bodies are acquiring strength and resilience as they engage in the contests, straining in resistance, and coping with the falls and the bruises which accompany the harsh and demanding activities. There is no lack of application from the two young men, and the sweaty, sun-browned skins which both lads now exhibit, coupled with the impressively sculpted frames which are beginning to emerge, bear testament to the toughness of the activities and the commitment both are showing.

James has his father's strong build, whilst Rupert has some of his father's strength, but much of his mother's litheness and grace. However, as much as Rupert tries, when they lock arms there is only ever one outcome. But the effort required by James to achieve his victories is not trivial, and, day-by-day, the duration of Rupert's resistance to the bigger lad's strength is increasing.

The other aspect in which the knights are educating the squires is the art of swordsmanship. And here again, the additional strength which James possesses is evident. But, in this arena the inequality is countered by Rupert's blossoming precision and speed. James can now regularly deliver blows that would leave an unprotected arm or chest badly crushed or bruised, but is finding that the target is never where the blow is directed. Rupert's anticipation and speed have developed to the point where James is finding difficulty in ever getting his sword past the resolute defence offered by Rupert. And not only is the lighter-build squire's defence almost impregnable, but his attack is becoming swift and precise. James may have the better of the unarmed grappling, but Rupert's swordsmanship leaves the bigger youth gasping.

And, as the education continues, the knights frequently switch partners, so that neither boy is allowed to fall into the complacency of dealing with a single opponent, and a single fighting style.

On the days the four are together, lunchtimes are a time for light-hearted camaraderie; however, the younger pair of the quartet usually talk little as they recover from their exertions of the morning. And, more than once, the knights have tousled the hair of the young squires and commented rudely upon their inability to handle the pace as well as the old men.

But it is during the afternoons when the tone changes from aggressive but restrained to all-out aggression verging upon violence. Averill has insisted to Gareth that there be no restraint in the build-up to the tournament, and, as the weeks have progressed, Gareth has taken the ever-improving Averill at his word and is now bullocking the lighter but faster knight with his greater strength. Averill is countering the big man's aggression with anticipation, precision and speed. Both are now wearing thick protective vests and carrying shields as they wield the blunted practice swords. The boys, required to practise the lessons of the mornings upon each other, are committed to emulating their teachers. But the temptation to stop from time-to-time and watch the increasingly aggressive contests between the knights is overwhelming... and understandable. And neither Averill nor Gareth objects, for both know that not only is diligent practice required, but also observation of skilled men engaged in serious tactical combat carries many lessons which need to be observed, as well as explained.

The thrust, the parry, the sidestep, the lunge, the stumble, the recovery, the slashing riposte are repeated, again and again. The clash of metal upon metal and the thud of sword upon shield resound around the clearing as, sucking breath into burning lungs, the two knights heave and strain; swords and bodies clashing in unrestrained aggression.

No quarter is given; and none asked. The occasional 'yeh' is the only concession from one to the other as a good strike is recognised. The more frequent 'ahh', punched from the lungs of the combatants, involuntarily acknowledges the power of the strikes being absorbed.

★

One week to go.

The target of the quintain shudders, and the arm swings wildly from the strike of the lance; the sharp crack of the impact immediately drowned out by the thunder of hooves as the knight, lance tucked tightly into right armpit and weight directed towards the target, roars under the slashing leaves of the overhanging branch. The sandbag at the other end of the quintain's arm is suddenly jerked from rest and flung dangerously around into the path just taken by the horse and rider; but they are well clear and no impact occurs.

"Oh, good hit, Gregory; good hit," shouts Gareth, applauding above the noise.

As the mare slows, Averill drops the lance and stands in the stirrups to relieve the cramp which is now wracking his thighs and right arm. Rupert and James, waiting at the end of the course, run to collect the lance and carry it back to the start of the run.

"I think I might have had enough for today," confesses Averill as he brings the mare to a halt and slides, with little grace, from the saddle.

"Yes, I think that's a good call, Gregory," replies Gareth. "I'm not sure that quintain could take much more without us doing some repairs on it."

Averill smiles. "It wasn't too bad today, was it?" he comments.

"Not too bad?" ejaculates Gareth. "For God's sake, Gregory, if you'd hit that target any more times and with any more force, I swear the bloody thing would have split into a hundred pieces."

"Yes, it felt pretty good, I have to say," replies Averill; a satisfied smile lighting up his face.

"James, Rupert," calls Gareth. "That's all for today."

"Can we have a go?" comes the chorused response.

Gareth looks to Averill, who replies with a chuckle, "Do you really think we could stop them?"

"Yes, of course," shouts Gareth back to the boys. "James, you set up for Rupert, first."

And, as James trots toward the central oak to set the quintain, and Rupert runs to the edge of the clearing to collect his grazing horse, the two knights walk away, Gareth's hand on Averill's shoulder, the latter gingerly leading his glistening mare.

"Let me," orders Gareth, picking up the large cloth from the pile of belongings where they stop, then stepping over to the mare to begin rubbing her down.

"Well?" asks Averill.

"Well?" replies Gareth, deliberately obtuse, as he starts to un-cinch the saddle.

"Well, what do you think?"

"I think it all depends upon what you think," the big man replies. "Are you satisfied?"

"I think so," replies Averill. "It feels good."

"Yes," adds Gareth. "I think so, too."

"Ready?" asks Averill, seeking confirmation.

"Are you?" counters Gareth.

A pause, as Averill stands, hands on hips, surveying the scene, as fifty yards away Rupert mounts and James passes up the lance.

"Yes, Gareth," replies Averill, turning back. "I believe I am."

"And you're sure you want to go ahead with this?" asks Gareth one more time, pausing in his task.

"Yes, Gareth; I'm sure. It took me a long time to realise that this is what's been at the bottom of all that frustration and anger that has been welling up recently. But you know, now that I'm going to have a go at the bastard, I can hardly wait. You wouldn't believe the sense of purpose I feel now."

"Oh, I think I might," chuckles Gareth. "I've been on the receiving end of your aggression for quite a few weeks now; and believe me Gregory, you've been aggressive."

Averill looks slightly abashed. "Sorry."

"No, Gregory," replies Gareth. "I wouldn't have had it any other way. And if you'd been less aggressive and less able, I would have carved you up just to prove to you that you weren't ready for him.

"Believe me, Gregory," he continues, "if you hadn't been ready, I would have cut you to pieces. I have no intention of letting you go out to get maimed by that animal."

A small silence as Averill watches Rupert gallop gently in... and miss the target, by a very small amount. "We're a good team, Gareth; aren't we?"

"Aye, captain; that we are."

"No, I meant the four of us; the boys too."

"Yes, Gregory," replies Gareth, "so did I."

CHAPTER THIRTEEN

The king stands, hands behind his back, looking out the window onto the courtyard below.

"Your Majesty," says Averill, with a bow.

"Ah, Gregory," replies Henry, turning and walking towards his visitor. "Thank you for coming. Pray, be seated..."

Averill waits for the king to seat himself, then follows suit.

"I'm not sure whether to be angry or just plain alarmed," continues the king.

"Sire?" queries Averill.

"I'm reliably advised that your name appears as a challenger for the tournament."

"Ah... yes, it does, Your Majesty."

"I also understand that you are drawn against Bijou."

"Indeed, Your Majesty."

"This worries me, Gregory," continues Henry. "This has all the appearance of an emotional, ill-considered dice with death; and... unless you provide me with very good reason, my friend, I will not permit it."

Silence, as Averill absorbs the words, and the king regains control over his breathing.

"Pray, give me one good reason why I should allow this brutal slaughter to go ahead?" continues Henry. "You have not held a sword for more than two years now, and although you may have been out riding your beautiful mare, a quiet jaunt through the forests is a far cry from the rigours of the tournament field. And how on earth do you intend to manage a lance? My God, Gregory," adds the king, in anguish, "what on earth are you thinking? Do you want to get yourself killed?"

A slight pause, as Averill rises. "May I, Your Majesty?"

"Yes, of course," replies the king. Then, to reinforce the point, "Gregory, you are more dear to me than any other knight in my entire kingdom. You have been through more heartbreak and anguish than any man should have to bear. You have lost the most beautiful creature we, all of us, ever had the fortune to know; and, I have watched as you and Odelia have picked up the pieces of your shattered lives and re-built them, piece-by-piece. But I will not watch you destroy yourself in front of your daughter, and all who love you."

Silence again as Averill watches the king, gauging when it is appropriate to speak again.

Henry waves his hand, resignedly. "Talk to me, Gregory; tell me I am wrong. Tell me that some magic has taken place, and this is all a bad dream, and you are the fearsome knight I once knew, when the world was a happier and a more beautiful place."

"You are wrong, Your Majesty," begins Averill. No response, so he continues, "And, although this life we now have is completely real and not just a bad dream, and although the world is not the happier and more beautiful place we both once knew, things have happened, my Lord, of which you are not aware."

"You have my attention, Gregory," Henry replies.

"There is a clearing, Your Majesty," continues Averill, walking towards the window, "some way off in the forest. I came upon it quite by accident some months ago. I had been lost within myself for a long time, and had taken to riding through the land, seeking some comfort from life itself; but I had found none, and gradually, I had let myself drift aimlessly through the days, not caring where my horse would take me, not caring how long it took to get there, or to find my way back again.

"But this I think you know, my Lord."

"Indeed, Gregory," replies the king. "We watched you from afar, our hearts crying out to you; but unable to help, it were better we stood aside and let time perform its healing."

"Thank you, my Lord; I was not aware you had watched so closely."

A quiet, reflective moment. "I stumbled upon the clearing one day, quite by chance. And beside this clearing, through a barely visible break in the trees, I found a glade; a soft, gentle green vision of sunlight and shade, of running water, and warm, beckoning stone... and, somehow, it began to restore me; somehow, as I spent time in this place, the coldness within my soul began to disappear, the pain of emptiness began to lessen, and the barrier I had created between myself and the world around me began to crack and crumble.

"My Lord, over time it began to feel to me that the hand of God, himself, had touched this place and had given it the power to heal."

A pause as Averill considers how to move the story forward.

"I have spent much of the previous months in this clearing and in this glade, my Lord, and gradually, I have found a direction to my life again."

A wan, almost benevolent smile from the king as he looks up at Averill. "That is good to hear, Gregory; I am pleased for you."

Averill smiles, a little self-consciously. "And, I have discovered my daughter again, my Lord. For a long time I had lost her. I had abandoned her, and it was only the kindness of Wendy and Gareth which ensured that Odelia was loved and cared for while I was lost. For that, I carry a guilt which will not disappear quickly, my Lord. I felt my own pain, but did not recognise my daughter's; I spent time lost in my own world, when I should have been inhabiting hers.

"But, thankfully, those times are past, and I see her again, and share her world again, and give her all the love I can; although it still does not match the love and happiness she would be now experiencing had her mother lived."

A pause, as Averill reflects upon his words, and chooses the next.

"My Lord, if you were to visit this clearing today, you would see changes which have occurred during these last several months; changes I could not have imagined that first day.

"From memory, I believe there are now twenty-five pells around the edge of the clearing; and all bear the scars of serious attack. They have been hewn from the trees of the surrounding forest, stripped of leaves, sunk into holes dug in the earth, then smitten without mercy... by me... and a small number of conspirators, my Lord."

The king's jaw is slack, mouth slightly open, as he absorbs the revelation being delivered by Averill.

"And, my Lord, in the centre of the clearing, on a slight rise, is a large oak tree, under which..."

Averill pauses, waiting to see if the king will remember.

Henry looks up, surprised by the abrupt interruption to the story, and finds Averill looking intently at him, expectantly.

A moment's reflection. "My God, Gregory," exclaims the king, standing. "You've built a quintain, haven't you? You've built a bloody quintain; just like the one we had as boys."

"Well, not quite, Your Majesty," continues Averill, smiling. "It was actually Joseph the carpenter who built it; and it's very much better than the one we managed to lash together, my Lord. But, yes, Your Majesty, there is a quintain; a very sturdy quintain; although, I have to say that it, too, is looking a little battered at this moment."

Slowly, the king advances toward Averill.

"This small number of conspirators, Gregory," he continues. "Pray tell me who is among them?"

"Only three, my Lord: Gareth, and James, his son... and Rupert."

"Gareth I know, of course; and James I have seen often in the courtyard, practising with the other squires; although now that you mention it, it has been several weeks since I last noticed him there.

"And who is Rupert?"

"My squire, Your Majesty; son of William the blacksmith."

"I know him not, Gregory. Tell me about him."

"A young, misguided ruffian, my Lord; at least, he was when I first met him. He'd been in with the wrong crowd for some time, and the good within him had not been permitted to see the light."

"And you changed that, Gregory?"

"No, my Lord," replies Averill, looking down. "I merely provided the opportunity. He changed that himself."

Piece-by-piece, Henry is assimilating the information.

"And have you fought Gareth, Gregory?"

"Oh yes, Your Majesty; we have battled each other many times now. He's still as strong as an ox, of course."

"Of course," replies the king. "But you had the speed and the agility, Gregory. Do you still have it?"

"It seems to have returned, Your Majesty," replies Averill, with a small grin.

"And swordplay?"

"Ah," replies Averill. "There I have to thank William. He has provided the most appropriate selection of steel one could wish for; light and manageable when I started, then much heavier as the weeks passed; exactly as you know he should, my Lord."

The king nods in understanding.

"And with Joseph, they produced one of the most beautifully-sculpted pieces of whalebone I have ever beheld.

"I owe them much, my Lord."

"Indeed, Gregory; it sounds as if you do."

Another pause as Henry paces to the window, in thought, and back again.

"And, are you really ready, Gregory?" he asks with sincere concern.

"Yes, I believe so, my Lord," replies the knight, drawing himself upright, as if to reinforce the words.

Another longer pause as the two men regard each other, directly.

"Well then, Sir Gregory Averill, my very dear friend, it seems that I should not meddle in the arrangements for this tournament."

"Thank you, Your Majesty," replies the knight, smiling. "I am grateful."

"I should have known, Gregory, shouldn't I?"

"Perhaps, Your Majesty," agrees Averill; then thoughtfully, "But then again, perhaps not; this has been a very strange road.

"You know of my loss, my Lord; there is no point in re-telling it; and I have visited depths I did not know existed; and yet somewhere along the journey I felt the hand of God upon my brow; in the sunlight of a glade, and the sound of a running brook, and the warmth of a rude stone bed. And... I have re-discovered friendships which I had taken for granted. I have found a young man of talent languishing at the bottom of a cesspool and have been brightened by his progress and, indeed, by his friendship; and I have found my daughter again, with a grace and a beauty which must have come upon her whilst I was lost in my grieving. She carries her mother's beauty and her spirit, in her own unique way, my Lord, and has provided the light to bring me through the darkness.

"All these things, all these blessings, could not have been foreseen, my Lord."

★

The beautiful, hand-carved wooden trunk is open. Piece-by-piece, Averill unwraps the oiled steel from the skins in which each piece had been packed away more than two years ago, and lays it upon the floor. He runs his finger across the breastplate, noting the smoothness of the polished steel, protected all this time by the thin film which William had applied as Averill had sat slumped in the corner of the room, watching, but not really noticing, what the blacksmith had been doing.

Gareth had called him, and together they had taken Averill's armour that day, and cleaned it, and oiled it, and packed it away in the knight's trunk; ready for use one day sometime in the future, when the horror of the recent events had receded sufficiently to allow the knight to contemplate donning it again.

Taking up one of the pieces of rag dropped in a heap on the floor, Averill begins to slowly wipe the metal dry. Lost in the memories unlocked by the activity, he does not hear the approaching footsteps.

A figure kneels quietly beside him and wraps her arms around his shoulders.

"So, it's true."

He looks into Odelia's eyes, noting the excitement, but also detecting uncertainty in her demeanour.

"Yes, Odelia, it's true," he answers with an attempt at lightness.

"I'm going to be so proud of you, Daddy," she continues.

"Well, I'm pleased about that," responds Averill. "I'd be very unhappy if you weren't."

"Oh, Daddy," she laughs. "Of course I'll be proud of you. It's just that… he's good isn't he? And dangerous?"

"Yes, Odelia, he is good. And, yes, he is dangerous. But didn't you tell me that I was the best?"

"Yes, but…"

"And didn't you also tell me that I could even beat Gareth?"

"Yes, but..."

"And didn't Gareth nearly beat him last time?"

"Yes, Daddy, but..."

"So, it should be alright then, shouldn't it?" he challenges, with a laugh.

"Oh, Daddy!" she exclaims. "Be serious."

"I am, Odelia," he replies, "I am." Then softly, "I wouldn't be doing this if I didn't think I could handle it. I wouldn't be risking injury if I thought I wasn't ready for it. And, I wouldn't be risking embarrassing both you and me if I thought I was going to get badly beaten."

"Are you sure, Daddy?"

"Yes, sweetie, I'm sure," he lies.

"I love you, Daddy," she coos, hugging him tightly again.

"I know, sweetie," he replies, stroking her hair. "That's what makes my life worthwhile, don't you know?"

"Now you're teasing me, Daddy."

"Am I? I don't think so."

She smiles demurely; pleased at the words.

"Now, off you go and let me finish getting all of this stuff ready. It's been a long time since it was used and I need to check everything; all the straps, all the buckles. Although I must say, William did an excellent job in packing it away; it still looks as good as new."

Still hugging his shoulders, she kisses his forehead, then rises. "Bye, Daddy. Make sure everything is perfect. We don't want anything to fall off now, do we?"

Averill chuckles at the light-hearted admonition, and still kneeling, watches as she walks lightly from the room.

He continues to stare at the empty doorway, remembering the origin of that light-hearted walk; then, wiping the dampness from his cheek, turns his attention back to the trunk.

The bascinet is next.

He holds it in two hands, moving the visor with his thumbs; pleased that the movement is firm, but smooth. He really does owe the blacksmith much for his craftsmanship and his dedication to his trade. No-one could have prepared the equipment for storage better than William has done.

The gauntlets are next. Slowly, he rubs the thin, oily film from the outside of each one, then tears the cloth into strips and, twirling them into fine fingers, stuffs them inside to soak up the slight residual traces of oil within the fingerplates.

Placing the gauntlets aside, he picks up another piece of clean rag, and, wiping the oil from his fingers, looks into the trunk once again. The ruffled material in the corner, visible now that the gauntlets no longer cover it, stares back at him. His heart lurches and fingers tremble as he reaches in... and draws out the beautifully coloured silk scarf.

The loss and the despair, so valiantly held at bay for so long now that he had believed he was on top of them, crash in upon him once again. Tears falls softly to the floor as he slowly leans forward and rests his forehead upon the dark wooden edge of the trunk, overpowered by the vision of Mariel, head back, eyes closed, swirling the same scarf above her head as a busy, gold-speckled hen pecked at the dusty ground at her feet. The moment is frozen in time as the scarf descends upon her long black hair, shining richly in the early morning sunlight.

He remembers how his heart had pounded, how their eyes had engaged, transfixed, unable to tear their gaze away from each other, how his body had strained at the paralysis immobilising it. He remembers the wild, giddy, boyish, uncoordinated lurch as he had broken free of the spell and stepped forward to retrieve the fallen scarf; how he had risen, hesitantly, leather gauntlets in one hand, scarf in the other, to find himself looking into deep, brown eyes set in almond-shaped lids, framed by the exquisite oriental features of a slightly upturned face, already flushing pink, only inches from his own. He remembers he was lost for words.

He remembers the feel of her fingers as she had reached out to touch the recent scar on his cheek. He remembers how, he, in turn, had reached out across a gulf of silence and placed his fingers beneath her chin, delicately turning her head towards his own; how a further slight pressure had raised her face, until warm, brown eyes, framed in almond-shaped lids and swimming in tears, had looked up into his.

He remembers falling in love.

★

Tomorrow.

There is no more to do now; no further preparation he can make, no further training he can usefully undertake; no further assurances he can provide to all of those concerned for his well-being.

The shock and the sadness of yesterday have settled now, and in their place a calmness has descended upon him; as if events are now beyond his control. There is a fatalistic undertone to his thoughts, which has taken away the anguish which had, once again, threatened to engulf him just hours ago.

Candles burn in the hallway, but the bedroom remains unlit as he gazes out into the deepening gloom. The moon shines intermittently through the trees as she slowly rises above the eastern horizon.

What are the chances of winning? What are the chances of serious injury? What are the chances that, when he confronts Bijou, all of the hatred and the anger and the torment and the despair of these last years will come to nothing? What are the chances that he is an imposter, about to be found out by a younger and a better knight; a knight whom he hates with a passion, but a knight who is the king's champion, and, as such, is no slouch in battle?

Doubt, emptiness, fear: all compete for dominance. And yet, the underlying serenity which has come upon him in these last few hours manages to push them all to the back of his mind.

Not even Henry had known of his progress; had known how much pain, and effort, and toil had been devoted to this task. And so, he knows that there is no expectation, by anyone else, that he will be anything other than entertainment value tomorrow. After all, he is, as far as the world is concerned, a relic of the past, a ghost from a time when the king was a prince, and an angel from the east had arrived to captivate a court; a time when the impossible was achieved with ease, and dreams were there to be lived; forever, it had seemed.

And so, he knows that there is no pressure upon him, other than that which he creates himself; knows that regardless of the outcome, he will continue to be loved by his daughter; knows that Gareth will remember, with affection, the efforts they have shared in furious combat in the clearing; knows that Rupert and James will urge him on with youthful confidence and eagerness, and be momentarily disappointed if he fails, but that it will not affect their young lives terribly much; knows that Henry will watch with affection borne of years shared in camaraderie and combat, but in all probability, expects him to fail.

He reflects further, and is surprised at what has happened to him; how the growing confidence and the eagerness of the past few weeks have been tempered by the emotions of yesterday; how the urgency and the excitement of the final days in the clearing have been replaced by a calm confidence that all will be well, and that, should he fail, as well he might, then so be it. The sun will not fail to rise in the east, nor the rains cease to fall in the wintertime.

Of course, Gareth and Rupert and James will be disappointed; they have, all of them, himself included, worked hard for this, and the boys, in particular, have revelled in the excitement. Odelia, he knows, will feel the loss most keenly. She is his life, his reason for being, and he has the growing feeling that, just at this moment, she loves him like a hero, and heroes are supposed to win. But she is young, and, given all that she has been through, his defeat will be easily absorbed by her young woman's confidence.

He continues to gaze over the scene outside the window, and slowly and without form, a feeling of melancholy descends upon him; a realisation that the picture tomorrow will not be complete, that the central piece of the tapestry of his life will be missing.

He wonders how he will handle her absence.

He recalls the tournaments of the past; the ones before he met her, when any number of women would claim his attention, but never his heart; and the ones after she had entered his life and become his beloved, when he would take inspiration from her presence, from her smile, from her beauty, and charge at his opponents, driven by the fearsome power of his desire, and obsessed with the commitment to deliver victory for her.

He sighs, long and deep, and, gradually, piece-by-piece, the sadness recedes.

The moon is above the treetops now; the garden outside bathed in pale, silvery light. Expectantly, he adjusts his gaze and looks into the trees, and finds her there; his owl, all fluffed and silent, looking directly at him.

The calmness is complete. He is ready.

CHAPTER FOURTEEN

The morning is cool and fresh as Averill strides, invigorated by a sound sleep, towards the pavilion, topped by the light blue pennant of his armorial bearings moving lazily in the very slight breeze. He nods, a little self-consciously, as two passers-by wish him well for the afternoon. *Strange*, he muses. *I feel like a new boy, and yet there are still one or two who seem to remember me.*

He is uplifted by the thought that, perhaps, there might be a few others in the crowd, who still remember the happier times, and would like to see him victorious; just for old times' sake.

He stops outside the entrance to the tall segmented tent, and, for a moment, allows his gaze to sweep over the collection of pavilions, laid out by the king for the participants in this afternoon's tournament. Henry has honoured him with a location which allows him a vista over all of the other pavilions. But, as protocol would demand, Bijou's tent is at the same level; but on the other side of the sloping field.

The thrill is still there.

Then, with his mind to the task ahead, he enters.

"Good morning, Sir Gregory," the squires chorus, as Rupert gets up from his knees, where he has been brushing the last of the dirt from the light, patterned carpet.

Averill does not reply as he gazes around the interior of the tent; suddenly silenced by the beauty and the quality of the appointments provided by the king. His gaze rests upon his armour; recently polished, and equally beautifully laid out.

"Thank you, Rupert," he offers, quietly. "The armour looks... outstanding."

"Thank you, Sir Gregory," the squire replies, bursting with pride. "James helped me with it."

Almost overcome with emotion at the unexpected splendour within the tent, Averill advances and wraps his arms around the necks of the two squires, hugging them tightly to him. "And, by God," he vows, "I will do my best to make you as proud of me as I am of you two."

"And so you bloody well should," adds a third voice, as Gareth strides in, flanked by Anthony and Thomas.

"Well Gregory," remarks Thomas, looking about. "It seems our king hasn't forgotten you."

"No," replies Averill, quiet again. "He has done me great honour here today. I only hope that I can repay him adequately; by not being a total failure when the time comes.

"But I also see some of my own pieces here; special things: the velvet cushions, the tasselled banner; things I treasured; things which I had forgotten. I just don't know how he found them all."

"No, nor do I," replies Gareth, looking about and nodding his approval.

"Nor me," add Anthony and Thomas, unable to keep the grins from their faces.

Suddenly the penny drops. Averill turns slowly back to the trio still standing at the entrance.

"You bastards. You've all had a hand in this, haven't you?"

"Well," drawls Gareth, hands upturned in appeal. "He did ask; and who are we to deny our king?"

"Well, hello," adds a new voice as three more figures make their way into the tent.

"My God," exclaims Bryan, looking around, and, for once, devoid of any smart comment. "Very nice, Gregory; very nice."

"Amen to that," add Charles and Robert, equally non-plussed.

A pause, then the obvious, and unstated, question from Anthony: "So, Gregory..."

"Indeed," replies Averill.

Another pause.

"Well, that was instructive," comments Bryan, looking from face to face around the group.

Averill chuckles and, one-by-one, the others join in as the tension is relieved. Then, spying Rupert, standing silently at the back of the pavilion, Averill continues, "Gentlemen, I'd like to introduce someone who has played no small part in bringing me to this point today; I'd like to introduce Rupert, my squire, to you all.

"Rupert is the son of William the blacksmith, whom you all know; and a swordsman of the future, I predict."

Each of the knights offers greetings, and shakes Rupert's hand, in turn. The young man glows with pride.

"That's some faith you have to live up to, young man," comments Thomas.

"Yes, Sir Thomas," replies Rupert, looking directly back at the knight. "I'm just starting to realise how big a task that will be."

"And of course you all know James," continues Averill. "Gareth's son."

And the assembled knights recognise the second young man's presence in the pavilion.

"I wouldn't wish to be anywhere else in the world this morning," blurts James, suddenly, then looks down, embarrassed.

Gareth smiles, and gently places his arm around his son's shoulder. "Nor I, my boy; nor I."

The atmosphere in the tent has the charge of a thunderstorm.

"How do you feel, Gregory?" asks Thomas.

"Strange," replies Averill. "If you'd asked me two days ago, I would have said 'raring to go.' But now, I feel this strange... peacefulness; as if everything is somehow under control. I don't know what it is. On the one hand, I can't wait for the next few hours to pass, so that I can get out onto the course and face the bastard. And yet, on the other hand, it sort of... doesn't matter.

"Perhaps it's my mind, preparing me for the ignominious departure I'm about to make," he chuckles.

"And perhaps it isn't," interjects a soft, feminine voice as Wendy and Odelia and Sarah enter the tent, all bearing folded bundles of predominantly light-blue clothing.

"Wendy, how lovely to see you," intone the group in various forms.

"Ah, more introductions," remarks Averill. "Odelia, you all know," the young lady curtseys, "and Sarah, Odelia's maid... and constant accomplice in trouble." The second young lady curtseys and blushes.

"Now, these are for you," continues Wendy, passing Averill's armorial doublet and surcoat to the knight.

"And these are for you," adds Odelia, taking two paces to stand in front of Rupert. The shock and embarrassment overwhelm the squire, who stands stock-still as Odelia proffers the garments.

"They're your squire's outfit... for this afternoon," she adds.

The young man takes the bundle and bows self-consciously. "Thank you... miss," he adds, quite unable to think of the correct form of response to a knight's daughter.

Wendy smiles. Averill notices and bristles. "No."

Wendy looks directly at him. "Time marches on Gregory; little girls grow up..."

"And these are for your horse," states Sarah; and the tent erupts into laughter.

Embarrassed for her, Averill looks toward the young maid. "Thank you, Sarah," he replies. "You have all done me a great service today; I am humbled by my family and my friends."

★

It is early afternoon. Averill has decided to retain the sleek, white mare for the joust. He feels that the bond between them is worth more than the strength of the other beasts in his stable. Whether this proves to be so remains a gamble, but he is comfortable with his decision.

The mare is ready now: the hard, moulded crupper of boiled and hot-waxed leather, known as cuir bouilli, protects her body, and the chanfrein of the same material protects her head. Resplendent in her trappings, she stands, contentedly, outside Averill's pavilion.

Inside, Gareth and Anthony are attending to the knight's final preparations. Rupert and James are assisting from time-to-time, but mainly attending to Rupert's first public outing as a squire. Rupert has a thousand questions of James, who has filled this role several times before, and is, without bravado, providing the benefit of his experience.

Averill has already donned the padded inner doublet, leather leggings and soft leather shoes. The hinged metal greaves and sabatons are already in place over the leggings and shoes, as Anthony and Gareth each fit a roundel over a knee joint.

"Right then, on your feet," instructs Gareth, as he and Anthony rise and walk over to take up breastplate and backplate. A few moments of gentle manoeuvring and the plates are in place and pinned.

Averill checks for freedom of movement. "So, you still think this is a good idea, then?" he comments, with a grin.

"Who better to cut the bastard down to size?" replies Gareth, without hesitation.

"Hmmm," replies Averill, "just checking. You know, in case you were having second thoughts."

Gareth mutters something very profane under his breath, whilst Averill looks over and winks at James.

"And now this," says Anthony, as he carries over the exterior doublet, bearing Averill's coat-of-arms – the black dragon passant upon bleu celeste – and helps the knight work his arms through the appropriate openings.

"Wow," remarks Rupert, as Anthony completes the lacing and stands back. "That looks so good."

Gareth, hands on hips, stands beside Anthony, inspecting the finished product, and nods quietly.

"Well, Gregory," he comments, "I wasn't sure I would ever see this day again, my friend."

Averill's eyes sparkle as he smiles. The delight is unmistakable.

A slight breeze stirs in the pavilion as the entry flap is withdrawn and three beautifully attired women step in.

"We just wanted to see you before you left," says Wendy.

Odelia, gorgeous in burnt orange silk, advances the few paces to Averill and stops before him.

"You look wonderful, Daddy; I am so proud of you."

Then, quietly, she allows the material clutched in her hand to unravel into view. "You always used to wear this, Daddy," she says, softly. "Would you wear it today?"

Overcome, and unable to respond, Averill nods, as his daughter ties the beautiful silk scarf, retrieved from the carved wooden trunk, to his upper arm.

Rupert stands, transfixed by the tenderness of the scene and the incredible beauty of the young woman. She turns to gaze at him; now a handsome young man with dark curly hair, resplendent in short black boots, dark blue leggings, and pale blue jupon emblazoned with Averill's coat-of-arms.

"Oh," is all she says.

Wendy wipes silent tears from her cheek, and wishes that another woman could also be here, to see the blossoming of her daughter's first love.

And Averill knows better than to comment as the two young people gaze at each other. Gently, he holds his daughter to him. Her eyes are still on Rupert. "Well then," he remarks, very quietly. "I suppose we should be about our business."

★

Rupert carries the tasselled standard with obvious pride, whilst Averill sits astride Damsel, surprisingly calm.

There are still two jousts to be completed before Averill's challenge to Bijou, but already he has heard whispers that suggest that the king's one-time champion has not quite been forgotten.

But, he has also heard whispers that there are fears for his life, since, there is no way he could be ready to take on the champion. He has been away from tournaments for so long, and has been seen as recently as last winter, trudging aimlessly over the cold, snowy ground, searching for God only knows what. There is concern that his mind has gone, and that this challenge today is the ill-conceived wish of a deranged man. There are even whispers that the king will intervene before the bout begins, to protect the life, if not the reputation, of his one-time champion.

The sound of applause impinges upon his thoughts as Gareth approaches. "It's time, Gregory."

Averill smiles a thin smile. He looks down at Rupert. "Walk proudly, my boy. This means a lot, today."

The young squire looks up at the knight, seated upon the sleek white mare and, for the briefest moment, recalls the first time he had seen him; the broken

259

down old man who used to slink out of the town in the early mornings; unshaven, lost, bereft of hope and sanity; the man his father had said used to be the king's champion, until something terrible and unfair had happened to him. He wipes the tear from his cheek. "Yes, Sir Gregory; I will."

Averill sighs, smiles at Gareth and looks around. He notices the varying greens of the closer and the more distant hills. He notices the blue of the sky; almost the same colour as his surcoat. He notices the soft, white clouds, and imagines that one of them might just be cradling the spirit of the woman who once defined his life; and that she may be here today, to watch over him.

He looks at Gareth again. "I wish I could remember her voice, Gareth," he says, quietly. "That is something I wish, very much."

Then, looking towards the stands, he breathes deeply, and almost imperceptibly touches the spurs to Damsel's flanks.

★

And so, at last, it has come to this.

PART 4

CHAPTER ONE

The column of knights canter along the cobbles of the market place, then around the corner and out of view as they head toward the east gate. The fluttering pennants show alternately bright and dark as the column passes through the long shadows of the early autumn morning.

"Well then," remarks Henry. "They've gone."

"Indeed, Your Majesty," replies Averill, standing alongside the king and also looking out from the map-room window.

"Still, in the scheme of things, it is nothing," adds Henry. "Bijou will return to France with his small band, and no doubt join the Armagnac cause, and a growing rift in our forces will be healed.

"As you see, Gregory; there is always a positive side to be found, if you only look for it."

Averill smiles. "You are not concerned, my Lord?"

"What, over Bijou's defection from my court? Hardly, Gregory; I have you, what more do I need?"

"Ah, Your Majesty," chuckles Averill. "As you know, full well, I am retired now. I have proven to myself, and, if I may say, to you, Your Majesty, that I still have a fire in the belly; enough to be dangerous on the odd occasion. But as for further campaigns, my Lord, I will leave that to younger and more gallant knights."

"So you tell me, Gregory," Henry replies with a laugh. "So, you tell me. But, as you know, I have further business in France, and I am raising an army, as we speak, to pursue this business. There is a role for you if you want it, Gregory."

"You honour me, my Lord, but my decision is firm."

"Yes," replies the king, unperturbed. "I thought you would stick to your stubborn views; which is why I have another requirement of you."

Averill's response is a mixture of interest and caution; knowing that the king gives his all to his office, and expects the same from those who serve him. He waits.

"Our last venture to France," continues Henry, "secured us the port of Harfleur, which was our first objective, since that gives us access to the Seine, and thence to Paris itself. And God, himself, walked with us as we returned home along the road to Calais, with its enforced detour via the fields near Agincourt. But, of France, there is much more to conquer, if we are to achieve our just rights and inheritances, both in Normandy, which is our next objective, and thence to Paris and the crown, which is our ultimate goal.

"And, achieving this, Gregory, will not be a trivial task. I shall be absent from England for quite some time to come.

"My brother, Bedford, and I have discussed his appointment as my lieutenant in England; to rule at home whilst I am engaged in France. And it is to his service that I seek your commitment. Your retirement from combat may be your wish, and I will respect your wishes, but your continued service to your king is my wish, and I would be greatly pleased if you would accept this post."

"Your Majesty," replies Averill, "I would be honoured to serve your brother in whatever capacity he requires."

"Good," continues the king. "And you know Bedford, as well as you know me. He is as passionate as I am about our cause, and, I think you will agree, a fine soldier. I think I could do no better than count upon him to act in my stead.

"Especially," he adds, "if I knew that he had access to your, often quite direct, counsel."

"Indeed, Your Majesty," replies Averill with a chuckle. "Bedford is a fine choice, and fortunately, he already has a familiarity with my, as you say, sometimes rather direct counsel."

"And he looks upon you the same way I do Gregory," adds the king to seal the arrangement. "You have been our valiant companion for many years now, and our love for you has never been misplaced."

Averill smiles in appreciation. "Then, by your leave, Your Majesty, I feel I should now depart and speak with the duke in order to better understand my new duties."

Henry waves him away with a smile. "Be gone then, Gregory... and don't disappoint me."

The words have a familiar ring. The map-room carries so many memories of times past, of meetings with the king, of challenges and charges. It seems a long time since he has walked from this room with purpose in his stride. But today is such a day.

★

Late September usually brings variety to the weather in England, and this year is no exception. The beautiful blue skies of the past few weeks have now been replaced by low, grey cloud, and the general feeling is that a long winter may be ahead.

Persistent, soft rain has been falling since morning, and Averill has had neither the opportunity nor the desire to venture out. But, as evening has approached, the rain has begun to clear, and Averill now stands at the first-floor window, transfixed by the beauty of the rainbow shimmering above the clouds scudding across the gradually clearing sky.

"C'est magnifique, n'est-ce pas?"

She stares, also mesmerised by the beauty of nature's spectacle, long auburn hair trailing down the sweep of her back, dark eyes focussed upon the beauty of the rainbow.

Then turning to face him, she continues: "Sir Gregory Averill, isn't it?" A pause, then, with a gentle, but almost challenging smile, she adds: "Recently retired, I understand."

"You have me at a disadvantage," replies the knight, smiling a little self-consciously, and noting the ease with which she carries herself.

"Perhaps I may be of assistance," interrupts an accented voice from behind Averill.

Averill turns to face a remotely familiar face; but a face to which he cannot put a name.

"I am Pierre de Montford, Sir Gregory; formerly, a member of the company of Sir René Bijou, and this…"

"I thought you'd all left," interrupts Averill, not particularly graciously.

"Mais non, Sir Gregory," replies the Frenchman, carefully. "Many of Bijou's circle left with him, but there are still a few of us who are Burgundians, first and foremost, and who chose to remain."

Averill is still bristling at the mention of the despised name.

An awkward pause, then: "I was about to introduce the lady, Sir Gregory."

"Oh, indeed," replies Averill, recovering slightly. "I apologise for my rather sharp tone, Sir Pierre; but there were reasons which…"

The voice fades, as Averill looks out the window; and once again, an awkward silence descends.

De Montford hesitates, then decides. "Sir Gregory Averill," he continues, "may I introduce my sister, Lady Elvira de Montford?"

Averill's attention is drawn sharply back. "Lady Elvira," he replies, taking the lady's graciously proffered hand, and bowing formally. "I saw you at the banquet, several weeks ago, although we did not speak."

"Yes, Sir Gregory," replies Elvira, curtseying, eyes sparkling as a ray of sunlight breaks through the thinning clouds, illuminating the trio. "I remember."

"I'm afraid I wasn't very good company that night," continues Averill. "I was a little tired, you might say."

Elvira laughs. "Dear Sir Gregory," she continues. "If I had been through what you had been through that day, I think I might have been a little tired, also."

Averill smiles, but says nothing, unable to understand the strange set of emotions building within him; a combination of interest and resistance.

De Montford continues, "Elvira has been at court here since summer, Sir Gregory. I invited her to join me for the May celebrations, and she has not yet returned home."

Averill stands still for a moment, torn between the uncharacteristic desire to talk further, and his more usual tactic of ending the pointless chit-chat as soon as possible.

"If you'll both excuse me, I really need to be getting on. I still have a number of things to complete before the end of the day. It was lovely to meet you, Lady Elvira," he continues, "and nice to know that you're still here with us, Sir Pierre."

"Of course, Sir Gregory," replies de Montford. "I'm sure we will bump into each other again soon."

"Goodnight, Sir Gregory," adds Elvira, with a soft smile.

Averill turns and walks quickly down the carpeted hallway, aware of Elvira's soft, gentle laughter in response to her brother's continued conversation. The strange, unsettling stirrings of interest persist.

CHAPTER TWO

The weeks have flown, and Averill seems to have covered the country from top to toe. Rupert and James have been busy with the other squires back at the castle, engaged in lessons from the elegance of courtly dance to the mucking out of the king's stables; all good character building activities, in Averill's view. Meanwhile, Averill, Anthony, Gareth, Charles, Robert, Thomas and Bryan have ridden hundreds of miles, visiting towns and villages in the twenty-odd counties around London, fulfilling the assignments allocated them by the Duke of Bedford. And, in response to at least one of the tasks, an impressive stock of goose feathers is now being assembled in the Tower of London. The manufacture of arrows for the coming campaign is now in full swing.

Meanwhile, at all points along the route traversed by the contingent, captains of local garrisons have been charged, in no uncertain terms, with the responsibility of achieving a fighting standard, in both men-at-arms and archers, consistent with the objective of winning the trail to Paris itself. The knights have, on more than one occasion, when the local standard was clearly inadequate for effective contribution to the forthcoming invasion, set the scene with frightening clarity in mock combat; between themselves, by way of example; and with the locals, for demonstration of the damage that a well-trained enemy soldier can cause. And none of the captains has been left in any doubt as to the assessment of the preparedness of his men; some congratulated, many given well-researched suggestions and advice, and a few taken behind the stables and verbally lashed until the perilousness of their situations penetrates the sometimes thick skulls.

And, in all cases, the promise of the certainty of a return visit by the troupe has been sufficient to cause the captains to take the message to heart.

★

A light snow is falling as the seven horses trot under the portcullis in the gathering gloom, and continue down the cobbles toward the eastern stables. Eager squires run forward to take the mounts as the knights dismount, and one-by-one stretch muscles cramped from sitting in the saddle through this last long push home.

"Oh, thank God," groans Gareth. "I feel as if I've been riding for weeks."

"That's because you have, you big git," retorts Bryan, falling over, obligingly, as the big man gives him a shove into the snow.

"Oh, that's really beautiful," comments Thomas, looking up at the castle.

The knights stop their banter, momentarily, and turn to follow Thomas's gaze.

"Yes, indeed," remarks Averill, looking at the lanterns and decorations strung from virtually every window and doorway of the castle. "It's good to be home for Christmas."

★

The light and merry sounds of the lute and the dulcimer are clear above the general babble of conversation from the assembling guests, even whilst Averill and his companions are still walking down the hallway approaching the Great Hall, in which the Christmas banquet in to be held. Frequent laughter carries from the direction of the hall as the guests begin to enjoy the occasion; and Odelia is as excited as Averill can remember. She is holding Wendy's arm tightly and chattering excitedly, as Gareth and Averill follow along behind.

At the doorway to the hall they pause, as Odelia turns to Averill.

"Oh, Daddy; it's absolutely beautiful."

"Yes, Odelia," he replies, looking across the scene laid out before them, then smiling back at her. "It certainly is."

The tables have been set around the hall, all draped with white linen, upon which wreathes of holly have been centrally placed. The king's table is laid out with pewter platters and goblets, and a centrepiece comprising a gilt tower, upon which Henry's royal arms, the lions of England quartered with the fleurs-de-lys of France, are emblazoned. The wall braziers have been polished and replenished with new torches; their light augmented by that from candles in the three pewter candelabra on each table. And stretching around on either side of the king's great chair, velvet cushions have been laid out on benches for the seventy-odd guests, many of whom have now arrived.

Gareth takes the Lady Wendy and leads her into the hall as a lithe, well-built young man stops in front of Averill and Odelia, and bows graciously. Dark curly hair has been washed and groomed. A doublet of muted crimson with long flowing sleeves offsets black leggings. Fawn doeskin boots complete the picture.

"May I escort you, Miss Odelia?" he enquires.

"Oh Rupert," she responds, blushing slightly and curtseying in response. "That would be lovely." Then, momentarily concerned, she turns to Averill. "Oh, Daddy, you'll be alone."

"My dear Odelia," he replies, "don't worry so. There are a hundred people here I know. There's no chance of me being alone tonight."

"Daddy, there aren't a hundred people here," she admonishes.

"Well, perhaps that's so," he concurs. "But there are more than enough to keep me company, I assure you."

Then to Rupert: "You take good care of my daughter, young man; she's very precious to me."

"Yes, Sir Gregory, replies the squire, seriously. Then, after a moment's hesitation, he adds, quite gently, "She's very precious to me, too, Sir Gregory."

Averill's heart lurches and he looks hard at the young squire. He isn't ready for this. For a moment he considers a brusque response, but then looks more carefully at the young man standing before him; well-groomed, serious, and displaying a degree of maturity which Averill recognises is a development for which he, himself, should accept a good deal of responsibility.

"Yes, Rupert," he replies. "I believe she well may be."

He stands alone in the doorway, watching as the two youngsters rush into the hall and disappear among the guests. *Where did they go*, he wonders; *all those years? One minute, she's a little girl, now, she's a young woman. And I just didn't see it coming.*

"It happens so quickly, doesn't it?"

The voice is warm and softly accented. He turns.

"Lady Elvira," he responds, taking her hand, and bowing slightly. "And Sir Pierre; how good to see you again."

"Yes, indeed, Sir Gregory," replies de Montford. "I foresee a most enjoyable evening ahead. It seems that your king has as fine a commitment to culture at home as he has to aggression in the field; I am impressed."

Averill smiles and nods. He hesitates, not quite sure how to move the conversation on, and thinks about excusing himself.

"Would you mind, Sir Gregory," continues de Montford. "I am required elsewhere for a few moments. Would you do me the honour of escorting my sister for a short time?"

"No," replies Averill, taken off-guard. "That is, no, I wouldn't mind at all," he corrects.

De Montford beams at them both, and then disappears into the throng of guests.

An awkward pause, then the Lady Elvira threads her arm through Averill's. "Well, Sir Gregory, shall we stand here in the doorway all night, or should we enter and join the party?"

Averill looks at her, uncertainly. Such poise, such elegance. Suddenly, he feels too much of a little boy to handle the situation. Then, warmly, she leans into him. "Come on, dear Gregory," she smiles, "it's Christmas; be happy."

269

He smiles back at her, confused by his own feelings, and allows her to lead him into the hall.

Across the room, Wendy observes... and smiles.

★

The feast was quite sumptuous. Swans and peacocks had been brought to the high table with their feathers still in place; having been thoroughly roasted before being slipped back into their skins for presentation to the king. And the several choices of main course for the entire gathering had included meat from a boar killed during the hunt at the start of the week, a carcass of beef stuffed with turnips and carrots and herbs, rabbits and geese caught wild, along with a number of pigs and pheasants reared especially for the occasion. Lightly fruited breads and mince pies with dried fruits and spices had supplemented the main dishes. Ale, apple cider and mulled wine had been served throughout the meal, and cheese and strawberries and stewed plums had completed the feast.

And behind each course, the musicians had entertained; and between the courses, the poetry readings had been enthusiastically received by the assembled guests.

Henry's speech, although pious, as befitted the occasion, had nonetheless been surprisingly light-hearted, given that he was preparing for war with France in the coming summer. Nothing, it seemed, was going to spoil the spirit and the revelry of the night.

Eventually though, the guests reached the point where more food could simply not be consumed, and more than one expressed the sentiment that if he ate any more he was sure to burst.

The arrival of the king's jester, accompanied by more musicians bearing flute and drums and tambourines, was greeted with noisy approval from the high-spirited bulk of the gathering. However, for others, this change of pace signalled the opportunity to retire to a quiet corner of the hall to either chat quietly, or to curl up and sleep off the effects of too much food and drink.

The corner to which Averill and Elvira have retired is gently lit by subdued light from the braziers on the opposite wall, and comfortably warm from the glowing log fire close by.

"Did you enjoy your first Christmas banquet in England, Lady Elvira?" enquires Averill, attempting to settle himself down into a comfortable position, as she sits gracefully on a floor cushion beside him.

"Yes, I did, Gregory," she replies, "although I found it a little more boisterous than the banquets to which I am more accustomed."

Averill is once again knocked off-guard, unsure as to whether he has just been reproached or not.

270

"I'm sorry," he replies.

"Oh no," she says. "I wasn't complaining; just commenting on the difference. In fact, I feel that I have enjoyed myself more tonight than I have at many of the banquets at home."

Averill smiles, relieved that the mood of the night has not been damaged.

"Perhaps it was the company," she continues, smiling back at him. "Pierre said 'for a short time' when he asked you to escort me, but I am pleased that he seems to have forgotten about me. I hope that I have not been a burden to you."

"Of course not," he replies. "It has been my pleasure."

She looks at him, seriously.

"Honestly," he feels compelled to add.

She is close to him now. She reaches up and touches his cheek. "Dear Gregory."

The food and the warmth and the wine seem to have gone to his head. He feels as if he is floating. Everything moves slowly.

Her voice is soft and gentle. "Pierre told me your story... last summer... sometime shortly after I had arrived."

He nods, silently, and looks back into her dark brown eyes.

"Such an evil man," she continues. "My young brother has been headstrong in his time, and has done things with which I have disagreed. But it was pointless to tell him. It would only have made him more determined."

Averill is looking past her as she speaks; watching the flickering light from a torch on the opposite wall, unwilling to focus on her words.

"But I know, from what he has told me," she continues, "that he and others of Bijou's group were appalled by what happened that day. How Pierre came to be mixed up with him, I will never know. But I thank God he is no longer associated with the man."

A pause, and in the silence Averill's gaze returns to Elvira's face. She looks up and sees him looking at her. She smiles, and reaches up, to gently brush a wisp of hair from his forehead.

"I remember you on the night of the tournament," she continues. "It was later in the evening. You were just a few metres from me, and I couldn't help wondering about you. You looked so tired and bruised, and yet, at the same time, you looked somehow... invincible."

Averill smiles. "You're too kind, my Lady," he replies. Then a moment later, he adds, "And I remember you, too, my Lady. I watched you... watching me. I saw you look away... and I saw you look back again; but I could not tell what you were thinking. And then you were gone, just like that."

He sighs.

"And I presumed that I would never see you again. It felt as if you had simply... sailed through my life; and all I had left were the fading ripples which confirmed that you had been there... for a moment."

Silence; then she speaks. "I was thinking..."

Another silence; then: "I was thinking, that night, that perhaps your victory had been a fluke, a once-off. I was thinking that you shouldn't have been able to achieve what you did that day."

"Perhaps I shouldn't," concurs Averill, nodding as he digests her words.

"No, that was my prejudice," counters Elvira; "because if I were true to myself, I was thrilled that you had won. But I was too bound up by the rules of polite society to let you know, Gregory.

"I wanted to take those few steps to reach you, and touch you, and tell you; but, instead, I walked away."

Slowly, she rests her head on his shoulder, and, hesitantly, he places his arm around her, and strokes her hair with his free hand. She snuggles closer to him.

He closes his eyes, confused.

Moments pass. "But you took those steps, tonight," he muses, quietly.

"We were alone," she replies. Then, with a slight giggle, "And... we had been introduced."

He smiles, then turns his head towards hers, and breathes in the scent of her hair. He gently hugs her to him for a moment, and feels her compliant response. She raises her head slightly; her lips touch his neck. He embraces the swell and fall of her breast as she breathes more deeply, and feels the sudden hammering of his own heart.

Unwilling to move and break the spell, he holds her, silently, listening to her breathing.

Time stops.

Has it been five heartbeats or five hundred? He neither knows nor cares. She reaches up and draws his head down until her lips reach his ear.

"Take me somewhere," she whispers.

★

He quietly closes the door and turns to see her standing at the window, looking out, silhouetted against the moonlit scene outside. The room is dark, apart from the soft, pale light reflected from the snow covered ground. He doesn't recall the few steps he must have taken to reach her, and stands behind her now, as she reaches back and takes his hands, drawing them around her. He lowers his head and inhales the scent of her hair, once again. Gradually, awareness of time and place recedes, as feelings, emotions, desires tumble over each other, and yearnings, long suppressed, find voice in the moment.

"Gregory," she whispers.

Intoxicated by her intimate presence, he lowers his head further. His lips graze her eyebrow as she turns in his arms, lifting her head. Hesitantly, they stand, gazing into each other's eyes; then suddenly, the tenuous restraint of shyness is overcome by desire. Lips meet, hearts pound, and the muted murmurs of passion escape into the night.

But the maelstrom in Averill's mind is only just beginning, and Elvira gasps as the knight wrenches himself free, and holds his head in his hands. He stands, apart and alone, whilst the lady watches fearfully, able to recognise but not comprehend the trauma of the moment. And, within Averill's being, a formless battle, between life and love and happiness, and death and purity and honour, begins.

Images of soft, flowing dark hair and warm, alluring almond-shaped eyes from another time appear, superimposed upon the softly illuminated tenderness of the lady who stands before him; images which he has loved and held and honoured since Choy Dip first entered his life on the dusty, bloodied ground of that field in France; images to which he has retreated time and again to cocoon himself against the harshness of reality, and within which he has relived the exquisite agony of his love and his loss; images which now conspire to debilitate the knight and hold him in the void between love forever lost and love never ventured.

Head still in hands he stands, looking past the lady, to the snowy scene outside, as he seeks to control the rising turmoil.

Elvira stands silent before him, hands clasped at her chin, searching his face.

Fluffed and silent, the owl holds his gaze, exuding wisdom and challenging him to understand. Many times she has maintained her vigil with him through the sad, lonely night; never forsaking him. But now he recognises that she demands one more effort from him; demands that he find a way to take the hardest step and discover a means to open his being to new love, without forsaking his past.

He stands, impaled by the unblinking stare of the owl and embraced by the memories of his lost love. Then, gradually, he becomes aware of the head resting gently on his chest, and the arms softly encircling his waist, as Elvira holds herself to him. And, slowly, he understands that she is blameless; a victim of the circumstances, not of her life, but of his. He recalls his encounters with her; the fleeting glimpse which set his heart racing the night of the tournament, the wonder of the evening several weeks ago when a rainbow and a sunset worked their magic upon two innocent individuals whose destiny had been determined the moment their eyes previously met, and now this night, when the joy of Christmas celebration and the loneliness of two solitary people, has brought them together through unusual circumstance, has fanned the hitherto unrecognised but nonetheless smouldering embers of desire, and led to this quiet, private, reflective and, now, intensely intimate moment.

And, slowly the dilemma resolves itself, as he recognises the familiarity of the feelings he now experiences; recognises that they are the feelings which ran through him every time he was apart from Choy Dip; and realises, with stunning clarity, that the angel of love is visiting him once again. And slowly he realises: there is no suffering he is causing, other than to the lady before him, in interrupting the tender moment she has created; there is no-one he has cast aside, no slight upon his former love, who has been carried to another, better place where he cannot follow; and so, little-by-little, he accepts that for his own sake, and for the sake of all who will come into contact with him, he needs to move forward; and, if that be towards a new love, then that is possible; and possible without diminishing anything of his former life and love.

Slowly, his hands fall from his face, to embrace the gentle creature standing close before him, her head upon his chest. Then, breathing deeply, and sure of himself at last, he moves to lift her chin and looks into eyes fearful of rejection, swimming in tears. He does not see the tears spill over and flow down her cheek, for his own eyes are closed as he kisses her trembling lips, and feels the passion of her response. Tightly, she clasps him to her, drinks him in, and presses her body to his.

Her breathing is ragged, as she repeatedly clutches his clothing in feverish fingers.

"Oh, Elvira," he murmurs. "What are we doing? How has this happened? I barely know you, and yet, you have touched me as I thought I would never be touched again."

"I don't know, my love," she replies, breathlessly. "It just seems so natural, so perfect. I want you so much."

The muffled sound of flapping wings barely impinges upon Averill as the owl disappears into the night. His attention is upon the lady he carries to his bed.

CHAPTER THREE

May is officially the end of spring and, although reducing in frequency, days of persistent rain continue to blow in from the north and the west. The heavy snows of the earlier, harsh winter are now a distant memory, as preparations for the invasion of France steadily gather pace.

Henry's personal attention to detail, already legendary, is complemented now by Bedford's determination that, this time, there will be no straggle of retreat, and no enforced heroics in the steady, relentless push across the French countryside.

The battle at Agincourt, two years earlier, had been forced upon the English army as, wearied and depleted by the siege of Harfleur, they had struggled to make their way back to Calais and thence to England. The Armagnacs, for their part, had sought to cut-off that path of retreat and had confronted the remnants of England with the might of France. But, as Henry had since declared, God had been with the English that day, and the French army had suffered terribly during those few awful hours.

Moreover, this time, the English army will not be resignedly accepting a battle it would prefer to avoid, but instead, will be putting itself, purposely, in harm's way, for the express purpose of committing France to English rule.

And yet, for all his bloody focus, the duke harbours a softness and a compassion for the general populace of France.

"Better to win their hearts," he says, "than to try to impose a tyrannical regime upon them. For such," he adds sagely, "would be doomed to failure in a foreign land, with long supply lines, and uncertain allegiances among the conquered armies and the hungry and deprived townsfolk."

Averill, for his part, is coming to appreciate Bedford's influence upon both the preparation and the direction of the campaign, and, somewhat surprisingly, is relishing the work of preparing for an invasion in which he will take no part. From time-to-time, of course, there are twinges of regret as he becomes caught up in the building enthusiasm and growing camaraderie of those preparing for battle. But it is nothing he cannot handle; and besides, the months since Christmas have seen the blossoming of a very good reason to remain in England. The Lady Elvira has provided a comfort and a purpose to his life, which, for a long time, had been absent. And the growing bond between Odelia and Rupert has not caused him the angst he had imagined it would. His daughter has shown a strength and an independence which has, frankly, surprised him, and Rupert has matured in a way his father could never have dreamed of during his youngest son's wayward years.

The preceding three months have seen Averill and his knights sweep in a massive circle through the counties to the east and the north of London, ensuring that men, from sixteen to sixty, are diligently preparing for the forthcoming invasion. In fields and archery butts throughout the country, enforced practice of battle skills is occurring every Sunday after mass, and small groups of the king's men, such as Averill and his knights, are descending upon villages and towns to ensure that the preparation and the discipline of the English army will be as good as they ever have been.

And now, on this last Sunday in May, Averill's troupe are beginning their final push, leaving Abingdon in Berkshire, and heading down into Hampshire; to Portsmouth, where the army will soon begin massing for embarkation.

Henry has decreed that there will be no Scottish, nor Irish, nor soldiers from Calais taking part in the invasion. He has, in fact, ordered that the defences of counties to the extreme north and west of England be strengthened, to ensure there is no second front required to deal with either border incursions from Scotland, or forays from across the Irish Sea.

And, as he did two years earlier, the king has ordered commissions of array for the clergy, taking advantage of the provision that the clergy may defend themselves when attacked, to boost the size of the assembling army by several thousand able bodies.

Working their way through the English counties, Averill and his men have witnessed the massive effort which is going into the preparations. Bows and arrows and strings are being packed into huge chests, covered in waxed cloth to protect their valuable contents from sea damage; mattresses, bolsters, and even latrine seats are being packed with the pavilions of barons and earls, who will command the larger contingents of troops; cauldrons, vessels, bottles and other tools of trade of the cooks of the land, who will feed the massive contingent, are being assembled and packed; pre-fabricated sections of trebuchets and mangonels, which will inflict devastation upon the enemy, and the belfries, which will protect the invaders from the excruciating defences of boiling oil and flaming arrows, are being manhandled onto ox-driven carts in preparation for transportation to Portsmouth.

And the personnel, themselves, represent such a vast cross-section of English society, that Averill momentarily wonders just what portion of the social fabric will actually be left behind in England: cooks and cartiers, masters of horse with their grooms and yeomen, carpenters and cordwainers, wheelwrights and labourers, smiths, saddlers, bowmakers, fletchers and armourers are assembling; a contingent of Welsh miners has been encountered on their way to the port; chaplains and friars, monks and minstrels are beginning to leave their normal places of work and begin the journey to the coast; heralds, who will judge the outcomes of the battles, record knighthoods in the field, make the lists of the dead, deliver messages, defiances, truces and surrenders, are preparing their trappings of office; physicians who will diagnose, and surgeons who will amputate and cauterise, are taking down their shingles and leaving their local practices for the greater good of England. And elsewhere, courtiers are pressing into service over a thousand vessels of the high seas, coastal traders and river boats, which will carry the many thousands of fighting men from England to the shores of France; to a specific destination, as yet, known only to the king of England.

Averill has heard stories of the preparations for invasion two years ago, which left the country reeling with their scope. But it now appears that the magnitude of this current endeavour exceeds even that, and, from time-to-time, the sheer scale of the activity leaves the knight speechless.

He recalls his early years with Henry, the gifted and self-confident young prince, whose penchant for battle was unquestioned but whose rashness and inconsistency were acknowledged, by more senior knights, as potential liabilities, if or when he became king. But, having seen the planning and the organisation which is evident in this new endeavour, Averill knows that there will be no such doubts now. He marvels at the transformation which kingship has wrought in his dear friend, and recognises that there are few who assume the mantle of greatness with ease; but the king of England is one of them.

A fleeting pang of regret that he will not be there with them catches in his stomach; but he brushes it aside and prepares to ride out.

★

In towns and villages across the south and east of England, goodbyes are being said, and countless men, some young and eager for adventure; some older, veterans of earlier campaigns and only too aware the horrors which will face them but, nevertheless, preparing once again to bear arms for king and country, are gathering together their pieces of kit, hugging tearful wives and girlfriends, and holding sleeping babies and wide-eyed young children in one last embrace, before walking steadfastly out of houses and falling in step with comrades already embarked upon the long journey to Portsmouth and nearby seaside towns.

For some, this will be the last time they see the green fields of England. For others, these fields will never look as beautiful as when they return, months hence, from the blood and the mud of the battlefields of France.

The usual directionless bustle of people on the roads going about their business has given way to a steady southward flow. Strong, tall, willowy figures, with broad chests and imperceptibly bent spines from years of drawing bow-strings, carrying bow and sword and dagger, walk purposefully along the edges of the roads, whilst slightly squatter, but equally barrel-chested men, sit astride powerful horses occupying the centres of roads, trailing yet more horses behind them, which carry carefully wrapped bundles of armour, swords, poll-axes and other fearsome weaponry.

As cross-road after cross-road is reached, the trickles of humanity merge and swell until the huge throngs of men on foot and on horseback, heading southward, leave no doubt that the preparations for the invasion of France are approaching their conclusion.

From sparse beginnings, where individual pennants flutter in solitary pride above small groups of similarly liveried men, the merging streams of the gathering army grow into spectacular patterns of colour as hundreds of pennants and thousands of men make their way south. And whilst memories of recent partings in some cases remain tearfully close to the surface, the underlying swell of pride begins to lift the vast contingents on their final approach to the south coast of England. The bravado and excitement of the untried adds a strangely positive edge to the steady purposefulness of the veterans, and once again those who have been here before begin to feel the power and the energy which permeates an English army gathering for war.

By Newbury, the mass of humanity has shaken itself into an orderly passage of archers, clerics, yeomen and others on foot occupying the left of the roads, and men on horse, along with the carts and drays and wagons carrying heavy goods claiming the right as their own. The minor traffic heading northwards finds itself consigned to the rough edges of the roads, and subject to the hearty humour of the army, as men who know they may soon die work to instil confidence in each other.

By Andover, the contingents of men from the western counties, and towns as far afield as Bristol, are joining the main southward stream; whilst to the east, even larger contingents are making their way through Surrey and Sussex; all converging upon the ports of embarkation.

By Stockbridge, the smell of the sea air is perceptible, and memories of small, rocking boats and hours of seasickness begin to rise again into the consciousness of the veterans. And here, for the first time, a stream of men departs to the east, toward Winchester, where they will assemble, whilst the main body of men continues on south.

Averill and his troupe also wheel east with the Winchester stream, before leaving them, several hours later, to start back up towards Windsor, confident that they have completed their mission and reassured by the knowledge that the capacity, organisation and discipline of the fighting men, first assessed during that worrying pass through the counties prior to Christmas, has now reached a level where each member of Averill's party has confirmed to his leader that he would be prepared to fall-in with the men, and stake his life upon their preparedness. And this is not an idle boast, since on occasions in the past each has been required to do just that. However, this time only the assurance, and not the commitment, is required, since Averill and his troupe will not be participating in the invasion, but instead will be remaining in England to be disposed of as it pleases the king's brother; John, the Duke of Bedford.

★

"Well, Gregory; we leave Windsor tomorrow, and make our way down to Winchester, then on to Portsmouth.

"Huntingdon has cleared the final obstacle by capturing or sinking the remaining Genoese ships which were blockading Harfleur, and the town is being re-provisioned as we speak.

"And, as you have recently witnessed, we have more than ten thousand knights, archers, men-at-arms and all manner of supporting trades and professions converging upon Southampton, along with several thousand more of the clergy who will defend themselves if or when they are attacked. So, Gregory, it seems to me that there is no reason to tarry any longer."

"Indeed, Your Majesty," replies Averill, nodding in agreement. "No reason at all."

"Clarence and Gloucester will accompany me," continues the king, "and Bedford here, with you by his side, will remain behind to govern England in my stead.

"A fair wind, and we will be off."

Averill and the Duke of Bedford exchange smiling glances as the king looks down at the charts spread across the table of the map-room.

"Take a look at this Gregory," says Henry, stabbing his forefinger at one of the maps.

"Touques! They won't be expecting that."

"I am surprised, Your Majesty," replies Averill, moving around to view the chart. "I wasn't expecting it, either."

"Ah, but it makes sense," comments Bedford, also walking over to the table, "when you remember what happened the last time we did this."

"Yes, it does," continues Henry. "You weren't there, Gregory, but we had our hearts in our mouths for three days while we carried everything from our ships to the shore. If the French had been more daring, they could have made life very much more difficult for us right there and then at the beginning.

"But this time, we're choosing a place where the beach is long and sandy, and where we can disembark men and equipment and provisions within a single day. And, I doubt they will have any fortifications within a bull's roar of us, from which they could despatch men, even if they were so inclined; which, from previous experience, I believe they will not be.

"But then," he adds, "we have to confound them further. We have to begin this campaign with such momentum that, from the very first battle, they never recover. It is imperative that we take Caen and Rouen, so these will be our primary targets. Rouen is our strategic objective, but we will take Caen first, as it will provide us with a port, from which we can continue to provision our army as we move further inland. It is only nine miles from the coast and the river is easily navigable. Provisioning from England will be a far better policy than plundering the land for supplies, and provoking the disenchantment and, quite probably, the resistance of the people. We will need a great deal of good-will, this time, if we are to avoid wastefully dispersing our forces to deal with ongoing uprisings among the French peasantry.

"Then, gentlemen," the king continues, with quiet, cold intent, "after we have secured Caen, we take Rouen, the seat of government for all of Normandy; for control of Normandy, which is ours by right of inheritance through the line of Guillaume Le Conquérant, is our principal objective!"

Once again, Averill and Bedford exchange glances, but this time there are no smiles.

★

"You're quiet, my love. Is anything wrong?"

Averill turns and looks directly into Elvira's soft brown eyes, before answering. Her fingers run softly over his bare thigh. He shudders at the pleasure, but continues to look at her; a bright, intelligent woman who fulfils the role of 'lady' perfectly, but, a woman of softness and warmth and surprising passion when they are alone; a woman who holds his heart in such a strange way, almost an otherworldliness which carries him away from the harshness of reality, into a soft vale of refuge and peace. He thinks carefully before replying.

"These last few months," he begins, "covering the counties as we did, making every effort to ensure the men were as prepared as they possibly could be, that their skills were as sharp as they could be, that their confidence was as high as it could be; these months, have been gruelling, and I am tired. But, I'm also happy, for I know we did a good job; I know we did what our king required of us."

"Yes, my love," replies the lady, continuing to stroke the knight's thigh. "I'm sure you did."

"And I saw it all come together during these last few weeks," continues Averill, "as the whole mass of our army began to make its way southward. But I was also amazed, and humbled, to see the organisation that our king has managed to oversee. Truly, in all the years I have been participating in battles, I have never seen such an achievement."

"But, are you really surprised?" asks Elvira. "After all, you have told me, several times, how thorough the king has been in his preparations."

"Perhaps I have always been too involved in the preparations to realise what was going on around me," says the knight, reflectively. "But this time, by not being consumed in gathering my own equipment, and that of my own knights, and in honing my own skills and those of my knights, I was able to open my eyes and observe. And I was overcome by the scale of what I saw; of what our king, and his brother, have achieved."

Elvira smiles. "You sound like a little boy who has just opened a wonderful Christmas present, Gregory."

Averill looks at his lady, then smiles in return. "Yes, my love; that's almost how it feels."

Then, more seriously: "In the past, I would have been confident in my own abilities, and in those of the men around me. But this time, I have seen an entire army assemble; I have seen those who will build, those who will cook, those who will try to keep our spirits high with music and laughter, those who will put us together again if they can after we are injured, and those who will lay us to rest if they cannot. And I have seen so many knights and men-at-arms who can wield a sword with strength and precision that I have begun to feel differently. I have always looked towards our king, but I have never turned around and looked back. But now, I see what I imagine he sees; a vast swell of committed and capable men, coming together for a single purpose, and I find I have a pride in these men, which I have never known before, and a belief in my country which exceeds anything I have ever felt before."

Once again Elvira smiles; but this time, she wraps her arms around Averill and confides, "I love you, Gregory Averill; and I love seeing you so passionate about your king and your country."

Averill returns the embrace of his lady, then quietly continues. "And, for the first time, I have seen the archers, up close. I have watched them practising; drawing bows and firing arrows, with unbelievable accuracy, almost at the rate of my breathing. I had always known that they were an important element of our army, but I had never really seen them for what they are; they are awesome, my love; and collectively, they are such a force as should strike fear into the hearts of any who face them."

The room is suddenly quiet.

Elvira rises until she is leaning upon one elbow, looking down upon her knight, naked upon the bed.

"Do you wish you were going with them?"

There is a long pause, as Averill looks up at her, outlined against the sunlight. He reaches up and gently cups her bare breasts in his hands.

"Would you believe me if I said 'no', my love?"

Elvira smiles and bends down to kiss her man.

"I love you, Gregory Averill," she answers, "and no, I would not."

Averill draws her down, hugging her to him.

"But, I have a duty to Henry, and to Bedford," he continues. "It is a duty of my own choosing, and therefore, I must meet my commitments as an honourable man. And so, my love, as much as my heart tells me that for the rest of my life I will regret not being there, my mind tells me that I could not live with myself if I failed our king when he is committed to defending me and those I love."

Elvira's tears of relief are sudden and overpowering.

"Oh Gregory," she cries. "I love you so much; you will never know what you mean to me."

Averill's mind is struggling with competing thoughts and emotions: too much desire to be here, too much need to be there; too much love for the woman he holds, too much commitment to his king; too much necessary work to be done for Bedford, too much accumulated skill and experience in battle to go to waste...

Senses heightened by the turmoil and passion inflamed, he rolls over, forcing Elvira onto her back. Her eyes are wide and as wild as his. He bends to kiss her and feels the rake of her nails across his back. She arches up to meet him as his fingers stroke the mound between her legs, already wet from her own inflamed passion. Her grip upon his hardness lacks gentleness as she bites his lip.

The agony of the turmoil both are experiencing feeds the desire they feel for each other, and, as the knight slides inside of his woman, her legs cross around him, drawing him to her. The violence of their passion reflects the need each has for resolution of the conflicting desires for togetherness and release. Wild, conjoined, thrusting moments rush by, giving vent to coarse, unintelligible utterings, until the sudden, pulsating, breathless ecstasy of the woman takes the knight over the edge to his own paroxysmal release.

Silent moments pass, as breathing gradually becomes steady once again.

Elvira slowly runs her fingers through her man's damp hair. "What will you do, my love?"

Face buried in his woman's breast, the knight answers: "What I have always done, my love; my duty."

Elvira turns towards the wall, as tears trickle slowly from her still-closed eyes. Averill's sense of duty is strong, but she knows his need for action, and fears it is stronger.

CHAPTER FOUR

"How stands the wind, captain?"

"Fair for France, my Lord."

Henry, hands on hips, looks out over the sea wall to the scores of boats, rocking gently on the early morning swell. All along Southampton Water, as far as the eye can see, small clusters of boats of all shapes and sizes are moored, awaiting the signal for departure.

The king turns, tunic flapping slightly in the gathering breeze, and smiles fiercely at his lieutenants.

"Well then, gentlemen; we sail on the afternoon tide."

The shouts of elation, which follow the long and intense build-up, reflect the tension which has been simmering for the last seventy-two hours as king and captains, knights and yeomen, have observed the light and fickle wind, and counted the cost of delay in terms of reduced readiness and fraying morale. But now, with the steady strengthening of the westerly breeze, and the king's decisive declaration, the mood has changed from ill-tempered agitation, to breathless anticipation.

"Go, therefore," continues the king, "and attend to those tasks which require completion before we depart; for once the royal standard is raised, we shall not talk again until our boots are caked with the mud of France."

"My Duke of Bedford; Gregory," calls the king, as the assembled court departs.

"John, my brother, and favourite above all... and Gregory, my brother in spirit and favourite knight, I detect in your long faces, a sense of despair at not being a part of the enterprise upon which we now embark."

"'Tis true, my Lord," replies Bedford. "I would give my right arm to be aboard your flagship when she sails this afternoon. And yet, should I do so, then I suspect that Your Majesty would find me of little value."

"Indeed, brother, I would," replies the king chuckling at Bedford's self-deprecating humour.

"But," continues Bedford, "I must also admit to being honoured with the responsibility of managing our England in your absence. And so, being unable to do both at the same time, I will keep my angrier self in check for another time, when, I trust, you will uncage me and allow me to stand beside you, as we regain this France which is, after all, English by right.

"God speed, my brother. Yours is an honourable cause."

"And I admit to a foolishness," adds Averill, "which has cost me the chance to accompany my king upon this just and mighty campaign. However, I have given my word to both Your Majesty and to my Lord the Duke of Bedford, that I will play my part in the maintenance of good order at home in England, and I will honour that commitment as I trust I have honoured all of the commitments I have made to Your Majesty, and place myself at the disposal of the duke in whatever capacity he would use me and my knights."

Henry smiles and wraps an arm around the neck of each of the comrades. "I thank you both, my brothers, for your commitment to our cause. But, it would be good indeed," he asserts, "if the day should arrive that we three were, once again, brothers-in-arms together. And I, for one, would not wish to be the foe who confronted such a trio as us."

★

Of the party assembled when the king declared the time to depart, only Averill now remains upon the sea wall, watching the activity below, and ruminating over his decision to retire from combat. The bustle of final preparations, as the last men board vessels nearing readiness to sail, echoes around the docks of the great port city. And crowds of artisans, farmers, women and children come to town to watch the spectacle, now gather near the water's edge ready to cheer the departing fleet as sheets are hauled and sails raised, to crack open when the now gusting westerly wind fills them.

For the solitary knight, absorbed in his own thoughts, it is difficult to separate the days since the departure of the king's entourage from Windsor. As before the first invasion of France, in 1415, Henry has, once again, been diligent in preparing the declaration that this war is indeed 'the proper execution of justice'. The cause is just, and the rights to France are being 'recovered' from a prior unjust usurpation. And so, the procession of nobles and knights and men-at-arms of the king's Home Guard, which had emerged from Windsor castle, had done so to deliberate fanfare as Henry had publicly declared the just causes for which the war was to be waged.

And, following the emergence of the entourage from the castle and its formal passage through the surrounding township, word of the king's coming had spread rapidly, so that from that point on hundreds had progressively flocked to the roadside, to line the route all the way to Southampton, and cheer their king in his mission to recover lost France.

Averill, riding in the vanguard of the procession behind the king, and Bedford, Clarence and Gloucester, had seen, first hand, the love with which the country folk regarded their king, and the enthusiasm with which they wished him well in this endeavour. And, once again, as he reflected upon the talented but erratic young man with whom he had grown up, Averill was struck by the completeness of the transformation which kingship had wrought upon this now formidable figure who ruled England, and was set upon achieving France as well.

The following day, at Winchester, Henry had paused for a private mass, conducted by his half-uncle, Cardinal Beaufort, the Bishop of Winchester. The occasion was simple, without fanfare, in contrast with the departure from Windsor when Henry had wished to convey a formal message to the watching dignitaries of Europe. But, on this occasion, as Henry had confessed quietly to his brothers, he wished to privately re-affirm, before God, his commitment to the just cause upon which he was now embarked, and to seek a moment's peace and solitude before plunging headlong into the final build-up before departure.

However, by the time they reached Southampton, entering through the arched portals of the Barbate to the roar of cheering crowds, the pomp and ceremony and grandeur of the occasion were again on display. And, once again, Averill marvelled at the perceptiveness of the king in recognising the occasions when private contemplation and prayer was appropriate, and those when public pageantry was necessary.

And it was here, in Southampton, yesterday morning, the 29th of July, 1417, that Henry had afforded Averill a vision of the future only known to a handful in the kingdom. The wind had, for the third day running, been unfavourable for France, and the king, in dismay, had turned to Averill and advised him that they were going sight seeing... alone.

And so it was that, moments later, two tall but otherwise nondescript figures in long, hooded robes, had descended quietly from the sea-wall, and walked deliberately towards Town Quay, where a huge scaffold had been steadily rising for the past eight months.

Entering the structure the pair had been challenged, but only momentarily, as the king threw back his hood and smiled with quiet charm at the young apprentice who barred their way. And, in the same instant, Master Shipwright William Soper had turned and spied the king.

★

Seventy feet... at least... straight up.

Averill's neck strains as he cranes his head back to look to the top of the forward castle of the mighty ship, still under construction. Henry, beside him, is also looking up and beaming with pleasure at the sight, while the designer stands alongside, a mixture of nervousness and pride.

"Tell us about her again, Master Soper," commands the king. "Sir Gregory, here has not had the benefit of any previous exposure, and I would like to confirm the details one more time."

"Well, Your Majesty," commences the ship-builder, "she's two hundred and eighteen feet long, per your specifications, with a beam of fifty feet. The forward castle, where you're looking now, Your Majesty, will be fifty feet above the waterline when she's afloat; higher than anything the Genoese have to throw at us, and as sturdy and well-fortified a platform as any, from which our archers can rain down destruction upon our enemies.

"I believe she can do us proud, Your Majesty."

"Yes, Master Soper, I believe she can," replies the king.

"She's clinker-built," continues Soper, warming to his theme, "but for a vessel this size, we've had to use three layers, Your Majesty. Would you like to see?"

Henry looks at Averill, who is shaking his head in amazement.

"What is it, Gregory?"

"I'm just stunned," replies the knight. "I've sailed in boats before, but I've never seen anything like this; it's almost... overpowering."

"Come on, then," replies the king. "Let's see how she's put together."

"This way, Your Majesty," says Soper, leading the way up through the maze of scaffolding, until the three men emerge into the morning sunlight, at deck level. The scaffold continues up either side of them, surrounding the forward and rear castles, still under construction.

"Please be careful, Your Majesty," warns Soper. "As you can see, the decking is still being laid. But from here you can get a very good look at the construction."

Averill moves to inspect the rough, unfinished edges where the side of the great ship merges into the forward castle, and notes the three layers of timber which Soper had mentioned; all made of planks, each about eight feet long and about eight inches wide.

"How do you hold these all together?" he asks.

The designer turns, picks up an item then walks to Averill. "With pitch and stuffing... and these, Sir Gregory," he replies, handing Averill a nine-inch iron nail.

"My God," ejaculates the knight. "How many of these have your made? And how many trees have you cut down to build this... this... giant?"

"Well, Sir Gregory, I don't know how many nails we've made, but it's quite a few. But I can tell you that there's over a thousand Beech trees, and two thousand Oak in this vessel so far; and that's not counting the specialist timbers from Latvia and from the Prussian forests, which we're using for the internal fittings."

Averill, still holding the massive nail, is looking incredulously at Soper, and shaking his head.

"Is it ready yet, Master Soper?" asks the king.

"Yes, indeed, Your Majesty," replies the designer. "Would you like to see?"

"Yes, I would." replies the king. "Come on, Gregory. Close your mouth or the flies will get in."

Once again, Averill shakes his head in amazement, then follows the king and Soper, and two apprentices the latter has called over, as they re-enter the scaffold and climb up towards the high prow of the ship. Nearing the top, Soper comes to a halt in front of a large, rectangular structure, covered by canvas and resting against the hull.

"This will be my flagship, Gregory," begins the king, with enthusiasm; "from which we will take control of the high seas, and never again be threatened, as we have been, by the French, or the Spanish, or the Genoese, or any others who would sail this channel with a view to attacking us."

Then quietly: "But, she will be mine, only by the grace of God, Gregory; by the grace of God, who put me on the throne of England, and challenged me to restore to our country that which has been unjustly taken from us.

"May we see, Master Soper?"

A nod from Soper and the two apprentices, having already untied the ropes holding the canvas, slowly lower the covering, revealing a large polished wooden board, bearing two words, beautifully scripted in gold paint with black shadowing: *Grace Dieu*.

"As I said, Gregory, she will be my flagship, but only by the grace of God."

The nameplate is breathtaking in its splendour.

"I wanted to see this before I depart; just in case I do not have an opportunity again."

The figures in front of the nameplate are silent, overcome by the moment: the huge ship, way beyond anything ever seen before; the name, imposing reverence and acknowledging the power granted by God, to a king, for the protection of a realm; and the occasion, the launch of an invasion of France, for the recovery of lands, unjustly denied England, by the convenient but inappropriate interpretation of Salic law, those eighty-nine years ago.

★

A hand on the shoulder returns Averill from his reverie.

"Second thoughts, Gregory?" asks the duke.

Averill stares, mind still filled with the awe and grandeur of yesterday, then smiles, uncertain how to answer diplomatically.

"Me too," continues Bedford, not waiting for a reply. "God, how I wish I were out there now, with Harry."

Both men turn to stare out over Southampton Water to where the *Holy Ghost* lies at anchor. But the vessel is not idle, there is much activity on deck, and the partly unfurled sails are beginning to thrash in the gathering breeze. And, as the duke and the knight watch, a ripple of excitement in the crowd at the foreshore becomes a roar of approval, as, hesitantly at first, then briskly, the royal pennant, three lions passant quartered with three fleurs-de-lys, begins its passage to the top of the central mast of the great ship. And, immediately behind, comes the unmistakable and inspirational red cross of St George.

The sound of anchor chains rattling across the deck comes distantly to the ears, above the sustained cheering from the foreshore, and, from ship to ship, as far as the eye can see, men bend their backs to the task of hauling sheets, raising the sails of vessels large and small along the length and breadth of Southampton Water.

The English invasion of France has begun.

Neither Averill nor Bedford recalls how their right fists came to be in the air, nor when their throats first became hoarse from cheering, but the gathering crowd of courtiers and administrators and minor functionaries on the sea wall are now sustaining the vocal support, as the duke and the knight, breathing heavily from the outpouring of emotion, looked at each other, with mixed emotions.

"My Lord Bedford," begins Averill. "Oh, what I would now give to recall the words I uttered so foolishly these several months past, when I thought that every good thing that had come my way, was over. I should be there with my knights, supporting our king on this righteous endeavour."

"Indeed, Gregory," replies the duke. "And I should be there also, for the battlefield is where I do my best work."

Then reflectively: "But, were we to go, then who would our dear brother, the king, turn to in order to ensure that the England to which he returns victorious is the England we know and love, and not some sad parody of former greatness, ruined by social unrest and lack of discipline?

"No, Gregory, we have an important job to do, and, by God, I intend to do it, until Harry allows me once again to take up arms for England."

Averill smiles. "Indeed, my Lord Bedford, your sentiments and your dedication are salutary lessons for all of us left behind. We will, indeed, preserve the England that our king left, so that she is as lovely and as welcoming as he remembers, when he returns."

CHAPTER FIVE

By Thursday, 1st August, Henry's boots were, indeed, caked with the mud of France, as he strode back and forth observing the disembarkation of the English army at the mouth of the River Touques.

And across the English Channel, a week later, another pair of boots is striding back and forth as a knight, with the demeanour of a caged lion, attempts to direct his energy into the training of young squires not old enough to form part of the invasion force, and bearing swords for the first time.

Alongside their leader, Rupert, Gareth and James, Anthony and Thomas, Charles, Robert and Bryan, all add their support to the effort of directing the boys in aiming their weapons at the charcoal marks on the pells in the courtyard of the castle.

And in the greater courtyard, surrounding the area set aside for the squires, the daily life of the castle continues as people bustle by.

Elvira, Wendy, Odelia and Sarah walk by in animated conversation; a fact not missed by Rupert who, momentarily, allows his grip to relax, his sword to drop, and his gaze to follow the beautiful young woman who has captured his heart. But the caged lion does not miss the fact, and within two strides has raised his own sword and delivered such a blow to the loosely held sword of the young man that the weapon is torn from his grasp and sent spinning and crashing to the ground some ten yards away from the young man.

"Pick it up," snarls the monstrously angry knight.

The courtyard has come to a sudden standstill, as passers-by, squires and knights react to the savage outburst from Averill.

Rupert is trembling at the ferocity of his mentor's anger. Backing towards the plundered sword, he maintains a wary eye upon Averill, who advances step for step with the young squire. Odelia is aghast at the turn of events and clings to Elvira, as tears well up in her eyes.

Gareth and company look on, unprepared for the sudden change in Averill's manner, but not willing to interfere.

"Every time you hold death in your hand, boy, so does someone else," snarls the knight. "And this time it's me! You get distracted by anything... or anyone... and your life comes to an end!"

Rupert has recovered the sword, but Averill continues to advance; slowly, menacingly.

"You forget that you are in a battle situation, and your chances of survival quickly diminish to nothing!"

Averill has assumed a stance of aggression. Rupert does the same.

Odelia screams in disbelief. She has seen this before; most recently when Averill faced Bijou in that bloody, ferocious battle last summer.

"Do you really need to do this, Gregory?" asks Gareth.

"Do not challenge me, Gareth," hisses Averill, without taking his eyes off Rupert. "This little shit still has much to learn... and I will not tolerate him losing focus because of some skirt, even if it is my daughter."

"Gregory, I think you're over-reacting," cautions Gareth.

"Then I'll fucking take you on as soon as I've finished with him," comes the savage reply.

And now there is general concern as to the extent to which Averill is prepared to go in delivering the lesson he clearly feels Rupert needs to learn.

The first strike is blindingly fast, and totally unexpected... except, apparently, by Rupert, who parries the advancing sword within inches of his face.

Averill advances a pace; Rupert backs off a pace.

The second strike is equally quick, this time descending towards Rupert's unprotected head, but the young squire is ready now, and slips sideways as he again parries Averill's sword with his own.

Averill's smile is cruel. "So, you've learned something, it seems."

Again, the knight strikes, and again the squire manages to deflect the blow. However, the next strike crashes through the young man's guard, and the point of Averill's sword stops an inch from the young man's right eye.

Odelia screams again and turns to bury her face in Elvira's bosom. Gareth heaves a sigh. Averill's attack is ferocious, but he is in control. He is not going to maim his squire; but he is clearly going to teach him a lesson he will never, never forget.

Another strike and Rupert's sword is almost torn from his grasp. Averill follows up with a grapple with his free hand and a hip throw which sees Rupert flung to the ground. The young man rolls away, terrified, as Averill's sword impacts the ground where Rupert's head had just lain.

And now, the young squire recognises that this is no drill; Averill is in such a foul mood that Rupert does not know if he can be contained. Gareth knows otherwise and observes quietly.

Rupert raises his sword and looks to Gareth for support. The big man shows no emotion and remains, arms folded, watching the unfolding battle.

And now the squire knows he is totally alone; abandoned by all whom he thought he could trust. He knows there will be no intervention to save him. He knows that his life depends upon his own capability. And so, slowly, carefully, he assumes the second stance of Fiore de' Liberi da Premariacco, and watches intently as Averill does the same.

For fully ten minutes, the pair trade ferocious strikes and parries. For fully ten minutes, an uninformed onlooker would have assumed that the two combatants were trying to kill each other. For fully ten minutes, the younger man fights with more concentration, more endeavour and more discipline than he has ever shown before. And for fully ten minutes, he manages to resist every attack mounted by Averill. It is not pretty, but it is effective. But ten minutes of sustained intense sword fighting is hugely taxing, and the natural talent of the younger man does not compensate for the equally natural talent and huge experience of the older.

The final blow is powerful and quick; incredibly quick. Rupert's sword is torn from his grasp and as Averill continues the serene fluid motion into the next thrust, the younger man leans the wrong way. The slashing sword scythes down upon the exposed neck of the young squire… and stops.

"Dead!" roars Averill, mouth inches from the young man's face. "You're fucking dead!"

Then, turning on his heel, the heavily breathing knight throws his sword to the ground, and walks stiffly from the courtyard.

Silence; except for Odelia's sobs.

Rupert collapses to the ground; drained of all energy now that the maelstrom has receded.

Quietly, as if afraid to further disturb the scene, the crowd across the courtyard return to their various activities. However, the squires and knights in the practice square remain silent, all focussed upon Rupert lying on the ground. With sudden pity, Gareth moves toward the young man, motioning James to join him, and squats down beside the prone form. Rupert looks up into the big man's eyes.

"What just happened, Sir Gareth?" he asks. "What did I do?"

"What you did or didn't do," begins Gareth, slowly, "is not important."

Then looking from one squire to the other, he continues, "Now, listen to me, both of you, and listen well. You have just seen what a trained man, who is not trying to kill you, can do; and you, Rupert, have just experienced the terror of real, single combat. Just imagine what it would be like facing a man who was trying to kill you. This is a situation which we all have to confront one day, and you, young man, have been fortunate to confront it in circumstances which were not going to cost you your life; although for a while there I wasn't so sure. Others are not so lucky.

"One day soon, you will both find yourselves on a battlefield, and, because of what just happened here, you might both just live through it. Now, the pair of you, for your own sakes let me say this: never again will you take up a sword without being ready to use it. Never again will you lose your focus, or relax your guard, or play and joke about war. Is that clear?"

Both squires nod, not prepared to interrupt Gareth's flow.

"Now I know you both may think that Gregory was a real bastard today, and I wouldn't blame you for thinking that. But believe me, if you take this lesson to heart, and if you are deserving of the wisdom you have just been shown, then one day, it may just save your life. Do you understand me?"

"Yes, Father, I think I do," replies James.

Rupert looks up into the uncompromising eyes of the big man. "I still have a lot to learn, don't I, Sir Gareth?"

The gentle giant relaxes and tousles the young man's hair. "Well, perhaps not quite as much now as a little while ago."

Then, because they are all still unsettled by Averill's uncharacteristic outburst, he adds, "And remember this: Gregory would not have been so furious if he hadn't felt that you were compromising your own standards; standards that he's drilled into you with his own blood and sweat and tears. He admires you a great deal, Rupert; I know it. And, I think we all know that, just at the moment, he's hurting badly: there's a war on and he's not part of it. That's not a good thing for a knight who used to be the king's champion."

★

Having Averill at home for the evening meal is generally an occasion for happiness, light-hearted conversation, and hugs. But tonight, happiness has not graced the table, conversation has been stilted and there have been no hugs.

"Excuse me, Father," says Odelia, evoking a mood of injured pride so reminiscent of her mother, as she leaves the table and walks purposefully to her bedroom.

Averill sits quietly, head bowed, staring blankly into the plate from which all food has been consumed and all gravy wiped away with bread.

"Have I hurt her that much?" he asks, without looking up.

"Well, Gregory," replies Elvira, "you cannot publicly humiliate her young man and not expect some reaction, you know."

"And you're not very pleased with me, either, are you?" he adds.

"It's not for me to determine how you treat your squire, Gregory," replies the lady. "I would simply say that I did not see any reason for you to be so boorish towards him, when he only looked at Odelia with love.

"And I thought you had got over the fact that your little girl is growing up, and has become desirable. In fact, I thought you had implicitly given your approval for Rupert to court her.

"But it seems that I might have been wrong about that," she adds, looking to extract some response.

"Of course you're not wrong about that," retorts Averill, sharply. Then: "Oh God, why is this all so fucking difficult?"

"Because, my darling," replies Elvira, "you're angry at being left behind, and you're taking it out on everyone else; that's why."

"I know, I know," nods the knight. "But it was my decision, so why am I so angry about it?"

"Dear Gregory," continues Elvira. "Don't you recognise how much you've changed? Don't you recognise that you're a different man now, from the one who fought Bijou a year ago?

"You're no longer the man who made that decision; the decision that you'd had enough of being a knight. You've healed, Gregory. You're capable of being everything a knight should be, once again. And now, you're hurting because there's a war on and you're not there."

Averill looks up, then reaches out to take his lady's hand. "Dear Elvira," he asks. "When did you become so wise?"

Elvira's smile is forced. She recognises the truth of the words she has just uttered, but also the pain that they will bring if her man does something about them.

"I was always wise, Gregory," she laughs. "It's just taken some time for you to recognise it."

★

The moonlight through the window fills the bedroom with a soft, pale glow. Averill gently knocks as he enters, to find his daughter lying face down upon her bed, whimpering quietly.

He sits quietly beside the still form and reaches out to stroke the shining black hair.

"I'm sorry, sweetie," he starts. "Sometimes, you lose your way a little, when things don't go the way you want them to; especially when there's no-one but yourself to blame."

The room is quiet; the whimpering dies away, but the breaths still come in occasional shudders.

"He's a good young man, Odelia," Averill continues, but then stops. The emotions are still too raw for words, and so he continues to stroke his daughter's hair, aching for the closeness they have always known, but unable to bridge the gulf he has now created.

★

They lie together, naked in the moonlight, gently stroking each other, but lost in individual thoughts. Togetherness is important, but lust and passion have no place here tonight. The events of the day have impacted both Averill and Elvira, and both are still coming to terms with the rage which Averill displayed, and wondering about the possible consequences.

"I want you to come with me tomorrow," says Averill quietly. "I have something to show you."

Elvira turns her head slightly to look at him. He lies, face up, eyes closed; as if he has already departed.

She feels alone, and turns further to embrace her man, holding him tightly. His arm encircles her and draws her closer; but the feeling persists.

CHAPTER SIX

Two horses and their riders canter out from the trees of the forest and into the clearing; Averill on the sleek white mare, with her cavernous saddle-bags, Elvira atop a slender brown gelding.

The lady is quiet as she follows the knight through the ring of battered pells with their slashed and chipped charcoal marks. The feeling of loneliness, which has persisted since last night, remains unabated, but now the strange, silent setting evokes a feeling of mystery; almost of... reverence.

"What is this place, Gregory?" she asks. "What are these?"

Averill looks around, so familiar with the circle of pells that he had not even noticed its foreignness within the clearing. For a moment, he stops, taking in the scene afresh; the cuts and slashes clustered at waist, breast, neck and eye levels, the charcoal marks; some clearly visible where early errant strikes have missed their target; others almost obliterated where the results of intense practise have concentrated the impacts.

He smiles at Elvira, and reaching out, takes her hand, hoping to ease her obvious disquiet. She notices the strangely familiar structure, with the swinging arm, under the central oak tree, but does not comment.

There scene is surreal, but strangely sad. The loneliness is almost overpowering. She turns in the saddle, overwhelmed by the feeling, and looks slowly around the ring of silent pells.

Moments pass; then, with a soft flick of the reins, they move forward again, towards a barely discernible gap in the trees, and pass through.

★

The sound of running water greets them. A stream gurgles and splashes as it flows over a low rocky outcrop which spans its path; the same rocky outcrop which culminates in two flat boulders, one behind the other, not two metres from the stream; one, knee-high and flat, the other, shoulder-high and upright, forming a wide, natural seat under the leafy boughs of a tree whose trunk stands on the other side of the stream. The scene is serene... and idyllic.

Averill dismounts, and walking around to his lady, reaches up to help her from the saddle. Together they stand, taking in the healing beauty of the glade. A feeling of peacefulness descends upon Elvira; so sudden, and so different from the persistent loneliness which has been with her since last night.

She turns to find her knight looking directly at her... smiling.

"Oh, Gregory," she cries, "what is this place? It's so... beautiful; so... so..."

"Peaceful," offers the knight.

She turns full circle, drinking in the incredible beauty of the glade, then walks to the stream, and bending down, dips her fingers into the water, watching the eddies they create in the swiftly flowing stream, which breaks and dances its way around the obstacles before tumbling over the low, rocky outcrop in the middle of the flow.

Her eyes are sparkling as she stands again, and turns to find Averill immediately behind her. He takes her in his arms. The kiss is long, and sweet, and feels like life, itself, returning to her body.

"How did you find this place? Have you been here many times before? Is it always like this?" The questions tumble over each other.

"Let's sit down, my love, and I'll tell you all about it."

★

The late afternoon sun flashes, intermittently, through the gently moving branches, waking them both.

She has made love outside before, but never with such tenderness and such intensity of feeling. There was no wild abandon; the setting was too powerful to permit that. Instead, there was a slow, poignant build-up which ultimately burst upon them, and washed over them and through them, until they lay depleted by the exquisite rapture which had consumed them.

And now it is time to talk; time to deal with the issues which have brought them to this place.

"This is where I found peace," begins Averill, "when I was lost. This is where I found the strength to come back to the world, after everything which was good and sweet and wonderful had been taken away. And, this is where I found God; or more probably, where He came to find me.

"And now I find that this is where I think most clearly, my love; and where I make good decisions."

Elvira nods quietly, fearful of what is about to come, yet somehow strengthened by the power of the glade; feeling as if she will be able to accept and deal with Averill's decision to go to war when he shortly announces it.

"You were right, my love," he continues. "The man who made the decision to end his days as a knight was not the man who is here with you now. I know that I have healed, and this glade is where that healing began. Here is where the spirit of God touched me, and revived me, and led me back to the world from which I had withdrawn.

"But there have been other influences too. My daughter led me through the darkness of those early days. She loved me, and waited for me, and held me together when I would otherwise have fallen apart. I love her more than I can ever express. I owe her more than I will ever be able to give her.

"And there have been friends whom I deserted, but who did not desert me: Gareth, Anthony, all my knights; even the king, whom I treated most shabbily, but who, as I should have known, showed the grace and the majesty which makes him the man he is today, brought me back to his bosom when I would have remained adrift.

"And you, my love: you have been the gift which life bestowed upon me, when I believed that all happiness had ended, and would never come again. You are the light, come so unexpectedly into my life, when sadness had given way to emptiness, and life had revealed itself to be but a pale shadow of the richness and the happiness I had previously known. I treasure you as much as I have treasured anyone in my life, my love."

A slight pause as Averill gathers his thoughts. Elvira watches her man, but does not speak, overcome by the poignant juxtaposition of the love of which Averill has spoken, and the love of which he has not.

"My love," he continues, "I am a knight again. I am capable of those things which a knight is trained to do. And yet, as we saw yesterday, I am still capable of rashness, and poor, emotional decisions. And so, my love, I have decided here today, whilst you were sleeping, that it is commitment to my word which is to be my principle from this point on. I have no need to wield a sword anymore; although I will gladly do so if asked.

"But there is more: to be knightly is to accept the challenges lain down by one's king, and to honestly and trustworthily execute them, to the best of one's ability. It is to find one's own Holy Grail, and to pursue it with honour and dedication. It is to be more than one thought one could be; it is to be better than one thought one could be.

"The king has commanded me to serve the Duke of Bedford, and that is what I shall do. If it requires me to go to France to fight, then I shall do so. But if it does not, then so be it. I shall remain in England, with my two most precious ladies, and serve my Lord the duke, for as long as he has need of me.

"And if that requires me to be a little more tolerant of young squires who have more romance in their bones than I, then I shall learn to do that too, my love."

Elvira's lower lip trembles as the joy in her heart rises up through her body. Reaching over to her man, she lays back down upon the grass, drawing him upon her.

"Make love to me again, Gregory."

CHAPTER SEVEN

On Sunday, 18th August, the English siege of Caen commences. And by the following Wednesday, word has reached Bedford.

"So, Gregory," begins the duke. "If Henry is at Caen, then it would seem that his landing strategy has surprised the lot of them, and they have all crumbled before him like so many overcooked biscuits. Clearly, he is now embarking upon his first objective; the securing of a port.

"But, these sieges are boring things: days and days of bombardment, weeks and weeks of very unpleasant starvation, but very little action to thrill the spirit, don't you think?"

"Yes, indeed," my Lord," replies the knight. "I do recall the months that we have spent on previous occasions when an enemy town did not have the good sense to surrender while they were still healthy. However, in a way, I'm not surprised; after all, this is the first real battle of the campaign, and it would be most unusual for the French to cave in at this point. But, you and I both know, and I suspect, a goodly number of the French also know from the siege of Harfleur, that, if they resist, then this will become a long and bloody action, which can only have one end. And I, for one, would not want to be a Frenchman when the king finally enters Caen. I suspect there will be a lot more bloodshed than the French are now envisaging."

"And what about you, Gregory?" asks the duke. "Do you wish you were there with him?"

"Actually," replies Averill, "I am surprised to find that, at this moment, I do not."

"Really?" exclaims Bedford. "Now that does surprise me; explain."

"It was an incident a couple of weeks ago," continues Averill. "I had let my feelings get the better of me – you may have heard about it. I allowed my disappointment at being left behind boil over, and Rupert bore the brunt of my anger."

"Yes, I did hear about it," replies the duke. "Rather unpleasant, I understand."

"It was," concurs Averill. "It caused me to take a good look at myself, and re-assess my feelings. And, after quite some agonising, I determined that I was actually sulking like a spoilt little boy; and so, I decided to start behaving like the knight I am supposed to be, and find some worthy challenge into which I could pour my energy."

"Very honourable," interjects Bedford, smiling.

"Very necessary," corrects Averill, "for me and for all those I love. I was becoming a boor, and risking the love of all who are important to me. In fact, there is still ice between me and my daughter, and I'm worried that I might have damaged that relationship beyond repair."

The duke smiles, and places his hand on Averill's shoulder. "Gregory, if there's one thing I know, it's how much your daughter loves you. Believe me, my good friend, there may be ice now, but it will thaw soon enough. Odelia is a young woman, with a young woman's emotions; and that includes protection of her young man. You still haven't realised how grown up she's become, have you Gregory?"

Averill looks sternly at the duke, then slowly smiles. "It seems that there are many wiser heads than mine on this matter, my Lord. Elvira said virtually the same thing to me when it happened."

"Well, there you go," retorts the duke, slapping Averill on the back. "Great minds..."

Averill shakes his head, and smiles again; recognising the hopelessness of his position and the futility of trying to defend himself any further.

He changes the subject. "So, my Lord; what now for England?"

"On the battlefield or here, Gregory?" asks Bedford.

"Here, my Lord. I have no lack of confidence in England's fortunes on the battlefield."

"Well then," considers the duke. "We have a huge accumulation of claims to file at the Exchequer. Are you up to managing that?"

Averill's look of horror has the duke almost rolling on the floor in mirth.

"Ah Gregory," he laughs, "if you could only see your face!"

Then as Averill smiles in relief, Bedford continues: "No Gregory, I would not inflict such boredom upon you."

A moment's pause, then: "But, do not worry; there is plenty of work, here at home, which will tax you physically and mentally, I assure you. But let us leave that discussion until tomorrow. For the moment, I want to bask in happy contemplation of Henry's siege of Caen."

Averill accedes; but, despite all the sincerity of his commitment to work honourably in England in the service of the duke, he knows, deep down, that should there come an opportunity to stand beside his king in battle, then he would take it in a heartbeat.

★

The weeks have passed well enough, and Averill and his knights have fallen into a routine which includes regular training of the young squires, periods of administration, frequent sorties into the home counties carrying important messages received from the king, requesting some service or another from those of his barons who have remaining behind, and, from time to time, the chance to let their blood rush and spirits fly as they pursue the quarry in the hunt.

The first meeting between the combatants of Averill's over-reactive outburst had proven easier than either had imagined. Averill, for his part, was truly ashamed that he had let his personal disappointment at not being part of the campaign cloud his judgement to the extent that he had inflicted violence and humiliation upon his favourite young man. Yet Rupert, in a mark of a young man maturing rapidly, had taken the lesson to heart; especially with Gareth's words of wisdom and explanation resounding in his head afterwards.

The two had met in the stables a few days later.

"Good morning, Rupert."

"Good morning, Sir Gregory."

"How's that shoulder of yours today?"

"It's fine, Sir Gregory." Then cautiously, "I believe you noticed my difficulty during our recent encounter and had the grace to make allowances."

And it was Averill who had been taken aback by this display of chivalry. A moment's though, then the knight had taken the necessary step and proffered his hand to the squire.

"You have become a remarkable young man, Rupert," he had said, quietly, as they clasped hands. "I am ashamed that I let my disappointment cause me to treat you so harshly; especially when all you did was look at my daughter, for whom I know you have much affection. Please accept my apology for my behaviour, Rupert."

"Oh dear, Sir Gregory," the squire had responded, searching earnestly for the words. "I am humbled that you, of all people, should think you need to apologise to me. I know full well that without you I would still be a bad-tempered ruffian, roaming these streets, with no hope of anything more than a short life of pain and dissatisfaction. And I am also just starting to realise how much missing this campaign is hurting you. I thought I was starting to understand what it takes to be a knight, but I see now, that I have not even scratched the surface."

Then, before Averill can interject: "I will take your lessons, Sir Gregory, in whatever form you deliver them, because I know that they will make me a better knight when the time comes. And if, along the way, I can make you proud of me, Sir Gregory, then I will have taken a small step along the road to becoming someone a little like you."

And then, to reinforce the point: "You once told me, Sir Gregory, that if I worked for you, then you doubted that I would regret it in the end; but that I would surely regret it more than once along the way. Do you remember saying that, Sir Gregory?"

Averill's eyes had become moist. He had not realised the impact his words must have had all this time. "Yes, Rupert, I do remember it; that morning, right here in these stables. You were a rather different young man in those days."

"Yes, Sir Gregory, I was," the squire had replied, standing tall. "And you were almost right: There have been many times when I felt so utterly sick that I could not push myself any harder, could not go any further... could not achieve the things you expected of me.

"But never once, Sir Gregory, have I regretted being your squire."

And, in a moment of rare defencelessness, Averill had placed his arms around the shoulders of the young squire and hugged him tightly. "God bless you, my boy. You have already made me proud of you; perhaps as proud as you have made your father."

And this time it had been Rupert's eyes which had become moist, as he thought of the simple old man who he had treated with such cruel disdain, but for whom Averill had embarked upon a crusade to recover a lost son.

★

"Caen has fallen, Gregory," exclaims the duke, as he reads the message from Henry. Then looking up: "'Tis good news, Gregory, is it not?"

"Aye, my Lord. 'Tis good news indeed."

A pause, then Bedford continues: "The king has need of another seven hundred men, Gregory. The town has been taken, but at a cost."

Averill is not sure where to look; not willing to do or say anything which will betray the lurch of excitement in the pit of his stomach. He says nothing.

Bedford is reading the message again, ensuring that he has assimilated all the details of the various requests from the king.

"I am going to need you to assemble a party to go and gather together such a group, Gregory."

Averill's sudden excitement is shattered by the dullness of the task proposed by Bedford. "Aye, my Lord."

Silence. Bedford finishes reading the message and looks up at Averill. "But surely, that is a task which Anthony or Gareth or Thomas could manage, is it not?"

"It is, my Lord," replies Averill.

Bedford is thoughtful, before speaking; very slowly and very clearly: "My role, Gregory, is to support His Majesty, in everything he wishes achieved here in England."

"Yes, I understand, my Lord."

"It is to manage the estates, to ensure the continuation of good government, and to support Henry in all things which he needs from these shores."

"Indeed, my Lord," replies Averill. "And, I believe that even though the campaign is young, we have discharged those duties in a manner which would be pleasing to His Majesty, my Lord."

"Yes, Gregory, we have," agrees the duke.

"But, Henry expects more. He expects me to use my initiative, to make sound decisions in his absence, and to take actions and do things that are consistent with what he would have done."

"Yes, my Lord," replies Averill, not yet sure where the conversation is headed.

"The king has need of fighting men, Gregory. My duty is to deliver upon his request. And your duty is to support me in my duty."

"Of course, my Lord. I am bound and willing to do your bidding and provide that support in any way that I can, my Lord."

"Yes, Gregory, I know you are, and I thank you for the constancy of your efforts. It has only been a short time that we have worked together in this endeavour, but it has, as always, been a pleasure."

"Thank you, my Lord."

A further silence, as Bedford sits, elbows resting on the arms of his chair, tips of fingers touching each other, as he ponders the matter occupying his mind. The solid frame contrasts with the taller, more slender figure of his brother, the king; but the intensity of his expression, as he ruminates, reflects the fraternal connection.

The handwritten note from Henry lies on the desk where the duke has let it fall while he thinks.

Once again, he looks up at Averill standing close by. Bedford's face is serious. "These men will come from a variety of baronial estates, Gregory. They will not be used to fighting together."

"Yes, my Lord; 'tis true."

And then, to make the point unambiguously clear: "His Majesty will need a good man to lead them, Gregory."

Averill does not speak; the emotions are too overpowering. He casts his mind back... further... further... He has not taken up arms for England since the skirmish in the village near Marquise; the day he rescued Mariel from the burning hut. And now, the opportunity to resume a career interrupted has been laid before him, interlaced with poignant memories of another place and another time.

"Well, Gregory?" asks Bedford, not yet appreciating the powerful emotions competing within the mind of the knight.

Then, as there is no answer from Averill, the duke looks more carefully; and begins to understand. "Dear Gregory, please forgive me," he begs. "I had not put the whole picture together."

"No, my Lord," replies Averill, unsteadily. "There is no need for you to ask such a thing." Then, as the emotion subsides: "It's funny how you long for some things, and you think you can handle them, yet, when they come, they suddenly overwhelm you... the feelings... the memories... it's all so much more than you have been allowing yourself to believe."

Bedford nods, bravely holding in check his own desire to join his brother on the battlefield. Then quietly: "I need an answer, Gregory."

And now the knight laughs out loud, carrying the emotion of the moment away with it. "Oh, I'm sorry, my Lord. I had already moved far beyond that point. Yes, of course. I would be honoured to lead such a group to France to fight alongside His Majesty."

★

"Gentlemen; a word."

Six knights and two squires call a halt to their activities with six groups of younger squires, and turn to face Averill as he arrives in the courtyard.

"Caen has fallen."

The responses are uniformly jubilant in their appreciation of the news.

Averill stands, feet apart, hands on hips, grinning at the group, who, having received the news and reacted to it as expected, now stand looking quizzically back at him.

"Is there something else, Gregory?" asks Anthony.

"The siege took its toll, gentlemen, and the king has need of a further seven hundred men from England. I have here a list of barons, and an order from the Duke of Bedford, requiring them to contribute agreed numbers of men to the cause.

"Anthony, I wish you to take Bryan and Robert and Charles, and, with all haste, visit the barons to make the king's demands known. The men and equipment are to be assembled in Portsmouth three weeks from today."

"Of course, Gregory."

"Oh, and gentlemen." A slight pause as Averill looks from each knight to the next. "I suggest you dust off your own equipment, too."

CHAPTER EIGHT

"Daddy, I don't understand..."

Odelia is standing in the doorway to Averill's bedroom, one arm over her head, resting on the doorframe.

"What is it, sweetie?" asks Averill looking up, carefully trying to hide his surprise at his daughter's gentle manner towards him.

"Well, I watched you and Rupert the other afternoon... and I was very upset," she continues; "and very angry about what you did to him. I felt as if you were humiliating him for no good reason."

Averill waits; certain that there is more to come.

"I love you, Daddy, but that really hurt me."

"I know, sweetie; it was not the right thing for me to do; and I apologise for it."

"So why does Rupert still think you're so great? I was with him just a day ago, and he's not angry at you, or anything. In fact, for some reason which I just don't understand, he seems to think you're even more wonderful than he thought before. I just don't understand."

"Come and sit beside me, Odelia," requests Averill. "And let me see if I can explain."

Odelia obliges; that familiar mixture of injured adult pride and loving little girl.

"Dear Odelia," begins Averill, taking her hand and looking at it as he strokes her fingers. "Rupert is a fine young man. In fact, I think he is one of the finest I have met in a long, long time. And, I believe that he has the ability, in time, to become a very good knight. I know from watching him and working with him, and seeing how he responds to the challenges I set him, and, from a recent conversation we had, I know that he is growing up, and acquiring grace and wisdom, very quickly.

"And, if I am truthful, I see a lot of me in him. He is good at what he does, he is strong and quick, and he is not satisfied unless he is doing things just right."

"Yes, I know," interjects Odelia, pouting slightly. "You have no idea how long I have to wait for him when he is practising. Sometimes I think he has forgotten all about me."

"Ah, Odelia," chuckles Averill. "You are finding out what a dedicated young man he is." Then looking directly into her eyes: "But remember, dedication is a mark of a man's character. If he is dedicated in his work, he will also be dedicated to the lady in his life."

"Oh!" Odelia's cheeks colour, as she reacts to an understanding of her feelings, which she never would have expected from her father.

Then, returning to the subject: "The other afternoon; I was wrong. I took out, upon Rupert, all of the frustration and disappointment which were building up in me, because I am stuck here in England, while the king and his army are fighting in France."

"But I thought you had retired, Daddy?"

Averill looks at his daughter. "Yes, sweetie," he admits; "that's what I thought too. But, sometimes a man finds that there are things that he has to do, even though it doesn't seem to make sense. It's as if, sometimes, what you have to do becomes so clear, it doesn't matter how hard you try to deny it, it remains, right there, in front of you, refusing to go away until you acknowledge it.

"Do you understand, sweetie?"

"I'm not sure that I do," replies Odelia, "but I think you're telling me that you're not retired anymore."

"Yes, my dear little girl," replies Averill, stroking his daughter's cheek. "That's exactly what I'm telling you."

"And Rupert?"

"Rupert is my squire, Odelia. He accompanies me wherever I go."

"Oh."

The young girl leans against her father's side. He wraps his arm around her as the tears fall silently onto the bed.

"Rupert is a very smart and a very capable young man, Odelia. He knows what this means, and so, he knows that his life depends upon learning every lesson as thoroughly and as completely as he can. He will be a knight soon Odelia. I want, and he wants, that he is the best he can possibly be.

"We understand each other, sweetie. He knows that even if I am in a foul mood, which I don't think happens very often, the things that I am telling him, the things that I am making him do, the things that we are doing together, will make him stronger, and better, and more able to become that illustrious knight that he so wants to be; and, one day, may even save his life.

"And this is why he accepts that, sometimes, I get things wrong, sometimes, I am not the knight that I wish to be, sometimes, my feet of clay show through, just like any other man's.

"And this is why I admire him so much. He has the capacity to understand and to forgive. And that is remarkable in one so young; especially one who was denied the opportunity to make something of himself for such a long time.

"He's an outstanding young man, Odelia; and I'm very pleased that you're so fond of him."

Odelia wipes away her tears and looks up at her father. "Thank you, Daddy," she says. Then, reaching up, she wraps her arms around his neck. "I do love you, Daddy; always."

★

Odelia's arms are still around her father's neck as a quiet cough is heard nearby. Averill turns his head to see Elvira standing in the doorway, where Odelia stood a few minutes earlier. The lady moves forward and sits on the bed, on the other side of Averill, placing one arm around his waist, and stroking Odelia's hair with her free hand.

"Do you have something to tell me, Gregory?" she asks, softly, knowingly.

A pause, as Averill takes a breath, and composes his words: "The king has taken Caen, my love; and he now has need of seven hundred more men. I have asked Anthony to take a note from Bedford to the barons, and to have the men assembled in Portsmouth in three weeks.

And now a longer pause; then: "Bedford has offered me the opportunity to lead them in France."

Elvira's eyes are closed as her head rests against Averill's; but the tears still escape.

CHAPTER NINE

"When?" asks Wendy.

"In ten days' time; on Saturday," replies Elvira.

"Oh, Elvira!" cries Wendy, "That is such wonderful news. But how is Gregory reacting?"

"Like any father about to lose a daughter, I imagine. He keeps telling me how young she is, and how much Rupert still has to learn before he can consider himself ready to become a knight. But I know it's all just words. I think that, deep down, he is as delighted about the prospect as I am; and, I imagine, as you are."

"Oh, yes," replies Wendy, still excited. "Gareth has watched Rupert for a long time now, and has told me, many times, how like Gregory he has become; the same dedication, the same insistence upon perfection. I imagine that they would both be a little daunting to live with," she laughs.

"Oh, they have their moments," agrees Elvira, smiling. "Not that I have seen that much of Rupert, but, yes, Gregory can be trying at times. However..."

"You wouldn't have it any other way," finishes Wendy.

"Exactly," replies Elvira. "I couldn't imagine him any other way. Is it the same for you with Gareth?"

"No, I don't think so," replies Wendy, considering. "Gareth is a very gentle man; not at all deep and intense, like Gregory. Gareth suits me very well; he loves me, and he loves our children. We have a wonderful life. He is big, and strong, but just so gentle with us. I cannot imagine what he is like when they are off fighting, but I suspect he knows how to take care of himself.

"But I do worry when he's not here. It's been so wonderful these past few years; having him home... and safe. But that was because Gregory suffered so terribly."

Then with sudden realisation: "Oh, Elvira; I'm so sorry. I didn't mean to imply..."

"Dear Wendy," comforts Elvira; "it's alright. I know very well what Gregory went through. I first saw him the night of the tournament, you know, after he had faced Bijou. We looked at each other, for just a moment, but it was a moment which burned into my soul. I think I knew then that he was the man for me. And, by last Christmas, I knew everything about him. And everything I learned just made me want him more and more. He had loved someone totally, without holding anything back; so much so that when she died, his whole being disintegrated. But he had found his way back. How could you not fall in love with such a man?"

Silence as Wendy regards Elvira with sisterly affection.

"Gregory is very lucky, Elvira. Twice, he has found a woman with a depth of feeling to match his own. Mariel would have given him such a beautiful life. I pray that, this time, he will enjoy a long and happy life... with you."

"Thank you, Wendy," replies Elvira. "That means more to me than you could possibly know."

Wendy smiles and holds out her hand. Elvira takes it, squeezes it, and smiles in return. "Now: we have a wedding to arrange."

★

"... And thereto, I pledge thee my troth."

"... And thereto, I pledge thee my troth," repeats the squire.

"Arise, Rupert. Arise, Odelia. In the sight of God, and before these witnesses here gathered, I now pronounce you man and wife."

And, for a moment, the bishop is transported to another time, when another young man from the west and another young lady from the east arose from his blessing and looked into each other's eyes as man and wife for the first time.

And now, a young squire, who is even more of a boy than the knight he remembers, and a young woman, who is so much the image of her mother, stand before him pledging their commitment to each other, before God.

And, behind the young couple, beside Averill and Elvira, the Lady Wendy sobs quietly onto the shoulder of her husband. The poignant memories are simply too much to bear.

Elvira turns to Averill and sees his clenched jaw as he works to contain the sadness about to spill over. Wrapping her arms around his waist, she lays her head gently upon his chest. Averill continues to look straight ahead, but draws his woman tightly to him. No words; just the immediate need of each other.

A heavily built older man walks slowly forward and stands beside Averill, waiting patiently until he is noticed. Behind him, two taller but equally heavily built young men move forward and stand quietly together.

Averill's jaw relaxes. The moment passes. He turns and smiles and takes the blacksmith's hand. "William, it is so good to see you. Have you met Elvira?"

"My Lady," responds the blacksmith, bowing. "And may I present my two older boys, Richard and Thomas."

The two young men also bow, and, one after the other, gently clasp Elvira's hand.

"Quite a day, William," remarks Averill, looking over to where Rupert and Odelia are engaged in conversation with the Duke of Bedford.

"Aye, Sir Gregory," replies William. "It is such a day as I will never forget. Never in my life did I imagine that my youngest would marry the daughter of a knight."

"Well, you might also have to get used to the idea that your youngest may also be a knight before too long."

The old man shakes his head and chuckles. "I will count my blessings one-by-one, if I may, Sir Gregory. Today's wedding is all my heart can take at the moment, I fear."

The young couple arrive breathlessly.

"Congratulations sweetie; how do you feel?" asks Averill as he lifts his daughter off her feet, and kisses her.

"Wonderful, Daddy; just wonderful."

"Rupert," says Gregory holding forth his hand.

"Sir Gregory," replies the squire, shaking it firmly.

"You mean 'father', don't you?" suggests Bryan, as the knights and their ladies walk forward to offer their congratulations.

Rupert, embarrassed, looks around, seeking direction. And James provides the relief: "Don't answer him, Rupert, it's a trick!"

The group laughs and Rupert turns to Odelia, to kiss her once again.

The bishop approaches. "I will take my leave now, Gregory. I have been honoured to marry these two fine young people, and it seems that this night will not lack for high spirits."

"Yes, indeed, father, I believe you are correct," replies Averill, walking with the bishop. "And, thank you for everything."

Then, a moment of quiet concern: "Are you alright, Gregory?"

A pause, then: "Yes, father; I am very well indeed. I am surrounded by people who love me, and my daughter has just married the young man I admire most in the world. There is little more that I could ask for."

Then, as he acknowledges his deeper feelings: "Perhaps, in the fullness of time, when the mysteries are revealed..."

The bishop smiles and nods. "Yes, Gregory; perhaps then."

CHAPTER TEN

"It is more than a year since I came to England to visit my brother, Gregory."

"Oh, yes; I suppose it is," replies Averill, looking up from the trunk as he lays the pair of greaves neatly upon the growing pile of equipment on the floor. "But you do like England, don't you?"

"Oh, yes; I love England," replies the lady. "Although I think the weather in France is much nicer."

Averill chuckles and nods. "Indeed."

"And England is where you are, my love," Elvira continues. "Although, not for much longer."

Averill stops, and looks carefully at Elvira. "Alright, my love; tell me."

"What?" replies the lady, feigning innocence.

"Tell me what you're scheming."

"Well," she replies, smiling, "I just thought that, since you'll be in France, and since I'm French, it doesn't make a great deal of sense for me to be here in England for the next few months, does it?"

"Elvira, darling," replies Averill, slightly exasperated, "there's a war on. It's no place for women."

"Not in Caen, there isn't," replies Elvira. "I imagine that the city will be starting to return to normal now that the siege is over."

"Have you ever seen a city after a siege, my love?" asks Averill.

"No, I haven't," replies Elvira. "But I imagine that they could do with all the help they can get in rebuilding the lives that have been so devastated."

Averill stares at his lady, thinking hard.

"I could make a difference, Gregory," she insists. "I know many of the English lords who would be there, and, of course, I would be among my own people. I could do a lot to help, Gregory."

Averill is struggling to find a counter-argument.

"We would be nowhere near the fighting, Gregory."

"We? Who is 'we'?"

"Oh," replies Elvira, momentarily abashed. "Well, you wouldn't want to leave Odelia here alone, would you; now that she is married? And just think of the poor girl; barely spent a night with her husband and he's off again. Now that's not very nice for your daughter, is it?"

Averill's mind reels at the thought of Odelia in a war zone.

"And, her French is as good as mine, Gregory; you know that, don't you? She would be a wonderful help to me, and to the women and children of Caen. We would be doing so much more than just sitting here in England, worrying about you and Rupert."

Averill sinks to his haunches and looks up at his lady. "You seem to have it all worked out, don't you?" he muses.

"No, not really, Gregory," replies Elvira, kneeling in front of him and placing her arms around his neck. "But, I do think that we could make a useful contribution to the city, rather than just being here in England, doing nothing. And, I believe we'd be quite safe. And... we'd be much closer to you and Rupert, which would be lovely for all of us, don't you think, my love?"

The conflicting desires, for the safety of his women and for their nearby presence, continue to trouble the knight. But, little-by-little, as he considers further, the dangers of their being in Caen seem to fade. The city will be under English control, and Henry will have made the rules of conduct exceedingly clear, under pain of death for those who disobey. And, both Elvira and Odelia will be quite comfortable speaking with and helping the French women and children...

"Have you mentioned this to Odelia?" he asks.

"No, my love," replies the lady, looking into his eyes. "I needed to know that you would accept the idea before I spoke with her. Or, perhaps you wish to tell her, yourself, Gregory?"

Averill ponders a little more, then: "No, my love. I see that you have thought this through, and I know that you would not willingly endanger Odelia. Let it be as you suggest, my love. Pray, go and ask her if she wishes to join us in France."

★

"So, you enjoyed the wedding, did you, William?"

"Ah, Sir Gregory," replies the blacksmith, chuckling. "You'll not be catching me out by hiding in the early morning shadows any more, my boy. I know you're back now, and I'll not be surprised where you turn up, these days.

"And, yes, seeing as how you're asking, I did enjoy the wedding, very much, Sir Gregory."

"It was nice to meet your other boys, William; Richard and Thomas," continues Averill. "Very much like their father, aren't they?"

"Aye, indeed they are, Sir Gregory. Strong as oxen; can go all day. They should be along in an hour or so. Got to tend to their families, see. That's why they're not here as early as I am these days. Got responsibilities, you see."

"As has your youngest, now," adds Averill.

"Yes, indeed, Sir Gregory," replies William. "Now that's something I didn't expect to see; Rupert with responsibilities."

He laughs at the thought, then stops and regards Averill, with curiosity.

"So, what is it, Sir Gregory? You don't come around here to pass the time of day with an old blacksmith. You've usually something biting you when you show your face here."

"Am I really that transparent, William?" laughs Averill.

"Oh, aye, Sir Gregory; that you are."

Averill pushes himself off the wall upon which he has been leaning and walks from the half-light into the early morning sunshine.

"I once asked if you'd be interested in a last hurrah with an old knight who doesn't know when to quit, William."

"Aye, Sir Gregory," replies the blacksmith. "I remember. But the old knight I had in mind is still some years off, it seems to me."

"Perhaps," replies Averill, almost absent-mindedly. "But then again, perhaps it's just that the time has come upon us sooner than we expected.

"Anyway, you seemed to be interested in the idea, William."

"Aye, I was."

"Well then?"

"Well then what, Sir Gregory?"

"Well then, are you still interested?"

"Oh, I would be if you had a battle to fight, but the word I hear is that you're stuck here with poor Lord Bedford, until the king decides he needs some experienced muscle."

"Is that the word you hear, William?"

"Aye, Sir Gregory; it is!"

"Amazing how the world can be turned on its head in such a short time, isn't it?"

William's eyes sparkle as he takes in Averill's words. Then slowly: "So, you're telling me that someone's let you off the leash. Is that it?"

"In a manner of speaking, William."

"Oh, aye, it was that, Sir Gregory; a manner of speaking."

"The king has taken Caen."

"So I hear, Sir Gregory. News does reach us here from time to time."

"And is in need of a further seven hundred men," continues Averill.

"And you have been tasked with finding them?"

"Already done," replies Averill.

"And now you're going to lead them to France," smiles William.

"You see," replies Averill, "there is absolutely no doubt as to where that son of yours gets his intuition."

"No, my boy," counters William. "There is absolutely no way that you can keep that smile off your face; and that gives the entire game away."

Averill laughs, self-consciously. "Well then?" he presses, again.

"Oh, I don't know, Sir Gregory," replies William, lightly. "It would mean packing up hammers, and anvils, and dismantling the small forge, and..."

"And?"

"And, all the other things I have to do when someone makes me an offer I can't refuse," responds the blacksmith, smiling hugely.

"Bastard," retorts Averill, clasping William around the shoulders. "So you'll come?"

"Well, I suppose someone has to look after you; seeing as how you're such an old knight now."

"This will be something to remember, William," replies Averill, excitedly, ignoring the jibe. "This will be an adventure to rival any we've had before, I wager: you, me, the French army. Oh, and we might let the king have a bit of the action too. What do you think?"

"I think I'd better get started, my boy. This is going to take some preparation."

"Perhaps I could help," suggests a voice from the doorway.

William looks up to see the strong, lean figure of his youngest son silhouetted against the morning sun. He smiles. "And what would you know about the insides of a blacksmith's works, my boy?"

"I may surprise you," replies the squire. "There was a time, long ago, when I would stand beside you, and look up at what you were doing and be enthralled; a time when I was a better son than I later became."

"Yes, there was, my boy," replies William, moving to place his arm around the young man's shoulder. "You were so bright; and I was so proud of you. But then, we didn't see eye-to-eye for a long time, did we?"

"No, Father, we didn't. I..."

"Enough, lad. Them days is over now. I've seen what you've become with Sir Gregory here, and I'm mighty proud of you now, my boy. What's past is past.

"So, come on then; there's heavy work to be done. Why don't you go and get your brothers. Tell them I have some packing to do. Then come back; I think I know just where you can start."

"Yes, Father," replies Rupert, quietly. "I'd like that."

And, as the earnest young man leaves, William turns to Averill: "'Father.' Such a simple word, Gregory, but one I haven't heard from those lips in such a very long time. I rather feel as if all my blessings have come at once, you know."

★

314

"You look exhausted, Rupert."

"I feel exhausted, Sir Gregory. It's been a tough day; tough, but very enjoyable."

"Yes, it has, Rupert; most enjoyable. Your father's a remarkable man."

"Yes, he is, Sir Gregory. I didn't see it for so long, but now I do. You have no idea how proud of him I am now, Sir Gregory."

"That's good to hear, Rupert; he's a man who deserves your pride. He's a man I've be proud to call my friend for many years now, and, I like to think that he's happy to have me as a friend."

"Indeed, Sir Gregory. I don't think there's any doubt about that."

"Well, goodnight, Rupert; sleep well. And... please say 'hello' to Odelia for me. I miss her very much; the house is so quiet now. It's taking some getting used to."

"I'm sorry, Sir Gregory. But, in all truth, I don't really want to give her back."

"Nor am I asking Rupert; just an old man coming to terms with the next phase of his life. Be off with you now... and say 'hello' for me."

"I will, Sir Gregory. Goodnight."

Averill waits, drinking in the early autumn night air as Rupert strides away into the gathering dusk; so relaxing, so peaceful. A moment's further pause, then the knight turns and starts to walk, slowly, toward the castle and his now rather quiet lodgings; quiet, but enticing, since the Lady Elvira will be preparing dinner for her man. And after that, an evening of soft, gentle time together beckons.

But something is not right, and he stops. The muffled sounds of aggression carry through the night air, and Averill feels uneasy. Something is amiss.

He turns and re-traces his footsteps, back to the corner where Rupert departed. He stops and listens. The sounds of low, baiting voices raise the hairs on his neck. Cautiously, he advances. The night is still, and as he steps slowly down the alleyway, the voices become progressively more distinct.

"So, it's that arsehole Rupert; the bastard who thinks he's too high and mighty for his mates now; the bastard we knocked the shit out of last time, and who's going to cop it again, this time. Only this time it'll be worse; much worse! 'Cos this time, we're angry; really angry!"

"Yeah, this time we're really angry," echoes another wheedling voice.

There are five of them, Averill notes. Careful to stay in the shadows, he watches. Three are taller than Rupert, but none of them has the solid build which the squire now possesses; and none appears to have the cat-like spring in his step which has become a feature of Rupert's growing prowess in the training arena.

The squire is encircled now, and he crouches just slightly, hands held loosely by his side, ready to respond. Averill can almost feel the cold calm descending upon his charge. The five ruffians surrounding the squire, buoyed by their numbers, remain totally oblivious to the menace of the squire's stance. Averill cannot help but think of a scorpion with its tail raised and ready, as the unwary five taunt their silent prey.

The three tallest of the group suddenly raise their voices in prolonged shouts of aggression, then, spurred on by gang bravado, rush at Rupert, intending to rain punches upon their isolated and surrounded target.

The hip throw to the first is immaculate. The body is still flying through the air as Rupert's clenched right fist drives in just below the rib-cage of the second, and follows up with an unrestrained straight drive into the face of the third. The crack of the nose breaking punctuates the hoarse cry of winded agony from the second, as the body of the first thuds onto the dirty cobbles, bouncing once.

And, in the instant that the remaining two turn to run, the squire springs over the mangled bodies and catches the departing pair; a hand tightly around each neck. A moment's cruel hesitation as the squire looks into their traumatised eyes precedes the crack of the two heads crashing together, as he throws the pair to the ground, then turns back to the first three.

One is on hands and knees, bleeding profusely from his smashed nose; the second is rolling on the ground in agony, not even able to gasp for breath, so complete is the collapse of his lungs. And the formerly loudest of the attackers cringes in fear as Rupert advances. He begins to cry. But with cold precision, the squire hauls the ruffian to his feet and then with a lightning-fast grapple, stretches the defenceless body across his thigh, bearing down upon the shoulder until the poor wretch wails in agony.

"I haven't even begun to take you apart," breathes the squire into his victim's ear. He looks into the terrified eyes and increases the pressure on the almost dislocated shoulder until the pinned young man screams in pain. Then, with a shrug, he drops the agonised body to the ground and turns back to the others, who have begun crawling away.

They stop as another pair of boots comes to a standstill before them. Now trapped between Rupert and Averill, the five terrified villains, fearing for their lives, lose control of their bodily functions.

Knight and squire stand and watch, while the stench of excreta rises from the cobblestones.

"Enough, for this time," comments Averill. Then squatting down next to the apparent leader of the gang. "But if there's a next time, and I sincerely hope there is, then I won't be stopping you, Rupert. You can do with them as you please."

Another moment to survey the damage, then Averill rises.

"It's no fun, is it?" comments Rupert, as they walk away from the convulsing forms on the ground.

"Very perceptive," replies Averill. "No, indeed. Just because you can destroy a man with your bare hands, doesn't make it pleasurable. It just gives you the confidence that you can do it, if you need to."

Rupert stops. "I've never done anything like that before. I mean, there was no emotion in it. It felt... cold. You could kill a man in that state of mind, and not even care, couldn't you?"

"Yes, Rupert, you could," replies Averill, placing his hand on the squire's shoulder, and leading him on again. "It's something we have to be aware of, that feeling of indifference. It's not something you want to let happen very often."

"Yes, I can see that," replies the squire, thoughtfully, as he walks. Then, stopping once again, he turns to Averill. "I think I'll go home now; I want to see Odelia. I need her very much now. I need to be with someone beautiful again."

Averill nods. "I understand, Rupert."

"This has been rather frightening. I've been in fights before, but not like this. This felt so cold; so... powerful. I'm a little bit afraid of what I'm capable of now, Sir Gregory."

"That's a very healthy attitude, Rupert. You're capable of a great deal now, my boy. And it's important that you keep it in check. That's something which defines a knight; the ability to deliver the worst, whilst maintaining focus upon the best. It isn't easy, Rupert. But then, nothing really worthwhile is easy. You'll learn that soon enough.

"Goodnight, my boy."

"Goodnight, Sir Gregory."

"Sir Gregory?"

"Yes, my boy?"

"Thank you... for being there."

★

The carts are assembled now, and the morning sunlight bathes the courtyard in a soft, early Autumn glow. Light-grey clouds move slowly overhead. Rain is on its way; but not for a few hours yet. The activity in the courtyard is purposeful, but not hurried; everything is almost ready now, and the first 'goodbyes' are being said.

"Ah, Gregory; it seems that everything is just about ready," booms the duke, as he descends the wide stone stairs from the castle.

"Indeed, my Lord," replies Averill. "I believe that we have everything packed, and everyone almost ready to depart."

Bedford looks around and nods. "Yes, Gregory, everything seems to be well under control.

"I have some despatches for His Majesty," he adds. "I'd be grateful if you would take them with you and deliver them personally to him."

"Of course, my Lord," replies Averill, taking the package and stowing it carefully in one of the cavernous saddle-bags hanging over Damsel's rump.

"It seems that William is determined that he will not have to say 'no' to any request," chuckles the duke, looking over towards the blacksmith. "I've never seen so much equipment piled onto one man's cart."

"Ah, well; you know how it is, my Lord," replies Averill. "If there's one thing a blacksmith prides himself upon, it's being able to provide an adequate supply of good armour when it's most needed."

"And William is certainly aiming to do just that," smiles the duke.

"He's a good man," comments Averill. "I'm very pleased he agreed to come with us. I feel quite happy that we have a very solid group here now."

"And your ladies?" enquires Bedford. "How are they coping with the preparations?"

"Well, I've had to stand back while the pair of them set about getting everything they wanted to take prepared, bundled and loaded. So, I'd say rather well, my Lord."

"Doesn't surprise me one bit," laughs Bedford. "They're a beautiful pair, Gregory. But woe betide any man who stands in their way, once they have their minds set upon a course."

Then, more seriously: "I know I don't really need to say this, Gregory, but do take care. This is a very special group of people you have here, and I'd be very sad of anything happened to any of them, you know."

"Yes, my Lord," replies Averill, quietly. "They are, indeed, a very special group. And, some of us have a rather long history together now. There are many memories here this morning, my Lord; many memories."

"But, you know as well as I, my Lord, that we will be going into battle in a couple of weeks' time, and, at that point, I cannot guarantee the safety of any of my men... or of the squires, my Lord."

"Yes, I know, Gregory. It was a foolish thing to say, since I know you will look after them as well as any man could. But, just for my own sake, I needed to say it. Just in case you didn't know how highly I regard every one of you."

"Thank you, my Lord," replies Averill, clasping the duke's outstretched hand. "I will remember this."

The duke turns once more and surveys the scene. All around him, men are saying their last goodbyes and mounting horses. Gareth hugs Wendy one last time, and kisses his little daughter on the forehead before swinging himself up into the saddle.

"My Lord," says Averill. "With your permission, we will depart."

"God speed, Gregory," replies the duke, turning back and shaking the knight's hand once more. And then, mounting the steps and looking out over the assembled group of travellers, families and well wishers, Bedford raises his right arm, and punching the air, shouts: "For king and country."

The response is loud and proud, as men, women and children raise their voices in support.

And so, one year to the day since Averill and Bijou met on the tilting field hard by Kenilworth castle, a party of seven knights and two squires, along with two ladies and a broadly smiling blacksmith driving an over-laden cart of equipment and chattels, accompanied by twenty-three yeomen and a contingent of archers and men-at-arms, rides under the gate of Windsor castle, heading south for Portsmouth, where they will join the nearly seven hundred men now assembling.

And thence to France...

PART 5

CHAPTER ONE

Caen.

The twin spires of Église Saint-Étienne come grandly into view as the lead ship slowly rounds the bend in the river, and the scene, hidden behind the trees for so long, is at last revealed.

Averill stands on the for'd castle with his lieutenants, catching the first glimpse of the recently conquered city. At his side, both Elvira and Odelia take in the French countryside once again. It has been a year and a half since Elvira saw her homeland, and more than five since Odelia last laid eyes upon French soil.

The young lady is quiet; memories of her mother revived.

"Do you know where Pierre is, my love?" asks Averill of Elvira.

"No, darling. He is with the Duke of Burgundy; but where they are right now, I do not know."

"Ah well. Let us see if we can find out more when we land," replies Averill. "I'm sure someone in the city will be able to tell us."

"It looks as if there'll be a party waiting for us," says Anthony, pointing towards figures running towards the docks still some half-kilometre away.

"I imagine there's more than a little desperation there," comments Thomas. "The poor bastards are probably starving."

"Yes, I think you might be right," replies Averill. "But the city gates are open again now, and hopefully, they're able to start planting and foraging and hunting again.

"However, I don't believe His Majesty will be allowing any of our cargo to go to the locals."

"No," replies Thomas. "We have an army to feed, and the king is nothing if not single-minded."

The ten vessels, inline and several hundred metres apart, one-by-one round the final bend and approach the city docks, where willing hands catch mooring ropes tossed from the vessels and one-by-one secure the ships. Within an hour, all ten are berthed and the passage of soldiers and the unloading of cargo are in full swing.

"It's good to see you again, Gregory," smiles Sir Gilbert Umfraville, recently appointed captain of the town, taking Averill's outstretched hand and pumping it vigorously. "It's been a long time since we've seen you on the battlefield, but, by God, it's good to have you back again."

"It's good to be back, Gilbert," replies the knight. "I'd forgotten the action and the excitement.

"By God, this place is a mess, isn't it?"

"Oh aye, it is, Gregory; but nothing like the mess it was when Clarence and the king had finished with it. Honestly, I've never seen so much blood in the streets before. I believe in our king, Gregory, and I believe God walks with us; but, my friend, this is not a pretty campaign."

"War never is, Gilbert," replies Averill.

Gilbert nods, soberly; then bright, once again: "Well then, let's head on up to the castle. I'm sure His Majesty will be very pleased to see you here, at last. Like I said, Gregory, it's been a long, long time; too long. It's good to see you back among us, my friend. It was shit when that bastard Bijou was leading us."

Averill is suddenly still. "I'll find him, Gilbert," he spits. "One day I'll find him."

Umfraville looks hard at Averill. "Yes, Gregory; I believe you will."

★

"Well, well; Sir Gregory Averill, on the battlefield once again.

"How are you Gregory," continues the king, embracing his old friend. "It's been a long time since you and I did this together, hasn't it?"

"Yes, Your Majesty, it has," replies Averill, smiling broadly.

"And the two prettiest ladies I know," adds Henry, turning towards Elvira and Odelia, who curtsey.

"How are you, Elvira?"

"Very well, thank you, Your Majesty."

"And my favourite young lady, Odelia. I hear you're now a happily married young woman."

"Yes, Your Majesty, I am," Odelia replies, blushing.

"Well, my dear," continues the king, "we'll see just what that young man of yours is made of over the next few weeks and months."

Then, as Odelia looks blatantly afraid, he adds. "Don't worry, Odelia; he's with your father, and I don't believe there's anyone who could protect him better. At least I hope not; I expect to be protected too!" he laughs.

Odelia smiles, unconvincingly, and Elvira places her arm around the young woman's shoulder.

"So, Gregory, shall we talk? I'm sure you have much news from my brother, Bedford."

"Yes, of course, Your Majesty."

"Then, by your leave, Your Majesty, we will depart," says Elvira. "I'd like to

324

start having a look around the town. I think Odelia and I can do some useful work here."

"That's very noble of you, Elvira," replies the king, gently. "I can understand that you want to help your people, and you have my full support in everything you wish to achieve. I've already told Umfraville that you're to be given anything you ask for."

Elvira and Odelia curtsey again, in readiness to leave. "Thank you, Your Majesty."

"Take care, ladies," waves the king. "I'm truly delighted to see you here."

Then, as the softer and prettier members of the gathering depart: "Now, Gregory, tell me all that is happening at home. Is my brother well?"

★

The light flickers slightly as the wall-torches in the room, where the war council is gathered, recover from the brief gust of wind. The floor has been cleared of the dust and rubble which had swept in during the bombardment, but the walls still show bare patches, where daubing has cracked and fallen away. Clarence, Gloucester, Umfraville, Lord Talbot – Captain General of the surrounding marches – and Averill, all sit, quiet but alert, as Henry speaks.

"Well, gentlemen, it's rather like old times isn't it?"

"Indeed," replies Clarence. "So good to see you, Gregory."

"Thank you," replies Averill, smiling. "It's a little daunting, actually. I feel so out of touch with everything."

"Ah, that won't take long to come back," laughs Talbot. "Come and spend a couple of days with me and we'll soon have you back in the thick of things."

The group chuckles amiably.

"Now then," says Henry, looking around the table. "To business!"

The chuckles die away and all attention is focussed upon the king.

"Gentlemen, we have Caen. The siege was bloody it is true, but not nearly as long or as costly as the siege of Harfleur, last time we were here. So, for that, God be praised."

"Amen," breathes Gloucester.

"But now we must consolidate what we have, then strike out again whilst the weather is not too unpleasant. I want to spend no longer than two more weeks here in Caen. Gilbert, I am looking to you to give me a secure town in that time."

"Yes, Your Majesty," replies Umfraville. "I will ensure that we achieve that."

"Our major objective is control of Normandy, and now that we have Caen, that means taking Rouen, the seat of government, almost due east of here," continues the king. "However, first, I plan to strike south, deeper into lower Normandy.

"As you know, gentlemen, the French forces are divided: Burgundians and Armagnacs, both at each other's throats. And this boon has become apparent in the last few days. We have been visited by the dukes of Burgundy and Brittany, and have reached agreement with both of them. We will not be harassed by either of their forces. However, there are still Armagnac forces at large and we need to be confident that this part of Normandy is under our control, before we set out to take Rouen. Hence the view that further conquest in southern Normandy is necessary.

"Do I hear any objections? Please, speak plainly, as we cannot afford to make decisions now, which we might otherwise not have made, had we known more."

"I have no objection," replies Talbot.

"Nor I," reply the others, in various forms.

"Gregory?"

"Too soon to really comment, Your Majesty. "I need time to understand what is happening here. But, certainly, no objection."

"Right, then," continues the king.

"So, in two weeks' time, we march. There are garrisons at Falaise, Exmes, Argentan, Sées and Alençon, which all need to be taken before we can consider this region friendly. We may then look to see if we need to show some muscle in Brittany, although I'd rather not, as that takes us further from our principal objective. Nevertheless, if it is required, then we shall do it."

"Wasn't the Duke of Alençon killed at Agincourt?" asks Clarence.

"Yes, he was," replies Henry. "Jean, First Duc d'Alençon. His son is now Duke, but he is only eight years old. So it's possible, but not certain, that there will be little organised resistance there."

"I understand that Falaise could be difficult, Your Majesty," remarks Talbot. "I believe it sits atop high ground with steep approaches, and is well defended."

"That is also my understanding," replies the king. "However, it is also my understanding that Exmes, Argentan and Sées, although well-manned in preparation for our attack, are not so geographically blessed, and would not present such difficulties. And Alençon we have already discussed."

"Perhaps then, we should then mark Falaise for later attack, my Lord," suggests Clarence.

A moment's pause as the king ponders. "Yes, perhaps we should. However, I would only go as far as making Falaise the last target of this region. I would not want to leave it in enemy hands as we pushed further south and then east."

There is general nodding of heads, which Henry takes as agreement.

"So then, for broad strategy, that is it: we take the five towns discussed, leaving Falaise 'til last. Then we review where to strike next, as we push toward Rouen. Gregory, I'd like you to work with Umfraville and Talbot, developing the details. I think it's time you started to become familiar with where we are and what's ahead of us."

"Yes, Your Majesty; that would be most welcome."

"Remember gentlemen; two weeks!"

The king rises, and the assembled group does likewise.

"I bid you goodnight, gentlemen."

"Goodnight, Your Majesty," is the chorused response as the meeting breaks up.

"I'll see you in the morning," remarks Talbot, clapping Averill on the shoulder.

"Yes, indeed," replies Averill. "God, it's good to back. I'd forgotten how much I missed all this."

"Still got that ugly crew with you?" asks Gloucester, walking by.

"Of course," replies Averill. "There's no-one else I'd risk going to war with.

"Well, there is one exception," he adds.

"Oh, and who might that be?" asks Clarence, stopping, intrigued.

"I'll introduce you in the morning. He's rather young, but very talented. And, I've just recently seen him see off five attackers, three bigger then himself... name's Rupert... he's my squire."

"I'll look forward to it," replies Clarence. "What's he like with a sword?"

"Tolerable."

"Oh dear, that good. Then I don't think I'll be challenging him, will I?"

That's entirely up to you, my Lord," replies Averill, smiling. "But I wouldn't."

★

"Gregory Averill; I'm so annoyed at you!"

"Why, my love; what is it?"

"I don't think I've ever seen you this happy. What is it with you men? The moment there's the smell of battle in the air, your eyes light up, you regain the spring in your step, and all is right in the world; while we women fall about, depressed, wondering if we'll ever see you again. It's so unfair! Why can't we be so happy about war?"

"Oh, my love," replies Averill, holding Elvira to him and gently stroking her hair. "If you could see the brutal side of it, you would not wish so. Yes, we become excited by the prospect of battle, of feeling the thrill of combat once again, of charging through the ranks of enemy soldiers, of duelling with a worthy opponent, of winning. But there's another side to it as well, and you wouldn't want to be part of that, my love; watching men being smashed and hacked to death, hearing the screams of the injured and dying, watching as men burn in boiling oil, or drown in suffocating mud. These are not things for a woman to see, my love, nor to think upon when her man is away.

"And that is why, it is better to be annoyed by the smile, and the spring in the step, and the glint in our eyes. These are our gifts to you, my love. This is the way we want you to remember us, in case we should not come back."

"Oh, Gregory, don't say things like that; they frighten me. I know this is your life, and this is what you are called to do, but, until now, it's never been so real. I'm scared."

"Don't be afraid, my love, we have two weeks yet; two weeks in which to put the detail into our strategy. And besides, you can see all around you, how comprehensive the victory was here in Caen, and this was a well-fortified city. Henry has a talent for war, and, God knows, his cause is just. We will be victorious my, love, I promise. And I will come back to you. This, I also promise."

CHAPTER TWO

Two thousand men remain to maintain order in Caen. Ten thousand are now assembling outside the city walls in preparation for the first phase of the advance into lower Normandy.

Averill and his lieutenants, along with Rupert and James, and scores of other captains and knights, have been up since before dawn, ensuring that the myriad activities are going to plan. Carts of equipment, prepared over the last few days, are now being arranged ready for departure. The larger units, carrying the components of siege engine and cannon, are being pulled into line by huge draught horses, brought especially for the purpose of moving such enormous loads. Hundreds of other horses, tethered in groups; destriers, large and powerful; chargers, sleek and fast; palfreys, docile but possessed of wonderful stamina; all stamp and kick at the ground as the excitement of the morning becomes palpable to man and beast. And everywhere archers, men-at-arms and knights move slowly into orderly arrangement, ready to move out upon the king's command. A hundred different pennants curl and snap in the breeze, as the rising sun begins to reveal the colour of the assembled army; each man wearing a jerkin bearing the coat-of-arms of his master; each knight resplendent in shining armour and emblazoned doublet. And on the back of every one, the red cross of St George.

The crowd of women and children and old men braving the early morning grows by the moment, as more and more arrive to view the spectacle. Odelia hugs Elvira tightly as they stand in the shadows, both reacting to the excitement and the foreboding of the moment.

"Oh, Elvira, I don't know what I am feeling. I feel so sick inside, and at the same time, I have this feeling like... like..."

"Like when Rupert touches you," answers Elvira, without thinking.

The young woman looks up, embarrassed. "Yes, Elvira; just like that; so powerful. Am I strange?"

"I don't know, Odelia. I've never seen my man off to war before, but that's exactly how I feel at the moment. I'm so scared for Gregory, but I also feel what you feel. It's not what I expected. In fact, I don't know what I expected, but not this; not this urgency, this intense desire to take him, and wrap myself around him, and..."

Elvira stops, suddenly aware that she is speaking to the daughter of the man she loves. But Odelia is no longer just Averill's daughter; she is also

Rupert's wife and lover, and has her own intimate knowledge of the passions which Elvira is describing. She smiles, "Oh God; me too."

A lone figure detaches itself from the mass and walks towards the women. Another follows.

Averill reaches Elvira, who throws her arms around her man, devouring his lips and grinding her hips against his, not caring if anyone is watching. Odelia and Rupert are more tender in their embrace, but no less passionate.

"We have to go, my love."

"I know, my darling, I know. This is so awful. I want you so badly. Please come back to me, Gregory; I couldn't bear it if anything happened to you."

"I'll be fine, my love. Rupert and I will take care of each other, I promise."

Averill and Elvira kiss again, as the tears begin to flow.

"Daddy?"

"Yes, sweetie?"

The young woman reaches up and ties the silk scarf gently around her father's neck. "You wore this once before for me; please will you wear it again? Mummy said it always brought you good fortune in the tournaments. I hope it will bring you safely home to us again."

Elvira senses Gregory's torn loyalties and placing her arm around his waist, leans her head upon his shoulder. "You are now part of a beautiful story, Gregory; a story of a knight, and three women, and a magic scarf which protects him. Please wear it for all of us who love you; those who are here, and those who are not. And come home safely to us, my darling."

And, just as the last time, overcome, and unable to respond, Averill nods his acquiescence to the request.

A last kiss and embrace, and each man walks back into the assembled mass. Neither speaks; the bond needs no statement.

A hush ripples out as Henry, flanked by Clarence and Gloucester, rides slowly through the mass of men and equipment. At the head, he stops, turns in the saddle, and looks back over the assembled English army. Then, with clenched fist raised high, he shouts "Onward, gentlemen. Now we take Normandy."

The army lurches into motion.

CHAPTER THREE

Heading south-east from Caen, the army skirts the heavily fortified Falaise and takes a wide, circular route toward Exmes. Word of the movement of the English army spreads rapidly. But this is no straggle of dehydrated wretches making their way home again, as it was two years ago; this is the collective might of England moving out against the fragmented and uncoordinated forces of a divided France.

And, six days and seventy-two kilometres later, the English army stands before Exmes, wagering with each other on the speed with which the town's elimination will be achieved. However, there is no resistance. A party of officials from the town, intent upon ensuring the survival of its citizens, meets with the English to discuss terms. The terms are Henry's: surrender and refrain from taking up arms again against the king of England, or perish now. Two days later, Argentan also succumbs, and three days after that, Sées does likewise.

And so, at dawn on the fifteenth day after leaving Caen, Henry and his army stand arrayed before the gates of Alençon. Not a sword has been raised, nor a cannon fired in the conquest to-date. However, Alençon has been well-fortified for resistance, and the English are itching for an opportunity to fight. But Alençon does not provide it. With stories of the brutality inflicted upon Caen fresh in the minds of the townspeople, and the advisors to the eight year old Second Duc d'Alençon unable to formulate any coherent defensive strategy, the town capitulates. The rout is complete.

★

Two weeks have passed; two weeks, in which, the entire duchy of Alençon has submitted to English control, and the Duke of Brittany, uncle to the now dispossessed young Duc d'Alençon, has once again visited the king of England, to sue for peace. The deal is done: Brittany is safe from attack, as is Anjou, and Henry is assured of the non-involvement of the two duchies for the next year.

The English now control a corridor from the coast through to the southern border of Normandy.

"Well, Gregory; we've had a pretty easy ride, so far, haven't we?"

"Yes, indeed, Your Majesty," replies the knight. "In fact, I'm beginning to wonder if you really needed me here, my Lord. We seem to be well in the ascendency."

"For the moment, Gregory; for the moment. But there is one fortress which stands in our way."

"Falaise?"

"Yes, Gregory; Falaise."

"Do we know much about it, my Lord?"

"Only by reputation, Gregory. It's the birthplace of my ancestor, William the Conqueror, you know."

"Yes, my Lord; I did know. I imagine that makes it quite a special place for you, my Lord. But, actually, I was asking more about its geography."

"Difficult, Gregory; difficult," replies the king. "The reports are that it sits on a plateau of land rising above the valleys of the Ante and Marescot rivers; a walled town, probably stocked to the hilt. But it's the castle that will be the greater challenge. It's built upon a steep, rocky cliff at the point of the plateau, where the two rivers meet. It's high, and overlooks the town. We'll know more when we see it, but, for the moment, it sounds quite foreboding.

"I fear that taking Falaise may be a costly exercise, Gregory. And, I don't think you need worry that you are not needed here. This next battle is going to test us, my friend."

Averill smiles. "Well, my Lord, it's been a long time since I fought for my country. It seems somehow fitting that the occasion should be... worthy."

Henry looks back at him, but does not smile, the blood of Caen still fresh in his mind. "Yes, Gregory; it's as you say: fitting, that it should be so."

CHAPTER FOUR

Campaigning in winter, although not unheard of, is nevertheless unusual, and the black branches of the leafless trees high up the hill to the left provide a stark and unfamiliar tone to the scene. But Henry is pushing to achieve control of western and southern Normandy, without delay, in order to release his army upon Rouen in the spring. And so, the campaign continues through the cold of late November.

Beyond the lake and the weeping willows, the ground rises steeply until a rocky crag emerges above the distant tree line. And then, as if to reinforce its dominance, the castle rises further above the rocky base; its large square keep and circular tower completely dominating the skyline.

"Château Guillaume-Le-Conquérant," breathes Henry, in muted admiration. Then, turning to the lords and knights gathered beside him at the head of the army, he adds, "This, as much as anything we have encountered to-date, belongs to England!"

But, even without advancing for a closer look, it is clear to all viewing the scene that there is no possibility of attacking the castle directly. The only viable approach will be through the walled town itself.

And so, although still two kilometres from their destination, the army gradually wheels right and begins the long, slow climb to the plateau between the two rivers, upon which the town is built.

Over the following two hours, the circular passage of the army gradually brings the castle into an alignment relatively behind and above the walled town.

"Magnificent," remarks the king. "Just look at it, Gregory; no chance of surprise, no chance of being caught out. There is only one way in. What mighty work has been achieved here by my ancestors, my friend? And how sweet it will be to reclaim our just rights and inheritances; our Normandy, and all that goes with it."

Averill looks at his king, amazed anew at the passion of the monarch for this quest.

"Your Majesty," he begins; "I wondered aloud to you, not eight days previous, whether I was really needed here. Well, whether I am needed her or no, my Lord, there is nowhere else I would rather be at this moment. This will be a battle to remember; and a prize more worthy than almost anything we have approached together over the years."

The king, hunched forward, resting his forearms on the saddle, looks over and nods. "Yes, Gregory; I feel the same."

And then, as if an afterthought, he adds, "I think it's time my army had its true champion back, Gregory. What do you say?"

"Ah... I'm an old man, Your Majesty," chuckles Averill; "well past my prime. There are others now who could fill those boots better than I, my Lord."

"Not while you're still wearing them," smiles the king.

Averill is suddenly quiet, remembering the circumstances which led to his losing the post in the first place. Henry, reliving the same painful memories, is also quiet... and inwardly still torn by the necessity of his actions.

Only a few moments pass, but, for the two men joined by common thoughts, it is as if time has stopped.

"It would be an honour, Your Majesty," replies Averill, at last.

"For me, too," replies the king, reaching out to clasp the gloved hand of the knight at his side.

★

Morning brings a crisp, cold day; bright sunshine, but a slight, chill wind that softly flaps and curls the tents of the English camp, hastily assembled the previous evening. Row upon row of tents, large and small, now occupy the gently sloping ground to the east of the city wall, but, owing to the urgency with which they were erected, the lines are ragged. This will be corrected during the daylight hours, today, as the serious business of 'digging in' proceeds. The royal pennant, lions and fleurs de lys, flies from the top of the large circular tent with protruding reception canopy, which sits within the northern quarter of the English encampment. And next to it flutters the red cross of St. George.

The king has despatched his negotiating party, two heralds, Lord Talbot and Averill, accompanied by Rupert, to deliver his message to the town council. As always, he has been punctilious, requiring the town to open its gates 'freely and without coercion', to restore to Henry the town 'which is a noble and hereditary portion of our crown of England', and referencing the twentieth chapter of the book of *Deuteronomy* to identify the consequences of refusal; the biblical provision to 'put all its males to the sword', and, for the rest, women, children and animals, to 'take as booty for yourselves; and... enjoy the spoils of your enemies, which the Lord your God has given you.'

And, predictably, Olivier de Mauny, Governor of Falaise, and his town council have rejected the king's demand, citing duty and honour as preventing them from complying, and referencing the king of France as the only authority from whom they could accept such a demand.

The formalities have been assiduously observed.

And now, the king, his ferocious and gifted brother Clarence; Talbot, who will command the town upon its capture; and Averill, who once again carries the honour of king's champion; ride in a wide arc, beyond the outer suburbs of Falaise, taking a good look at the defences: the great stone outer walls, several kilometres long, encompassing the dwellings of half of the town's six thousand inhabitants; the regularly spaced watchtowers at which defences will be concentrated and counter-attacks co-ordinated; the four gates, each protected by fortified bastion and portcullis; then, deep within, the huge castle walls, which are probably several metres thick at the base, and look to be about ten metres high, and no doubt just as deeply set into the earth to thwart attack by mining; the huge protruding, circular defensive turrets at the north-east and south-west extremities of the castle wall; and within that enclosure, no doubt separated into fortified outer and inner baileys, the massive square keep, looking to be about twenty metres broad, and just as high, reinforced by huge stone buttresses running the full height of the walls, apparently comprised of three floors, most likely for storage, living and defence; the smaller or 'lower' keep, rectangular, and built hard against the larger structure, occupying the ledge of land atop the high cliff of the natural rock spur at the end of the plateau, upon which the whole castle and its enclosure have been built; and, finally, the great circular tower, almost fifteen metres wide and forty metres high, added by Philip Augustus II, King of France, in 1204, to strengthen the castle's defences, and eliminate the blind angles which restricted the coverage of the rectangular keeps.

In truth, Falaise appears almost impregnable.

"This will be a battle to reflect upon in years to come," remarks the king, smiling fiercely. "Mark my words, gentlemen: whoever comes through this with me will remember this battle for the rest of his life."

"'Tis a fearsome task, my Lord," adds Clarence, also grinning with relish. "But if not fearsome, then what is the point?"

"Two phases," adds Talbot. "The town will take some time to breach, and then we will have to start over again upon the castle."

"Well then," remarks Averill. "Two chances for glory." And the group erupts into high-spirited laughter.

"Ah, my brothers," cautions the king. "Let us not get too carried away, just yet. True, we will take this, this... pebble, but let us not diminish the magnitude of the task which awaits us. There will be losses, gentlemen; there will be losses."

And quickly, as if upon a cue, the mood changes from high-spirited anticipation, to the serious business of war.

★

At eleven o'clock, on the morning of Sunday 1st December, following morning Mass, the battle for the town of Falaise begins.

Three thousand archers, with arrows dipped in pitch and set aflame, launch a barrage of fire upon the wooden dwellings outside the city wall; the objective being to clear three wide paths in towards the defensive walls, so that cannon and siege engines can be brought within range of the walls, to batter the town from different directions, thereby dividing the defences which can be mounted against any single source of attack. Within hours, the sky is dark overhead from the thick smoke which emanates from the numerous gutted structures and smouldering heaps of ash, which only this morning were the homes of the poorest of Falaise.

And, incensed by the attack upon their property, hundreds of ragged, displaced homeowners launch counter-attacks upon the archers, with anything to hand; spades, pitchforks, and all manner of farming implements. But this frenzied reaction was anticipated, and the response by the English men-at-arms is swift and brutal. By the end of the first day, the paths have been cleared, and many of the town's menfolk lie dead. The pitiful scene is made more horrifying by the wailing of women clutching lifeless bodies and rocking backwards and forwards as they shriek their anger and grief at the devastation which has been visited upon them. Wide-eyed children with tear-stained cheeks, stumble, trance-like, through the carnage, looking for parents, or pets, or anything which might bring back just a little of the life they knew only hours before.

The eerie glow of embers continues through the night, punctuated by groaning crashes as larger timbers finally succumb and crumble into ash.

As morning breaks the land is revealed, covered in a grey, smoky haze. Already the echoes of hammering resound as carpenters begin the building and erection of huge wooden screens, behind which the construction of the siege engines, brought in pre-fabricated sections from Caen, will commence. Bolts from crossbows fired from the town walls fly overhead, occasionally finding their target as the work force swells. Today, there are English dead lying face-down in the grass. And still others commence digging, as earth is removed to create huge ditches around the areas where the siege engines and cannon will sit, and the removed earth is packed, between the ditches and the rising weapons, to become ramparts, behind which the machines of war can be operated, and from which any counter-attacks can be quickly quelled.

The labouring continues, day and night, for two more cycles of the sun, until the massive structures one-by-one begin to groan and strain as the operators test first the capacity, and then the range, of the weapons.

336

The repeated crashing of huge flying stones upon stubborn, unyielding masonry, and the sharp splintering of timbers confirm that the walls are now within range of the English siege engines.

And then, late on the fourth day, the thunderous roar of exploding gunpowder adds to the violence, as the newest generation of weaponry becomes active. The stockpiles of some of the ten thousand gun-stones brought from England are now higher than a man's shoulder, and ready to be unleashed upon the defenders of Falaise.

★

Eighteen days.

The high stone walls of the town no longer appear impregnable. The inevitable end is near, and yet, the ferocity with which the French defend their town remains undiminished. At points along its perimeter, the crumbling wall has been shored up with timber and stones, earth and dung. At night, the defenders slave feverishly to repair the damage of the day's onslaught, creating screens within the ruins behind which they can fight the next day. Tree-trunks driven into the ground and lashed together on the outer side of the wall cover the weakest points. The streets of Falaise now reek with the stench of mud and clay and dung, mixed together and spread in a thick layer to lessen the impact of the huge gun-stones which pelt the town mercilessly. Many beautiful buildings within the town have simply vanished, blown to pieces by the relentless bombardment. Others remain mere shells, imminent collapse inevitable.

"A few more days, at most," remarks the king to Clarence and Averill and Talbot as they walk between the twin trebuchets closest to the town wall. "I cannot see them holding out any longer."

"Aye, my Lord," replies Talbot. "They are defeated but refuse to acknowledge it. It seems that we will be forced to pursue this siege to its bitter end. And that will mean much bloodshed in the final hours."

"So stubborn!" retorts the king, as he stops and stands, hand on hips, looking at the battered walls and shaking his head. But then he relaxes and turns to Averill. "But would we be any different, Gregory? Would we capitulate, or would we fight on even though the odds were impossible?"

"You know the answer, Your Majesty," replies the knight, smiling. "There is a spirit within England which I, for one, would not wish to meet on the battlefield; a spirit which, even in the most dire circumstances, will not let us take one single pace backwards. And, my Lord, I have to say that the citizens of Falaise are showing that same spirit. It seems that your ancestor, William the Conqueror, has imbued this town with his own mighty spirit, and that these, are honourable and worthy opponents, my Lord."

The king nods and claps Averill on the shoulder. "Then let us have done with this, Gregory; and quickly."

★

Upon a signal, the sky bursts into light with the trails of a thousand flaming arrows as they rain upon the eastern bastion. And under cover of the pre-dawn darkness, five hundred men-at-arms storm the gate within the now flaming tower. At the head, led by Averill and Gareth, pairs of axe-men hack into the burning portcullis for several minutes before giving way to the next team, and so on. One hundred yards behind the attackers, archers crouch behind wooden screens, launching death at any defender who raises his head above the crenellations of the adjoining wall.

Gradually, the burning timbers give way to the axes being wielded by strong, muscular foresters, accustomed to felling trees much thicker in girth than the heavy lattice-work of the gate. And, from within the smoke come the sounds of shouting and running as the surprised defenders recover and sprint towards the conflagration.

The gate begins to splinter, then breaks, and knights and soldiers stream through.

"Stay behind me, and stay alert!" barks Averill to Rupert; "Things will happen very quickly now."

Eyes wide with excitement and glowing with the reflection of the flames all around, Rupert charges through the gap immediately behind Averill.

"How the fuck would you not stay alert, here?" he shouts.

"Just be careful!" replies Averill; humourless.

"Shit," shouts Gareth, "another wall!" as they come up against huge rocks, packed together with earth and dung to form another line of defence.

"The ram!" shouts Averill, and the command is echoed back through the press of attackers.

Valuable minutes pass as the battering ram is manhandled through the bastion; minutes in which the assembly of defenders on the other side of the wall increases significantly.

Once again, the foresters, used to hauling huge loads, take up the attack. The ram is some fifteen feet long, and almost two feet in diameter. And, in the arms of twenty muscular men, it becomes a fearsome weapon. The recently constructed secondary wall begins to crumble after the tenth blow. And, buoyed by the success, the attackers together put their shoulders to the failing structure every time the ram strikes. The noise of falling rock is ear-shattering up close, and the dust billowing up from the falling stones turns an eerie orange in the light of the flaming portcullis behind.

Battle is joined as English men-at-arms charge through the gap and clash, in ever-increasing numbers, with French defenders, wielding axes and swords. The torrent of men pouring through the gap is swelled again as archers, having dispensed with their bows, now join the fight armed with short-swords and daggers. And as the struggle rages, and the hacking and maiming and death continue, the gradually lightening horizon to the south-east heralds the dawn.

Little-by-little, the defences weaken and give ground, then finally succumb to the relentless advance of the attacking force. By the time the sun is fully above the horizon, the ground is littered with dead and wounded.

The gradually materialising scene of horror slowly brings the attacking force to a halt, as men from both sides take in the cost of the night's battle. Everywhere they look, they see shattered buildings, crumbling, burnt-out structures which used to be homes, and the as yet unburied bodies of yesterday's conflict, now augmented by the freshly dead and wounded of the night.

"My God!" says Averill, to no-one in particular.

An unearthly silence descends upon the battlefield, as wounded French lay on the ground, uncertain as to what will become of them, and bloodied English stare in morbid disbelief at the scene before them. There is no exaltation in the victory, only horror at the extent of the carnage.

The bastion and the area surrounding are now in English hands. No further walls remain between the attackers and the centre of the town. But between this point and the centre, there are a hundred or more buildings and ruins, from which fierce resistance can still be expected. The major breach has been achieved, but the slow, brutal mopping-up phase of the siege remains ahead.

Many of the attackers collapse to the ground in exhaustion. Some stand and talk quietly, counting themselves lucky to be alive. Others sit and take in the scene, while reinforcements clamour, en masse, through the breached bastion. Surgeons arrive and begin attending to the injured, both English and French. It is hard to tell the bloodied bodies apart.

★

Time has passed since the battle ended; how much, is hard to gauge. Averill and his lieutenants, with Rupert and James, sit quietly, watching and waiting. No-one is talking.

The regalia of a herald gradually becomes clear as a figure advances through the smoky haze which permeates the town. Behind him, a group of three, dressed formally, walk with slow dignity towards the English line. Averill rises to face them.

"We have a message for your king," begins the herald. "Pray tell me who will take it to him?"

339

"You may take it to him, yourself," booms a voice from the still-burning remains of the bastion, as Henry, accompanied by Clarence and Talbot, emerge through the breached fortifications.

"Your Majesty," replies the herald with a gracious bow and elegant sweep of the headdress in his hand.

The king grimly surveys the scene, then, followed by Clarence and Talbot, climbs down through the rubble of the destroyed towers, and continues forward until he stands beside the grime-covered Averill.

"Your Majesty," repeats the herald, "I stand before you, representing the Governor of Falaise and his town council."

"But surely," replies the king, "the governor can speak for himself, for I see behind you one who bears the badge of that office."

De Mauny bows and steps forward, replying in formal terms, "Your Majesty, King Henry of England, we have defended our fair town with all endeavour and with all available resources, but to no avail. We have seen the loss of many hundreds of our citizens, and I fear the loss of thousands if we persist in resisting your advance; again to no avail. Therefore, King Henry, I, Viscount Olivier de Mauny, Governor of Falaise, take full responsibility for placing our town at your mercy. I beg that you treat our citizens with kindness and charity; for you are known to be a just and righteous king.

"Your Majesty, we are defenceless. The town is yours."

"Governor de Mauny," replies the king, equally formally. "We do hereby accept your surrender of this fair town, much injured by recent events, and we commit to treat, with kindness and charity, those of her citizens who lay down their arms immediately. But, for any who resist, there will be death, without recourse to any authority, for my word and my word alone, for the moment, is the law in Falaise."

De Mauny nods, soberly.

"There are further conditions," continues the king. "For any who are found to have fought against us before, and whom we have pardoned, and who have made their way to Falaise to fight against us again, there will be no second pardon. They too shall die. And, for any we pardon today, should they depart Falaise, and be found fighting against us again in the future, their lives shall also be forfeit, regardless of any charity offered here today. These are the conditions, upon which, our grace and our charity shall be extended to the citizens of Falaise. Pray have your herald convey this message to all corners of this fair town, so that we may, together, begin its reconstruction."

"We understand these conditions, Your Majesty, and recognise the justness of them," replies de Mauny, bowing. "We shall comply."

"And, finally," continues the king, placing his hand upon Talbot's shoulder, "allow me to introduce your new town commander, Lord Talbot. He will command in my name. But I would be pleased if you, Governor de Mauny, would agree to continue to serve, under his direction, for it is by working together, that we can best repair the damage done here these three weeks past; for this is a town which I would value, greatly, in the coming English Kingdom of Normandy."

"If Your Majesty will permit," replies de Mauny, "I will consider my position, and reply to your gracious offer before the day is done."

"Of course," replies the king. "This has been a difficult day, and I understand the need for careful consideration. Nevertheless, recognise that should you decline, there will be no place for you in Falaise, governor."

Then, abruptly: "And what of the castle?"

"The garrison commander is not with us, Your Majesty. He will not surrender. He defies you to take him in his keep."

"Indeed," replies Henry. "That is a brave move, but a foolhardy one, for there will only be one outcome, and he must know it."

"He is a proud man, my Lord; and a particularly violent one, if I may say. You would do well to heed his boast that you will have to fight every centimetre of the way to take him from within the keep. I think he will not surrender easily, my Lord."

"Well, we shall see," replies the king. "Pray tell me, Governor de Mauny; what is his name; this fearsome and violent garrison commander?"

"Bijou, Your Majesty; Sir René Bijou."

CHAPTER FIVE

"I thought I would have felt angry," says Averill, "when I knew he was here. But, strangely, I don't. Somehow, it all seems to fit; as if the last piece of a puzzle which has been before me for such a long time has, suddenly, dropped into place. He is here, and we will confront each other, as I have known, for so many years, that we would. I had not known where or when, but I had known. At last, it will be settled."

"Yes, Gregory; it will be settled," nods Henry. "But first, you will have time to think about it," he adds, "for I intend to return to Caen, and there celebrate Christmas. We leave tomorrow."

"Oh!" replies Averill, in obvious surprise. "I thought..."

"Ah, Gregory," smiles the king; "have you no sense of history?

"Yes, we have work to do, and yes, we do not want to tarry here too long, but Gregory, just think about it: this year's Christmas may be the way it will be for years to come now; our family, spread across a new kingdom, spanning Britain and France: Thomas and Humphrey in Falaise, John at Windsor; and Harry in Caen. And all of us descended from Henry Plantagenet, himself descended from William the Conqueror, before whose castle gates we now stand. But it is from Henry Plantagenet that I derive my desire to spend Christmas in Caen. I have an affinity with France, Gregory. I have a feeling for this country which is almost as strong as my feeling for England; and Henry, with our many-times-great-grandmother, Eleanor of Aquitaine, did spend Christmas in Caen in 1182, with their sons, the illustrious Richard the Lionheart, and his brother John, and a company of one thousand knights, when this vast Anglo-Norman Kingdom encompassed Normandy, Anjou, Aquitaine, Limousin, Brittany, England, Wales and Scotland. And both Richard and John did spend time here at this very castle in Falaise, and did contribute greatly to these defences which now stand against us.

"Can you not feel them, Gregory? The ghosts of our past, demanding that we pause and consider; that, as we celebrate the birth of our Lord, we also reflect upon all that has gone before us, and all that now awaits us.

"What mighty power we have with us, Gregory."

Averill looks at his king and smiles. "Sire, it is no wonder that men follow you to the ends of the earth. Your vision, your passion, your commitment are such that most are taken out of themselves, to live your dream alongside you. And I, Your Majesty, confess to being one of them. So, yes, I feel it, and, yes,

342

I want to be part of it, and, yes, I will reflect upon our heritage as we celebrate Christmas in Caen, my Lord."

Henry smiles in return, then adds: "Of course, there is one other reason for going to Caen, Gregory."

"Your Majesty?"

"There were a number of young squires with you when you stormed the bastion, who, I understand, acquitted themselves rather well, under quite trying circumstances."

"Indeed, Your Majesty," replies Averill. "They were..."

But Henry cuts him off: "It seems to me, Gregory, that such a confluence of circumstances as we have here, may not happen again for a very long time. It seems to me, therefore, that a Ceremony of Knighthood should follow, a day after our Christmas observances, before we return to take this castle of Falaise."

"My Lord..." commences Averill.

"Make sure the boy's father is present, Gregory," interrupts Henry again. "He deserves to see his son knighted."

"And James, too; Gareth's son," adds the king, turning to depart. "For the rest, I charge you with drawing up the list of names of the worthy."

"Well, well," muses Averill to himself; "Sir Rupert and Sir James..."

He pauses, then smiles. "And, why not?"

★

There are two hundred and twelve in the entourage which arrives in Caen on the evening of Monday 23rd December 1417, having ridden the thirty-five kilometres from Falaise during that day. Thomas, Duke of Clarence, and Humphrey, Duke of Gloucester, along with Lord Talbot, the town commander, and the newly reappointed Governor de Mauny, have remained in Falaise along with the vast bulk of the English army. Their task is to ensure that, over the next six or seven days, no person enters and no person leaves the castle precincts. Notwithstanding this duty, the celebration of Christmas, by those remaining in Falaise, is expected to be fulsome. A Mass is to be conducted, and sufficient supplies from Caen have been accumulated to ensure that the English army will enjoy a hearty Christmas dinner. And, most probably, the French inhabitants of the town will also enjoy more food these next few days than they have seen since the beginning of the siege.

Meanwhile, in Caen, a greeting party emerges from the city gate as the column arrives; forewarned of their coming by the messenger despatched by Henry immediately Falaise had been taken.

343

"Welcome, Your Majesty," calls Umfraville, bowing graciously, as the first horses reach the gate. And in the press of people behind, Averill spots Elvira and Odelia, craning forward to see if their men are among the arriving party. Within seconds, the two women are jumping up and down and hugging each other as first Averill, and then Rupert, are spied among the travellers.

"A little better welcome than we received at the last place," remarks Averill, smiling.

"Yes, indeed," replies Rupert. "I can't wait to hold her again."

He suddenly looks at Averill, embarrassed. "Sorry."

"No, my boy," replies Averill leaning over and tousling the young man's hair. "Odelia is your wife now, Rupert. You and she should be overjoyed to see each other, and to take each other in your arms. You have my blessing, my boy. Love her as dearly as you can."

Rupert nods, and smiles, but remains embarrassed; still unsettled by the way his love bursts through his composure from time to time.

The riders pass through the gate, surrounded by an ever-increasing crowd, all wishing to catch a glimpse of the king.

"Let us all meet in the morning," calls Averill to his knights. "We have some arrangements to make."

Anthony and Gareth wave their acknowledgement and with Thomas, Robert, Charles, Bryan, and William, the ever-jocular blacksmith, wheel left, as the column begins to separate into smaller groups heading for their respective destinations.

Minutes later, and before his feet have touched the ground, the breath is almost knocked out of Averill as, dismounting, he is pounced upon by the breathless Elvira, who grips her man with a fervour which tells of absence, and abstinence.

"Oh Gregory," she cries, "we only heard yesterday that the king was returning, but no-one could say who was coming with him. I was so desperate."

"Well," replies the knight, lightly, "it's lucky we came with him, isn't it; otherwise, you'd still be desperate."

Rupert is similarly embraced by Odelia, but, once again, as when the army departed, the younger pair, not yet certain of their ground in public, show more decorum than the older.

Then, as grooms lead the horses away, and the four walk towards the castle, Averill moves between the two women and places an arm around the waist of each. "By the way," he announces, "I have some news for you, concerning our young squire here; which not even he knows yet."

★

Two nights and two days have passed since the king and his entourage arrived in Caen. And now, with the sun already set and braziers lit, the grand hall of Château de Caen is warm and alive, resounding to the bonhomie of the gathering about to partake of the Christmas meal.

By contrast, the Mass, begun at midnight the preceding night and conducted in the beautiful Église Saint-Étienne by the Bishop of Bayeux, Jean Langret, had set a ritual tone, with 'Le Sacrement de l'Eucharistie de Noël', 'The Sacrament of the Christmas Eve Eucharist', beyond anything which Averill had ever experienced. Sung in both Latin and French, and made all the more inspirational by the presence of the king of England, it had touched the knight more deeply than ever before, engendering a mood of brotherhood, in which he had glimpsed just a little of what Henry was trying to achieve with the unification of the kingdoms of England and France.

For a moment, the knight had sensed what it was to be a king, had sensed what it was to have a vision for an entire people, and had sensed just a little of the enormous burden of responsibility that such grand designs carry with them. And then, looking at his king, he had recognised that there, on that night, Henry, for all his plans, for all his ambitions, was acknowledging that all of this was as nothing, before his Lord, the king of Kings, the Messiah. And, through moist eyes, Averill had understood that the brash young prince of yesteryear was no more, and that in his place now stood a mighty and a pious and a humble king, who might yet achieve his 'just rights and inheritances', and, in the process, succeed in creating a new kingdom of England and France to rival that of Henry and Eleanor before him.

In Falaise, Averill had promised his king that he would 'reflect upon our heritage as we celebrate Christmas in Caen'. But he had not expected to be so moved by that reflection.

And, as the reverie fades, he recognises that Elvira is talking to him. He smiles as she comes into focus again, then asks, politely: "I'm sorry, my love; what did you say?"

★

The meal is over, but for Averill, comparisons with last year hang in the air before him. The company is smaller of course, and the meal not as grand given only two days' preparation, but the setting, the grand hall of Château de Caen, is as beautiful as any he can remember. The influence of last night's mass has not yet worn off, and echoes of the past still haunt him. He looks around and can almost see Henry and Eleanor, Richard and John, and the thousand knights of that Christmas two hundred and thirty-five years earlier.

The warmth of Elvira leaning into him adds to the surreal nature of the scene. And then, for a moment, for just a moment, a pang of sadness as he reflects upon how much Mariel would have loved this. It is always like this; at the edges of every moment of happiness, when he is least prepared for it, comes the tinge of sadness for what might have been.

"A penny for your thoughts, Gregory?" smiles Elvira, as she wraps her arms around his neck and kisses him deeply.

"No thoughts, my love," the knight replies, softly, willing the sadness to pass. "I just feel so much a part of all this that I cannot believe how lucky I am. It's like a dream."

"Yes, my love," says Elvira. "It is for me too; being home again, but in the company of Henry and his knights, one of whom has given me more happiness than I ever thought possible. I love you, Gregory Averill. You mean more to me than I thought any man could. There are simply not enough words..."

Moments pass as Averill and Elvira sit quietly, gazing into each other's eyes, fingers entwined.

Around them, the babble of conversation is steadily increasing in volume as the night transitions from meal to revelry.

"Where did I find you?" asks Averill, softly.

"Under a cabbage... at the bottom of the garden," replies a lady in love.

Moments pass. Neither wishes to break the spell.

"Tell me about tomorrow," asks Elvira, eventually.

"Ah, tomorrow," sighs Averill, recognising that the world must continue to move forward; the sun rising and setting without cease.

"Tomorrow evening, Rupert and James, together with the other five squires who are to be knighted, will arrive at Église Saint-Étienne. For each of the squires, a sword of their choosing and a shield will be placed upon the altar, then the seven young men will retire to nominated points within the church, where they will spend the next ten hours in silent vigil.

The following morning, Henry will conduct the Adoubement Ceremony. Each candidate will have two sponsors. Gareth has asked Anthony to assist him with James; I have asked Thomas to assist me with Rupert."

Elvira smiles. "Perfect choices, Gregory."

"Yes," agrees Averill. "I thought so, too."

Then, continuing on, "Their dress will be symbolic; a white vestment for purity, a red robe for nobility, and black hose and shoes for death, the constant companion of a knight."

Elvira nods, and Averill continues: "There will be a Mass conducted by Bishop Langret, and a sermon on the responsibilities of knighthood. Then, for each candidate, the sponsors will take the sword and shield from the previous night's vigil, and present them to the bishop for blessing. We will then bring our candidate before the king. The candidate will recite his vows and swear an oath of allegiance to the King of England. Henry will then perform the accolade.

"Then, finally, we will attach the new knight's spurs, and gird him with his sword."

"Oh Gregory," exclaims Elvira, squeezing his hand. "It all sounds so magnificent."

"Yes, I believe it will be," replies Averill. Then, with quiet intensity, "I just hope our young man recognises the fortune which has befallen him; the wayward son of a castle blacksmith, being knighted within sight of the tomb of William the Conqueror. It is such a rags-to-riches story, I can scarcely believe it myself."

He pauses, "I remember his first words to me."

"Which were?" prompts Elvira.

"'Who the fuck are you?'" laughs Averill.

"Oh, Gregory; that's awful!"

"We didn't know each other very well at that stage," chuckles the knight.

Elvira looks closely at her man. "You're very proud of Rupert, aren't you?"

Averill looks directly at her, then smiles. "Yes, my love, I am; very proud. He could have turned out so differently. In fact, there was a period, early on, when I wondered if he would ever make it. But, you know, I couldn't believe that a son of William would fail; especially after I first saw his intensity, and his objection to the privilege he felt some boys unfairly enjoyed whilst others didn't. It seemed to me that this was a wretched young man, who had been deprived of opportunity, and who felt injustice, deeply. I think this was why I made the decision I did; this, and the fact that he was William's son, and William had been such an influence in taking me from a spoilt, self-centred child of privilege, and turning me into someone who understood the meanings of grace and humility."

"Yes, Gregory," murmurs Elvira. "I have seen, time and again, how alike you two are. I don't think there is any doubt that Rupert was going to turn out well."

The two sit in silence, holding hands, looking at each other; then Elvira rests her forehead against Averill's and whispers: "It's Christmas, Gregory; take me somewhere."

CHAPTER SIX

Long cloaks flap in the early morning breeze and low grey clouds scud swiftly overhead above a light drizzle as the quartet approach the church. But, despite the inclemency, eyes are still drawn to the tops of the twin towers, reaching nearly three hundred feet into the air, which surmount the rectangular and buttressed western portal of Église Saint-Étienne.

"I still find it awesome," remarks Elvira, as she hugs her knight. Behind them, Odelia shivers slightly as the cold momentarily defeats the warmth of her father-in-law's embrace as they hurry toward the shelter of the church.

Inside, candles suddenly flicker as the door opens and the breeze bursts in, then return to their serenity as Averill and William force the large wooden door closed again.

Silence.

The four stop just inside the doorway, momentarily overcome by the magnificence before them. Without the Christmas congregation, the true size of the building becomes apparent, as does the beauty and the grandeur of its architecture. The nave stretches for more than fifty metres before them; high vaulted ceiling once again drawing eyes upward in awesome contemplation of things ecclesiastic. Eight bays, three levels high, incorporating high semi-circular arches at ground-level, surmounted by first-floor galleries, and topped by a celestory, are over-arched by four high segmented and ribbed vaults. An even higher eight-segment dome crowns the intersection of the nave and the transepts, establishing the fundamental Roman cross of the design. And, at the far end, light streams in through three levels of Romanesque arched windows, completing the Gothic choir, and illuminating the altar, already adorned for the ceremony to come.

All along the central arcade of the nave, figures sit, heads bowed in quiet prayer; people of Caen, come early to witness the spectacle. Beyond, a gathering from the English court in Caen sits beneath the central dome.

Hushed and reverent, the quartet move slowly forward. To the left, facing the outer wall, a red-robed figure stands, head bowed, hands together in silent supplication. To the right, a second figure stands in silence.

As they move forward, a third is found kneeling, silently, beyond an archway to the right, eyes raised to the invisible heavens, mouth moving in silent prayer. On the left stands James, head bowed, hands clasped before his breast.

As they reach the dome and prepare to sit with the others, Rupert is visible in the transept to the left; kneeling, head bowed, hands clasped together, oblivious to his surroundings. Another figure on the right is standing, similarly focussed.

And behind the altar, facing away, the final red-robed figure stands upright and silent, head bowed.

The large oak door opens again and another burst of wind tears at the candles; then silence, except for the footfall of six knights walking slowly forward; three to witness the forthcoming ceremony, and three to participate in it. None of the squires moves. Ten hours have almost passed.

Now seated between William and Averill, Odelia suddenly feels faint, and leans upon her father's shoulder. Averill turns, and taking his daughter's hand in his own, looks at her with gentle love.

"Are you alright, sweetie?" he asks

"Oh, yes, Daddy," is the breathless response. "I'm just finding it almost impossible to remain unaffected by all this. I don't think I have even been in a more magnificent place, nor awaited a more important occasion."

Averill smiles. "Well, your wedding was rather special too, I thought."

Odelia looks at her father with undiluted love. "Yes, Daddy; it was, wasn't it?" She reflects for a moment. "Then, you were escorting me. Today, you're escorting Rupert. It all seems rather fitting doesn't it?"

Averill gently strokes his daughter's head; running his hand down through the long, silky-smooth, black hair. He draws her to him and kisses the top of her head. No words are needed; the understanding is complete.

Elvira stares at the altar, mesmerised. Gregory had mentioned that swords and shields would be placed there, but the reality is powerful beyond all expectation. A large pennant covers the entire altar: gold lions of England on red, quartered with gold fleurs-de-lys of France on blue; Henry's royal standard. And, arranged in a crescent, seven shields lie face up upon the standard; newly-emblazoned coats-of-arms glistening in the pale morning light. To the right of each shield, lies a sword. Pommels outward, tips converging, they create an arc, which although in a setting of Christendom, still hints at the magic, and mystery, and mysticism of the old world. Overcome, Elvira reaches out and takes Averill's free hand.

"Oh, Gregory; this is unbelievable."

A door opens, and the herald emerges, followed by six pages, then Bishop Langret, and behind him, Henry V of England.

★

Five newly-appointed knights, now fully accoutred, stand facing the congregation, a sponsor on either side and half a pace behind. The smiles on their faces say it all. James also faces the congregation as Gareth and Anthony kneel at his sides, each affixing one of the pair of spurs. Only Rupert remains facing the altar, with Averill and Thomas half a pace behind him.

And, as Gareth and Anthony rise, and Sir James Littlewood, at last, breaks into the smile that has been suppressed during the long and demanding ritual, Averill leans forward and whispers to Rupert. The squire moves forward to stand before the king, whilst Averill and Thomas take up the last remaining sword and shield from the altar and turn to the bishop for the blessing.

A nod from the king, and the herald steps forward and, holding the ceremonial scroll before him, addresses Rupert. "Squire, repeat after me: I do hereby swear..."

"I do hereby swear..."

"To fear God and to maintain His church..."

"To fear God and to maintain His church..."

"To serve my liege lord in valour and in faith..."

"To serve my liege lord in valour and in faith..."

"To protect the weak and the defenceless, and to give succour to widows and orphans..."

"To protect the weak and the defenceless, and to give succour to widows and orphans..."

"To be a light of chivalry unto the people..."

"To be a light of chivalry unto the people..."

Henry smiles as the oath proceeds, with only a few minor stumbles. Then, upon its completion, and, as with each of the others, he leans forward to talk privately with the candidate.

"Yours is a particularly wonderful tale, Rupert; the son of a blacksmith, become a knight; the event consecrated within sight of the tomb of Guillaume Le Conquérant. Do you recognise the significance of this occasion, Rupert? And, do you understand the importance of the journey upon which you are about to embark?"

"Yes, Your Majesty; I believe I do," comes the solemn reply.

"Then, I have some words of advice for you, Rupert," continues the king. "As I said, yours is a wonderful story. But, it carries the seeds of its own destruction, if you let it, Rupert. You are the son of a blacksmith, and you may be tempted to forget your heritage; to forget it, because you believe it to be too common for an illustrious knight. Allow me to correct this impression, Rupert, before it has a chance to take root in your mind. Sir Gregory Averill is the knight he is because of your father and others like him; and I am the king I am because of your father and others like him. Each of us was born a son of privilege, and each of us had the great potential to misunderstand who provides service to whom. It was your father, and the others like him, Rupert, who taught both of us the lessons which we still hold dear today; lessons, and understanding, which we believe make us better men; understanding, and sympathetic, and above all, useful to those who look up to us, Rupert; to those whom we serve."

Then, as the young man lowers his gaze in embarrassed recognition of the truth in the king's words, Henry continues, "Rupert, I charge you with this today: be as proud, always, of your father, as he already is of his son. Confirm to me, here and now, that you will never deny your father and your mother, who sadly is no longer with us, as the source of everything which is good and decent about you. Confirm to me, that you are worthy of the knighthood which I am about to bestow upon you."

The young man's eyes glisten as he looks up and utters his last words as a squire: "Your Majesty, I confirm that I will never deny my father; that I acknowledge my mother and my father as the source of all that is good and decent in me; and, that I understand that, as a knight, it is I who serve."

"Well spoken, Rupert," replies the king. "Now, kneel."

Then, drawing his sword, and in full voice, so that all in Église Saint-Étienne can hear, he strikes the flat of the blade upon Rupert's right shoulder, and, mindful of the occasion, issues the colée dating back to the knighthood of William the Conqueror: "Rupert Black, son of William, and protégé of Sir Gregory Averill, in the name of God, Saint Michael, and Saint George, I dub thee 'knight'. Be valiant, bold, and loyal. Speak the truth, maintain the right, protect the defenceless, succour the distressed, champion the ladies, vindicate your knightly character, and prove your knightly bravery and endurance by perilous adventures and valorous deeds. Fear God, fight for the faith, and serve your sovereign and your homeland faithfully and valiantly."

The king lifts the sword.

"Arise, Sir Rupert."

The young knight stands, and, as dictated by protocol, turns to face the congregation. Thomas takes the shield, bearing the newly-emblazoned black dragon and hammer crossed, upon bleu celeste, and places it before Rupert, whilst Averill girds the young man with his sword. Then, both kneel to affix the spurs.

They rise to stand with the other sponsors, half a pace behind and to the side of each of their protégés... and seven new knights face the congregation; their smiles unrestrainable.

A moment's pause to allow for reflection by all, then the king kneels, and within Église Saint-Étienne, only Bishop Langret remains standing: "In nómine Patris, et Fílli, et Spirítus Sancti, Amen."

And as the reverberations of the benediction fade, a large man slowly stands, as does a beautiful young woman with almond-shaped eyes and long black hair, beside him. He looks with love and pride upon a young man he had once believed lost beyond redemption, then, hand-in-hand with the young woman, walks forward to embrace Sir Rupert Black; son, husband, and knight.

★

"Such a beautiful country, you have," says Averill, as he looks out the window onto the moonlit scene before them.

"Yes, I like it very much," replies Elvira, dreamily, warmed by her lover's embrace from behind. "It's different from England, isn't it, Gregory. Even in winter, it still feels... light."

Averill continues to gaze for a few moments before replying. "Yes, my love, winter here seems not as heavy as at home." Then, with slight chuckle: "But then, perhaps it's the effect of the wine we have enjoyed tonight, which makes everything seem lighter; including me."

The lady turns in her man's embrace, and raises her lips to his. "It was wonderful today, wasn't it, Gregory? And tonight too. I've never seen Odelia look so lovely, nor Rupert so bashfully proud. What a beautiful couple they make; and what a beautiful life they have before them, my love."

Averill draws his woman to him and continues to gaze upon the scene outside. "Yes, indeed," he replies, softly; "all their lives before them; all their dreams yet to be unwrapped; all their desires yet to be fulfilled."

Then quietly; almost in a whisper: "I remember what it was to be young; to be invincible; to know that everything was possible."

"I also Gregory," replies Elvira, reaching up and placing her hand around the back of her man's neck. "I, too, remember what it was to be young, to be desired, to be the belle of the occasion, to be the object of every young man's attention. Oh, we were so naughty, we girls. We toyed with their emotions, those poor boys, and cast them off as if they were nothing. We were so, so... innocent then; nothing mattered; everything was a game.

"But I also recall how things changed as I became older," she continues, quietly; "and how, I could never find the boy, or later the man, who could hold me for more than a few days, or a few weeks. And I became convinced that I was destined to go through life alone and unfulfilled; knowing so desperately what I wanted, but unable to find it. Until that day, late one summer, when a man I didn't know faced a cold and brutal beast I did know on a tournament field in England, and surprised all who watched by doing what I believe even he did not really believe he could do."

Averill is silent for a moment as thoughts of that day tumble through his mind, then slowly he lowers his gaze from the scene outside and looks directly at the Lady Elvira. He thinks hard before speaking, then: "He is here, my love."

"Who, Gregory?"

"René Bijou."

Elvira's breath catches in her throat. She feels suddenly cold.

"He is in Falaise," continues Averill. "He commands the castle we are about to take."

The warm, dreaminess of the evening is suddenly gone; replaced by fear, and Elvira's sudden, desperate need to be held close by her man.

Averill gently strokes her head, now resting upon him, and feels her arms tighten around his waist. Was he right to mention it? Should he have kept this small piece of information to himself? Should he have returned to Falaise the day after tomorrow, without so much as breathing a word?

But Averill's uncertainty is in stark contrast to Elvira's growing need. The sudden, initial coldness has been replaced by a heat, reflected in the flush of the lady's cheeks, and her shortness of breath. Somehow, the knowledge of Bijou's imminent presence has slashed through the civilised fabric of the night, and released the animal passion of a woman whose beloved is threatened.

The distance to the bed is but a few paces; covered in seconds as the woman forces her man down and falls upon him, grinding her hips and mouth against his as she tears clothing from them both. The knight is momentarily taken aback by the sudden change; then responds in kind, uncertain no longer.

Aroused by his woman's passion, he grasps the long auburn hair and, almost cruelly, drags Elvira's head back, exposing her throat. Now upon her, he bites down on her neck, as fingernails rake his back and naked legs entwine tightly about his waist.

Driven by urgent need, Elvira suddenly releases her scissor-hold upon her man and reaches between his legs to grasp his rising manhood. The exquisite agony forces Averill to cry out; pleasure indistinguishable from pain. Forcing him onto his back, Elvira turns and straddles him as she lowers her mouth to engulf the object of her passion. Beneath her, Averill clasps the soft, full buttocks to his face and drinks in the strongly-scented liquid now flowing from his aroused woman. Her mouth and fingers, his tongue and hot breath bring whimpers and groans from bodies engaged in giving and taking pleasure. And, slowly, the exquisite sensations begin to move inward as rising passions move towards inexorable climax. Toes curl, hands grasp buttocks with force which, unfelt now, will leave bruises later, and hips gyrate as internal tensions mount. The working of Averill's tongue and the intensity of the passion generated by the night bring Elvira to her climax first. She loses control of her senses, releasing her man as her body spasms and contorts in ecstasy. She falls moaning, head thrashing from side to side, legs trembling as wave after wave of pleasure engulf her. The knight withholds his touch, watching as his lover rides the sensations to completion, her violent movements easing back to long tremors and shuddering breaths. Wild-eyed she looks up at him, as he slowly turns and lowers himself onto her, sliding easily into her silky hot wetness, and begins to thrust; slowly, lest the next wave of pleasure overtake them too soon. But the love and the fear and the need of the woman all combine to heighten her sensitivities and Averill can feel himself drawn in by the hungry clasping of his woman's body. And once again, without volition, the sensations become focussed, and awareness of surroundings fades. With arms wrapped around each other's sweating bodies, and mouths joined in delirious, passionate exploration, the man and the woman thrust and strain unaware, delirious, without volition, without restraint. And then as the inevitable ecstasy overtakes the man, he bursts within his woman; the hot stream triggering her own convulsive coming as she wails and screams and rocks from side to side in shuddering, paroxysmal ecstasy, while he climaxes in gradually diminishing groans of deep-throated, hoarse, spent relief.

Silently, the lovers lay entwined in abandoned disarray, breathing slowing, but still occasionally punctuated by shudders of release. Minutes pass, with no word spoken. Averill's eyes are closed as he slowly twirls his fingers through his lady's hair. Elvira's eyes, too, are closed as she lies in the afterglow of love making. The urgent desire is now assuaged; body, mind, spirit, soul all calmed, and in this dreamy, almost disconnected state, she recognises a question, long within her, which now needs to be answered.

"Do you think about her, Gregory?" she asks quietly. "Do you think about Mariel?"

The knight is silent; still falling softly from the peak to which ecstasy has transported him.

Elvira turns to her side, and, opening her eyes momentarily, strokes her lover's head, drawing him close to her.

Time passes, then, eyes still closed, the knight speaks; slowly, softly. "There was a time, after she had gone, when I thought of no-one else; a time when the world was so dark, and a pain burned in my breast with such intensity, that I could not be comforted. I retreated into a shadow world; a world in which I would re-live all of the beautiful things we had done together; a world which made me cry with its sadness, but a world from which I did not want to emerge. I was clinging to a dream.

"It took a long time to return from that world, my love; a very long time. And, as I told you once before, when we were together in the glade, I sensed during that time that I was being cared for by someone I should have been caring for; a little girl who never knew her father, and who had now lost her mother, but who loved me so dearly that she pushed aside her own pain in order to hold me together whilst I grieved."

Averill opens his eyes and looks directly at Elvira. "I shall never be able to repay her for that, my love."

The lady's embrace tightens as she caresses her seemingly fragile lover.

"And, every time I look at my daughter, I see her mother," Averill continues. "Sometimes it makes me smile, because I recognise little things she does; the way she holds her head when puzzled, the shape of her lips when she smiles, the sparkle in her eyes when she laughs, the irreverence she shows for the more pompous members of our court. And sometimes it makes me cry, because I see Mariel so clearly in her gestures; the concerned way in which she sometimes regards me, the toss of her head when she feels slighted, the sudden, unexpected breaking of a smile when I think she has been hurt; all gestures of the woman I loved, perfectly reflected in her daughter.

"And sometime I cry for all of the beautiful new things in Odelia's life; for the grace she has acquired, and for the happiness I see her now experiencing, which her mother will never see.

"Yes, my love; I think of Mariel."

Elvira continues to stroke Averill's hair. The knight remains still; then: "And in my quietest moments, I would be lying if I said that I did not wonder what might have been."

Another pause, as the knight tries to understand, in one broad sweep, a lifetime's pleasures, delights, pain, suffering, hopes, despair, loss, redemption.

Unable to ask the next question, Elvira lies silent. And in the silence, Averill finds the answer. "I cannot tell you apart from her, my love. Is that strange? I cannot say 'these are the feelings I had for Mariel' and 'these are the feelings I have for you'. I cannot say 'this was my greatest love' and 'this is my second love'. I have found that when I am in love, I am in love. There are no degrees of love. And it is not something which I initiate or which I control. It is not that I have found love, but rather, I think, love has found me; as if it has descended upon me, and overtaken me, and transported me to a place like no other. It is as if there is an angel of love, who comes to us in forms we do not recognise until she is with us. And when she touches us, she does so utterly, and completely, so that love burns within us. It is as if each of us is a vessel for the angel, and that she enters us, and stays with us, and, through the grace of God, brings us peace, and delight... and warmth and comfort. She becomes... the sunshine of our days, and the bright star of our nights."

Elvira lies silent as the tears escape. At last she knows, as she had hoped but not quite believed, that the love Averill feels for her is not a secondary love, subservient to another, but is as real as the love he felt for the figure who has always been at the periphery of her mind. She knows that he has not, will not, ever forget Mariel, but at last she feels that, perhaps, the love she shares with this man, who is so different from any she has known before, is complete; that there is no reservation on his part, no holding back. And, as she lies with eyes still closed, she feels her breathing deepen, and becomes aware of a peacefulness spreading through her breast, which, until this moment, she had not truly realised was missing.

She opens her eyes to find Averill looking at her; gently, lovingly. He smiles, and kisses her tears.

Elsewhere within the castle, two young lovers consummate a raw passion not yet complicated by life's strange twists and turns. The young woman offers her naked self to her young husband, without restraint; and the knight, of less than a day's standing, responds with gentle intensity; body taut and straining, mind overcome with the sheer delight of the soft sensuality of the vision beneath his touch.

Overhead, a pale moon momentarily disappears behind a slowly moving cloud, before re-emerging to shine equally upon the castle and the houses of Caen. Such a day this has been. One wonders what tomorrow will bring.

A long, whimpering wail of pleasure floats softly through a room of Château de Caen as a young woman's experience of earthly delights reaches new heights; and a young knight shudders in ecstasy.

A smile, a giggle, a sigh, then... silence.

CHAPTER SEVEN

The morning of Sunday 29th December 1417 is as beautiful as any Elvira can remember. It is one of those unique winter mornings for which France is renowned, when the pale golden-pink behind the eastern horizon spreads upward onto a clear, cloudless sky, bathing the land in gradually brightening splendour, and when not a breath of breeze stirs the leaves. And, as her preparations for the early morning Mass continue, memories of similar mornings long ago fill the lady with warmth and pride in her heritage. But hovering just beneath the surface of her emotions lies the sadness which comes from the knowledge that the king and his men return to Falaise today. She sighs, and returns to the final brushing of her hair. Averill, fixing the clasps of his doublet, watches her tenderly, then reaches for the beautiful armorial surcoat: the black dragon passant upon bleu celeste. She looks up to see him still watching her, and smiles; a woman in love.

★

And now, as the mid-morning sun warms the courtyard and the bustle of activity comes to its conclusion, the knight and the lady stand together, hands clasped.

"Be careful, Gregory."

"I will, my love; I will. And besides, I have a valiant young knight beside me now, so we are twice as formidable as we were when we arrived," he jokes.

The approaching group of Averill's lieutenants wave a greeting as they lead their horses towards the pair. And, from the direction of the castle, Rupert and Odelia approach with James striding beside them.

"Well then," remarks Averill; "it seems we're all here and ready to go."

"Be careful, Daddy," says the young lady as she arrives and flings her arms around her father's neck. "And don't you let anything happen to my new knight," she adds.

"We'll look after each other," replies Averill. "How will that do?"

"Perfect," she replies, transferring her smile and her embrace to Rupert.

A sudden fanfare from six trumpeters announces the arrival of Henry, and the entourage prepares to depart.

"I love you, Gregory Averill," says Elvira, holding her man, earnestly. "Don't you ever forget that."

"And I love you, my beautiful Elvira," replies the knight, drawing the lady to him. Then, recognising her angst, he adds, "Wait for me, my love; we won't be long."

The king mounts. Averill takes the reins Anthony has passed to him and follows suit. The others are already mounted. The smiles on the faces of Sir Rupert Black and Sir James Littlewood have never been so broad.

The king looks around, and, satisfied with what he sees, raises his voice: "My Lords, we have a castle to take. To Falaise." And the ground reverberates with the impact of a thousand hooves.

Elvira stares after the departing group. "I hate this; this watching them ride off... so much," she confides.

But Odelia is too young and too much in love for the worries of life's uncertainties to dampen her mood.

CHAPTER EIGHT

For twelve days now, the battlefield has resounded to the roar of cannon, and the crash of huge gun-stones shattering against the castle walls.

"That wall must be fifteen feet thick if it's an inch," remarks the king shaking his head. "No wonder William regarded this as his most defendable asset."

Further back, the trebuchets continue to launch their payloads over the walls and into the inner bailey of the castle, threatening life and limb of any who venture outside the three keeps. Smoke from the cannon fills the air, mixed with dust from the shattering stones and the walls which are now irregularly smashed at the top, but which, as yet, carry no significant damage at the lower levels. There is still no possibility of storming the castle.

"I'm beginning to see what de Mauny meant when he said 'centimetre by centimetre'," adds the king.

"Indeed," replies Averill, shouting above the noise. "I think we're going to be forced to go in via the gate-house. That will get us into the inner bailey, but then we'll still have the job of breaching the entrance to the castle."

"Not a pretty picture," adds Clarence, "but I think you're right, Gregory. This battering away at the walls will take forever; and aside from eventual starvation, we're putting no real pressure upon the French."

The informal war council of the king, Clarence, Gloucester, Lord Talbot, and Averill winces collectively as another cannon erupts and another massive stone shatters violently against the castle wall, adding yet another cloud of choking dust and falling rock fragments to the swirling, man-made storm.

"That entrance is going to be difficult," shouts Gloucester. "As far as I can tell, the ground level is completely closed, and the entrance is at the first floor level. It's going to mean taking the inner bailey, then building a scaffold to reach the entrance before we can storm the individual keeps. Sounds very bloody to me."

The five men duck, involuntarily, as another trebuchet payload flies overhead and crashes unseen into the inner bailey, causing unknown damage.

Henry turns. "What do you think, Gregory? Do you fancy having a go at the gate-house?"

"I think it's the only way, my Lord," replies Averill. "As my Lord Clarence said, we'll be here until kingdom come if we just keep battering away at these walls. My God, but they're strong."

"Alright, then," decides the king. "We'll maintain the bombardment whilst you prepare to attack the gate-house. How much time do you need?"

"Give me tomorrow, and we'll be ready to go Friday morning."

The king nods and turns away from the scene. "So be it; Friday morning."

★

Once again, the forces are assembled; archers to fire the wooden structures of the gate-house and men-at-arms to hack their way through the ensuing firestorm. But, unlike the last operation, when open space was on the other side, this time the attacking force will find themselves contained in the blind inner bailey, where the castle's defending forces can rain arrows, burning oil, and all manner of maiming and death upon them. And, to make matters worse, they will have to work their way through the fallen rock and shattered timber from the damage they have caused by the bombardment to-date. But, with destruction of the castle walls proving nigh on impossible, the building of a scaffold to the first-floor entrance has become a necessity. And to build the scaffold, the inner bailey must be taken.

Two thousand men crouch in readiness as the gradually lightening sky to the south-east heralds the dawn. The regular creak, strain and whoosh of trebuchets is periodically drowned by the massive roar of cannon as they launch the huge gun-stones, which crash and shatter in thunderous violence against the unyielding castle walls.

Men standing on the mud ramparts built around the siege engines watch for the signal which will halt their bombardment, and initiate the assault.

"Well Gregory, it's in your hands now. God's speed."

"Thank you, Your Majesty. We will do our best."

And with that, a thousand flaming arrows are launched into the dawn sky, arcing slowly across the distance between the English army and the fortified gate-house to the east of the castle.

The thunder of the barrage ceases, and three hundred men-at-arms begin to run, as fast as their armour will permit, across the exposed ground towards the now-burning timbers of the gate-house. Seven hundred others, in reserve, wait in the pre-dawn gloom, ready to pour through the opening as soon as the entrance is breached. And in the cold morning air, shouts of alarm ring out from the upper reaches of the high circular keep as lookouts react, first to the shower of flaming arrows, and then to the swarm of men-at-arms converging upon the gate-house below. The second phase of the siege of Falaise Castle is under way.

★

The inner bailey, bounded by the now flaming gate-house to the east; the outer defensive wall to the north; the great square keep to the west; and, to the south, the buttressed curtain wall atop the steep hill, which runs down to the wide water-filled ditch separating the inner precincts of the castle from the outer bailey, has become a confined battlefield of chaotic and frenzied activity.

Archers, taking refuge behind and beneath whatever cover is available in the destruction which litters the ground of the inner bailey, are firing upwards at any movement within the castle that could be an enemy soldier preparing to fire back, or to hurl some deadly abomination upon the English men-at-arms working below; those same men-at-arms who are man-handling into position the pre-fabricated sections of the belfries, transported from England for just such a purpose; to provide the initial defensive platform, under which the construction of the scaffold will commence.

And from the top of the large square keep, arrows and bolts are being fired, rocks hurled and boiling oil poured upon the armoured but still vulnerable soldiers below. The screams of the burned continue to penetrate the cacophony of noise which accompanies the construction. But, little-by-little as the sections of the belfries are hammered and pegged and lashed together, and the cover becomes more substantial, the frequency of damage inflicted upon the attackers diminishes.

★

Two more days have passed; days in which the huge scaffold has climbed two-thirds of the way to the first-floor castle entrance, and the accompanying ramp, up which the attackers will make their way when the breach is achieved, has begun to extend forward from the English line. Calculations are that both the scaffold and the platform will meet within another day-and-a-half, at which point, the business of breaching the entrance to the great keep can commence in earnest. Thereafter, the work will be like disposing of so many rabbits in their warren.

Teams of carpenters protected by men-at-arms work during every available daylight hour, driven by the need to complete the construction before the weather worsens. So far, the attackers have been blessed with cold but dry conditions; but all know that this situation will not last much longer, and that, soon, January storms will be upon them.

★

The light is fading in the early evening, and the noise of construction diminishing with it. The watch for the first phase of the night will soon be in place, and carpenters, labourers, archers and men-at-arms will retire, gratefully, for another night's hard-earned rest.

The scaffold and the ramp are within a man's jump of each other now. Tomorrow they will be completed, providing a continuous path from the English lines to the castle entrance on the first floor of the great square keep. But for tonight, rest and reflection are the order in the English camp.

The first torches are lit, and, for a moment, the surreal beauty of the long, inclined line of light from the ground to the castle distracts thoughts from the grim business ahead; the business of hacking their way into the castle and through the enclave of defenders within.

"Sometimes I find the most beautiful sights coming from the basest of conditions," remarks the king, as he stands, hands on hips, surveying the scene.

"Yes, Your Majesty," replies Averill; "I understand exactly what you mean. There are times when the vision before you is quite disconnected from the reality it hides. It is hard to realise that in the next day or so, hundreds of men will die here. And yet, right now, in this fading light, those torches provide a scene more beautiful than most people will ever see when looking out over a valley towards a castle."

Henry looks at his favourite knight and smiles. "You've become a romantic, Gregory," he chuckles.

Averill's boot traces out a small circle in the dirt as he considers the king's remark. He looks up, a smile on his lips. "Yes, Your Majesty; I think I have. I suspect it's something to do with my daughter and her young man."

"And your lady?" queries the king.

Averill continues to smile, taking in the surreal beauty of the scene.

"And my lady," acknowledges the knight.

Clarence and Gloucester approach.

"What do you think, my Lords?" asks the king, sweeping his hand across the scene before them.

"Strangely beautiful," replies Clarence, looking out.

"Yes, Your Majesty," adds Gloucester. "Amazing how such a scene of impending devastation can appear so calm and beautiful before the event."

The four stand; confident and relaxed. But within, the first tingles of anticipation begin to manifest themselves as thoughts turn towards the forthcoming attack, now only a day or so away.

★

The shouts and cries of men fighting, and the clang of steel on steel shatter the peace of the night as French men-at-arms burst from the castle and begin to hack their way through the night watch of the English army. Behind them, in the now-open entrance, other French soldiers stand poised with buckets of oil ready to hurl over the scaffold and the ramp, and archers with flaming arrows stand behind, ready to create an inferno of both structures.

Averill and his knights, only partially attired for battle, are already charging up the ramp with Clarence, Gloucester, and Lord Talbot's troops fifty paces behind.

Forcing their way up the inclined ramp, Averill and Anthony and Gareth reach the French first. Within seconds, battle has been joined by tens of English and French. Less than half a minute later and the rearguard of the English arrives.

Further back towards the base of the ramp, soldiers are struggling with buckets of water, while still others are charging forward carrying bags of sand. The threat of fire is well understood, and no effort is being spared in preparing to smother the impending flames.

Unnerved by the rapid English response, the French on the scaffold begin hurling their buckets of oil onto the structures even whilst their own soldiers are engaged further down the ramp in close conflict with the English. The French archers respond, on cue, by launching their flaming arrows, point blank, into the now-slippery timbers.

Mayhem ensues as the gathering flames begin to consume the ramp at the top, and the English make their way up the ramp from the bottom. The fighting becomes ferocious as the English attempt to clear a path to the flames for the water and sand carriers, and the trapped French, recognising the impossibility of their situation, between the now mounting flames and the advancing English, determine to sell their lives at the greatest possible cost.

Averill looks around wildly, cutting, thrusting, defending, attacking in turn, despatching French soldiers, all the while searching for Rupert. Thick, oily smoke now covers the scene as the heat from the flames becomes intense.

And suddenly, there are no more French between him and the flames. He ducks, as men carrying water and sand hurl their loads past him, then retreat for others to do likewise. The skirmish is over, but the flames continue.

Greasy, sweaty, dirty and coughing from breathing the smoke-filled air, the knights stumble back down the ramp.

"Everyone here?" asks Averill.

"Not sure," replies Gareth. "I couldn't see a bloody thing in all that smoke."

"Have you seen James and Rupert?"

"Yes, they're just ahead of us; I pushed them both back when I saw that we had their numbers covered."

"That's good," replies Averill. "Thanks for that."

The pair move down the ramp as other soldiers continue their rush up the ramp to deliver their payloads to the fight against the fire.

Anthony is on his knees as they approach. The two forms on the ground are both still. Another knight kneels and, wrapping his arms around one of the forms, begins to weep.

Rupert and James, smudged black from the fire and the battle, stand, slightly apart from the rest, looking on in uncertainty. Death has never been this personal.

Averill kneels, looking into the lifeless eyes of Thomas; the deep slash from the Armagnac sword running from his neck to his unprotected chest. Charles' sobbing is muffled as he cradles the body of his brother, Robert.

The mind struggles to assimilate the scene. Averill, Anthony, Gareth, Charles, Robert, Bryan and Thomas have been together for so long, have been through so many battles together, have survived and cared for each other, protecting each other, acting as one unit for so long now that each feels a part of the other, and each feels incomplete without the other. Without stating it, the feeling has been of invincibility. And now, in an instant, the bond, the brotherhood has been torn apart, in a futile attempt by an outnumbered enemy to delay the inevitable.

Averill stares in numbed disbelief, and then, slowly, the fatal reality of the situation descends upon him: this is the way it is, and this is the way it always will be; this is how armies are built, and damaged, and repaired; this is how they move forward again. Two knights die and two new knights take their places. Two close, dependable bonds are severed, and two new fragile, tentative bonds are born. And none knows when his turn will come, but each recognises that, almost certainly, it will come.

Thomas, who stood beside Averill at Rupert's knighthood; who chuckled at Gareth when he tried to prise from Averill more information than Averill was prepared to reveal. Thomas, who always saw through the superficiality of the situation and understood the deeper meaning of each encounter. Thomas, who more than anyone, provided Averill with a mind against which to test his ideas; whose soft, calm, gentle intelligence gave Averill the confidence that the plans being evaluated and the paths being followed probably did not contain any fundamental flaw. This Thomas, upon whom Averill relied so much, in such an instinctive way, lies before him, still, silent... no more.

And the siblings, whose fierce but loving rivalry brought such intensity to their endeavours and their actions, are a pair no more. For Charles, Averill knows, the loss will be exceedingly harsh, for never before has one brother been without the other. They have always thought in unison, acted in unison, celebrated in unison, grieved in unison. Now, Charles will grieve alone.

The quiet confidence of the early evening, in the presence of Clarence and Gloucester and the king, seems far away; seems almost callous now, given the sacrifices made here tonight.

Standing, Averill slowly turns away, anger building in his chest. His roared "No-o-o-o" reverberates through the night. But the violence within his breast remains unabated. There will be no mercy when he confronts the French, after the repairs to the scaffold and the ramp are completed.

His mind has only one focus now: Bijou.

CHAPTER NINE

Shock had given way to numbness, but the numbness has faded now, leaving the pain, real and raw. Seven knights sit staring into the flickering flames. There have always been seven, but tonight is different. Yet among those present here tonight, there are none whom Averill would send away. But the pain and the emptiness remain, for there should be nine. Now, the seven knights of numerous shared encounters should be welcoming Rupert and James into the brotherhood of men preparing to fight together; for king, for country, and for each other. Now, there should be tales of heroic battles, of close encounters, of single-minded bravery in the face of overwhelming odds, to inspire the new knights to give of their all; of their best. But, this is not the mood tonight, this is not the substance of the animated conversation which should be occurring, and the raucous bonhomie of close, trusting comrades preparing for battle. Tonight, the mood is sombre, and the conversation is almost non-existent. Tonight, seven knights sit quietly, reflecting upon the events of the last encounter with the French. Tonight, the number remains seven, but the composition is new.

"He never could keep his breakfast down," remarks Bryan, in a small attempt to lighten the mood.

"True," replies Averill. Then, after a little thought: "It's funny the things you remember about them, isn't it?"

"He understood you better than any of us," adds Gareth. "He knew that you would come back, but in your own time. He once said to me, 'Don't push it, Gareth. It won't achieve anything. Just have faith. He'll be back.'"

Averill looks over at the big man. "Then he knew me better than I knew myself, Gareth."

The big man smiles, but does not respond immediately, bending his head again and leaning forward, forearms resting on his thighs, staring into the ground. "Aye, Gregory; I suspect he did."

Quiet reflection.

"Are you alright, Charles?" asks Averill.

The bereaved brother looks up and smiles, wanly. "Yes, Gregory; I'm alright. It's just going to take some time." He pauses, then: "Quite a long time, I suspect."

"Yes, I understand," replies Averill, gently. "You two were always what I thought brothers should be; intense, competitive, but above all, loyal. I couldn't have asked for a better example of family, for all of us to observe. We

366

have been blessed by your presence, Charles; yours and Robert's. I will miss him very much, but his spirit will not be gone. You know that, don't you?"

Charles looks directly back at his captain. "Yes, Gregory, I know that. I just wish it wasn't so."

"I remember when I lost William the bowman," begins Anthony. "He was not a knight, and so you would not have known him well, but he was a friend, and I used to rely upon him so much. He was always the first one I would choose if I had to put a party together. I remember how it felt when I arrived back at the castle that time; when he did not return.

"I recognise the same feeling here tonight... but I think this hurts even more."

A figure steps quietly from the surrounding blackness into the illumination of the fire; and all stand, to bow.

"Be seated, my friends," says Henry, gently motioning to the seven. "There are heavier matters on your minds tonight than the protocol of greeting your king.

"Gregory, a word."

Then, as the pair step away, the king, on an impulse, turns and walks back into the firelight. "Sir Rupert, Sir James," he calls. The two stand.

"This is not the preparation I know Sir Gregory wanted for you, but it is what you are getting nonetheless. Every time I lose a knight, I feel it personally. And when I lose some of my household, then I feel it very keenly indeed. These were good men, Robert and Thomas, who gave their lives the other night. They leave big shoes to fill, gentlemen; big shoes. But, I knighted you in the firm conviction that I could rely upon you when times got tough. Well, they are a little tougher than I had anticipated; but, I expect that you will respond to that challenge tomorrow morning when we storm the castle. Are you ready?"

"Yes, Your Majesty," reply the pair, in strenuous support of each other.

"That is my view also," replies the king, taking another pace toward them. Then, hands on hips and looking directly at the two new young knights: "You are more fortunate than almost every soldier here this night, for you are being led by my champion and his chosen knights. Don't you ever forget that, gentlemen. You are in the company of the best. I have high expectations of you tomorrow."

Then, suddenly, he is gone, along with Averill.

"Well, there you have it, lads," says Gareth, looking up at the pair. "The king, himself, has charged you with excellence tomorrow. And mark my words: he will know how you perform.

"Now, I suggest we all go and get some sleep. We'll be arming before dawn."

CHAPTER TEN

The miners have completed their work; not underground as would normally be the case, but here, where the restored scaffold abuts the castle wall. Great metal plates have been laid to protect the underlying timber of the scaffold, and upon them the miners have stacked the materials which will begin the destruction of the great castle doors. Accustomed to preparing materials for the burning of tunnel supports to initiate the collapse of a besieged castle's walls, the miners are well-versed in destruction by conflagration. However, with the walls of Falaise castle being some fifteen feet thick, and the foundations known to be some thirty feet deep, the miners have been thwarted in their art; until tonight.

And arrayed in the pre-dawn gloom at the end of the long inclined ramp which leads to the scaffold and thence to the castle entrance, the Majesty of England stands waiting; Henry, the king, encased in steel, overlaid by the battle doublet bearing the three golden lions passant on red, quartered with three golden fleurs-de-lys on blue. And, beside him, also fully armed, stand Thomas, Duke of Clarence; Humphrey, Duke of Gloucester; Gilbert Lord Talbot, Commander of Falaise; and Sir Gregory Averill, King's Champion.

Averill turns, running his eyes over the second rank: Gareth, Anthony, Charles and Bryan; and safely ensconced between them, Rupert and James. Suddenly, he mourns the absence of Thomas's calm, studied features; features he would always seek out, to hold his eyes for just for a moment, to ensure that nothing was amiss with the plans for action.

For an instant, Averill's searching eyes catch Gareth's. The big man smiles a little smile, and nods in sympathy with Averill's suddenly forlorn features.

"They will be with us today, Gregory," he murmurs. "Have no doubt about that."

Averill forces a brief smile, and nods in return, then turns his attention to Rupert and James.

"Are you two feeling alright?"

"Yes, Sir Gregory," the pair answer, almost in unison; but the nervousness is obvious.

A familiar touch on the shoulder and Averill moves off; walking in-step beside Henry as the pair pass back down through the ranks of fighting men, just as they have done on so many occasions before, but which, for a long time now, both Averill and the king thought they might never do again. And, as they approach each rank, the quiet, nervous chatter ceases, as men-at-arms respond to the intimate presence of the king and his champion, knowingly inspecting the troops now arrayed for battle. These are the touches, the little touches, which generate the belief and the camaraderie and the confidence for which Henry's armies are known and feared.

★

And now, back at the head of the assembled force, the king and Averill resume their places.

"Ready, brothers?"

"Ready, Your Majesty," reply both Clarence and Gloucester.

Then, turning to his favourite knight: "It's been a long time, Gregory."

Averill looks directly into his king's eyes. "Indeed, Your Majesty; it has. But we are here now, and we will turn back the clock one more time."

"Dieu et mon droit," whispers the king, raising his sword in the dim, early morning light.

"Yes, Your Majesty," replies Averill, raising his own sword in reply; "by God and by your right."

Then, at a signal, ten archers standing close by dip their bulbously-prepared arrows into the flaming pot, and hurry up the long ramp, toward the shadowy outline of the scaffold, and the dormant payload waiting at the base of the great castle door. Within the scaffold, the second wave, the foresters, wait with axes and the huge battering ram to inflict devastation upon the great door as it succumbs to the flames.

Moments later, the sustained dullness of the morning is pierced by a brilliant illumination at the base of the massive castle door, as the huge packed and oiled mass of combustible material catches fire, then roars into life; tongues of flame licking twenty feet up the great door.

And now the growing tension is palpable, as knights and archers and men-at-arms watch, in fascination, as the gathering firestorm scorches the great wooden door, and spreads thick black smoke upon the high stone walls above the castle entrance. It takes time, but then, one-by-one, angry glowing coals begin to fall from the centre of the great door where the heat from the flames reaches its highest, and the timber structure begins to fail.

And, as each glowing mass falls onto the metal plates protecting the scaffold, the disjointed mutterings of the watching troops begin to aggregate themselves into muted shouts of encouragement. And then, as the destruction continues, each glowing, red-orange falling mass is greeted with a growing roar as the massed army involuntarily psyches itself for the impending assault.

Suddenly, the conflagration erupts into a huge spray of brilliant yellow sparks as the foresters, now silhouetted against the flames, drive the huge battering ram into the already weakened base of the door. And as the sound of the heavy crash reaches the ears of the assembled troops, another mighty roar ensues; the energy of the early morning destruction infusing the hearts of the gathered English army, lifting spirits and readying loins for the action about to commence.

A brief retreat, another charge at the base of the door by the foresters, another brilliant burst of sparks as the structure begins to disintegrate, and Henry determines that the time has come. He raises his sword: "For God, England, and Saint George!"

The roar in response is overwhelming, and immediately the massed body of English men-at-arms begins to rumble ominously up the ramp, towards the flaming, cascading wood which used to be the great castle door.

The foresters are attacking the flaming structure with heavy axes now, forcing an opening at its base, and working furiously at widening it for the advancing troops, so that a veritable torrent of armour can pass through and wreak havoc upon the defenders waiting on the other side. And hundreds of archers positioned at the sides of the ramp are firing almost without pause at every visible opening in the Great Keep's wall, ensuring that as few missiles as possible are fired or hurled upon the first of the assaulting troops now reaching the entrance below.

The waning fire-light at the castle entrance is both a product of the receding flames, their job now completed, and the morning sun, breasting the south-eastern horizon and announcing another fine, crisp winter morning.

The castle wall is now illuminated by the strengthening sunlight as Henry and Averill charge through the flames and into the enclosed battle arena beyond.

The timing is perfect.

★

For a moment, Averill and the king are exposed as they burst from the flames and plunge into the darker interior of the castle. But the huge number of knights which crash through behind them makes the task of the defenders impossible. Within an instant, the king's guard has caught up and re-grouped, and the momentary opportunity to maim or kill the two English leaders, has disappeared. Rampant knights continue to pour through the shattered and burning hulk of the great door, screaming vile threats and base obscenities, and swinging swords, cudgels and maces at anything that moves.

The clash of metal, the grunting of close combat and the dull crack of flesh and bones being severed are horrifyingly intimate in the enclosed space of the great keep's reception chamber. The shrill screams of injury and the muted moanings of prolonged agony add to the mounting horror. Visors up, the attacking knights continue their ferocious slashing and advancing as defenders are pushed back against castle walls, and finding no path of escape, are cut down and mauled and crushed and trampled into non-existence. The progress is frightening and brutal.

Then, suddenly, the deafening cacophony of enclosed battle is over; the pile of dead and writhing the only remnant of the initial line of defence. And, one-by-one, the agonised screams are silenced as viscously wielded swords are thrust into the bodies and heads of the victims where they lay.

The floor of the chamber is littered with the weapons of the defeated; swords, crossbows, a handful of maces, and a small number of daggers. Without exception, the weapons are sticky with slowly-congealing blood.

Averill turns to find Rupert, sword raised, but face petrified, looking with horror into his eyes.

Almost together, Gareth shakes James by the shoulders and Averill strikes Rupert with a gloved hand to the face, breaking the spells which threatened to immobilise the young knights.

"Stay alert," shouts Averill grasping Rupert's shoulder. "Remember, these bastards want to kill you. And they will if you freeze again!"

Faces stinging and eyes watering, the two young knights shake their heads, in desperate attempts to push down the horror and the nausea and regain control of their shocked limbs.

"Are you alright?" shouts Averill again, looking from one to the other.

The two young men nod in unison, but the fear in their faces remains unabated.

"Talk to them, Gareth," commands Averill, turning his attention back to the king.

The big man takes the two young knights by the scruffs of their necks and half-walks, half-drags them to the castle entrance, for fresh air and a chance to regain their equilibriums. Imperviousness to the horror of such close combat is not easily acquired, but acquire it they must, and quickly... or perish.

The character of the game has now changed, as Averill and Henry recognise the obvious next phase of the siege; the slow, methodical and particularly dangerous pursuit of the enemy deeper into his lair.

In keeping with castles of this nature, the attackers expect several chambers at this level: a main private chamber, several household chambers, and, no doubt, a chapel. Above, the accommodation for the defenders is expected, whilst below, the ground floor will contain storage rooms for food and weapons and treasure. And, at some point, there will be narrow and dangerous passageways to the adjoining keeps, where well-placed defenders can pick off the advancing knights and men-at-arms as they move in single-file through constricted openings.

From this point on, the attackers need to split into smaller forces, each seeking out and destroying the defenders congregated in the various locations. Now that the initial resistance has been smashed, one can confidently predict the successful outcome of the battle; however, the number of the losses which will be sustained along the way is still completely unknown.

Henry, with Gloucester and Anthony and a substantial contingent of men-at-arms start towards the stairs leading to the massed concentration of defenders above. Gareth and Bryan lead a second large group down to work their way through the storage rooms below. Clarence and Talbot direct their forces into the passages leading to the smaller lower keep and the great circular tower, where further fierce resistance is expected.

Averill looks to Charles and indicates the path ahead, to the residential chambers of the first floor. A quick scan back and he finds Rupert re-entering the castle and hurrying towards the assembled group. The young man raises his hand and nods his recovery to Averill.

★

Now that the reception chamber is taken, the principle of passive defence, wherein each line of resistance is backed up by another, has been overcome, and the fighting now fractures into multiple concurrent battles; the three separate floors of the great keep, the lower keep, and the multiple levels of the great circular tower. The English have the numbers, but the French have possession of all the vantage points, including those most dangerous of places, the narrow passageways, through which the English must pass to reach each objective. But numbers count most, and although the losses are considerable, the inevitability of the English advance soon becomes apparent as one-by-one, the defensive positions fall and the remaining defenders are forced back into enclaves of resistance.

Gareth's sword is raised as he and James and five men-at-arms round the corner of the passageway and charge into the next store-room. They pause, momentarily, listening; but no sound greets their ears.

"No-one here," shouts Gareth above the surrounding din of battle, and the group turns to leave.

A bin clatters to the floor, and Gareth turns. The others have all moved on.

The Frenchman is armed and bristles in defiance. The bin clatters again as the young boy tries to disengage his foot. His father crouches, facing Gareth with the desperation that only a parent knows. The shock of red hair on the youngster momentarily softens Gareth's resolve as he recalls James, so similar at that age.

The Frenchman roars and launches himself at Gareth, who backs away, still confounded by the presence of the youngster. But Gareth is between the Frenchman and the doorway, and there are only two possible outcomes: death to one of them, or the Frenchman's surrender.

But it is clear that the Frenchman will not countenance surrender.

Another roar and this time a clash of steel as Gareth's decision is made. His own son is somewhere close by, possibly engaged in battle, and Gareth needs to find him again, quickly.

The big man advances, and the Frenchman recognises that the decision is now no longer his. The slash and the thrust of swords in the confined space of the storeroom is terrifyingly close, and brutal. There is little opportunity for retreat, and Gareth is by far the stronger. The imperative of getting back to James is increasing by the moment. Swords clash again, but this time, the combatants are close and Gareth grasps his opponent by the throat. The young boy screams and launches himself at Gareth, who brushes him violently aside. The youngster crashes against the storeroom wall and falls to the floor as Gareth tightens his grip around the other man's throat. He throws the Frenchman to the floor and follows up with the fatal sword-thrust. The young boy crouches, whimpering as the life flows from his stricken father.

Panting from the sudden exertion, Gareth stands, bloody sword in hand, looking across at the miserable creature, whose red hair is matted with dirt and perspiration.

"Fuyez d'ici," he roars at the boy, pointing toward the door. "Get out of here before I change my mind and do you in, too."

Frozen by fear, the youngster does not move. Gareth takes a step, then picks the boy up by the arm and hurls him towards the doorway. The boy looks back in terror, then scrambles upright and begins to run.

Gareth looks back at the body of the Frenchman, now trickling blood from the wound just inflicted, then charges out of the storeroom in search of his son.

★

Henry's progress is methodical and decisive. The initial resistance as the English poured up the stairs and into the upper floor sleeping quarters, was short-lived. This was the last refuge, and once the defensive line at the top of the stairs had been smashed, the opportunity for resistance rapidly diminished as scores of men-at-arms poured out of the stairwell and into the fray.

The shouted capitulation of the French comes quickly as the captain recognises the inevitability of slaughter if he chooses any other course.

The collection of weapons commences as the French are disarmed, then, slowly, the escort of prisoners down the stairs and out into the courtyard begins.

The garrison commander is still at large.

★

Averill's movements are slow and cautious as he enters the small, intimate chapel. No sound returns, but there are numerous places where a man might wait, concealed.

The battle for the castle is clearly almost over. The private chambers have been taken, one-by-one, and now only the chapel remains unsecured on this floor. Rupert has fought in the thick of battle, and Averill, concerned for the young man's safety, has despatched him, with Charles and a contingent of men-at-arms, to escort the prisoners outside. But, inwardly, Averill also admits to the other motive behind his decision; and further admits that, although perhaps foolhardy, the thought of encountering Bijou, before the victory is declared and the fighting ceases, is driving him on.

He stands, quiet but alert, knowing that, regardless of where the battle took him today, this is where he would finish up; waiting here, in the chapel, where some unseen force has been drawing him; knowing almost instinctively that the same force will be driving Bijou to confrontation, and praying that the Frenchman has not succumbed to another's sword.

He stands, head bowed, listening; alone and still.

The voice is clear, and accented, "I have waited a long time for this, Averill."

The hairs on the back of his neck stand with the reckless thrill of the encounter.

"As have I, Bijou," he replies, without looking up; "as have I."

Then, at the sound of slow, steady footsteps, he turns, and watches as the knight, in Armagnac colours, emerges from the long, crimson drapes framing the small central altar, so incongruous given the battle now coursing through the castle.

"Luck, Averill," calls the Frenchman as the heavy curtain falls back into place. "It was merely luck that saw you victorious in our last encounter.

"And all for what? A woman? A memory? Honour? What was it for Averill?" he goads. "What made you think that you, a relic of the past, could stand up to me in any field of combat?

"And now you seek me out again. Why? Perhaps because you, too, recognise that, on any level field, you are no match for me? Perhaps you have carried the embarrassment of your hollow victory all these years, and know, as I do, that but for a momentary loss of footing by my steed I would have despatched you like so much cattle fodder. Is that it? Is that why you stand here alone, waiting for me; waiting to bring this chapter, and your embarrassment, to an end?"

Averill ignores the jibes. "You and your army are defeated, Bijou. That should be enough for me. But it is not. This is personal. This is for what you did to my lady."

"Oh, really?" replies Bijou, "For what I did to your lady; and what I shall do to you. You are nothing to me, Averill; and nor was your lady.

"Yes, the army is defeated, and, yes, Falaise Castle will fall, and, yes, I shall be ransomed. But not by you, Averill, never by you."

"So very true," replies Averill, "for I will not spare your life this time."

Bijou laughs. "You dream, Averill; you dream."

Another sound. Averill turns, as another knight, also in Armagnac colours, steps into the chapel doorway and advances up the small aisle towards him.

Averill's heart jumps.

"Oh, do not worry, Averill," remarks Bijou. "He will not intervene; unless absolutely necessary, of course. A precaution, you understand, but hardly a necessary one, I suspect."

Averill looks from one knight to the other, mind racing, gauging distances, then slows... and relaxes. He knows that Bijou understands the chivalric principles at stake here; knows that Bijou's pride will not let him claim a victory unearned. He remembers the Frenchman waiting for Henry's word to launch him into combat with Averill the last time they faced each other; remembers turning and drawing his own sword first, to obviate the need for the king to make the decision; and so knows that there will be no interference whilst he and Bijou are engaged. But he also knows that he could well be cut down by the second Armagnac sword, a moment after he despatches Bijou. But that is a step too far for consideration now.

And so he readies himself; retreating moment-by-moment into the small sphere of focus which he inhabits in battle. The chapel fades, the Armagnac knight ceases to exist, only Bijou remains, standing quietly and confidently before him. There is no bravado from either man now. For all his arrogance, Bijou is not a pretender; he is a formidable opponent. The two face each other; Bijou, supremely confident in his ability to destroy Averill; Averill, focused, intense, knowing that all those years of pain and hatred have resolved down to this moment; from which, this time, only one will walk away.

The older knight draws his sword and crouches, waiting. Bijou smiles; the same cruel, supercilious smile Averill saw the last time they faced each other. Suddenly, and with frightening speed, Bijou's sword is in his hand; ready. He spins the weapon in his grip and laughs, mocking the older knight facing him... then crouches.

Yet, within the sphere, a soothing calm descends upon Averill. His heart-beat slows, his mind clears; he relaxes. Senses heightened, body calm, mind cool, he waits.

The first strike is sudden, and violent, and crashes into Averill's upheld shield with a force which Averill had forgotten. But the older knight now possesses a battle hardening which he did not have last time, and counters with a thrust which penetrates Bijou's defence and skids off the shoulder-plate of the Frenchman's armour.

"Very good, Averill; very good," mocks the Frenchman.

He advances a pace down the short aisle of the chapel; Averill retreats a pace. The second Armagnac knight, with sword drawn and positioned between Averill and chapel doorway, also retreats, maintaining his distance from the combatants; close, and ready, should the need arise, to advance and deliver the fatal blow. The battle-space is frightening in its intimacy.

Bijou thrusts again. Averill's shield blocks the thrust, as he follows up with a powerful forehand cut of his own. The sword strikes the Frenchman's shield half-way along the blade, the tip of which just catches the edge of Bijou's helmet and continues on upward in a graceful arc. And, then, without pause, the sword is descending again in a powerful backhand slice as Averill flows from one stroke to the next. Bijou ducks and backs off, hurriedly, as the blade passes before his eyes, barely missing his face.

The Frenchman sucks in his breath.

He snarls. The supercilious smile has vanished.

Averill waits, slightly crouched; ready. Bijou strikes, and once again the sword crashes into Averill's raised shield, forcing Averill back a pace. But the blow is not quite as powerful as Averill had expected; not quite as bone-jarring as he recalls from their first encounter. A momentary image flashes through his mind; an image of severed metal, crushed fingers and shredded flesh; of finger plates of a shattered right glove dripping blood. And suddenly he knows; knows that the beautifully executed last stroke of their previous encounter has left Bijou debilitated; his sword hand weaker; not much, but enough.

It has taken but an instant for the realisation, and in that instant Averill has countered with his own thrust. Still riding the momentum of the strike, he cannons into Bijou with his shield and bringing his sword down again, smashes the pommel into the Frenchman's face. Bijou roars in pain, anger and surprise. But Averill has survived a hundred more battles than Bijou, has experienced a hundred more opponents than Bijou, and can fight dirty a hundred times more effectively than Bijou. This is not a tournament, and prettiness is not part of the script.

Angry now, the Frenchman raises his sword to slash down upon his opponent, which, with visor raised, leaves his face exposed. For Averill, the Frenchman's face, at the exact level of a charcoal mark on a pell, is an irresistible target. Focused as Averill now is, the Frenchman's sword appears to descend in slow-motion. He sways sideways, sensing rather than watching the passage of the sword, and thrusts his own sword at the target.

Not quite close enough to inflict serious damage, the tip of Averill's sword, nevertheless, grazes Bijou, and the Frenchman's face begins to drip blood.

Behind Averill, the Armagnac knight is becoming uncertain. Should he allow this unexpectedly tough encounter to continue, or should he intervene to tip the balance slightly in Bijou's favour?

Bijou dabs at his wounded face and looks, angrily, at the slash of blood on the back of his gauntlet. Behind the scene, Rupert appears in the doorway to the chapel, and stops, rooted to the spot.

Bijou raises his sword, and the Armagnac knight behind Averill begins to raise his sword also.

The powerful strike crashes into Averill's raised shield and glances off again. No damage done. But Averill is in no mood to give the Frenchman any time to re-group, and puts all his strength into another blow, aimed at disabling his opponent's right arm. The blade crashes down upon Bijou's armoured forearm, and Averill notes, with satisfaction, the grimace of pain that passes across his opponent's face.

Bijou flexes the fingers of his right hand. His grip is momentarily weakened, and Averill noting the pain, seizes the moment and strikes again, aiming not for Bijou's body, but slicing down the arm and onto the gloved hand behind the cross-guard of his opponent's sword. The sword is torn from Bijou's grasp and clatters to the chapel's stone floor, as Averill's sword-point reaches the Frenchman's face.

Behind Averill, the Armagnac knight raises his sword higher, and Rupert, spurred by the sight, reaches out to push the tall candelabra to his left, which crashes to the floor, shattering the candles into flying fragments, and starkly announcing his presence.

The Armagnac knight turns. "And who are you, boy?" he calls. "Come to save your master, have you? A boy on a man's errand, I fear."

Averill's focus remains on Bijou.

Rupert is silent as he now advances; coldly drawing his sword back and cocking his wrist ready to strike. The Armagnac is facing Rupert now. He crouches in readiness, only slightly discomforted by the litheness with which the young knight approaches. He strikes, but there is no-one at the point where the blow lands, as Rupert, with speed and grace, side-steps the blow and slashes viciously at waist level as he passes. The Armagnac folds and crashes to the floor. Rupert crouches, and Averill recalls the scorpion he was reminded of on a previous occasion.

The Armagnac rises, quickly raising his sword to parry the almost immediate thrust from the young Englishman as he steps forth from the crouch. But the defence is inadequate as Rupert flows fluidly into a follow-up slash, which slices across the armoured chest of the Armagnac, knocking him to the floor once again.

And now, there is concern in the face of the grounded knight; concern that this young man is not as green as he at first seemed, but rather carries a cold, malicious intensity and a fierce commitment to kill, clearly matched by an ability to do just that. Rupert has still not uttered a word.

The Armagnac rises to his feet again, raising his sword against the next strike. He is still bringing his weapon up as Rupert's thrust pierces his throat. He collapses to the floor, hands tearing at his helmet, gurgling and writhing hideously as he slowly drowns in his own blood.

Silence.

The new knight's youth and prowess are not lost on Bijou, who now, in this moment of realisation, responds with rage.

In sudden rebellion against the fates which have deserted him, the enraged Frenchman charges at Averill, who reacts, instinctively, thrusting his sword full into the face of the Frenchman, who cries out, and falls.

But the blow has merely passed through the Frenchman's cheek. He recovers his sword and rises, now bellowing with unchecked fury, and slashes at Averill, who parries the blow and responds with another short thrust to the head, striking Bijou's helmet and stunning the Frenchman. Bijou's response is another wild, ferocious slash, delivered with unrestrained aggression. But his inertia carries him forward onto Averill's powerful counter, which is short, swift and precise. The blade penetrates deep into the Frenchman's stomach and wedges between the plates of his armour. Bijou groans horribly and falls to the floor. He rolls painfully to his side, then, inch-by-inch, drags himself to the wall, clawing himself up into a half-sitting position as Averill stands over him. Blood flows from his fatally wounded body.

He lies, propped against the wall, breathing in gasps now.

"I've never forgiven you for what you did to me on the tournament field, Averill," he spits. "I've hated you for as long as I've known you."

Averill looks down at the stricken knight, but feels no pity.

"She was too good for you, Averill," Bijou continues, still goading.

Averill does not respond, as memories tumble through his mind, then, with quiet dignity: "You're wrong Bijou. She was too good for all of us."

Bijou looks hard into the other man's eyes, then, as his strength begins to leave him, he motions Averill to come closer.

"I've hated you, Averill, not only for what you did to me, but also for what you had. I had women, I had glory; but you had love, Averill; you had love. I hated you for that.

"And did you love her; your woman; the one I took from you?" he rasps, mercilessly forcing the knight to remember.

"Yes, Bijou," Averill replies, thinking back; "more than anything or anyone I had ever known. She was..."

But he is talking to no-one. The Frenchman's head is inclined as far as the helmet will allow. His lifeless eyes see nothing. And in the silence, Averill cannot tell whether the emptiness he feels is from the raw memory of his lost love, or the absence of the burden of revenge.

Drained of all emotion, he slumps beside the body of Bijou; exhausted, impotent. His long and anguished quest to avenge the death of Mariel is over. Suddenly, he feels old again; as if all reason for living has deserted him. He removes his helmet and lets it fall to the floor.

Rupert comes closer and stands, looking down at him. Then, quietly he removes his helmet also, and sits, still without speaking; not wishing to disturb the thoughts of his mentor.

Averill's voice is distant. "It's over, Rupert. It's all... over."

And, resting his head back against the cold stone wall, he looks up, noticing the chapel again, and, slowly, the realisation dawns that he is in God's house. He remembers the special moments he has experienced in God's house: Christmas Mass and Rupert's knighthood in Église Saint-Étienne; his daughter's wedding in the chapel of Windsor Castle; his own wedding in the same chapel, so long ago, it now seems. All swirl through his mind in floating, disconnected unreality.

He thinks of the glade, where he felt God's presence, so powerfully, and where, piece-by-piece, he felt his life being restored. He closes his eyes as the images pass before him. He remembers the candles in a chapel, and the exquisite pale beauty of the woman who brought love and joy and meaning to his life, as she lay still and silent... and unbelievably beautiful... the last time he ever looked upon her.

Then gradually he begins to emerge from the shadows of the past. He remembers Elvira now; remembers that life is not all lost; that it has moved on since those awful days when the beauty of the world departed and life became a pale reflection in a darkened landscape. And he remembers Odelia; her smiles, her hugs, and her delight in the young man sitting quietly beside him. He smiles and feels a little better; a little more hopeful; a little more able to cope.

"Come on, my boy," he says, quietly; raising his arms and stretching. "Perhaps we should go and see how the others fared."

Rupert looks in surprise at the man sitting beside him; the man he will never fully understand, but who he owes so much, then rises and, offering his hand, hauls Averill to his feet. Arm-in-arm, the two knights trudge from the chapel towards the castle entrance, and thence, out into the morning sunshine.

"It's a good day to be alive," smiles Averill at the young man.

"Yes it is, Sir Gregory," replies Rupert, smiling back.

"Yes it is, Gregory," corrects Averill, with a wink.

CHAPTER ELEVEN

Dappled light filters through the trees, but the ground remains cold and the young boy shivers as he wakes. He looks up at the leaves overhead, struggling to remember. Then, in an overwhelming instant, the images of his father's death crash in upon him again.

He recalls his terrifying progress from the castle basement, crashing into oncoming English soldiers, who brushed him aside with rasping threats and foul curses. He recalls crouching in a darkened corner of the reception chamber, taking in the surrounding devastation; slashed and broken bodies lying in odd, unnatural positions; grotesque masks of faces; swords, crossbows, daggers strewn about the floor; dark pools of sticky, drying blood. He recalls escaping through the charred and smouldering castle door and out into the cold, bright morning; rough voices shouting abuse at him, but no-one bothering to stop his progress. He recalls running crazily across the outer bailey of the castle, a dense grove of trees beckoning, the horizon tilting wildly as he feels himself falling; then nothing.

He rolls over, burying his head in his arms, sobbing softly in despair. Thoughts, hitherto beautiful, but now agonising, run through his mind. With no mother to comfort him these last three years, his father has been his world. They have hunted together, killed and dressed game together, laughed together, and ultimately, as the hated English began to destroy their town, retreated into the castle together.

His father had been a soldier, and a good man; had been concerned for his son's welfare, had taught him to be considerate in his treatment of people, had taught him how to hunt and trap, how to wash and cook and clean for himself, and more recently, had started to teach him how to handle the weapons of defence; the short sword, the dagger, and the cross-bow. Life, although harsh, had not appeared impossible, and the boy had believed that, in time, he might have emulated his father and lived in a small house, with a family, and perhaps even a son like himself.

But now the dream, if that's what it was, is gone; destroyed by the English. Now, he knows himself to be an orphan, with no-one to care for him, no-one to provide shelter, no means of obtaining food, aside from begging, or thievery.

He sits up now, looking around. The noise and confusion of battle has subsided. Groups of men make their way through the expansive courtyard of the outer bailey; some, seriously injured, are being carried, some are limping from wounds sustained earlier in the morning, and some, French, are being herded together and marched, presumably outside to the English camp, where they will be held as prisoners until their ransoms are paid sometime in the future. This he knows from the stories his father has told him about war, and the way it is conducted, and, ultimately, resolved.

In the middle distance, another group of men stand talking. With sudden anguish, he recognises the big man from the morning; the one who screamed at him to flee; the one who killed his father. His body stiffens and his eyes water from the concentrated effort of staring, just to make sure that it is him. But, there is no doubt: he was a big man, taller than most, and built like an ox; a powerful man who despatched his father with a short, violent sword-thrust which is still imprinted upon his mind.

The others are unknown; but one wears battle-dress which offends the boy. The fleurs-de-lys are French; they should not be on the surcoat of an Englishman. The three gold lions upon red, and the three fleurs-de-lys upon blue do not belong together. He knows this man; his father had warned him about this man; this Henry of England.

Shaking, with tears welling in his orphan eyes, he looks down. There, in the grass, a cross-bow lies cocked and ready, just as it was dropped when its bearer died. He reaches out to grasp it, then hesitates.

What are his options? To quietly slink away, unnoticed; but to what? What is there ahead for him? What will he do tomorrow when the cold of the night and the sharp pangs of hunger reduce him to the beggar he knows he must become? He could kill the big man; the one who killed his father. But what would that achieve? Would it bring back his father? Would it bring back the life which has now gone? And besides, he is only here now, alive, because the big man took pity upon him, for some reason, and told him to run; to flee, before he changed his mind and killed him too. Or, he could kill the English king; the imposter with the fleurs-de-lys of France upon his chest; the man who started all this when he brought his army to France; the man whose actions led to this battle, in which his father died this morning; the man who is now responsible for his miserable life ahead.

He wipes away his tears with the torn sleeve of his ragged coat... and takes up the cross-bow. Indecisive, he lowers it again, and observes. Two targets. But only one can be taken, for he has no wish to be captured and probably killed; and that is certainly what will happen if he tries to re-load the cross-bow. And then he realises: he only has one bolt anyway. No, he has to make a decision; the big man, or the king; the one who took his father's life, or the one who caused this whole fucking mess in the first place.

He decides, and raises the cross-bow again. He places the butt firmly against his shoulder, just as his father taught him, and sights the target: the upper of the three lions. Then, not certain of the distance between himself and the king, he raises the weapon a little further, just to make sure that the bolt strikes the chest, and does not fall lower. He has learned his lessons well: he breathes in deeply, then slowly and steadily exhales, and in that smooth continuous motion... squeezes the trigger.

★

The unmistakable twang of a crossbow, and Averill, instinctively, launches himself at his king, taking them both heavily to the ground. And, in the same instant, the bolt strikes the castle wall just about shoulder height, spraying dust and stone fragments into the faces of the group.

Henry rises, shaken but unhurt, and angrily brushes the dirt from his clothing, looking around to see from whence the attack came. Averill rises... and stumbles... and falls, again.

Suddenly, Gareth is on his knees, holding his captain's head. Rupert also kneels, looking with concern at Averill, as the knight struggles to rise again.

The king, now realising something is amiss, quickly kneels beside his favourite knight. "Gregory, what is it?"

Averill's eyes look back, but uncertainty clouds them. "I don't know, my Lord. I suddenly feel faint."

Gareth's hand is warm and sticky from the blood flowing from the long gash in Averill's neck.

The king roars for his surgeon.

"I'll go," calls Rupert as he turns and runs.

★

"I cannot cauterise this, Your Majesty, nor can I bind it. This carries blood to the head; one cannot just stop the flow."

"Then what can we do?"

"Nothing, Your Majesty; I have never seen men recover from such wounds as these."

"There must be something we can do!"

"Make him comfortable, Your Majesty. These are precious minutes you have with him now. They will not last long."

Henry takes the hand of his favourite knight and clasps it to him. "Oh Gregory; not like this!"

Averill lies quietly, looking up at his king. "It matters not how or when, Your Majesty; it comes to us all. And where better to fall than here, in the company of my king? Not alone, in some nameless field, writhing in the mud, but here, where, as you yourself pointed out, so much of our history began.

"No, my Lord, I think I could not have chosen a better place to leave this world."

He closes his eyes as the strength begins to wane.

"I would have liked to see my daughter one last time," he continues. "She has been my life, and my constant companion for so long now. I miss her so very much, my Lord. Does time pass quickly, I wonder? I hope so; I will want to see her again, very soon.

"And Elvira. Pray tell her gently, my Lord, for I fear she will suffer my loss as much as I would suffer hers."

He lies silent for a while, as Gareth looks from Anthony to the king and back again. But no-one is doing any better.

Averill stirs. "Who is that approaching, my Lord? The sun is behind her and I cannot see her face. But her hair... so soft, so beautiful..."

Henry looks around, but there is no-one there. It is an illusion of the knight's mind, made real by the depth of feeling he has for those he has loved.

The king looks down again. A smile hovers over the knight's face.

She is with him now. He lovingly absorbs her features; the auburn hair, the dark eyes, the graceful sweep of her back. She holds him gently, then lowers her head onto his shoulder.

"Oh, Gregory, my love."

He smiles, and wraps his arm around her, stroking her hair with his other hand. "Be strong, my love. We have had a wonderful time, you and I; two Christmases together, wonderful nights in England and France, a daughter's wedding, her young man's knighthood; so much beauty, so much happiness, so much love..."

She lies quietly in his embrace as he remembers the first time he saw her, standing some few yards away, looking at him, as if not quite able to believe what she had seen that day; not quite able to believe that he had walked from the field of the tournament victorious. He remembers standing at the first-floor window, transfixed by the beauty of the rainbow, shimmering above the clouds scudding across the gradually clearing sky, and hearing her first words to him: "C'est magnifique, n'est-ce pas?" He remembers being unable to understand the strange set of emotions building within him; a combination of interest and resistance. And he remembers their first Christmas together; how after the feast they retired to a quiet corner, she resting her head on his shoulder; how her lips touched his neck; how he embraced the swell and fall of her breast as she breathed, and felt the sudden hammering of his own heart; how she reached up and drew his head down until her lips reached his ear; how she impaled him with her words: "Take me somewhere."

Muted voices break through, and Averill's eyelids flicker, then hesitantly open as he searches out his younger self.

"Rupert," he calls, softly, urgently.

The young knight bends close. "Yes, Sir Gregory?"

"I will not see my daughter again... and I love her so very much."

"My boy... if I could choose anyone, at all, to care for her... I would still choose you; the once angry young man... who put all of that behind him... and finally understood what it means... to be his father's son."

His voice is weak now, and Rupert strains to hear.

"She is yours now, my boy; just as you are hers. Love her as dearly as I have done, Rupert," whispers Averill. "That is all I ask... my boy... love her as dearly..."

"I will, Sir Gregory; of that you can be assured," replies the young knight. But the reply goes unheard.

★

There is no sound now; no footsteps, no voices. The whisper of the breeze has faded. She lifts her head from his shoulder and rises, looking bashfully away, and holds out her hand for him to follow.

The long, black hair shines richly in the brilliant sunshine.

He reaches out across the gulf of silence and places his fingers beneath her chin, delicately turning her head towards his own. Her face is a soft oval, lips rich and full, skin smooth; a slightly olive complexion; pale no longer. On her right cheek, he remembers the smudge of flour where her hand had wiped at tears. A further slight pressure and her face is raised until warm, brown eyes, framed in almond-shaped lids and swimming in tears, look deep into his soul.

A thousand fathoms of suppressed grief and despair wash away as he reaches for the exquisite creature before him.

A blink, and the brimming tears cascade down her softly flushed cheeks, as Mariel smiles and takes his hand: "Come, my love..."

★

Across the outer bailey of Falaise castle, bloodied and weary soldiers make their way back towards the town. Some limp, some carry the lifeless bodies of comrades, while still others herd groups of French prisoners before them. But here, at the edge of the castle, in the bright midday sunshine of a cold winter's day, a small group of men, whose number includes a blacksmith and a king, stand or kneel in muted shock at the final act of the morning.

385

He lies in peaceful repose now, hands crossed over his chest, neck wound hidden by the blood-drenched silk scarf which had become his battle emblem, but otherwise unmarked; the pale beauty of an elegant man, greying at the temples, apparently sleeping, in silent preparation for the adventures of the coming day.

CHAPTER TWELVE

The cart comes to a halt at the steep incline leading to the St Nicholas Gate, in the eastern extremity of the wall of Falaise Castle, where only yesterday, Gregory Averill, with his king, had led the English forces to victory. Anthony and Elvira have been silent for most of the journey from Caen; each lost in private grief. Behind them, Odelia's body shudders from time to time as her agony spills over. Her head is buried in her young husband's gentle but futile embrace.

Beset by pain and doubt, Elvira raises her tear-stained face and softly asks: "Was he mine, Anthony? Was he ever mine?"

"Oh, my Lady," replies the knight, taking her hand and looking gently at her.

A moment's thought, then he continues: "Gregory never did anything, but completely, my Lady; he lived life to the full. In battle, I have never seen anyone so fearsome, or so committed. And in love, my Lady, I never saw a man so devoted."

A longer pause as Anthony reflects; searching for the words, then: "Life dealt him a hand which, once, shook his being to its core; a blow from which I thought he might never recover. And yet, she also dealt him favours which most of us will never experience. I have seen the way his ladies looked at him; with such tenderness and love. No man could have received such love and remained untouched by it.

"I have seen his princess from the East cradle his head in her arms, when she thought we were not watching, and lay her head upon his, with such tenderness that no-one in the room spoke, for fear of breaking the spell. I have seen his daughter gently pull him down to her level, and wrap her arms around his neck, and tell him 'I love you, Daddy,' with such deep affection, that I have felt my own life diminished for not having been blessed with such love. And, my Lady, I have seen the look in your eyes as you have sat with him, with your hand upon his shoulder, and your face just inches from his, telling him with your smile how complete he has made your life.

"Yes, my Lady, for the period of time he was with you on this earth, he was yours; totally, and unconditionally."

"Thank you, Anthony", replies Elvira, as her tears fall softly to the ground. "I am honoured to be included in such company. And, yes, that is how I felt about him; he made my life complete… and wonderful."

She pauses for a time. "I pray that, one day, the sadness of today will fade, and I will smile again as I recall the beautiful times we spent together... in love."

Silence, as both reflect within private thoughts. Then Anthony continues, "We will miss him, my Lady; we will miss him, greatly. Oh, Gareth will defend us, of that I have no doubt, and Bryan will remind us, frequently, of the wonderful times we shared. But there will be no-one to lead us; no-one to urge us on; no-one to inspire us to do better, to make us more than we ever thought we could be.

"I wish Thomas were here. I miss him, too. He would know how to express the feelings which my words struggle to convey."

"No, Anthony," replies Elvira, gently. "Your words are from the heart; there is no need for any others. I understand you completely."

Anthony is quiet as his thoughts broaden.

"I am sad, my Lady," he continues, "and I have a pain in my breast which sits like a heavy stone; and life will never be the same again, without Gregory. But, our king is a mighty warrior, and a truly just and pious man, and I know that his courage and his inspiration will continue to carry us all forward; even those of us who have felt the awful pain of loss here today."

Then, as the thought evolves, Anthony continues, "Yet, one day, my Lady, even Henry will be gone, and I wonder if our country, our England, will feel as we feel now. I wonder if an entire nation will feel as bereft as we do today, through the loss of one man."

Silence, again; then, quietly, with tenderness and compassion, and a brave attempt at a smile, he continues: "Mark my words, Lady Elvira, this time will not come again. We must grasp it, and hold on to it, and live it as completely and as passionately as Gregory lived his time, my Lady; for we are fortunate, indeed, to have lived when Gregory Averill was our friend, and Harry our good and courageous king."

★

The governor's dwelling is arranged along the northern wall of the castle, and within it, the private apartment is separate from the other living quarters. Soft, muted sunlight now filters through the window of the apartment, so different from the cold, clear brightness of yesterday.

The figure before them looks completely peaceful. The armour has been removed, and William has cleaned and oiled it, as he did once before, when Averill's need for it faded. And Gareth has honoured his captain in the same manner Wendy honoured Mariel; the doublet bearing the black dragon passant upon bleu celeste is spotless. The silk scarf, now washed free of blood, graces the knight's neck, covering the wound which cost him his life. Black boots and leggings complete the picture. He lies still and silent; the image of knightly grace.

Elvira lies alongside her beloved, her head beside his, weeping quietly as the agonising pain of loss spreads through her chest. Her hand brushes his cheek, tracing the line of his lips, then strokes his forehead as she has done on so many nights when they have lain together; without talking, just being.

Close on the other side, Rupert sits, cradling his wife in his arms as she begins the next phase of life's journey. Her hand reaches out to rest on the once strong arm which had scooped her up when terror struck; the arm which had held her, supported her, carried her from all manner of danger; the arm on which her same hand had lightly rested the day her father had given her away in marriage to Rupert, those few months – or was it hours – before.

Tears drop, noiselessly.

Time passes, and slowly, gradually, within Elvira's mind, a thought takes hold: "I know a little about solitude, for I have known a man who knew that condition well, and who showed me, daily, how one can both love life, and love a memory, and be a better person for it." And a commitment slowly forms: "So now, how could I do any less? How could I not continue to live, loving his memory; for he was everything to me, as I know I was to him, for the period of time that we had each other. I will remember every minute, every hour, every soft touch, every whispered word, every moment of joy, for these are the true treasures of life. These are the moments in which we are blessed; and these are the memories which will sustain me, and bring me love, and warmth, and peace, until we are together once again."

★

Thus the trio stayed; for an hour, perhaps more.

The late afternoon sun was setting slowly in the clearing sky to the south-west, bathing the land in rich ochre and violet tones, as Elvira and Odelia and Rupert rose and quietly left the room where Sir Gregory lay in peace. Arm-in-arm, they walked down through the outer bailey of Falaise Castle, past a small, innocuous grove of trees, and out into the town, to make the arrangements for the final, requiem celebration of Sir Gregory Averill's life on earth.

The order of the world has changed once again: another central figure has passed on to the next, unknowable phase, and those who remain behind have begun the task of living for the future, embraced by the memories of the past, just as Averill had done all those years before; setting the example, and providing the proof that life is, indeed, liveable without the beloved; for they never truly depart, but merely pass into a place close by, and there, can be found by the loving mind, in those quiet moments of solitude, when the warmth of the morning sunshine, or the haunting call of the owl, or the soft touch of the evening's misty rain, pushes aside the curtain, and gently ushers us in... to eternity.

---end---

EPILOGUE

Summer has returned and the English countryside is redolent of life and love and happiness. Elvira talks quietly with Odelia and Rupert, reminiscing upon beautiful, other-worldly times spent with Averill.

Her once-vital outlook upon life is quiet now; subdued.

"I recall a glade where Gregory once took me. It was so beautiful, so peaceful. He said it was where he found the peace and the strength to come back to this world; as if God himself had been present with him. It is somewhere I so wish I could visit again; to sit quietly, and be with him again. It carried his spirit, and I believe it would still be there. But sadly, I have no idea where it is. We rode through a forest to get there, but apart from that, I know nothing of its location."

The room is quiet, as Elvira and Odelia and Rupert drink in the summer sunshine streaming in through the south-facing window of the castle.

"I never saw such a place," remarks Rupert. "Sir Gregory showed me many things, but not that. It must have been a very personal place for him."

Elvira smiles, lovingly, as she watches Rupert gently running his hand over the slight bulge of his newly-pregnant wife.

"I was amazed," she continues. "We had passed through what seemed to me like an altar; like somewhere something magic had happened. There were all these poles in a rough semi-circle; poles which, for some reason, had been cut and slashed. And there was a tree in the middle; a beautiful tree. I think it was an oak; with some strangely familiar structure beneath it. I asked Gregory about it all, but he just smiled and said, 'Boys' games.'"

Silence again, as Rupert battles his emotions. Then, smiling through his tears, he offers: "That is a place I know, Elvira; I can take you there."

Elvira looks up, and smiles; her heart beating a little faster at the thought. "That would be lovely, Rupert; that would be very special."

★

The pells are mossy now, more than two years since they played their part in Averill's recovery. A few have already been reached by creepers from the forest's edge, which have stretched forth their tentacles and started to wrap themselves around the bases, seeking stronger sunlight.

Rupert walks slowly among them, his hand trailing across each one as he passes. The seasons of rain have washed away most of the charcoal marks, but one or two remain. The young knight recognises his first pell, and stands before it now, recalling the slow, studied movements of Fiore de' Liberi da Premariacco, which Averill had instilled in him. Ghostly voices echo in his head: *Lucky...; Jealous...;* and he smiles; sadly, wistfully.

Faint images hover before him; of Gareth and James... and Averill... sweating and straining in the summer sun, then lying exhausted together at lunch, the knights commenting upon the inability of the young squires 'to keep up with the real men'; and the afternoon battles, when he and James would stop their practice, and watch in awe as Gareth and Gregory threw everything they had at each other in the controlled violence of truly awesome soldiers at work.

He turns, no longer able to control the tears which tumble freely down his cheeks, and walks back to where Elvira and Odelia are standing, watching him, unwilling to intrude upon his poignant, bittersweet memories.

"Please show me the glade," he asks of Elvira. Then, wrapping his arms around Odelia, he looks intently into her eyes. "Don't you ever let me forget him, my love," he gently instructs.

"How could I, my darling?" she responds. "He was my father."

Elvira turns slowly, uncertainly, overwhelmed by the power of the surroundings. There is an incredible sadness about this place, with its ring of sentinels, standing silently, as if guarding some timeless secret. She looks carefully around the ring of trees surrounding the clearing... then smiles. A barely-perceptible gap catches her eye, and she walks towards it.

And, as they pass through the ring of trees, the sound of running water greets them. A stream gurgles and splashes as it flows over a low rocky outcrop which spans its path; the same rocky outcrop that culminates in two flat boulders, one behind the other, not two metres from the stream; one, knee-high and flat, the other, shoulder-high and upright, forming a wide, natural seat under the leafy boughs of a tree whose trunk stands on the other side of the stream. The scene is serene... and idyllic.

The three sit quietly, not speaking, overcome by the silent intensity of the glade.

And, as the afternoon sun traverses the sky, its light momentarily strikes the wet rocks, over which the stream is tumbling, at just the angle to reflect the sparkling pattern into Elvira's face; just as it reflected the same pattern into the face of a man seated cross-legged on the grass at the feet of a sleek, white mare, that first afternoon, three springtimes ago.

She feels him look over at the rocks, dazzled by the rapidly changing patterns which shimmer and dance and break and fold before him.

He gazes, mesmerised, and then smiles.

A small piece of the wall encasing her bereaved mind breaks away. A chink appears. Sunlight and beauty stream in...

ACKNOWLEDGMENTS

I wish to sincerely thank Gary Smailes (bubblecow.net), for the painstaking editing and sound advice provided in bringing this work to publishing standard. I wish to also thank Ned Hoste (www.nedof2H.net) for the outstanding cover design, which captures so much of the essence of the story. And, to the team at Troubador Publishing, I record my gratitude for their guidance and support during the production phase of the book.

I also wish to acknowledge the historical works of Juliet Barker (julietbarker.co.uk), in which I found both the factual data and the inspiration so necessary for the creation of the world in which this story is placed. The following works, in particular, were of inestimable value:

Agincourt: The King, the Campaign, the Battle

Conquest: The English Kingdom of France 1417-1459

The inspiration for the chapter on Henry V's flagship *Grace Dieu* came from the ITV4 *Time Team* television series; specifically, Series 12, Episode 6, 'In Search of Henry V's Flagship, *Grace Dieu*'.

The meeting of eastern and western cultures, which for personal reasons was so central to the story, needed to have its roots somewhere. The selection of Rhodes as this point is directly attributable to the television series and DVD by Francesco da Mosta, *Francesco's Mediterranean Voyage*.

Finally, I wish to acknowledge the efforts of the many people who have created the huge body of knowledge which is the internet. From this, I have gleaned facts and figures pertaining to Rhodes, Falaise, Église Saint-Étienne, the Ceremony of Knighthood, boar hunting and food preparation in medieval times, and so many other many precious pearls which I have been able to incorporate into the story, to add detail to the world in which it occurs. As is fitting for the technology, these sources are acknowledged at the internet site www.knightthebook.com. All links are valid at the time of initial publication of this work.

Ian Anderson, February 2013